Anita Notaro is a TV producer, journalist and director and worked for RTE, Ireland's national broadcasting organization, for eighteen years. She has directed the Eurovision Song Contest and the Irish General Election, as well as programmes for the BBC and Channel 4. Her first novel, *Back After the Break*, is also published by Bantam Books.

BEHIND THE SCENES

Anita Notaro

BANTAM BOOKS

LONDON • NEW YORK • TORONTO • SYDNEY • AUCKLAND

BEHIND THE SCENES
A BANTAM BOOK: 0 553 81478 8

First publication in Great Britain

PRINTING HISTORY
Bantam edition published 2004

1 3 5 7 9 10 8 6 4 2

Copyright © Anita Notaro 2004

Set in 11.5/12.5pt Garamond by
Falcon Oast Graphic Art Ltd.

Bantam Books are published by Transworld Publishers,
61–63 Uxbridge Road, London W5 5SA,
a division of The Random House Group Ltd,

For my mother
Teresa

whatever my achievements, your love
and support have made them possible

Chapter One

The image in the mirror said it all in a single word. Hooker. A pair of anxious jade-green eyes surveyed it one last time. It was one hell of a fashion *faux pas*. Black clumpy, strappy, too-high sandals. Painted toenails that had seen one coat too many. Short, tight, Lycra skirt. Wonderbra only partially hidden by a flimsy cheap top. Pushed up, fake-tanned boobs. Garish jewellery, lots of it, in gold that was several shades too bright. A hard, caked face. Enough eyeliner to have kept Cleopatra going for months. Ruby-red lips outlined with a pencil that didn't quite match. Hair that tried too hard.

Annie Weller would normally have had a good laugh at herself, especially given the amount of time and energy she'd invested in perfecting the call-girl look, but today nerves got the better of her so she turned away quickly and belted her sensible, grey tweed coat tightly as she headed out the door. The respectable outer garment didn't quite manage to disguise the trailer trash image, even with the collar turned up. Immediately she sensed people were looking at her, and she was right. It was nine-thirty on a cold January morning. The steamy bus had shed its workforce and was now crammed with damp-smelling bargain hunters anxious to beat the post-Christmas blues. An elderly lady sniffed as Annie sat down beside her, pulling her parcels and her coat edges closer as if to protect herself. A spotty young Goth opposite chewed gum and gawked. The bus driver winked.

Almost an hour and two bus rides later Annie arrived at the main entrance to one of the country's biggest independent production companies, in an affluent suburb of south County Dublin. It was a bitterly cold, blustery morning and her bare fake-tanned legs were tinged blue with cold, the inky streaks hinting at varicose veins where none existed. Annie was oblivious to the stinging sensation, however, and to the pins and needles pricking her numb toes.

Glancing at her watch she saw that she was miles too early but it had been difficult to calculate the journey from the centre of Dublin. Anyway, it was a relief to be indoors. A bit more time to mentally prepare, she told herself as she was directed to a large nondescript holding area and took her place amid twenty or so girls all around her own age and all looking way too respectable: masses of virginal white blouses and leather pumps and real jewellery and even the odd ribbon. She wondered again if she'd overdone it. Too late now, she thought as she fell upon the coffee machine, realizing just how cold she was as her hands cupped the flimsy plastic beaker and started to sting. A surreptitious glance round the room told her that no-one here needed the job as much as she did, judging by the number of shoes similar to those worn by Carrie Bradshaw, and the handbags with letters on. Several pairs of eyes stared openly at the newest arrival; others feigned indifference, but what none could have guessed was that her nonchalant head toss hid a steely determination and a burning ambition.

Annie tried to psych herself up but the information they'd provided had been scant. All she knew was that they were looking for a late twenties or early thirties actress to play the part of Bobby, a part-time barmaid and prostitute under the control of a wealthy nightclub owner. It was a tiny part but Annie felt it had potential and the amazing thing about it was that 'they' were the producers of the country's number one drama, *Southside*.

Originally lauded and laughed at in equal measure when it burst onto Irish screens three years earlier, it had gradually won acceptance as a brave attempt to capture the notoriously fickle 25–40-year-old audience. It wasn't like other soaps or drama series in Ireland or the UK. The characters were expertly cast. The storylines were shorter and sharper and the issues harder. Set in contemporary Dublin, it was shot mostly on location by young, innovative directors and had slowly built itself into an award-winning series with an audience of almost a million. It now had major clout and Annie wanted in badly.

As she huddled in a corner to wait her turn she tried not to think about how much she needed the work. Things were tough, money was tight and the worst thing of all was that she was becoming disillusioned for the first time ever. At twenty-nine she should have had her life sussed, but fate had dealt her a difficult hand, although Annie herself never saw it that way.

The youngest child and only daughter of Joe and Anne Weller had not found it easy growing up with four brothers, in a working-class south County Dublin household where money was tight. When she was ten her mother died and from that day on Annie was expected to assume the role. After they got over the initial shock, life went on as normal for the Weller men. But for Annie, things were never the same again. She lost what remained of her childhood. Her teenage years were a blur. There was no question of going to college, no chance to indulge her passion for drama and the theatre, which had lurked at the back of her mind since the day she'd been introduced to her grandmother's trunk in the attic. Only about six at the time, she must have been driving her mother bonkers, because she was dispatched to the tiny attic and told to amuse herself. Hours later, when her mother shouted at her to come downstairs immediately and no slacking, Annie appeared in full theatrical garb. The bug had bitten, even if she didn't yet know it. For years afterwards, if Annie went missing, it was always 'Try the attic.' She pored over diaries and photos and begged for stories about the granny she'd never known – Nora Kane, who had been a showgirl and a budding actress. Anne Weller indulged her daughter's fantasy and allowed her to join a dance class, without ever imagining it would amount to any more than a little girl's daydream.

All those dreams became submerged by the lead weight of domesticity and for a long time after her mother's death Annie's heart was too bruised to successfully nurture even the weakest fairytale. One by one the boys left home and got good jobs. Tom was a chef and now lived in Australia where he had eventually managed to buy a small bar and restaurant. Donal, a builder, had married his childhood sweetheart and moved to London with his three sons. Jim was trotting around the world as manager of a travel agency and Greg was a struggling artist who still lived in Dublin. Annie was closest, in a not close at all sort of way, to Greg and didn't doubt for a minute that he'd succeed, but he was flaky at the best of times and had never offered much support to a gawky young sister.

Because they were men they just got on with their lives, assuming that Annie would look after everything but never once asking if it was what she wanted. And like her mother before her, the day-dreaming teenager wasn't good at pleading for help. Yet the seed that had been sown that first day in the attic flourished. The dance classes gave her an opportunity to put on a mask, and she shone at many auditions and junior shows. Years later, television drama became a passion, and *Coronation Street* was her first favourite soap. She couldn't afford to go to the theatre and anyway, her family would have laughed themselves silly at such grand notions. The pub was their only form of social entertainment, so Annie spent the winter evenings in an amateur dramatic society and no-one even noticed. She saved every penny to further her dream and the local library became her second home where she gobbled up anything to do with her secret craving.

Finally she plucked up the courage to leave home on her twenty-first birthday, scared that she'd never be able to go. Joe Weller, to his credit, had eventually realized what was happening and encouraged – no, insisted – that Annie move out and learn to be independent, assuring her over and over again that he'd be OK. She cried when her father gave her a bank book with an account in her name. It had been opened by her mother when she was born and topped up every time there was a spare few bob in the kitty. 'She planned to let you have it when you left home, wanted you to have a nest egg in case you still had those flights of fancy about being on the stage,' Joe Weller said, his bottom lip quivering.

It was a relatively small amount of money but Annie knew exactly what it would buy – a place on a course in one of Dublin's oldest and most respected acting schools. So she left with great plans and a head chock full of hopes and dreams of her life as a mature student. With a huge circle of friends and a determination to succeed, she'd repay her mother's faith.

Things took off slowly, much more slowly than she'd expected, but were moving along nicely when she discovered a lump in her breast two months after her twenty-third birthday. Everything came to a big fat full stop. Cancer. It was the scariest thing she had ever had to face up to, but she was well used to coping with whatever life threw her way. Once she could see through the thick fog of fright and loneliness – not helped by being surrounded by men who didn't know how to deal with the tears and were embarrassed by the problem – Annie discovered that she was one of the lucky ones. After a long, gruelling spell in hospital when she lost every single bit of hair, including her eyelashes – yet miraculously didn't lose her breast – and over a year in recovery she managed to pick up the pieces of a life that had never really got started.

Her father was amazing: she moved back home and he looked after her. Her brothers had rallied round as best they knew how, and gradually things improved, but it was a long time before anyone saw a spark of the old Annie and even longer before the tiredness left her bones and a little of her former energy returned. Only her determination and natural optimism had kept her going during that first long, icy winter, when all she could do was read and watch TV and dream.

So, at almost twenty-seven she left home for the second time and started again. It wasn't nearly as easy this time round. For one thing, she wasn't a kid any more and cancer had given her a perspective on life that most seventy-year-olds had only recently acquired. Her world seemed a million miles away from that of the carefree students she bumped into at auditions and she felt decades older and no wiser than most. But Anne Weller had been a strong, Irish mother and everything that happened to her daughter somehow made her more stubborn, more ambitious and hungrier than most. So now Annie had a tiny but solid former council house in a quiet area in the north inner city, close to O'Connell Street, in the middle of a settled community who minded each other as only true Dubs can. She'd tried to pick up the pieces of a fledgling acting career but jobs were hard to come by so she worked part-time as a front of house person in a posh restaurant to keep things ticking over. Mostly she felt lucky and happy and content. And best of all, after what seemed like a lifetime in remission, she was now considered cured of cancer.

Nothing exciting had come up on the acting front, which was her one regret. Contacts were everything in this business and most of Annie's friends had stopped calling after the first few weeks of her illness. She tried not to let it make her

16

bitter. They were young, carefree and selfish and the sights and sounds of their world didn't include drips and tubes and noisy bedpans; nor did they gravitate towards the pungent smell of dis-infectant. But people were kind once they realized she hadn't died – cancer still carried a death sentence in most people's minds. A gradual resumption of acquaintances led to a number of roles in amateur productions but none had pro-vided her with the much-needed break. She knew she was good, and she desperately wanted a chance to prove it. Maybe today, she thought longingly as she sipped a second beaker of the comforting liquid that looked like cough syrup and tasted like consommé and tried not to get too excited.

One of the producers on the mega-successful soap had seen Annie in a small production and suggested her for this audition. She didn't have an agent so they'd gone to considerable trouble to track her down, which pleased her enormously. Getting any audition was usually the most difficult part and she'd heard tales of people who were offered other roles once they'd been seen by the major producers and directors. Still, it was a long shot, she knew, as she recognized some of the faces around her. There were several established names being considered and she wondered for the twentieth time what her chances were. An attack of nerves threatened to overwhelm her but a quick prayer to her mother helped. It always did.

Chapter Two

A very different face stared out from an ornate mirror in a stunning period bathroom a couple of miles away, in a huge Victorian house located on one of South Dublin's most prestigious roads.

'God, I look wrecked.' Libby Marlowe was her usual critical self. But she didn't really and she knew it.

She looked exactly what she was, a stunning, confident, thirty-eight-year-old woman who had everything, including porcelain skin, masses of pale gold hair, big soft boxer-puppy eyes and lips that smacked of collagen but had, in fact, been pouty since birth.

As she slipped off her silk robe in readiness for her shower, she surveyed her body in one of many mirrors, not really liking what she saw. Yet the image that stared back would have delighted any artist. Tall, slim torso, long legs, softly rounded hips, flat tummy, big boobs, all covered in a light sprinkling of gold, courtesy of a two-week holiday in the Maldives at Christmas. Libby wrinkled her nose as she stepped into the scalding jets of a power shower and lathered herself in expensive foam.

Forty-five minutes later she was in the kitchen almost ready to face the day, sipping freshly squeezed pink grapefruit juice and nibbling at wheaten toast, prepared by her housekeeper. She was dressed in a tailored, pinstripe trouser suit, her make-up was flawless and her jewellery to die for. Mrs O'Connell made herself scarce as a tanned, immaculately dressed man entered and slapped his wife playfully on the bottom.

'You're looking good, what's on today?' David English smiled.

'More meetings, I'm afraid. We start shooting the new series the week after next and we still haven't thrashed out the formula and the stylists haven't produced one decent image yet. I think I'm about to kick ass.'

'That's my girl. Go get 'em.' She saw he was engrossed in a sheaf of papers. Absently he picked up a piece of her toast and she smacked his hand.

'You've had yours. Go away, glutton.' He dodged her and smiled in a preoccupied way. 'Yeah, I'd thought I'd start by having the producer castrated,' she joked.

'Sounds good.'

'You're not listening to me.' It was a childish, singsong reprimand.

'Sorry, darling, actually I need you to sign this.'

She accepted the gold fountain pen but used the smooth metal to stroke his cheek.

'You look tired, what's up?'

'Just a temporary hitch. I need to transfer some funds . . . One of the companies I've been dealing with is operating—'

'Do I need to know this?' Libby moved closer to him, sidling up seductively. She loved the aura of power that surrounded him.

'No.' There was the faintest sigh before David bent and kissed her upturned lips, but she knew it was an automatic peck.

'Want me to beat someone up for you?' she asked as she signed both copies and replaced the slim pen in its casket.

'I'm afraid there are too many. Things are tough out there at the moment.'

She pulled him closer via his expensive tie. 'I know how to make you forget all those bad guys, but only after you've helped me with my personal plan for world domination of the airwaves.' Her smile was suggestive but her tone was tinged with the faintest hint of criticism. 'You've been promising for weeks to look over those papers for me. So, how about dinner tonight? I can promise you a truly scrumptious dessert.' Libby was stroking his thigh as she spoke, but it was clear his mind was elsewhere.

'Not tonight, I'm afraid. I won't be home until late, I've got clients in from New York so it's dinner at the Grasshopper and probably drinks afterwards. I did mention it to you the other day.'

'No, you did not. Who are they?'

'That big American multinational that I've been trying to persuade—'

'I'm bored already.' She gave a playful yawn and her eyes were teasing. 'Couldn't I persuade you to dump them early and come home to me?'

'I wish. No, I'm going to have to give them the royal treatment. Fine wine, Armagnac, the lot.'

'Well, make sure you don't drive.'

'I've got a car booked for the day, in fact he's probably outside now. I'd better shoot.'

'OK. By the time I've spent the day discussing food I probably won't cook anyway, so now that you're not coming home I'll ask Mrs O'C. to dig out some of that gorgeous wild smoked salmon you got as a present and I'll take a tray to bed early.'

'See you around midnight so, love you lots.'

'You too. Have a good day.'

Libby gave him a shiny, happy kiss and smiled to herself as she watched him pick up the papers and head for the door. David English was gorgeous and powerful and sexy and she loved him to bits. At thirty-nine he was one of the country's most successful financial brains and between them they were a magical couple. Even their looks were a perfect foil for each other, her blond, high-school prom queen image contrasting brilliantly with his sultry movie star appeal. It had been lust at first sight for both of them and the fact that he was extremely wealthy and she was one of the country's up and coming celebrity chefs meant their relationship had been front-page news from the start.

There'd been a lot of speculation when one of the most eligible, high-profile men in Ireland had started dating a 'cook' and most people, especially the tabloids, had felt it was merely a dalliance on his part. Privately Libby felt it could have ended up as just that, but she was a funny and intelligent companion, a million miles away from her dumb blonde image. She had a way of looking at the world that kept him laughing from the start and he secretly liked the way she could be tough as nails sometimes and didn't suffer fools easily. Within weeks he realized they were a powerful combination and a great team and the sex was amazing. He was hooked.

They'd married within six months of their first meeting, more than eight years ago. She'd just turned thirty and had wondered if she'd ever meet the right man, when David came along. Neither of them felt the need to wait. It had been a blissful few years. His wealth and power fitted her like a soft leather glove: it was a life she'd always felt she was destined for and she blossomed. Her career had really taken off and she'd started to do serious TV, as well as books and videos, which kept her extremely busy but was fabulous for her profile. Barely a week went by without some article or photo or speculation in the papers. Suddenly she was a heavyweight and everyone wanted her. She honed her image carefully and was seen as cool and untouchable. As a couple they were on everyone's A list and Libby exploited her status fully.

They'd agreed to wait a few years before

thinking about children, which suited them both. She was beginning to wonder if they'd ever get around to it. Things were just too good at the moment. They were constantly in demand socially, with friends including aristocrats and politicians (his) and rock stars and celebrities (hers). Life was a caviare and champagne sushi counter and neither was anxious to halt the merry-go-round. It was a litany of parties and holidays and shopping and playing and hard work, although less so for Libby now. It seemed the more successful she became, the more people were on hand to do the slogging for her, but she was careful not to let her career get too far out of her control and David was usually happy to advise her.

Pinning him down was the problem. He was travelling extensively and working horrendous hours and she was worried that he looked tired all the time. 'I'm fine, stop fussing, I'll sort it out,' he'd told her more than once recently and she was content, happy to be in partnership with her whiz-kid husband as long as it only involved using a solid gold fountain pen for a split second every so often. Nevertheless, she made a mental note to ring his rather tiresome secretary later in the day and get her to write him out of his diary for a week next month, despite the fact that it was less than that since they'd had a break. The ghastly woman was always telling Libby how busy 'Mr English' was and she knew the dowdy forty-something had been in love with him for years.

Tough old boot, Libby smiled as she dialled the

number of his office and finished her breakfast, preparing to be nice simply because she was feeling generous today. A week in Colorado, skiing in the pure mountain air, was just what they needed and she had a two-week break in her shoot schedule around the end of next month. She'd check it all out later with her PA.

Her mobile rang. It was the producer of the new series, Jeremy Scott-Thomas, enquiring what time she'd be available.

'See you in about an hour or so darling, OK?' She was always teasing him for his plummy, 'my father is a lord and I'm only doing this as a hobby' accent.

'Fine, I've got a draft running order ready and the stylists will be here all morning.'

'Oh God, not the stylists again,' Libby laughed. They were everywhere – for food, hair, make-up, clothes. Secretly, she loved them. They made her and her food look delicious even if neither did need much effort. She hung up, still smiling, and checked her other appointments. She resolved to get her husband alone the following evening and make him forget his worries, although what she'd planned would diminish his energy levels further.

'You're even scrummier than the tastiest morsel,' David had teased her the other night as he nibbled her ear while she prepared a quick duck stir-fry with crunchy vegetables and crispy noodles; they'd abandoned it in favour of another, altogether more tasty quickie and then stretched out on the feather bed and sipped ice-cold Bolly.

After a few words with her PA and a tiresome ten minutes spent discussing a long, detailed list with her housekeeper, Libby travelled the short distance to the office in her new shiny black Merc, a surprise Christmas present from David. She was mildly irked that someone had parked in her reserved spot and soon had a middle-aged uniformed officer scurrying about. Within two minutes a preppy, college type emerged, flushed and stuttery, to where Libby stood.

'What part of reserved do you not understand, I wonder?' Libby gave the spotty youth the full benefit of her 'don't fuck with me, earwig' look, then let him squirm for a few seconds before turning away. 'I trust he won't be in a position to keep me late for a meeting again, Joe?' Libby always knew the names of the unimportant people who were important to her.

'He won't, Miss Marlowe, I can assure you. If you'll leave me your keys I'll park the car and have them delivered to your office.'

Libby gave him one of her helpless little girl looks. The ignoramus involved would be banned from driving on the complex for at least three months. She sashayed in past a room full of hopefuls, at least one of whom smiled at her. 'More auditions for that ghastly soap, I suppose?' Libby shuddered at the receptionist, wondering how people watched such drivel, much less believed it.

Chapter Three

Annie Weller was the smiler. She just couldn't help herself. Everyone knew Libby Marlowe and in real life she was even more striking. Annie sat entranced, without a trace of envy as the woman emerged from the shiny black panther to chat to the security guard. She took in the endless legs, designer sunglasses pushed back on top of her silky blond hair, and the soft leather bag and matching briefcase swinging jauntily as she handed over her keys and strolled indoors.

As an entrance, it was something else and everyone who watched it wanted to be her.

'What is it about her?' a soft-spoken girl sitting near Annie asked no-one in particular.

'Apart from the fact that she looks like a beauty queen, has a model figure, superstar husband and as much money as Bono, d'ya mean?' A much younger girl laughed sarcastically and the group joined in.

'I think it's that she has an edge about her.' A

young guy in his early twenties, who was obviously one of the production minders, hit the nail on the head. 'She's sassy and looks like she could have a laugh with you or have you fired, and that's incredibly sexy when you've got all she's got.' Everyone wanted some.

She can't be much older than me, Annie thought. She looked away immediately, knowing that the other woman probably hated it when strangers smiled at her.

But for Annie it was an omen. Libby Marlowe had somehow become her lucky mascot. She was everything the younger girl was not – stunning, confident, sexy, vibrant; and everything she wished she could be – namely a star. Well, an actress really, but a little bit famous all the same, although Annie wouldn't have admitted that to anyone, because apart from one fierce, burning ambition she was a mass of vulnerability and insecurity, always had been. Being an actress meant you got to wear a mask a lot of the time and Annie was a brilliant performer. Hence the outfit today.

She'd first seen Libby while she was in hospital recovering from cancer. After months of pain and drug-fuelled sleep and retching and discomfort, one day Annie had finally felt well enough to sit up and watch some mindless television. It was the first time she'd been interested in anything in months and as she flicked channels she came across the ultra-cool Libby Marlowe. Annie Weller fell in love in that childish, girl on girl way peculiar to females. She decided that Libby was lucky, because that day she felt better than she had in yonks. From then on Annie secretly wanted to be just like her. She'd kept an eye on her career and day-dreamed more than once, especially when she saw the fairytale wedding pictures featuring her heroine in a back copy of a glossy magazine.

There were other stupid coincidences, at least in Annie's star-struck head, like years later, when Annie was reading an article in a Sunday news-paper entitled 'The Sexiest Women in the World'. She had just noticed that Libby Marlowe was the only Irish woman in the top twenty when she glanced at the date and realized that her period of remission was over and she was finally considered 'cured'. Libby became her good luck charm all over again.

I wonder if you get sick of all the attention after a time, the younger girl speculated now, with some sympathy for the celebrity chef, knowing she was constantly hounded by the media. They seemed to print a different story about her every week, the most recent of which speculated on whether Libby had been spoilt as a child, since she had no sisters or brothers and had gone to a private school.

Oh well, not something I'm going to have to worry about in the near future. Annie grinned, wondering if her local free community paper would hound her for an interview if she got the part. Some chance, although half our street will want signed photos of the stars in *Southside*, Annie thought and tried to picture her neighbours' reactions. They instantly deserted their doorsteps once the opening music of the programme came belting out from cheap, leather-sofaed living rooms and steamy, cabbage-smelling kitchens. 'What's the appeal?' Annie had asked more than once, intrigued that her older, settled neighbours were fascinated by the racy drama series.

'We can all dream, love,' Mrs Morgan smiled.

'Makes me feel young and sexy,' Lucy O'Neill added and blushed.

'And horny.' This from mad Madge Thompson. They all fell about. Laughter was what kept them going.

'Annie Weller, please.' A friendly voice startled her out of her daydream.

'Hi, I'm Rosa, one of the secretaries on *Southside*. Sorry to have kept you so long. We're running way behind today, yesterday wasn't half as bad.'

'You mean there are even more people auditioning?' Annie felt deflated.

'Lots, although not for the part of Bobby. The series is to run two nights a week instead of one after Easter so we've had to create a number of new parts to help our storylines.'

They had arrived in a small room full of people, who all looked at her in that way you do when you're not quite sure of someone. Annie quickly shrugged off her coat in an effort to convince them that this was definitely not her normal interview suit. A tall, gangly blonde was the first to recover.

The men simply stared at her breasts and then made a huge effort to keep their eyes on her face.

'Hello, I'm Isobel Ryan, production assistant and this is Max Donaldson, executive producer and Dave Gordon, script editor.' Isobel went on to introduce Annie to a number of writers, directors and others. It was all quite scary.

'How do you feel about the part?' Max enquired, glancing through Annie's résumé. 'I see you haven't done any TV before but I've heard good things about you from Mike, who saw your last theatre performance.' He indicated a younger man, who smiled encouragingly up at her. Annie suddenly thought she must look like a clown: she'd been holding the same 'please like me' grin on her over-made-up face for ages.

'I'm really excited by it, although I only have the single page you issued. She sounds like a gutsy character who's been through a really rough time and I think I'd enjoy playing her. I like the fact that she's not your normal TV heroine . . .'

'What makes you think she's a heroine?' The producer looked intrigued.

'I think she could be. The character has great potential. She's a star in the making.' Annie was sure she'd gone too far with her fantasy. She cleared her throat and tried to return to planet earth. 'Eh, she probably doesn't care too much what people think of her but I'd like to make her a little bit vulnerable underneath, just to give a bit of depth to the details you provided.' Annie felt she was waffling and wondered if she'd misinterpreted the brief.

'That's fine, we're very unsure as to where she's going, to be honest. At the moment we've written her into four episodes only and we may or may not go further with her. Anyway, here's a scene we'd like you to read for us, and let me introduce you to Stephen Wilson, who plays Ted Doran.'

Max indicated a tall, angular man, who now strode quickly towards Annie with a broad grin on his face. She knew the smile well from the box.

'Why don't you take a couple of minutes to talk and read it through and let us know when you're ready,' Max said and Stephen led her over to a corner of the room, filling her in quietly as they walked away.

'Let me tell you quickly what I know about the scene. Ted has just started to get involved in this whole business. On the surface he's a respectable nightclub owner who has recently realized there's big money to be made behind the scenes. A number of wealthy businessmen want to be "entertained" privately and he's on the lookout for girls. Bobby is a waitress but has clearly been around. She's flashy enough for him to think she might have done this kind of thing before, although that's obviously an assumption on his part. The men all seem to fancy her, so he decides to offer her a job.'

'OK, it seems quite straightforward, but from the dialogue she could think he's trying to come on to her, so I might play it a bit suggestive at first and then pull back once I learn what he really wants. How does that sound to you?'

* * *

Max and the others watched Annie's performance intently. The executive producer asked them to read a second scene and in a couple of minutes it was over. She had no idea how it had gone, although Stephen seemed enthusiastic as he shook her hand. She glanced towards the table.

'Thanks for coming in, we'll be in touch as soon as we've made a decision, which might even be today, as we need the actor for costume checks and a read-through at the end of next week.' The executive producer was already looking at his notes for the next person and Annie felt dejected as she moved towards the door.

'Oh, by the way, I should have said, just in case . . .' She smiled nervously at the expectant faces, 'I sort of . . . dressed for the part, although I may have overdone it just a little.'

'That's a relief.' Max smiled at her and then decided she'd taken him seriously. 'Only joking, I think we all gathered you had much better taste, judging by the photos you sent us.'

She couldn't think of anything else to say so she slithered out, feeling very flat and acutely conscious of the cheap Lycra skirt riding up around her ample bum.

Chapter Four

Libby was having an exhilarating and exhausting day. They'd finally agreed on a format for the show. It was to be set in a dream house and the idea was to deal with all aspects of entertaining – everything from baking luxurious breads to laying the perfect table. An entire programme would be devoted to the ideal pantry and store cupboard. Unusually, Libby wasn't entirely sure about it but they'd investigated every conceivable idea to do with cooking. Perfect pantries and beautiful breads weren't really her thing: she was happiest trying out new ideas, finding exciting combinations, using a simple *mélange* of the freshest local ingredients to create something magical. She knew she had a way with food, things just seemed to work for her and sometimes they worked amazingly well.

During a break for coffee, Libby phoned her friend Moya, who was the wife of one of David's business colleagues. Libby had as many friends as others had takeaway coffees. She could click on her e-mail any evening and find thirty personal messages. She was air-kissed and breathlessly hailed as somebody's 'darling' several times a day. Her voicemail was permanently crashing under the volume of 'let's do lunch' messages.

Moya and Libby had liked each other instantly when they were first introduced years ago, although their relationship had never really progressed. Now they kept in touch mainly by phone and e-mail and were forever promising to meet.

'Libby, I was only thinking about you the other day.'

'Hi, Moya. How are things?' They chatted easily for a few minutes and Libby ran a few ideas for the show by her.

'It sounds fabulous. I can't wait.'

'You don't think it's a bit too pretentious, too middle class, do you?'

'God, no. Most of my friends would be glued to it looking for ideas. And everything you promote will be copied in hundreds of ghastly mock Tudor mansions in south County Dublin.'

'Most of your friends have two cleaners, a housekeeper, an au pair and a lady who comes in to do the ironing,' Libby laughed, knowing that she was exactly the same.

'That's true, but you know, so many people have more disposable income now. My domestic had lunch in a sushi bar the other day, for heaven's sake. Everyone's entertaining and the food is becoming more and more exotic. Even barbecues now have monstrous equipment – patio heaters, citronella candles and God knows what else.'

Libby could almost feel her friend's nose turning upwards. They chatted on for a while and Libby felt a bit less unsure of the idea.

Later, she phoned Carrie Ferguson, her old and probably closest friend from college whom she hadn't seen in at least five years. Carrie had met and married Peter, a farmer, and they'd quickly moved to a small village near Galway and had three baby girls, one almost every year.

'Libby, it's great to hear you. How the hell are you?'

'Carrie, I'm so sorry I haven't been in touch. Things have been just crazy here.'

'I can imagine. Every time I open the newspaper I see your photograph. How's David?'

It took them ages to catch up and Libby asked her opinion too.

'Well, I wouldn't do much entertaining out here in the sticks, to be honest, but I'd definitely watch it and dream, for the same reasons I buy all the glossy magazines. I think that with a bit of effort I could be like all of you lot. Some chance.' She laughed good-humouredly.

'I'm just not completely convinced,' Libby told her friend.

'Well, you're selling the dream of the perfect lifestyle – log fires burning, candlelit table, crystal glasses and a woman who throws together an exquisite four-course meal when people arrive unexpectedly. I'd happily sit down to watch it in my oldest jeans and eat a packet of chocolate biscuits and think that I could do it too.'

'Me, I just call in the caterers,' Libby laughed without a trace of self-consciousness.

'And then you go down to your well-stocked wine cellar and choose a vintage champagne to greet your guests with. I ring Peter and beg him to go to the off-licence in the village where they sell nothing but Chardonnay.'

'Bet you wouldn't change a thing, though.'

'That's only on good days. Sometimes I feel like selling up and moving back to civilization.'

'I wish we saw more of each other.' Libby had a sudden longing for an evening out with a real friend, instead of the sort she usually found herself seated next to at dinner parties. Moya was great, but you wouldn't be telling her secrets.

'Is everything OK?' Carrie had heard something in her old friend's voice.

'Yes, fine, too busy if anything.' The rare moment of reflection was gone. 'Too many parties, so little time.'

'Wish I had that problem.'

They promised to stay in touch and both knew they probably wouldn't. Still, Libby felt better about herself and, more importantly, about the new series.

Next up was a discussion on key crew members. The production company had hired a hot new director and Libby wasn't convinced he was right for this job, although so far she'd only met him twice. She had never been one to play safe with crew. Some presenters liked to work with the same cameramen, directors etc. all the time. Libby, however, had worked in TV long enough to realize that a look could quickly become dated.

Nigel, the latest hotshot, seemed to think the series should look like one long pop music video and was talking about using only hand-held cameras and fast cutting sequences, which Libby felt might look great but not show much of the food.

'Our audience are twenty-, thirty- and forty-somethings who wouldn't normally watch MTV on a regular basis,' she'd reminded him coldly at their last meeting. To her annoyance he didn't seem to take her seriously. Libby's instinct was to have a second director who had a good knowledge of cooking and food presentation but, as usual, it came down to money, as it seemed to more and more on this particular series.

Luckily, her fee had been negotiated months before the present round of cutbacks and her agent had already secured a substantial figure plus a generous wardrobe and personal allowance. Libby was now at the stage where she could command huge extras such as her own private car and driver, nominate her own team of hair and make-up artists and select her clothes and stylists from almost anywhere in the world. She knew the TV channel were selling her whole lifestyle, hoping to attract a huge audience and bring in a considerable amount in sponsorship to boot. She felt justified in asking for all that she wanted, but of course she did none of the negotiations herself.

It was one of the things she'd learned from David, who advised her to get herself a first-class agent, in a top firm with offices worldwide. She had insisted on a clause in her contract whereby her approval was needed when deciding on a new format – almost unheard of in television – which was where she was at now.

During the morning David phoned and Libby retreated to her private office to take the call.

'How's it going? Are you giving them hell?'

'You know, suddenly I'm not sure about this one. I think they're skimping on resources and the lead-in time is not as long as it should be. I'm a bit worried.'

'Well, get Melanie on to it, that's what you're paying her for.'

He sounded preoccupied as always these days. Phones buzzed and doors banged in the background and he was tapping on a keyboard as he spoke. Even though she was used to it, it irritated her today, for no reason.

'David, could you just stop what you're doing for a second?'

He was quick to respond. 'Listen, why don't we go out for a quiet dinner tomorrow evening and you can tell me all about it?'

'When did we ever get to have a quiet dinner in

our lives?' She felt silly being so tetchy. 'I need to sit down at home and go through it all in detail but then I will run it by you, thanks.'

'OK, hon. Gotta go. Clients arriving. This could be make or break time.'

'What do you mean?' She was annoyed more than concerned, wanting David to show more interest in her project.

'We've got a lot of their money tied up in pharmaceutical companies and the market—'

'Sorry darling, now I've got to say ciao. Jeremy is prancing about like a hyena. Must go. Big kiss.'

'Remember, don't agree to anything you're not one hundred per cent happy with. Your career is too important, much bigger than one miserable series.'

'Don't worry, I've a lot more fight left in me yet.'

'That's my girl. See you tonight. Don't wait up, I think it'll be a late one.'

'Love you.' She knew he was already somewhere else.

'You too.' She heard a sharp click.

'Bye-bye darling,' Libby said to no-one, smiling as she hung up.

She knew why she relied on her husband so much. As usual he got straight to the nub of the issue and was positive and assertive without being the least bit truculent. She always felt guilty about showing so little interest in what he did. It was just so boring compared with the razzmatazz of her world. Still, she thought as she gestured at Jeremy to come in, once she'd run through everything with David she'd make the right decision. She always did.

Much happier, she went back to the meeting.

The rest of the day went off without a hitch. Some great hot looks were proposed for Libby and the new fashion stylist certainly seemed to know her stuff, even if she'd taken a while to get going. She had finally prepared a mood board to give a feel of the look she wanted to achieve for the series. Libby liked it – and her – immediately. It was a sort of Salma Hayek meets Cameron Diaz look, sexy in a very laid-back 'I could be anyone's mother/lover/wife' type way and it was a radical new approach for Libby, who tended to go for a classy, slightly conservative look on television. This was all layers and colours and textures, and much more funky than she normally went for.

Also, the food stylists had some clever ideas for the menus and food presentation. There was to be a book to accompany the series and the proposals for the website looked great.

The producers took Libby to one of the top French restaurants for lunch and a photographer was spotted snapping away through the front window, much to the owner's chagrin. He lowered the slatted wooden blinds and apologized profusely, but Libby waved him away.

'Don't worry, Charles, I'm used to it by now, they just want to make sure I really do eat occasionally,' she said and smiled, tucking into the most amazing boeuf bourguignon, tender slivers of the finest organic fillet of beef cooked slowly in perfumed claret with herbs and baby vegetables. It was divine and the deep, velvety Châteauneuf-du-Pape was exactly the right accompaniment.

Libby was not unaware that the entire restaurant was watching the incident. She licked her lips and her laugh became huskier. Might as well ensure it was a decent photo, she decided, spotting the photographer at the opposite window and angling her head in a flattering way. She noticed a good-looking man opposite staring at her breasts suggestively. Despite her protests, she was enjoying herself.

'George, do stop fussing, I'm fine,' she told the annoying waiter, who was clearing away imaginary crumbs and trying to protect her. She shooed him playfully away and went back to pretending she wasn't looking at the young man who could have been Orlando Bloom's brother. Running her fingers along the back of her neck and allowing her hand to rest just above her cleavage, she could see him sipping his wine and ignoring the two older men who were trying to keep the conversation going. She felt powerful and sexy and was enjoying the harmless flirtation until a young woman approached their table.

'Excuse me, I wonder if I could have your autograph.'

'Of course.' Libby smiled and decided to be extra gracious. She took the biro and notelet offered and signed with a flourish.

'Your programmes are fantastic.'

'Thank you.' She handed back the pen and paper.

'And your books are really beautiful.' Libby smiled vaguely and said nothing, simply picked up her knife and fork in a gesture of dismissal obvious to everyone, but the woman wasn't daunted.

'This is for my mother, she's nearly eighty and she never misses any of your shows. How would she get a photograph of you?' Libby didn't particularly want to be associated with eighty-year-old grannies, it was bad for her image. She decided she'd had enough. One ever so slightly raised eyebrow in Jeremy's direction and the producer sprang into action.

'If you'd like to give my office a call, I'm sure my secretary would be happy to oblige.' He handed her his business card and placed his hand firmly at her elbow. Libby looked away and began to talk animatedly to Ben, their trendy new accountant, and when she looked up again her admirer had gone. The granny reference cast a faint shadow on the proceedings and everyone sensed their star was slightly miffed.

The waiter insisted they have a second bottle of wine on the house, but they all wanted to keep a clear head for the afternoon, so they made do with dessert, Libby treating herself to chocolate *crème brûlée* with champagne vanilla cream.

The rest of the day passed in the blink of an eye. Libby was feeling pleased with herself again as she made a couple of quick phone calls, signed the last of her fan mail and sipped a cup of peppermint tea while her secretary fussed about, preparing a file of photos and notes for her to take home and study the following day.

'Hurry up, please, I need to be out of here in ten minutes.' Libby gave the temp a filthy look. It irritated her enormously that her own secretary was on extended maternity leave, abandoning her to a series of irritating impostors.

She had a massage and facial booked for five and as she entered the luxury salon she felt the tension in her neck easing.

'Hard day, Miss Marlowe?' the receptionist asked as she helped Libby slip off her coat and took her keys to have her car parked for her.

'Busy enough, Laura, I can't wait to have someone stretch out my back and dance on my shoulders. I've been looking forward to this all day.' Libby liked the reverential tone so she was sweet as pie.

'Well, everything's ready for you.' Laura opened the door to a treatment room and Libby's senses were assailed by the scent of essential oils and fragranced candles and fresh flowers. She undressed and sipped from a crystal glass a relaxing elixir of fruits and herbs and berries that was supposed to have many restorative qualities. Libby slipped between the cool cotton sheets and smiled as she always did at the old-fashioned touch – a hot water bottle for her feet. Music played softly: it was a magical sound of waves lapping and birds singing, and she could almost feel the sunshine on her shoulders even though she was indoors and it was dark and January.

For two hours she was pampered with creams and oils until her whole body felt stretched and supple and soft and her skin tingled and smelt wonderful. She had brought a pair of fine, cotton stretch pants and a big fluffy sweater in her gym bag and now she dressed snugly and tied her hair back in a ponytail. She emerged feeling no pain and stepped into her car, which was parked outside the door waiting for her. Normally they had the motor running on a cold evening. Libby turned on the engine and shivered slightly and resolved to complain to the owner, a friend of David's. The young man who had been on duty for the last couple of weeks was just not up to scratch.

Mrs O'Connell had left supper ready, a snack as Libby had requested, on an inlaid tray dressed with snow-white linen, silver cutlery and sparkling crystal. Food was in the fridge – a dish of home-made brandy pâté and a plate of wild smoked salmon with lemon wedges and capers, needing only a crack of black peppercorns. Crusty ciabatta bread had been sliced thinly and was already in the toaster, ready to pop, and there was warm, moist brown bread and country butter for the salmon. Everything exactly as she liked it.

God knows it had taken long enough to train the housekeeper, who had been with David's family or yonks and was used to doing things her way.

Libby recalled the battles she'd kept from David in the early days of their marriage. She poured herself a glass of chilled Cloudy Bay, jumped into her thick white dressing-gown and flicked through the post. The best part of getting a facial was not having to take off your make-up that night. Libby sighed happily as she arranged the tray and took it to her bedroom where she curled up like a baby on the massive cream couch and flicked channels happily as she ate.

Chapter Five

The day passed agonizingly slowly for Annie, who was afraid to move from the flat in case *they* rang and didn't like talking to machines. She didn't have a mobile, the charges were simply too horrific to contemplate. She'd stopped on the way home to do some shopping, feeling even more self-conscious about her 'party' look, if that were possible.

Annie lived on a very tight budget and knew she ate all the wrong things. Largely her trolley contained convenience foods – tins of beans and spaghetti, frozen brown burgers and plastic chips, packets of cheap biscuits and plenty of processed white sliced bread. She bought all the own-label value brands rather than the well-respected and expensive ones and only ate meat once or twice a week. She hardly ever bought fish or fresh vegetables. Frozen everything was a hell of a lot easier and, she wrongly assumed, cheaper.

She struggled onto the bus not sure which was heaviest, her shoes or her shopping. A well-dressed woman gave her a pitying look and another of the ubiquitous teenagers a longing one.

Walking from the bus stop to her home always made Annie smile and despair. Sometimes, the teenage kids kicking a football gave her a wolf whistle and today they had something to whistle about. Annie burst out laughing at the 'Jaysus, where'd ye get those knockers' delivered to her retreating back. She stopped to nuzzle the horse kept in one of the tiny front gardens and felt sad as usual as she saw the frayed rope that ensured he stayed home alone. She knew the family looked after the animal, it just never seemed right that he should loom like a giant in his tiny playpen and as always she saw the faraway glazed look in his beautiful face.

She nodded hello to the elderly man trying in vain to sweep up the litter dancing about in the January wind, lurid ice-pop papers, cellophane-covered blue and red cigarette boxes and brown, oily, chip shop bags that formed the basis of their late winter gardens.

The flat was freezing. As a rule she didn't turn on the heat during the day, so she quickly washed and scrubbed away her heavy make-up, wincing at the cold water but feeling instantly better. Shedding the shoes was like putting aloe vera on sunburn and pulling on thick fluffy leggings was instant balm for cold, chapped legs.

I need a good haircut, Annie thought, eyeing her unkempt tumbling, reddish locks, back to normal after vigorous brushing and shaking out of th gluey hairspray she'd applied lavishly that morning in order to complete the trashy look. She was of average height and weight with sparkly, emerald green eyes – her only good feature, she thought savagely, as she glanced disgustedly at her freckles in the cracked mirror on the back of the wardrobe door, thinking she looked like a real scrubber. Today was not a good one: her eyes were puffy from all the washing and a faint trace of liner still lingered no matter how hard she rubbed. She scurried around cleaning the house in comfy, faded tracksuit bottoms and several layers of well-worn, nobbled jumpers, hair caught up in a ponytail in a vain effort to tame it.

It was a funny little place she called home, one of a row of tall, thin houses, just a door and two narrow windows, one on top of the other, designed to create maximum capacity living in minimum space. Not a palace, but the rent was cheap. Large families had been reared here, Annie knew from her neighbours, in the two tiny bedrooms, so small that one barely held a double bed and the other groaned under the weight of a wardrobe and chest of drawers. Most people used the parlour – the one good room if you avoided looking at the brown and beige tiled monster that dominated one wall – as another bedroom and many of the sofas that listened to gossip and innuendo during the day provided the only privacy and place for procreation at night, as the partition walls upstairs were almost translucent.

The kitchens were small and badly equipped, although a few were home to the Belfast sink, a huge ceramic basin now much sought after by designers of country kitchens and whipped out by most of the council tenants as soon as they could afford a shiny, stainless steel model half the size of the original.

Annie's house had been painted magnolia and furnished sparsely, which suited her ideally. It had been a luxury renting a house rather than a flat, but months in the close confines of a hospital ward with no privacy and a commode as the only piece of furniture in her eye-line had made Annie slightly claustrophobic and desperate for something more than a bedsit when the time came to start over. She'd hunted in markets and junk shops, gone to every car boot and jumble sale for miles and had furnished her home with style on a shoestring, making cushions and curtains from remnants and begging plant cuttings from her green-fingered retired neighbours.

Now she washed and dusted and polished furiously, just in case she got the job and had no time to do anything for weeks, then began her usual half-hour of floor exercises, partly to keep her circulation going.

She didn't have to worry about her weight. Since her illness her appetite had never really been the same and anyway she was always rushing about, using up valuable energy. Because she still got tired in the evenings she tended to go to bed as soon as she could, so late night binges in front of the TV never happened. She rarely drank, simply because she couldn't afford to.

Lunch today, later than normal because of the audition, was a processed burger, beans and fries with too much salt, as usual. A watery sun poked its head through the kitchen window as she dunked her chips in lurid red sauce. She resolved to spend the afternoon cleaning the grimy glass in anticipation of a sunshine-filled spring.

At five she applied a little make-up, stuffed her hair into a bun, changed into her one good, cheap black suit and white shirt that had become just a touch faded recently, and headed for work. She worked from six to about eleven five nights a week and the restaurant treated her well and fed her even better. Owen Kerrigan, the manager, knew he had been lucky to get Annie; she was remarkably pleasant and efficient and remembered most of their regulars. They all seemed to like her.

Tonight was busy but manageable and she was glad. January was always quiet; everyone was recovering from the excesses of Christmas, even if most of their clients were not concerned about credit card bills. There were a few early diners, but many of their regulars came between eight and nine. Annie buzzed around, checking everything, her mind elsewhere. She really wanted this part – if she didn't get it she'd have to consider giving up and getting a proper day job, one where she could afford all the things that most people took for granted. Or even just not to have to struggle all the time, watch every penny, would be nice. She was still daydreaming as Sarah, one of the waitresses, approached.

'So, where will you go to celebrate if you get this job, then?'

'Oh, I dunno, out for a few pints, I suppose.' Annie had no intention of doing any such thing, but her acting skills came in handy.

'Go on, you must have loads of famous friends.'

'Well, I have met one or two . . .' Annie stopped herself. 'Actually no, I'm lying.' They grinned at each other and continued working.

'Still, it must be great being an actress. It sounds so glam.'

'It's not, trust me, though it is quite a social business, but it's also very competitive, at least where I'm at. As well as that, I'm a bit older than most of the studenty crowd you meet in the regular actors' haunts.' She looked at the younger girl with the kind, smiley face. 'I was a late starter.'

'How come?'

'I was sick for a while.' It was out before she realized.

'Oh, was it serious?'

'Not really,' she lied easily. Already she'd said too much. 'Anyway, enough about me, tell me about the new waiter you fancy.'

As they chatted she wondered about celebrating if she got this job. A party would be nice. She thought of all the friends she'd had at school, Anne Rooney and Kate O'Halloran and Brenda Smith. She'd been very popular, no doubt about that. Most likely to succeed, they'd have written in her

51

yearbook if this had been America. They'd lost contact when she left home, really. Where she came from girls left school early, got a job in a shop or factory, nabbed a boyfriend, got married and had babies, although not necessarily in that order. Her three oldest friends had about a dozen kids between them, and they were still under thirty. Annie saw them sometimes when she visited her dad and they'd have a good chat at the front door. Sometimes they even went for a sly drink in the afternoon, but not too often as money was tight. They all lived locally and relied on their parents to babysit. None of them were working but they were all happy, still buying clothes each Saturday and going to the pub at weekends, still ensconced in the same gang.

When Annie first left home she had been the most sociable of them all and was always the last one to leave the pub while on the drama course. When she started doing amateur productions she was the one who organized the party at the end of each run. Her illness had changed everything. Friends had come to see her often at the start, but they were embarrassed, breast cancer was not on anyone's agenda. Seeing someone so ill made them feel old.

Being sick had robbed Annie of her confidence. She'd once felt untouchable, bulletproof even. But for a long time after coming out of hospital she was scared. Oh, she was still good in a crowd and great at putting on an act but not so good in a one to one situation and useless at really talking about herself.

It simply made her feel too vulnerable. People treated you differently once they knew you'd had cancer: it was almost as if you might pop off on them any minute. Annie had tried it out on strangers once or twice but quickly learned to keep it to herself. And holding back robbed her of some of her vivaciousness.

Stop feeling sorry for yourself, she chided herself, and resolved to ring round everyone she knew for a drink to celebrate, if she had cause to. 'If' was an enormous word. She said a quick prayer again, her favourite: O sacred heart of Jesus, I place all my trust in thee. Maybe if she got this job it would be a new start, she'd be back to her old bubbly self, she thought hopefully as she greeted clients and prepared to act the part of confident hostess for Owen Kerrigan once more.

At eight-thirty David English arrived with a party of seven guests. She knew who he was and greeted him warmly. She liked him.

'Good evening, Mr English, how are you?'

'Fine, thanks, Annie. You?'

'Great, thank you. Can I take your coats? Would you care for a drink upstairs or would you rather go straight to your table?'

'I'd murder a gin and tonic myself. Now, gentlemen, how about you? They do a great vodka martini here.'

They trooped upstairs and David winked as he passed. 'Thanks, Annie, make mine a double, will you? I think I'm going to need it.'

'Sure, I'll send Geoff right up to take your order and talk you through the specials, you know most of our menu by heart anyway.'

David English was utterly charming, as usual, she thought although she noticed he looked tired and drawn tonight. He smiled his perfect white toothpaste ad smile and she smelt the cool, clean smell of him. He oozed wealth and sophistication and old money and she thought once again that he and Libby were a fabulous couple, although she'd rarely seen them here together.

The evening was hectic. Just when she thought it was never going to end, things quietened down and Owen, surprisingly, told her to go home. She was amazed to get off so early: it was not yet ten o'clock.

'You look tired, go on, I can manage here.'

'You're an absolute star, I am wrecked. Thanks.' She'd told him about the audition and he knew she was dying to get home in case they'd called.

Annie made her exit quickly. The wind chill cut right through her thin coat and she hurried along, pulling up her collar and blowing on her hands, anxious to catch the five past ten bus. A drunk sat down beside her and serenaded her throughout the entire first part of her journey, then she had to wait twenty-five minutes for the second bus, her connection having sailed by three minutes early as she charged towards the stop.

She made it home by eleven-fifteen, not at all worried about the gangs of youths she encountered as she walked from the bus. Tonight they had a fire going on the only patch of green for miles and she smelt the thick, chemical fumes of burning rubber. Tyres, she rightly suspected. Exhausted, she let herself in quickly, glad to escape the wind and the fumes, and switched on the electric coal-effect fire after checking the answering machine twice. Nothing. It made her feel restless. She didn't really want to go to bed, even though she was knackered, but it was the warmest place in the house, so she switched the fire off again and made herself a cup of cocoa, with half milk, half water, wishing she had some wine or beer in the house. She brushed her teeth, filled two hot water bottles and tucked herself under a mound of blankets and an old duvet, to read and sip her hot drink and eventually to chase dreams.

Chapter Six

The intercom at the front gate buzzed viciously rousing Libby from a delicious dream and she really minded the intrusion. She assumed it was students on their way home and turned over, rooting in the darkness for a warm body that she sensed wasn't there even before she'd found the cold spot.

Blinking, she fumbled for the alarm clock light. Almost 3 a.m. Where on earth was David? she wondered, feeling a nervous sensation in her stomach. The buzzer sounded again, and this time it was insistent.

Struggling out of bed, trying to wipe away the grogginess, she fumbled towards the huge bay window, pulled back the heavy curtains and looked out over the vast shadowy lawns. She could see the beam of a car at the electronic gates, headlights pointed searchingly towards the house. She fumbled for the dimmer switch and picked up the intercom. The image in the small TV screen was blurred, or maybe it was her sleepy eyes.

She uttered a croaky 'Yes?'

'Ms Marlowe?'

'What is it?' She cleared her throat, wondering who was using her name at this time of night.

'This is John Reynolds from Blackrock garda station. I'd like to have a word with you, please.'

'What's happened?' Her voice rose a fraction and she felt her heart quicken.

'Could you let the car in, please? I need to speak to you in person.'

She pressed the button and flung herself into her dressing-gown, pushing back an untidy mound of hair as she dashed barefoot over the thick cream pile of the carpet. The house was silent except for the fierce wind that made a strangled sound as it skated round the building. Libby's hand was sticky as it glided along the highly polished banister but the only thing she was conscious of was her heart, now thumping out a warning. She needed to get to the messenger quickly. A neighbouring dog barked in the distance, otherwise the city snored.

Throwing open one of the huge old double doors she knew she looked frightened as she waited for the police car to curl around the sweeping driveway and deliver its unwanted information.

It must be her mother, she was breathing heavily now. Please don't let her be dead. I haven't called her for a few days and I meant to. Guilt threatened to consume her. She never seemed able to hide her irritation with her mother these days and maybe this was God's way of punishing her.

John Reynolds hated these calls, was absolutely useless at them, and as he walked towards the tall, almost transparent woman in cream silk, her shocking blue eyes almost navy with fear, he wished he was anywhere else in the world. One glance told him she wasn't prepared for what he had to say.

'Please tell me, it's my mother, isn't it?'

'May I come in for a moment?' He held out his ID.

'Yes, of course ... I'm sorry.' They stepped quickly inside and she closed over the door, but left it ajar as if sensing they'd be using it shortly.

'Miss Marlowe, I'm afraid your husband has been taken ill. I need you to come with me to St Jarlath's Hospital.'

'My husband?' She was completely thrown. I don't understand ... how, where ... what happened?'

'I don't have much information. He was in a restaurant and he collapsed and they called an ambulance. They need you to get there immediately.'

'Why didn't they just call me themselves?'

'All your numbers are ex-directory. The only identity your husband had, apart from credit cards, was a bill with your address on it. The people he was having dinner with were foreigners, apparently, they only knew his office and mobile number. So, the hospital rang us.'

'Why didn't they just ask David for his home number?'

'I'm not sure, I didn't speak to them myself . . .'

'But he's OK, isn't he?'

'I don't know anything else. I'm very sorry. If you could get ready as quickly as possible I'll take you there now.'

Libby continued to search his face for another clue but he was young and clean and he looked tormented enough so she dashed upstairs, pausing halfway to turn and ask in a curiously calm, flat voice, 'You're sure it's my husband?'

'Yes, ma'am, certain.'

'David English?'

He nodded silently and she felt stupid for wasting time.

Quickly she pulled on black trousers, a sweater and socks and her suede boots, not bothering with underwear. She seldom prayed but she did so feverishly now as she grabbed her long cashmere coat because suddenly the house felt icy cold, even though the temperature was controlled twenty-four hours a day. Stopping only to pick up her bag and keys from the polished Edwardian table, she was back at the door in less than two minutes. The waiting policeman was already in the car and pointed in the direction of the gate. He genuinely didn't know any more but he'd seen enough in his short career to know it wasn't good.

It took the longest few minutes Libby could remember to reach their destination, even though the flashing blue light made what little traffic there was around give way immediately, the last of the late-night revellers and taxi drivers staring at their car enquiringly. She was huddled against the back window, remembering all the times she'd seen an ambulance or police car or fire engine pass her by and wondered about the casualties. As a child her mother had always told her to say a prayer when she heard the nee-naw and she hoped someone was doing the same for her now.

They reached the main entrance to the hospital and to her surprise the garda continued driving.

'Where are we going?'

'Accident and Emergency's over the other side.' He spoke quietly.

Libby never realized that two words could strike so much fear into an already racing heart.

'But he's in the private hospital, surely?' She stopped, reminding herself quickly that there was no point in getting angry with him.

'Everyone is admitted through A & E initially—' He broke off as the car came to a halt and she was out the door in an instant, before he had time to explain that his duty ended here. Libby made up her mind to pull whatever strings were necessary to ensure David had everything he needed. John Reynolds followed her inside.

The scene that greeted her made the televised medical dramas look under-resourced. It was chaos. The throng of damp, fearful bodies, the smell of sweat and blood and alcohol and vomit and the harsh orange light would normally have made Libby recoil, but she simply looked around blindly then made a beeline for the desk. 'My husband, David English, was admitted a while ago.'

The clerk didn't have to ask for her name. Everyone knew who she was.

'If you'd like to take a seat I'll have someone to talk to you as soon as possible.'

'Can't I just go to him?'

'If you wouldn't mind waiting, I'll check.' But Libby had already turned away.

'Can't you do anything?' This to the young garda.

'I'm sure they're doing all they can. Someone will be along in a minute.'

'They'd better be. I can't stand this waiting much longer.' She fell onto a seat like a disgruntled child but he could easily see that she was frightened. He decided not to leave now as he normally would have done. Several pairs of eyes were staring at her and one or two swaying bodies looked as if they might weave a path in her direction. She didn't belong here, but then he wondered if many people did.

'Mrs English, I'm staff nurse Ann Jones.' Libby looked up, taken aback slightly. Nobody ever called her that. She rose to her feet.

'I just wanted to let you know that the doctor will be along to speak to you shortly.'

'What happened?' She couldn't bear it for another minute.

'Your husband was admitted as an emergency

at about one forty-five. Apparently, he collapsed in a restaurant and they called an ambulance.'

'But, was it something he ate, did he choke, what?'

'We believe it may have been a heart attack.' The nurse knew exactly what it was but was drip-feeding the information.

It was the worst possible news and Libby wasn't prepared. She stared at the woman with a puzzled expression on her face.

'How bad is it?' a voice she recognized as her own asked calmly. The lights were hurting her eyes and making her head feel dizzy, on top of an already queasy stomach.

'I'm afraid it's serious.' The brown eyes were solemn. 'Maybe you'd like to sit down over here. Can I get you anything – cup of tea, glass of water?'

Libby shook her head and silently did as she was told. She wished this had happened to her: David would have been much better able to cope. She had a sudden aching longing to be close to him at this awful moment.

'Is there any way I could just look at him? Please?' she begged the older woman.

'I'll let the doctor know you're here,' the woman said. She moved off quickly.

The young policeman moved over and knelt down beside her. 'Is there anyone you'd like me to contact? One of your family, a sister or brother maybe?'

She shook her head.

'A friend then, someone who would be able to come and sit with you while you wait.'

'I'm an only child,' she murmured as if that explained everything.

'Are your parents alive?'

'Only my mum, but she'd have a heart attack if anyone called or telephoned at this time of night.' Libby smiled sadly at the irony. All her earlier arrogance had gone. She felt helpless and the feeling was unusual for her, as was the sensation of being utterly alone that hit her then, as she realized there really was no-one she could call on. There were loads of people in her life, in their lives, a telephone book of couples to have dinner with or go on holiday with, but no-one close enough. Maybe Carrie, if she lived in Dublin. Not Moya though, she'd be irritating. Strange to think that she could have called the wife of a government minister, or the girlfriend of one of the leading rock bands in the world, or pull any amount of strings to get the attention she required, but she couldn't think of one person she really wanted now.

'What about your husband's family?'

'His parents live in Dubai and his two brothers live abroad as well, I'll have to ring and get them over.' She fished in her bag for her phone, anything to stop her mind playing the cruel tricks it was playing at this minute.

'Don't worry about that for now, wait until you've seen the doctors first,' the garda said reassuringly, wishing he could be of more help. He'd known who she was the minute he'd heard the name, but she looked much more vulnerable than he'd imagined. He knew it was shock, she'd crumpled when the nurse had told her, and now she was like a child with her tousled fair hair and china blue, saucer eyes, innocent of the scourge of sickness and accidents and obviously unused to dealing with this kind of authority.

The nurse with the kind face returned with a mug of strong tea, 'to keep you going'. She smiled gently. 'Doctor Noonan is on his way to see you.' It sounded deadly serious.

'I should have you call his own doctor, he'll want to be informed . . .' Libby went fishing again.

'Fine, we can do that.' She moved aside as a tall man came slowly down the corridor, looking as if he'd stepped off the set of a hospital drama, white coat flapping and leads dangling, although as he got nearer Libby knew he was too tired and worn out for a romantic lead.

John Reynolds stood up immediately. 'I'll leave you to talk. I'd better get back to the station. I wish you the best of luck and hope things will be OK.' He was anxious not to intrude, in view of her celebrity status. Libby barely heard him, so intent was she on trying to read the approaching doctor's face.

'Miss Marlowe, I'm Donal Noonan. Perhaps we could talk in here.' She wished he'd called her Mrs English too, because at this moment that's all she was, somebody's demented wife.

She'd stood up the minute she saw him

approach, searching his face for clues. There were none.

People stared openly at her as he led the way to a quiet waiting room with comfortable chairs and took her cup away as she almost sent it flying in her haste to hear what he had to say.

'Is there anyone with you?'

She shook her head. 'Please tell me.'

'I'm afraid your husband suffered a massive heart attack in the restaurant tonight.'

'How is he?' It was all she wanted to know. She wondered why he wasn't smiling at her; people were usually kind once they realized who she was.

He sighed and shook his head. 'I'm sorry, but . . .'

'He is going to be OK, though?'

He tried again, this time more slowly.

'I'm very sorry to have to tell you this, Miss Marlowe, but I'm afraid it was too late . . .' He paused for only the slightest moment, putting off what he knew she didn't want to hear. 'I'm afraid we couldn't save him.' Her navy eyes flickered with fear.

'What does that mean?' She knew what it meant but she had to believe she was hearing him wrong.

He swallowed and looked at her with the eyes of someone who'd done this before. 'He was dead on arrival at the hospital.'

Libby made the smallest movement of her head, almost afraid to shake it and communicate a sign that she had accepted what he'd just told her. She tried to scream but nothing came out and she struggled to keep him in focus as she felt a lightness wash over her. After a long time she spoke and her voice was barely audible.

'No.'

She grabbed his hands and never took her tormented eyes off his face, just in case he tried to leave it like this. She couldn't let him do that to her.

'Please.'

'I'm very, very sorry, Miss Marlowe, there wasn't anything we could do.'

'No. Please God, no.' She shook her head wildly from side to side. She closed her eyes and screamed, 'Noooooooooo.'

There was nothing else to say after that so they simply stayed as they were, holding hands for a few more endless seconds, the doctor looking at her bowed head, Libby staring at the floor, silently willing him not to take away all her hope. And normal life went on all around them, if the sounds were anything to go by. After a few moments she looked at him with tortured eyes and spoke softly.

'He can't be, he's only thirty-nine . . .'

The doctor nodded silently, his eyes telling her he'd seen far worse.

'He's always been so healthy.' She was begging him.

'I'm very sorry. There was nothing we could do.' He was repeating himself, new words were scarce. 'Will you let me call someone?'

She shook her head and went back to staring at

the floor. 'Can I see him?' It was very important all of a sudden. It wasn't definite yet, not until she saw him. She clung to the ridiculous hope that they'd made a mistake.

'Of course.'

'Now?'

'Perhaps you'd like someone with you?'

'There's no-one, honestly.' The truth was, there was no-one she wanted.

He wondered how someone so sought after could seem so alone. He stood up, disentangling their hands, then he opened the door and led her gently, like a much older woman or an invalid, down a never-ending blank corridor, slowing down to her pace. She sensed his hand at her back, guiding her.

'Would you like me to wait outside?' He was always unsure at this moment. Everyone seemed to handle it differently. Some were scared, others wanted to ask questions, a good few needed his support and more simply wanted to be alone with their loved ones and hold onto them.

Libby nodded and he held open the door. She saw David, lying quite still, but otherwise looking exactly as she'd last seen him, except that his hair was tousled. He looked healthy, relaxed even. He looked alive.

'Was he in any pain?' She'd only just thought of it.

He shook his head quietly. 'No.' She left him then.

*   *   *

Just for a brief second she thought that maybe her husband was playing a trick on her and her heart started pounding with anticipation. Until she touched him.

And then she knew and she simply lay down beside him and tried to get him, and herself, warm again.

She stayed with him for hours, talking and pleading and fixing his hair and telling him how much she loved him, how desperately she needed him in her life, and it was a cold bright morning when she finally left him – refusing all offers of help – to make her way home to a life that no longer existed.

Chapter Seven

Annie woke to the shrill of the telephone. She got a fright as she always did when forced alive. Usually it was the doorbell ringing: every kid in the neighbourhood seemed to enjoy playing chasing at her expense. Groggy and bad tempered, she skidded across the cold, hard floorboards and grabbed the offending article.

She offered a muffled greeting and waited, expecting to hear the usual 'Is that the maternity hospital?' It happened to her several times a day. The numbers were almost identical and she'd had more than her fair share of irate or scared or drunken husbands over the years. But not today.

'Hello, is that Annie?'

She came to very fast. 'It is, yes.'

'Oh hi, Annie, this is Max Donaldson from *Southside* here. Sorry to ring you so early, I hope I'm not disturbing you?'

'Oh hi Max, no not at all.' Disturb me any time you like, was what she wanted to say, just as long as it's not the electronic equivalent of a Dear John letter. Surely they didn't ring people with bad news? The thought was just too depressing to even contemplate.

'. . . just calling to let you know we'd love you to play Bobby, we all agreed you were terrific yesterday.' Her head started buzzing. 'We really enjoyed your performance . . . not to mention the outfit . . .' She could hear laughter in his voice and knew he was teasing '. . . and Stephen said he felt very comfortable playing opposite you.'

Just like that. A couple of short sentences and everything changed.

'Oh my God, I can't believe it, that is just fantastic. Thank you so much.' She knew she was supposed to play it cool but she was hopping around in a skimpy T-shirt with numb fingers and a toe that was slowly turning gangrenous with cold. Acting cool was out of the question.

He laughed and she liked the sound. 'I take it you accept?'

'Yes, yes, *yes*. I'm absolutely thrilled and eh . . . honoured,' she felt she should add.

'Well, wait till you hear the terms first. I know you've no agent, so I'll ask one of the assistant producers to call you later today with dates and a proposed fee. As I think I mentioned yesterday, it's only for four episodes at the moment, but we do think the character has a future, depending on how this session goes. I don't want to get your hopes up though, you know what this business is like.'

'Yes, of course.' Her voice still sounded two octaves too high.

'OK then, that's it, congratulations. You had some stiff competition there yesterday, by the way. We're really looking forward to having you on board and one of the others will explain it all in more detail later, OK?'

'Yes, fine and thanks again.'

'Pleasure. Talk to you soon.'

'Bye, thank you. Bye-bye.' Shut up, Annie before you blow it.

She hung up, shouted 'yes!' and threw a victory punch, then slid down the wall and hugged her knees to her chest and rocked back and forth screaming in delight, eventually sticking her fist in her mouth in case the screams brought her next-door neighbours running with a hatchet. She could hardly believe that she'd finally been given a break. Her first TV part, and what a one to start on. She was scared then for a split second, knowing that if this didn't work it was definitely the end of the line.

Annie jumped up again quickly, realizing she was about to have icicles dangling prettily from her nose, grabbed her ancient woollen dressing-gown and faded slippers and made for the kitchenette and the kettle, turning on the heat to celebrate. She stretched lazily on the couch and sipped the scalding tea, enjoying the indulgence of morning TV as only someone with a proper job can. She didn't see or hear anything. She was dreaming with her eyes open, picking a new outfit, maybe a good bottle of wine, perhaps a moisturizer not from the super-market, definitely some mugs so that she could throw away her brown-ringed ones and maybe even a few fresh flowers that weren't a guilty garage impulse buy. The day now seemed filled with possibilities and she felt giddy.

*

The morning rush was almost over as Libby walked along a quiet road near the hospital on the outskirts of Dublin. She swayed slightly as if she'd been drinking. A car pulled up beside her. John Reynolds jumped out, looking tired and dishevelled and slightly embarrassed.

'I just called to the hospital. They said you'd left but that you wouldn't let them call anyone. Are you OK?'

It took her a second to recognize him. She shook her head silently.

'You're miles from home. Let me drive you.' She nodded and he opened the passenger door. 'You shouldn't be on your own at a time like this.' His face was full of concern.

'I was just thinking about that.' She spoke more to herself than to him. 'I am on my own, actually. Oh, there are hundreds of people who'll come rushing round as soon as they hear. But they're all social acquaintances, or business friends of David's.' Her voice was barely audible. 'At our level people use each other and he always warned me of that. When they want us to go to a dinner party, or a launch, it's mostly not us they want at all, it's who we are. The entrepreneur and the celebrity chef. We're a much sought-after duo,' she snorted. 'Guaranteed to make the papers. Top of everyone's list. Or at least we were,' she corrected herself and continued to stare straight ahead like a zombie. 'In a way, though, it suited us. We liked keeping people at a distance. We only wanted each other. And David was always slow to trust people, so I never really let my guard down in public.' Her face distorted. 'Look at me now.'

They drove for several miles in silence. When they eventually reached the house Libby got out in slow motion to punch in the code and open the gates to let the car through, but made no move to get back in. The garda drove on ahead, sensing she needed to be alone, but kept his eye on her in the mirror as she walked up the drive behind the slightly battered Ford Focus, head bowed as if practising for walking behind her husband's coffin.

His gorgeous silver Jag was where it always was, his pride and joy, and she ran her fingers over it tenderly, hoping to magically spirit him home. She could picture the two of them standing there beside it as they had many times, she teasing him about loving his car more than her. He simply could not be gone from her for ever. He just couldn't.

'Thank you,' she said, turning to the young man who'd been a stranger until a couple of hours ago. 'You're very kind.'

'Let me see you inside, make sure you're all right.'

'Where's your police car?' It seemed important, the sort of trivial detail that meant your brain was still functioning.

'I'm actually off duty now. I was on my way home to sleep. I just wondered what had happened.' He looked at her half apologetically, as a pink tinge stained his face. 'My mother loves you, she watches everything you do, so I felt I should make sure you were OK.'

She gave him the ghost of a sad smile. 'I don't think I'll ever be really OK again.'

'You will, I promise. Now, let me get you inside and make you a cup of tea.'

'Mrs O'Connell will be ... Oh God, I don't think I can face anyone right now, I don't want to have to ...'

'I'll deal with it, just show me where the kitchen is.' He was much better at the practical details.

Mrs O'C. came bustling out as soon as she heard the door. 'I wondered where everyone had got to.'

'Good morning, Mrs O'Connell, I'm John Reynolds, I wonder if you'd be good enough to make Miss Marlowe a cup of tea and perhaps some toast, please.' He was glad he'd changed out of uniform, it was less frightening for the older woman.

'Yes, of course.' She came to an abrupt stop, wanting to say something but too well trained, or maybe too used to being discreet in a house where she'd gleaned many nuggets of information over the years.

Libby led the way to the breakfast lobby, a warm, sunny, Victorian garden room filled with plants and flowers and oversized chairs. She plonked down woodenly in the nearest one, as if someone had pushed her.

Garda Reynolds simply stood facing the window, seeming to admire the exotic vista of tree ferns, huge palms and fat-leaved castor oil plants. In reality he didn't see any of it, he was simply giving her space and time to regain her composure.

Minutes later Mrs O'Connell entered silently, sensing the mood. She left a silver tea service with a pot of fragrant coffee and strong tea and a silver rack with slivers of white and brown toast. There was strawberry jam and bright yellow butter along with a small porcelain plate of handmade biscuits, Libby's favourite.

'You should try and eat something,' John Reynolds urged as he brought her a cup of strong, sweet tea.

She simply shook her head again. 'What time is it?'

'Shortly after nine.'

'There are so many things to do, people to tell. I don't know where to start. How am I going to tell his parents?'

'Is there someone who could help you with all of this?'

Another fringed-lash look that tugged at his heartstrings. Then, after a moment or two, 'My mother, I suppose.'

'Would you like me to call her?'

'No, it's a bit too early, she lives alone and I don't want to frighten her. Her housekeeper will be there at nine-thirty, I'll call then. I wonder what time it is in Dubai?'

'I can check that for you.' He was on the phone in an instant, leaving her with a fast beating heart and sweaty palms at the thought of having to speak to David's parents.

'I'm going to go and see my mother.' Suddenly Libby jumped up, grabbed her bag and headed for the door.

'I'll drop you there.'

'No, honestly, I'm fine, really.'

'You're not in any fit condition to drive. I can just leave you off and then I'll head home.'

She nodded, already at the door, then turned in realization. 'I'll have to tell Mrs O'C. . . . people will start phoning . . . I don't want her to find out that way . . . she . . .' Libby gave a soft moan, sorry now that she'd never really made any effort to get to know the woman. It would have made what she had to do now a lot easier. '. . . She loved him, was with his family before they went away. She's known him since he was a child.'

Garda Reynolds nodded sadly, 'I'll wait in the car.'

Libby moved like a robot jerkily towards the kitchen, where the older woman was working quietly. She stood looking at her back for a moment, realizing there was no easy way to do it.

'Mrs O'– a pair of inquisitive eyes faced her

instantly. They were cautious, as usual. When Libby came into the kitchen like this it was usually to complain, or to give her an order, and she disliked the former and detested the latter.

'I'm afraid something awful's happened. It's David, he . . . he had a heart attack last night.' She bit her lip, knowing that if she gave way to tears now she'd never stop. How can I say these words? she thought, afraid to speak them aloud for the first time and make the whole horrendous thing real, yet knowing that she had no alternative. 'I don't know any other way to tell you.' She could barely get the words out, they seemed so treacherous.

The housekeeper had never heard her sound so . . . she struggled to find the word . . . so soft. She knew it must be very bad.

'I'm afraid he died within a short time.' A million questions flooded her woolly brain at that moment. Who had been with him? Had he said anything? Where were his things? She felt hysterical.

'Ah, no.' The tortured words jolted her back to reality. Her housekeeper's worn, lined face had dealt with a lifetime of bad news but she wasn't prepared for this. She sank tiredly into a chair and put her head in her hands. Libby started to move then stopped, wanting to give her a hug but knowing they weren't close enough.

'I know how much you cared for him. It must be a terrible shock. Will I make you some tea?'

What was it about tea, that it was always

automatically offered as a magical potion to cure all ills?

The other woman shook her head and Libby saw she was crying.

'I'm very sorry to have to tell you this way, but people may start calling or phoning and I didn't want you to hear it from anyone else. Would you like a brandy, perhaps?'

'He was such a beautiful boy, I held him when he was only days old and he grew into a lovely, lovely man.' The old eyes were glassy; her voice was barely audible and sounded incredibly weary.

'I know.' Libby poured a brandy from the bottle of ten-year-old that she kept in the kitchen for cooking.

'I just can't believe it. He was so young and always so healthy.'

Libby sat with Mrs O'Connell for a few minutes longer and let her reminisce about her beautiful baby. Eventually she stood up uncertainly.

'I'm sorry to leave now but I have to get to my mother. She doesn't know. Will you be OK here by yourself?'

Mrs O'Connell nodded.

'Please just take it easy. It's probably better to let the machine take calls. A lot of people will start ringing once it gets out.'

'Don't worry about me. Will you be all right yourself?'

'Yes.'

'Right so.'

'If I'm calling I'll use the code.' David always

made the three of them use his code – let the phone ring twice, hang up, then immediately ring again. Strange to think she'd never share that with anyone again.

'I'll go then.' Libby didn't know what else to do.

'God bless you.' It was the friendliest they'd ever been.

Chapter Eight

Libby slipped quietly out of the room, out of the house, into the only safe haven she knew at the moment.

'Are you OK?'

'Yes, thank you.'

John Reynolds drove off slowly. She gave him directions and huddled in the corner for warmth, grateful he wasn't expecting her to make small talk.

Twenty minutes later they arrived at the large modern house in Foxrock, which her parents had bought for their retirement ten years ago. It was an exciting building, if you liked that particular style. Libby never had. All white and chrome and glass, it was much more suited to a young architect type; she'd been surprised when her parents had decided they loved it. The wide sweeping drive was bordered by truly magnificent lawns that owed more to the constant attentions of a gardener than to mother nature.

She got out awkwardly. All her movements

seemed puppet-like this morning. John Reynolds jumped out as well. 'I'll say goodbye, then.'

She shook the outstretched hand. 'I can't thank you enough, you've been more than kind.'

'No problem at all. I'm very sorry for your troubles. Good luck to you, now.' He had a funny, old man way with words and she suspected it was the product of a country upbringing.

She headed for the door, dreading seeing her mother yet needing her badly.

'Hello Vera, is Mum in?'

'Libby love, what brings you here so early?'

They were standing in the big open-plan hall with winter morning light threatening to blind them.

'I need to talk to Mum, Vera. Is she up yet?'

'Yes, I've just brought her up a cup of tea. Would you like a coffee?'

'No thanks, I'll go up.' She moved away quickly as the situation almost overwhelmed her again. Her heels clicked out a warning on the polished maple floor.

'Elizabeth, darling, what are you doing...?' Her mother turned and caught the first glimpse of her daughter's ashen face. 'What's wrong?'

'Oh Mum.' All the pent-up emotion came out in one great, shuddering sob.

Christina Marlowe was a tall, handsome, sixty-something woman with good skin and poker-straight silver hair that hung just below her ears and was kept from her face by a thin navy velvet hairband, by now a sort of trademark. A widow for some five years, her greatest regret was that she'd only had one child. She'd always seen herself with lots of daughters, instead of a single busy one, who didn't stay in touch as often as Christina would have liked. She was putting the finishing touches to her already immaculate make-up when the unexpected visitor hurled herself at her and buried her face in her chest.

'Please Libby, tell me, what is it?' she said, reverting to the childhood name she hadn't used for years.

'It's David.'

'What's wrong, have you had a row?' She fully expected Libby to announce a minor upset in a major disaster way. She knew her daughter had a very good marriage but throughout her life Libby had always felt that total happiness was hers for the taking, that she deserved nothing less. Even the smallest thing that went wrong became a drama. She also believed she was nearly always right, which sometimes made her a difficult mate, Christina suspected.

Libby shook her head and great gulping sobs racked her body as she searched for the right words. There were only wrong ones.

'He's dead.' It was bald and cold and brutal, which was exactly how she felt.

'No.' All colour drained from Christina's face as she sat her much-loved baby down on the bed. 'Oh my God ... Libby please ... darling, tell me what happened?'

'I got a call in the middle of the night, he had a heart attack in a restaurant. The police came to the door. By the time I made it to the hospital he was . . . oh Mum, what am I going to do without him?' It was a pitiful plea and there was simply no answer that could comfort her.

'Shush now, it'll be all right, I promise.' They sat together, arms wrapped around each other, mother stroking child's head, until Vera, who wasn't nearly as discreet as Mrs O'Connell, strolled in and found them.

'Anyone for a nice cup of cof— what's wrong?'

'Vera, be an angel and make a pot of strong tea and bring it up here, please. I'm afraid David's had a heart attack and . . .'

'Oh my God, I'm sorry. Libby love, come 'ere to me. Is he OK?' Vera knew of no ailment that a hug couldn't cure.

Christina shook her head wearily, a warning sign and Vera moved backwards, shocked yet not fully understanding why. Her mind began to race with fear, but she quickly shook the offending thoughts away and hurried downstairs as fast as her sixty-year-old arthritic legs would carry her.

'I simply cannot believe what you're telling me, Libby,' said her Mother. 'My poor baby, what a terrible shock for you, why didn't you ring me? I'd have come to the hospital to be with you.'

'I didn't want to frighten you. Besides, it was too late, there was nothing you could have done.'

'I could have helped you shoulder the burden.

My God, not David, he'd never been sick a day in his life as far as I'm aware. Had he been complaining of anything?'

'Not that I know of.' Racking her brains for a moment, Libby realized they'd never really talked much about the ordinary inconsequential things. Strange as it sounded, she probably wouldn't have known if he'd been feeling unwell. Anyway, he was always so healthy that she'd have had no sympathy for him if he'd complained. He'd probably have gone straight to Mrs O'C., who'd have fussed over him for ages, or his frightful secretary, who'd have done exactly the same thing. She felt guilty but wasn't sure why, because her role had always been to make him laugh and tell him the latest celebrity gossip, or drag him shopping or on holidays or out to play. Business discussions and pampering sessions weren't her style.

Telling his parents was awful. Luckily, his father answered the phone. Libby didn't think she would have found the courage to tell his mother that she'd lost her youngest child.

'Hello Libby, nice to hear from you. How are you, my dear?' Charles English boomed, sounding every bit as aristocratic as Libby knew him to be. 'What's the weather like in Dublin?'

'Charles, I have the most dreadful news.' Libby couldn't control her tears and gave up trying. 'It's David.'

'What's wrong with him, Libby?' That voice again, calm, questioning, concerned.

'He had a heart attack last night. Oh Charles, I'd give anything not to be telling you this.'

'How bad is it?' She could feel the fear from the other side of the world.

'I'm sorry, so very sorry, Charles.'

'Please Libby, no.'

Her voice was almost a whisper but she had to get the words out fast, lest he think there was any hope.

'He ... he didn't make it.' She was almost uncontrollable now. 'I want him back with me. I need him. I can't go on without him.' They both knew it might be true. David had been her protector, and all his cosseting would make it much harder now.

She told Charles everything she knew. She felt completely numb. Her mother came and put a cashmere shawl around her shaking shoulders.

'Oh, dear God. How can I ever tell this terrible thing to Monica?' Libby could hear the grief.

'I don't know. I just knew I had to get you so that you could break it to her gently. I haven't told Robert or Trevor either.'

'It's all right, I'll do it.' His voice came down the line with a lead weight attached. 'Have you someone with you?'

'I came straight to Mum's. I didn't know where else to go. She's here beside me.'

'I can't talk to her now, Libby. I need to get my head together before I face my wife. I'll call you back in a couple of hours, if I may.' Still as polite as ever.

'Yes of course. I'm so very sorry, Charles, I know how much he loved you both.' She was inconsolable now. They talked for a few minutes longer and agreed to speak again later in the morning.

With each phone call it became more real to Libby and she felt more and more out of control. She rang Alex O'Meara, the chief financial officer in David's main company. He was devastated. John Simpson, his solicitor and childhood friend, was distraught.

Her old friend Carrie squealed when she heard Libby's voice. 'Did you get my message?'

'No.'

'I only found out after we spoke yesterday. Oh Libby, I'm pregnant, can you believe it! And, I know it's too soon and all that and I'm dreading the terrible sickness I'll have for the entire nine months but I really feel this time it might be a . . .' Her voice trailed off. 'Libby, are you there?'

'Carrie, something terrible's happened.' It all came flooding out and in a warm country kitchen Carrie sat and cried with her friend and cursed her own stupidity and wished she wasn't pregnant and miles away.

'Oh Libby, I just don't know what to say.'

'I can't go on without him, Carrie. He minded me.'

'I know he did.' She wasn't the first that morning to wish he hadn't shielded Libby quite so much.

*　*　*

It was all so unlikely: everyone was caught out, dumbfounded even, and no-one could find the right words to say to the broken-hearted woman left behind. Libby didn't know what to do about her own work or how to handle the media interest. She decided to go straight to one of the heads of RTE, Ireland's national broadcasting organization. She was, after all, a major star and he was an old friend.

Leo Morgan was gobsmacked. 'Oh, Libby, Libby, I am so sorry. Is there anything I can do?'

She bit her lip; the sadness in his voice made her want to cry again. Funny how kindness has that effect. 'I just didn't know who to call. I can't face everyone. Would you mind talking to the production company, please? And I suppose the Press Office will have to issue a statement of some sort. Just keep them away from me, Leo, I couldn't face a photographer today.'

'Of course. I'll handle it all myself. Don't give it another thought, please.'

'Oh, and I've just realized one of my programmes is on transmission tonight. I don't think it should go ahead. It wouldn't be appropriate.' In fact, it would freak her out, she knew, seeing herself happy in another lifetime.

'No problem, Libby. I'll keep in touch with you, if that's OK.'

'Just call me on the mobile from your mobile, that way your number will come up. And tell people not to ring me just yet.'

'Don't worry and please, call me if there's anything else I can do.'

'I will.'

'And Libby . . .'

'Yes?'

'I cannot tell you how sorry I am. He was a fine man.'

'I know.' She was off again.

She made several more phone calls while Christina went downstairs to give Vera instructions just in case anyone tried to intrude on their grief. In between calls Libby simply sat and stared.

It was eerily calm for a while in the warm sanctuary of the bedroom. Surprisingly it was almost midday. She knew she needed to keep going but all at once a terrible tiredness enveloped her body, forcing her down on the bed. But stillness brought its own torment and the icy clutch that gripped her every time she paused for an instant now threatened to suck the air from her.

She paced up and down holding her stomach and as she passed the TV she flicked it on, unable to stand the silence any longer. The early lunchtime news was just ending and she stared unseeingly at another scene of carnage. The picture cut back to the newsreader, a cool brunette with a false smile whom Libby had never liked. She wasn't smiling now. Libby heard the Dublin 4 clipped voice as if from a great distance.

'And finally news has just reached us that the

well-known businessman David English has died suddenly in hospital in Dublin.'

Libby was unable to resist watching. The picture changed to one of David walking into Dublin Castle with a group of politicians. It had been filmed a few months previously and he looked fit and tanned and gorgeous.

'Mr English, seen here on the right, was guest speaker at a major international conference held in Dublin last September and was highly regarded in business circles.'

It was seeing his smile that did it. Libby jumped up and ran to the screen, trying to erase the awful reality with some stupid remote control that wouldn't work now. The voice droned on.

'Mr English is survived by his wife, television presenter—'

She hit the off button just as everything turned white in front of her eyes. She fainted.

Chapter Nine

Annie had had a delicious morning. After she'd channel-hopped for an hour, she dressed quickly, took the phone off the hook in case *they* rang, then dashed to the local shop for a treat for a very late breakfast. The indulgence came in the form of a thick brown block. She spread it on the table, smoothing out the silver foil wrapper just as she had done many times as a child. Eventually it sat on a mirror and she snapped a few squares crisply and popped one into her mouth, revelling in the silky smoothness. No 70 per cent cocoa solids, no organic rubbish, just plain old Cadbury's milk chocolate. She stretched out on the hard, lumpy couch and felt only feathers as she scoffed her luscious prize, each mouthful of velvet washed down with a gulp of hot tea.

Annie felt not a trace of guilt as she finished the entire bar and poured her third cuppa. She'd also allowed herself the glossiest magazine in the shop, not a difficult decision where she lived, as there were only about three on sale. Expensive titillation was not an everyday purchase for the customers of Lucky's Newsagents, an unfortunate name given that the premises was nearly always boarded up after yet another attempted robbery. Still, she'd managed to find one with a limited number of thumbprints and settled down to read about the lives and loves of the rich and famous, imagining her own face in one of the photos some day. *Annie Weller, newest star of the mega-successful* Southside, *seen at the première of Colin Farrell's latest blockbuster, where it's rumoured she spent several hours in the company of the rugged Irish heart-throb.*

She pictured the caption and her floaty, designer dress and laughed out loud at the fantasy. Still, as daydreams went it was pretty fantastic and she speculated again on where this particular career move would take her. After a while she was desperate to tell someone so she rang her dad.

'Hi, it's only me.'

'Hello love, how are you?'

'I'm good, in fact I'm terrific really. I've just been offered a part in *Southside*.'

'The TV drama series, you mean?'

'That's the one.'

'You never mentioned anything about that. When did all this happen?'

'It happened really quickly, actually, I only auditioned yesterday. They just rang this morning. It's only a small part, so don't get carried away. At the moment it's for four episodes, but you never know, they might like me.'

'Well, I'm delighted for you, love. What sort of part is it?'

'Eh, not one you'll be mad about, I'd say. She's called Bobby and she's a sort of . . . a good-time girl.' That should put an end to the conversation, Annie thought ruefully, knowing her father.

'I hope you won't be taking your clothes off?' He sounded slightly agitated.

'So do I or the public are in for a shock.' Annie laughed and her father cleared his throat, a sure sign he was embarrassed. 'Don't worry, it goes out early in the evening, they can't broadcast nudity before the nine o'clock watershed.' Annie hoped she was right.

'Well, you deserve a bit of luck, girl. That's all I'll say.'

'Thanks, Dad. I was going to call around on my way to work this evening, if that's OK?'

'Fine, I'll be here, as usual. Not going anywhere.'

'OK, I'll see you about half-three then.'

As soon as she'd hung up, the phone rang.

'Hello, Annie Weller speaking.' She'd no idea why she said that. She was obviously getting notions above her station already, she chided herself, feeling foolish.

'Oh, hi Annie, this is Isobel Ryan from *Southside*, we met at the audition.'

'Yes, of course, hi, how are you?'

'Good, thanks. Congratulations, by the way. You were terrific.'

'Thank you, I'm really thrilled, although my

father is slightly worried, no, make that very worried, that I might have to take my clothes off.'

'Well, not in these four episodes, anyway, I've just finished reading them. I was wondering if I could send them to you by courier, so that you have a chance to go through them.'

'That would be brilliant. I was wondering when I could get my hands on them.'

Annie gave her address, wishing it was a posher one and then felt guilty for being a snob. Isobel asked if she wouldn't mind holding while she transferred her to Mike Nichols, one of the producers, who also wanted to speak to her.

'Hi, Annie, it's Mike Nichols here. How are you?'

'Hi, Mike. I'm great, thanks.' Annie was unsure what to say to the man who had helped turn her life around. 'I really want to tell you how grateful I am to you for getting me the audition in the first place.'

'Oh listen, I was just looking after our interests. I saw your performance in that play at the Everest Theatre a couple of months ago – can't remember the name of it even, but you stood out, so I was delighted when this part came up. It sort of seemed right for you, not that I'm saying you look like . . . hell, I'd better stop before I dig a hole for myself.'

Annie was enjoying herself. 'Well, I was playing a girl who had just left a religious order so my acting must have been seriously flawed if you saw me more as a prostitute.'

'Let's just say you looked far too good to be left to the celibate life. I had to try to broaden your horizons somehow.'

Annie blushed but was delighted. 'Well, I'm glad you did. It's a big break for me and I'm really happy. So thanks.'

'Pleasure. Now, I need to talk to you about money and I hope it won't put you right off me. TV doesn't pay that well, as you're about to find out.' Annie was glad he didn't know that she'd do it for nothing, just for the experience.

'At the moment we'd like to contract you for four episodes, as I think Max explained. If we decide to take the character further we'd probably commit to a six-month contract, but don't hold me to that.' He mentioned a figure per episode that was more than Annie earned in a month at the restaurant. Not huge, but mega to her.

'How does that sound?' he asked half apologetically.

'That's fine.' Annie was not going to argue.

'There are a few perks, though they're tiny. We'll provide taxis to and from studio on recording days and we have a full breakfast available if your call is early. We offer vouchers for lunch and the food here is quite decent, to be honest. Also, anything we might ask for, such as, say, a change of hair, will naturally be taken care of.'

'Are you thinking of a change of hairstyle?' Annie was intrigued.

'I'm not sure. I heard Max talking to design yesterday. I probably shouldn't have said anything because wardrobe and make-up will want to meet you and discuss the part . . .'

'That's fine. I was just thinking that I needed a

good haircut anyway.' And good cutters charge a month's wages, she thought.

'Well, don't do anything till you talk to them and don't worry, it's all negotiable. We're not going to turn you into a peroxide blonde and then turf you out after four weeks.'

'That's a relief. My father is rather proud of my "Irishness" – at least that's what he calls red hair and freckles.'

They laughed together and chatted for ages. Mike Nichols gave her dates and promised to send her a rehearsal schedule and all the relevant info nearer the time. She took a deep breath and risked asking a favour because he sounded so nice.

'There's just one thing. I don't know what time recording finishes on the studio days, but I was wondering if there's any way I could be free at five. I'm sorry to have to ask and if it's a problem . . .' She bit her lip, trying to work out what the silence meant, then rushed on anyway. 'It's just, I work at night and . . .' She paused, flustered and definitely not willing to let him know how much she needed her paltry earnings.

'I'm just looking at the schedule but I see we don't have your episodes finalized yet. Most days, we don't finish in studio till seven-thirty, but look, leave it with me and I'll see what I can do.'

'I don't want to cause any problems.'

'No worries. I'll give a note to the PA and tell her you need to be finished by five. I'm sure we can accommodate you, given that it's only for four episodes and if we can't then it might only be on one particular day, so you should at least be able to make other arrangements. To be honest, it's a bit of a nightmare trying to keep everyone happy and usually we say no, but I'll tell them you're accepting the part on the basis that you'll be free at five.'

Annie was horrified. 'Oh, no, please I . . .'

'Don't worry, we'll work something out. Leave it with me and I'll talk to you later in the week. Meanwhile, I've just been handed a note to say that wardrobe and make-up would like to meet you on Thursday, if that's OK with you.'

'Yes, that's fine, I can be available any time you like.' She was waffling again.

'Listen, it might be a good idea if you come in and see the place. We're recording all day on Thursday so you could spend a couple of hours in studio in the morning and see the others in the afternoon. How does that sound?'

'Perfect.' She had to bite her lip to stop herself offering to sleep with him to make up for the hassle she was inflicting on them at this early stage.

'Great, that's it then. Oh,' he laughed. 'I've just been handed another note asking what size you are, top and bottom, so I think I'll hand you back to Isobel 'cause if I know any more about you I might have to marry you. Here she is. Bye for now.'

Annie was smiling as the other girl came back on the line. But five minutes later she was anxious again that she'd been too demanding. They'd probably be dying to get rid of her after four episodes, and she hadn't even signed her first contract. She considered ringing Mike Nichols back, but couldn't decide what to say.

She got out her diary and made a few more calls to friends who had been supportive over the past few months. After talking to quite a few answering machines she finally got lucky. Angie answered immediately.

'Hi there, it's Annie.' She almost said Annie Weller, because she didn't see Angie that often, but they usually had coffee after an audition, to catch up.

'Annie, how are you? What's happening?'

'I'm great, Angie, how about you?'

'Fine, although I've had two auditions this week and neither has been in contact. Still, I'm in rehearsal for a small play in the Civic so I'm kept going.'

Annie wasn't sure about dumping good news on her, so, but she couldn't help herself.

'Well, guess what, I've just been offered a part in *Southside*.'

'Oh my God, that's fantastic. I knew they were casting at the moment and my agent's been in touch with them. Tell me everything.'

Annie did.

'That sounds brilliant. You deserve it. It's just a pity there are so few good parts for women our age, at the moment. And it'll probably get worse. It's so much easier for men, it's just not fair.' They moaned for ages. Annie felt great to be part of it all and able to contribute properly.

She was delighted when Angie suggested they

meet up for a few pints the following week to celebrate. Angie was the kind of girl who had a million close friends and Annie always felt good to even be considered part of her circle. She hung up, delighted with herself, knowing her news would be all around Dublin by this evening. Brushing her hair and grabbing a jacket, she left to visit her father happier than she'd been in years.

Chapter Ten

'Annie, come in, love. You look well.'

'Thanks, Dad. How are you? How's the leg?'

'A bit better today. No use complaining.' Joe Weller was a tall, handsome, weatherbeaten man of seventy-four who always wore cardigans. Although he suffered badly with arthritis and his daughter knew it got him down at times, he never moaned. She noticed he was using a stick more often, even around the house. Still, he'd been a doer all his life so now he simply got on with things and accepted that life was tough. It always had been.

'The kettle's on. Would you like a sandwich?'

'No thanks. I brought you a fruit brack. Your favourite.'

'What did I do to deserve this?' He was pleased.

'You know I'm celebrating my first TV part.' Annie grinned at him. 'But I can't afford champagne just yet.'

He left her to make tea and Annie looked

around the room that had been home to her for ever. It was spotless and tidy, but cluttered, and she knew better than to suggest a bit of feng shui. Piles of newspapers were neatly stacked in a corner beside the gas fire that was always on. Annie sat down on a heap of pink velour in the corner, and felt the spongy seat give way underneath her. Did they still make pouffes any more? Did they still call them by that ridiculous name?

The room smelt of pipe tobacco and mothballs and the faded pictures and fussy smoke-stained wallpaper added an air of gloom. All the furniture was too big and too dark and an oversized ancient TV didn't help, nor did the dog hairs and feeding bowls littered about, but it was still her father's favourite place to be of an evening. Especially in the winter.

'I tried calling the boys,' she shouted towards the kitchen.

'Any luck?'

'Well, in Australia it was the middle of the night. I only realized after I'd dialled, so I hung up again quickly. In London Donal's machine was on so I left a message. I have no idea where Jim is at the moment and I tried four different numbers for Greg and no-one had seen him.'

'Don't worry, they'll ring from Australia on Sunday week like they always do. Jim was in Mexico last time I heard. And Greg rang last night and said he'd call round tomorrow, so I'll tell him then.'

'Where's he staying at the moment?'

'In Kilkenny with some other struggling artist.' Her father emerged from the kitchen, tea towel in hand. 'I dunno about him at all sometimes.'

'He'll be fine, he's a survivor.' Annie only ever kept in touch with her brothers through her dad, so she wasn't worried that she hadn't managed to speak to even one of them.

'You don't want to be getting too fond of that stuff, now.'

'What stuff?'

'Champagne. And mind yourself in that TV place. I hear they're nearly all alcoholics and everybody is supposed to be sleeping with someone else's wife.'

'Chance would be a fine thing, Dad. Anyway, it's only for a couple of weeks.'

'Well, I wish you luck, you know that. Now, come into the kitchen and we'll test this cake out for freshness and you can tell me all about the audition.'

An hour later Annie left, feeling glad that she'd called. Home was a great leveller. Her father was terrific and she owed him a lot. He waved her off and she promised to call over and help him cut the front hedge at the weekend.

As she walked along the neat, littered street, its row of identical council cottages all with their brightly painted front doors and windowboxes and hanging baskets of fading winter pansies, Annie remembered her childhood spent skipping along these streets, playing beds and kick the can

101

and relievie-i-o. Days when the only pain was tiredness and your worst fear was being called in early. Until her mother's death it had been a happy time, with long sunshiny days spent in the grass-scented air and evenings curled up in someone else's house, scoffing Kimberley and Mikado biscuits and drinking diluted Mi Wadi orange. They were always hungry and always craving an adventure, preferably Enid Blyton style.

All that had changed overnight for Annie when her mother passed away but she didn't resent it. It was simply what was meant for her. Maybe all that's happened has been preparing me for what's about to happen now, she was fantasizing as she sat on the bus from Dun Laoghaire, smelling the faintly stinky sea breeze and recalling the long walks along the pier with her mother and brothers, licking HB ripple ice-cream wafers. Or Neapolitan if you were really lucky. She felt a faint trace of regret that life hadn't stayed that simple.

It was five minutes to six as Annie approached the restaurant, still dressed in casual clothes and swinging the bag containing her suit and white blouse. She planned to change when she got there and was hoping she'd remembered her shoes when she noticed the sign over the main door wasn't lit, the inkwell-blue streak not casting its usual chilly evening glow.

The front door was locked, which was also strange. Annie rang the bell and a hassled Owen opened up. 'Oh Annie, I'm sorry, I meant to ring you but with all that's been happening it completely slipped my mind.'

'That's OK. What's wrong? The sign isn't on.'

'We're not opening tonight. Last night, after you left, David English collapsed. It was terrible. We had to call an ambulance. There was chaos.'

'That's awful. Is he OK?' She still didn't understand why they were closed.

'You didn't hear any news bulletins then? He was dead on arrival at the hospital.'

'No.' Annie was shocked.

'I'm afraid so. The police called round this morning. Just routine. They wanted to take a statement, check what happened.'

'What did happen?'

'Heart attack. He was unconscious when he left here and died shortly afterwards. Obviously, by the time his wife got to him it was too late. Must have been an awful shock for her.'

Annie felt numb. 'I saw her yesterday, when I went for the audition, she looked so sexy and aloof and carefree, every inch the star. I wanted to be her.' She felt guilty just saying the words. 'Who'd want to be in her shoes today?' Annie felt as sad as if it had been one of her own family.

'You were talking to him when he arrived. Notice anything unusual?' Owen asked, leading the way to a table and removing a full ashtray before pouring two coffees from the half-full cafetière.

'No, he was charming as always. Although, come to think of it,' she was remembering his slightly grey tinge, 'I did think he looked tired and sort of ashen faced.'

Owen filled her in on what had happened after she'd left.

The party had been drinking till well after midnight, although Owen had noticed that David English himself was drinking relatively little and had passed on the after-dinner brandies that his guests were downing like water. He'd got up, presumably to go to the bathroom, then suddenly slumped over and fell to the ground. Owen had been on his own, having sent the last of the staff home at twelve-thirty.

No-one really knew what to do. They didn't try to move him, simply loosened his clothing and dialled 999 for the gardaí and an ambulance. He was still breathing when the ambulance arrived, within two or three minutes of the call.

Owen persuaded the rest of the party to return to their hotel and took their number. The gardaí promised to make enquiries at the hospital and let the businessmen know the outcome. No-one had believed it would be so gruesome.

'I didn't know what to do after they'd gone. I went home and couldn't sleep, ended up drinking brandy myself at 4 a.m.' Owen was still upset. 'When I heard he'd died, it didn't seem right to open tonight. Anyway the police were here and the place is still a mess. There wasn't much clearing up done after what happened. I called all our customers and explained.'

Annie and Owen cleaned up upstairs, tidied

stuff away, and answered the phone. At eight-thirty he suggested they call it a day.

'I'm sorry you had to come all the way in. Naturally, I'll pay you anyway.'

Annie felt tired. This had taken the edge off her perfect day and she couldn't stop thinking about how Libby Marlowe must be feeling tonight.

'Come on, I'll drop you home. I'll just put a message on the machine explaining that we're open tomorrow, in case anyone rings.' Owen stood up and Annie got her coat.

Normally she'd have refused his offer, as her house was miles away from Sutton and he could have taken the toll bridge, but tonight she was very glad not to have to make the two agonizingly slow bus journeys home.

He took a bottle of red wine from the giant rack near the cash register. 'There you go, a present. You look like you could do with a drink.'

'You are an angel. I was going to stop some-where on the way home. I don't think I can simply go to bed. It's funny, but I feel as if I knew them, which is ridiculous.'

They drove in tired silence and Annie was relieved when Owen dropped her off. She switched on both the heating and the electric fire to try and ease the chill that had crept into her bones. Within five minutes she was in her dressing-gown snuggled up on the couch, wine open, watching the main evening news, anxious for more information. Sleep was not an option, she was way too wired. The report at the end of the bulletin was dissatisfyingly brief, the station obviously anxious to protect the privacy of one of its biggest stars.

*

That star was now heavily sedated, following a day of intense emotion. Her mother had tried to persuade her to stay in bed after she'd heard a thud and found her on the floor. But phones kept ringing and cards and flowers started to arrive and neighbours called to see if they could do anything and Vera and Christina were exhausted from talking and Libby went from being very quiet to crying uncontrollably. She refused to see anyone until at last her mother had followed her instincts and called Donald Barton, their family doctor, who'd known Libby since her MMR vaccine. He was a calm, gentle giant with a mop of grey hair and a moustache that Libby used to twiddle as a child and he sat on her bed now and held her hand as if she was still five years old.

'Please, give me something to take away the pain, please Barty,' she begged.

He stroked her head and made soothing noises. 'I wish I could, child. I really wish I could.'

'But it's not fair. How could he leave me like this?' She sounded as she had when she was a little girl and things weren't going her way. Back then she'd usually managed to turn things to her advantage somehow and the pattern had continued throughout her life.

'I won't be able to cope on my own.' She was crying softly. 'He did everything for me.'

The doctor knew it was true. She'd gone from an adoring father to a husband who had indulged her and now, for the first time, she was truly alone. Maybe it would bring mother and daughter closer, he mused, but Libby was a man's woman, always had been, and David's loss would have a huge impact on her life. He listened to her rambling on about her husband, and hoped the future wouldn't be too difficult. She was a woman of extremes and he felt life could go either way for her now.

Eventually, he gave her something to help her sleep and promised to call round in the morning, after she pleaded with him not to leave her alone.

'You'll feel a little better once you've rested, my dear, I promise.'

'I want him back. That's all I want.'

'And I'd do anything to be able to give him back to you. I know how much you loved him.' He'd been at their wedding and felt angry that such a young life had been quenched. For the millionth time he was baffled by the ways of this God of theirs. Being a doctor and seeing life and death at such close quarters was never easy and he felt that now might be a good time to retire. Either it was getting harder or else he was getting too old. Seeing gorgeous Libby, always one of his favourite people, lying like a battered rag doll and begging for his help was difficult to bear. He kissed her forehead, something he'd never done before. The equivalent of the lollipop he always had for her when she was little. This time, however, he couldn't make it better.

Chapter Eleven

The morning of the funeral dawned suspiciously bright. Libby woke at six, feeling drugged. The pain hit her like a physical blow. She closed her eyes tightly then rolled over and clutched her stomach, curling up like a baby. She wished herself dead: the day ahead was just too impossible to contemplate.

The previous night at the removal had been bad enough. A silent queue had snaked its way up the centre aisle and sides of the church as friends and family and colleagues came to pay their respects. A million hands to hold and endless sad eyes to mirror her own. Today she had to face it all over again and at the end of it he would be gone away for good, swallowed up by the black, wet, cold earth.

Libby jumped out of bed and threw herself into the shower. She dried herself roughly and wrapped a dressing-gown tightly round her icy body. Her mother appeared with a cup of tea, already dressed in draining black.

'Did you sleep?' She was gentle.

'I don't know, I think so. I had so many dreams. When I woke I thought for a split second that it was all a nightmare. Then I realized where I was, not tucked up safely in my own home, listening to David in the shower.' She sat down heavily. 'I don't know how I'm going to get through the day.'

'You will, don't worry. I'll be there beside you.'

'I want *him* beside me.' She almost stamped her foot.

'I know. I know, darling.' Christina sat down on the bed and smoothed her daughter's hair and wished she could make it all right again. 'Come down and have some breakfast, it will help.'

Libby shook her head.

'You've eaten nothing for three days. You'll make yourself ill. Please.'

'I can't.'

'Try, for me. Just some toast and juice.'

Libby followed her mother listlessly to the kitchen, where everything had already been prepared. She poured coffee and sat with her head in her hands.

'What am I going to do, Mum?' She gulped the coffee and searched for answers. 'Why did I let myself rely on him so completely? I don't even know how much money is in my bank account.'

'Don't worry about anything for now. Just let's get through today.' Her mother poured some freshly squeezed juice and buttered small slices of toast, pushing them gently towards her daughter. Libby continued to stare at the table.

'Please just try and eat something.'

'I feel sick all the time. I can't face food.'

'Just one slice, it's warm and comforting and you always ate masses of toast as a child when you were ill.'

Libby bit into what tasted like a piece of cardboard.

'Good girl. The hair and make-up people will be here shortly.'

Her daughter jumped up, eyes glassy. 'I don't want anyone near me. I told you that last night.' She was crying now, and lashing out. 'I don't want to look my best saying goodbye to my husband. Can't you understand that? Are you stupid? I want to look wrecked because that's how I feel, all smashed up inside.'

'I know, darling. But there will be a lot of people to meet and you'll feel better if you're not worrying about how you look.'

'I couldn't care less about how I look. My life is over. It's all gone. He took it all away, everything. He took it with him.'

'It's OK, shush now.' Her mother was at her side in an instant and Libby let herself be led back upstairs, where she sat at her old dressing-table. She didn't recognize the grey, shadowy face that stared back at her.

The house was soon alive again. Vera bustled about as usual. Her mother's two sisters had stayed overnight. The doorbell sounded continuously. Jonathan, Libby's current favourite hairdresser, and Laura, an old friend who'd been doing her make-up for TV for ages, arrived together. They all tiptoed round her. No-one said anything and somehow that made it all worse. Everyone was trying to pretend it was OK.

She sat like a child while her hair was blow-dried. 'I'd like it straight, please,' was all she said. David had seen it like that once and loved it. Jonathan nodded, unsure. Normally her hair was tousled and urchin-like and very sexy. He didn't ask.

Laura smiled sadly at her.

'Hi.'

'Hi.'

Libby wondered why some people preferred not to refer to it when someone died; she assumed it was because they were afraid of upsetting the bereaved person. Or reminding them. But she wanted to talk about David, wanted them to understand how ripped apart her life was, wanted them to know how very much she'd loved him, but in a funny way she was afraid of upsetting them, so she said nothing either.

Laura did her make-up, her touch gentle and strangely comforting, probably because as Libby sat in the chair cocooned in a black plastic sack she felt normal. She was well used to having her face done. She sat like this three or four times a day when they were recording a show.

111

'Not too much, please. I don't want to *look* made up,' was all she said.

Libby thanked Laura and Jonathan and they left as silently as they'd arrived.

She put on a simple black dress and matching coat, a Gucci classic, with sheer black stockings and high heels. She wore the heavy pearl strand with the magnificent clasp and slender chain around her neck and added matching earrings that David had bought her as a mini-surprise in her Christmas stocking weeks before. Her hands she left bare except for her platinum and diamond wedding ring. She didn't bother to check the finished product in any mirror. Had she done so she would have seen a tall, gaunt, beautiful woman with poker-straight, shiny hair, dark blue, swollen eyes and a pale, lifeless face, despite the faint hint of false rosiness in her cheeks and the muted, damson lips. The only touch of light about her came from the natural sheen of real pearls.

The ceremony itself was exactly the way David would have wanted it. A truly magnificent string section played some of his favourite pieces of music, little-known works that he'd listened to regularly, and his all-time favourite, Bruch's First Violin Concerto, which brought memories tearing back for Libby. Sarah Jansen, an internationally renowned soprano who had been at college with David, sang some of the classic, old-style hymns. His brothers, so like him in their gestures that Libby kept wanting to touch them, did the readings. Before communion his father read one of his favourite poems and broke down in the process.

Just as the ceremony finished the priest announced Libby, as she had requested. Her mother had been very unsure but Libby was insistent. She needed to speak about him. They had to understand what it was like for her.

'I've known David for less than nine years, which is probably a lot less time than most of you here. Love caught both of us unexpectedly, and I think I fell first, although David always told friends that I should have come with a health warning.' She gave a little smile, remembering. 'I was feeling bored at a party and wondering how I could make my escape when I saw him and I . . . I just knew. Oh, I had all the usual symptoms – wildly beating heart, stomach churning, everything – but I didn't need them to tell me that this man was going to be very important in my life.

'He was gorgeous to look at, as you all know, but more important he was lovely inside as well. He was a mass of contradictions and made me laugh from the moment I met him. The way he could be as coarse as a sailor at rugby matches, but melted into putty when we once found an injured fox in the woods. The way he adored opera yet his singing at parties often caused a riot – for the wrong reasons. How he loved his parents and wasn't afraid to tell them. How he danced Mrs O'Connell round the kitchen one morning when she won 5,000 euro on the lotto. The way he told jokes when he was drunk and always got the punchline wrong. Or once slept in the bath with a towel over him because we'd had a row, then laughed like crazy when I turned the tap on him next morning because I was so angry. The way he jumped out of the car one night when we were on our way to a function because a dog was trying to cross the road in the rain and almost got killed. He was wearing black tie and I was in a see-through dress and we ended up in the vet's till ten o'clock and missed dinner, yet he was deliriously happy because the dog had a chip and the owners were traced and it turned out he'd wandered over thirty miles and a little girl had been crying somewhere for nearly a week.'

She closed her eyes for a moment as the memories flooded in. 'When he asked me to marry him I was the happiest girl alive. And the love between us grew until it threatened to overwhelm at least me, sometimes.

'And just as he came into my life without warning, the other night he left me the same way and a light went out and the warmth of him around me faded. And now, there'll never be a full moon for me again and the stars will never shine quite as brightly and the sun will never feel as good on my shoulders and the sea will never have that shimmery, perfect blue haze. And I'm angry. I want the birds to stop singing and children to stop laughing and flowers to die and Santa not to come and no dog to ever lick me and no baby to smell sweet.' She looked out into the overflowing crowd and couldn't see a thing.

'But I know he would hate that, would kick and scream and fight against it, so even though my love, my best friend and my greatest ally is being buried today, I know he'd want me to keep going until somehow, a light switches on inside me and I come alive again. In fact,' she managed a thin smile, 'I'm sure he's up there right now using one of his favourite expressions and telling me to go kick some ass.'

She lowered her head and swallowed hard, then slowly returned to her seat, touching his coffin as she passed, a bit taken aback to find people crying all around her. Her own eyes were empty.

In the cemetery it was grey and raw. Libby stood, hand in hand with his parents as the final prayers were said. The tears finally came as she laid the traditional single rose and stood and looked down at his coffin and said her final goodbye to the man of her dreams.

Chapter Twelve

Annie felt she was really living for the first time in years. She was excited, exhilarated, scared, challenged. The morning spent in studio was terrifying, although everyone greeted her warmly and she felt as though she knew them all already. She was being ultra-careful not to call them by the name of their character, a classic newcomer's mistake.

The sets looked tiny, even the pub, which seemed huge on TV. A large crew was involved and they were clearly working under pressure, yet appeared relaxed. The running order showed that there were eighteen scenes to be recorded that day. This morning all the bits in the pub were being done, out of sequence and from different episodes, which made it very difficult for cast and crew. For each scene there was a walk-through with the director, then a rehearsal for cameras followed by a dress rehearsal and then finally it was recorded. It was all over in about twenty-five minutes. Annie couldn't believe it. No time if you forgot a line, or hit a wrong mark. It just didn't happen, from what she'd seen so far.

Later in the morning all that changed. Actors forgot whole pages, a light went in the middle of a take, an extra entered at the wrong moment and all hell broke loose as the director got more and more irritated. A coffee break was called to restore humour and Annie trooped off with the rest of the cast to the green-room, where hot tea and coffee with scones and jumbo sausage rolls were pounced on eagerly.

At twelve-thirty Mike Nichols stopped by.

'Seen enough?'

'Enough to ensure I don't get a proper night's sleep until I've recorded at least one episode. It's so busy.'

'I know, and believe me this is a quiet day. It's a bit like working on a production line, the machines keep turning, churning out the product and you've just got to keep up.'

'Don't worry, I won't let you down. I'll be word perfect.' Annie smiled shyly.

'Would you stop it, you don't owe me anything. I didn't make the final decision.'

'No, but usually the hardest part is to even get considered for an audition.'

'Enough. Come on, a couple of people from the office are heading off to the local pub. It's Isobel's birthday so we're deserting the canteen. I told them I'd bring you along. We only take an hour, same as studio, so we'd better get going.'

Annie was delighted to be included. Max

Donaldson was there along with most of the others she'd met at the audition.

'Annie, welcome, sit down.' The boss greeted her warmly. 'How did you find this morning?'

'Terrifying.' She grinned. 'Everyone is just so good and the speed at which you record scenes left me breathless.'

'Well, they don't all go so smoothly. We have one or two prima donnas and boy, do we have our moments.' He had no intention of elaborating.

'Well, I'll try not to give you any grief.' It was so great to be part of all this. 'Happy birthday, by the way Isobel.'

'Thanks, Annie. Glad you could join us. We don't get to socialize with the cast that often at lunchtime. Usually they go off together and bitch about us and vice versa.'

'And then whoever's around on Friday evening at the end of recording goes for a pint where we all kiss and call each other darling and make up,' Max grimaced. 'I usually have to grovel to somebody or other because I've made life hell for them.'

'Don't mind him,' Mike interjected. 'He gets us to do all the dirty work. The cast love him and hate the rest of us.'

On and on the banter went as they tucked into quiche and lasagne and thick cuts from the joint of the day. One or two people had a glass of wine, including the birthday girl, but most of them drank no alcohol, it was all Diet Cokes and sparkling mineral waters. Annie was surprised. So much for her father's theory.

In the afternoon, she met with wardrobe and make-up. Eileen Waters was the senior costume person on the show. 'I'll be on for your four episodes,' she greeted Annie warmly. 'Come through, I'll show you what I've bought so far.' She opened a copybook at a page with the name BOBBY in large letters in gold ink, surrounded by tiny, scribbled flowers. On the following few pages, she'd stuck in cutouts from various magazines and scribbled notes beside each one.

'It's only rough, I'm afraid. We're so short of time and there are ten new characters coming on board in the next few episodes. But at least it will give you some idea of the way I'm thinking.'

'No, it's great to see anything.' Annie was surprised to find it wasn't that far off the look she'd come up with herself for the audition.

'I thought we'd go cheap and just a bit tacky to start, rather than opt for the all-out trailer trash look. Bobby has a lot of street cred and you're a good-looking girl so I'm assuming she would have a bit of taste and be well up on fashion but not have a lot of money. I think she would show off a bit where men are concerned, so I thought I'd buy a few coloured bras, maybe red, tigerskin, that sort of thing, and get a couple of slightly see-through blouses. Then, some tight jeans, maybe a pair of cheap, plastic leather-look trousers and a short skirt or two. How does that sound?'

'Sounds just like my wardrobe at home.'

'Mine too, come to think of it,' Eileen joked and they laughed easily together. Annie liked her. They talked about sizes and shoes and jewellery and arranged for Annie to call for a proper fitting the following week.

Next up Susannah Browne, chief make-up artist. She was older, in her late forties, perfectly groomed and she looked over her silver-rimmed specs at Annie with just the faintest hint of disdain. It was as if she'd just detected a slightly off smell. 'Hello, dear, come in, sit down. Now, tell me, what sort of look do you normally go for?' She obviously thought Annie was just like her character and didn't think much of either, despite the fact that Annie had deliberately dressed down for today, to show them all the real her.

'I don't really wear much make-up, to be honest. Just a tinted moisturizer, some blusher and a bit of lip gloss.'

'And what brands do you use?' That look again, the nose held slightly too high.

'This and that. I haven't really got any favourites.' Annie didn't want to admit she used the cheapest ones she could find in Boots or the supermarket.

'What about on the eyes?' She was scribbling notes in a leatherbound notebook.

'Em, nothing really.'

'Not even mascara?'

'Sometimes, but very seldom. It usually runs or stings my eyes.'

'Are you allergic to anything?'

'Only mornings,' Annie tried. It was wasted.

'I see, well, talking to Max,' she said the name protectively, 'I think we're going to have to go for quite a pronounced look. Have you done television before?'

'No, but I've done a lot of theatre,' Annie offered, hoping to impress.

'Totally different. I'll tell you what, why don't I think about it and chat further with Max. Then I'll try out some stuff on you next week and we can take it from there.' She closed the book and took off her glasses. 'I'll give you a call early next week.' Annie was dismissed and was just about to skulk off when she was summoned again.

'Oh, I almost forgot. Hair. Let's have a quick look before you go. Over here.'

She led Annie to a swivel chair in the main make-up area, so that she could examine her under strong lights. Annie pulled her hair out of its scrunchy and shook her head.

'Yes, I see.' She gazed at Annie's head as if she was discovering nits for the first time. 'It's rather, em, dull for the strong lights of TV.' She continued to poke around with the pointed edge of her tail comb, giving the impression that she was half afraid of catching something.

'I think you mean mousy and you're right.' Annie's normally vibrant hair looked lifeless.

'Nonsense, you've lovely hair, really. Sort of auburny, would you say? It's just that television can be so cruel, sometimes . . .' She trailed off and smiled weakly.

Can't be much worse than this. Annie didn't say it.

'How would you feel if we gave you some different coloured highlights, just to sort of liven it up.'

'Fine, no problem, just as long as it's done by a professional.' Annie wasn't prepared to let her away with everything.

'Oh, of course. In fact, if you give me the name of your own hairdresser I can talk to him and arrange everything and naturally we'll pay for it all.'

'I was thinking of going to Paul Hession.' Annie mentioned one of the top stylists in Dublin, whose name she'd only ever seen in one of her glossies. 'My regular guy has recently moved to London and I need a good cut as well.' Annie could feel her face turning hot at the outright lie. What was wrong with her, she wondered. She wasn't usually like this.

'Oh yes, Paul is a friend of mine. He's wonderful. I'll phone him and discuss it and tell him to expect a call from you.' She smiled sweetly. 'And of course you know you mustn't do anything to your hair during the weeks of recording, because all the scenes are shot out of sequence and it would be a disaster for continuity.'

'Of course,' Annie said through gritted teeth.

'OK then, that's it for today. Bye.' She was dismissed for a second time.

Annie swung by the office then to collect some more paperwork.

'How did you get on?' Isobel greeted her warmly.

'Fine, I think. I've to meet them again next week. Eileen has some nice ideas, if you can call that look nice.' She grinned. 'And Susannah wants to talk to Max a bit more.' She didn't like to say too much.

'Eileen's a dote,' Isobel smiled at her brightly and Annie immediately felt better that she hadn't said the same about the older woman.

They spent time going through the schedule again and it was after six when Annie finally left, exhausted, wishing her tiny house had a bath. She'd been on her feet since 7 a.m. and she'd have given anything for a long soak in bubbles.

Still, at least she wasn't working tonight. She stopped at her local garage for a tin of meatballs in gravy and treated herself to a packet of bourbon creams. It had been a great day overall and she was very happy.

Chapter Thirteen

For Libby it was a day filled with anguish and heartbreak and invading, scalding memories. Being so close to David's family and all his friends made his absence unbearable. She missed his smile and his touch and his breath on her neck and his arm around her. She couldn't stop thinking about him, and each thought dealt another blow to her already battered heart.

Christina had invited family and close friends back to her house for lunch. It seemed a strange thing to do, Libby thought. She couldn't understand why anyone would want to eat or drink today. But of course they did. She wanted to lock herself in her room and scream at them all to go away but instead, she wandered around and kept her head down and tried not to listen to the everyday, if subdued, inconsequential chatter.

'How are you holding up?' Robert English, David's brother, smiled sadly at her, looking so like him that it sent a red-hot poker scorching through her stomach.

'Badly.' She hadn't the energy to pretend and knew she didn't have to with him.

'Me too. I keep wanting to tell him something.'

'He'd have livened this lot up, that's for sure.'

'It must have been a terrible shock for you, Libby.'

She nodded, a bit more resigned now. 'For all of us.'

'I'm worried about Dad. I don't think he's that well and I'm not sure how he'll cope with this. Although she pretends otherwise, Mum is actually a much stronger person.'

'I know. David used to say your mum was as tough as overdone roast beef and your dad as soft as mushy peas. Oh, Bob, what am I going to do without him?'

He said nothing, simply folded her tightly in his arms and they stood like that for ages and people around them tried not to notice her open display of grief as she sobbed on his shoulder.

Lunch was an exquisite buffet. Libby tried to concentrate and kept forgetting and staring blankly into the distance. Most people left soon afterwards and by mid-afternoon only family and one or two of David's close friends remained. Vera and Mrs O'Connell bustled about, vying to be top dog, making coffee, discreetly topping up wine glasses and generally driving the caterers mad.

Her friend Moya glided around, calling

everyone darling and rubbing Libby's back every time she passed. It felt as if she was being burped and it irritated her no end.

A pregnant Carrie had travelled up from the country, in spite of her all-day sickness.

'Libby, I wish there was something I could do for you.'

'I know, but there's nothing anyone can do. Oh Carrie, I need him here with me.'

'I just wish I didn't live so far away.'

'Me too.'

Carrie sighed. 'We've sort of lost contact, in a way. I don't really know much about your life any more. So, let's start by staying in touch. Damn, I wish I wasn't pregnant right now. I'm not much use to anyone.'

'Maybe I'll come and visit you.' Both of them knew she wouldn't.

'Promise me you'll think about it?'

'I promise.' Libby was like a schoolchild agreeing to do her homework. They hugged each other tightly.

The endless day at last gave way to darkness. Libby was glad to be surrounded by the inky black night with no magical stars and not even a fingernail of a moon. The hired chef had left a comforting home-made steak and kidney pie with tiny dumplings and a featherlight puff pastry, to be accompanied by steamed, fluffy potatoes, kept warm in an industrial hostess trolley. There was also a spicy baked organic ham, salads and an array of freshly made breads, as well as a mouth-watering display of puddings. Nobody felt like eating but they sat round in the formal dining room for the sake of it and attempted to do the food justice. They sipped the wine mostly because it softened the hollowness.

By nine o'clock Libby couldn't stand it any longer. 'I'm sorry, I think I'll have to go to my room. Please excuse me.'

Everyone got up together, it seemed, and it made her feel claustrophobic. She backed away with a haunted look. John Simpson, David's solicitor and closest friend, was the first to sense her panic.

'I'll walk Libby to her room,' he offered, smiling at her mother in an attempt to avoid any argument. Charles English put a gentle hand over Christina's in a gesture that seemed to speak only to parents.

She walked slowly, glad to have John beside her. He was a soft, lovely man and he'd loved David too.

'I need some fresh air. Think you can brave it?'

He followed her out through the sliding doors and they stood for a moment, gazing at the garden in silence. It looked bleak and shadowy in its winter overcoat and Libby shivered, glad there were no comforting sights or scents to try and tempt away the anguish.

'I'm sorry I didn't really get to speak to you all day. This must be terrible for you, too. I know how close you two were.'

'I'm OK,' John said. 'I'm going to miss him. He

always made me laugh, no matter how bad things were. And he was usually so confident, so definite, that he sort of swept you along with him.'

'I know.'

'What will you do?'

'Try to survive, I suppose.'

'You have to do more than try. It's what he'd want, you said so yourself earlier.'

'And he usually got what he wanted.' She said it kindly, with a smile, remembering David's powers of persuasion. She was going to miss him so much.

Someone walked on her grave again and she shivered and made her way indoors. John followed, shadowing her protectively as she mounted the stairs.

'I'll call you tomorrow,' he said as they got to her room. Tilting her face up to his he kissed her forehead and smiled at her tiredly. They'd always been a bit like brother and sister.

'And Libby, I'm around for the next few weeks, so lean on me, OK?'

'It's the next fifty years or so I'm worried about.' She kissed him on both cheeks. 'Thank you.'

'I mean it.' He held her for a moment.

'I know you do. Good night.'

Libby stripped off her clothes quickly. Her skin felt tight and her underwear hurt and her shoes pinched. Then she stepped into the cubicle for a shower because she couldn't face the loneliness of a king-size bed, even though she desperately wanted this day to be over.

Her nightly cleansing ritual offered no comfort either and she slipped between the sheets and felt the warmth of the electric blanket and shivered. Then she lay, teeth almost chattering in the snug haven, and tossed and turned and dreamed horrible dreams that were still better than reality.

Chapter Fourteen

The next few days both sped and crawled.

Annie felt as if she'd been given wings. Her whole outlook changed and she realized just how much she'd been struggling and for how long. Her contract arrived and the promise of a decent amount of money was exhilarating. She knew she'd have to be careful: the temptation to spend had been lurking inside her for years and could do serious damage to her frail finances. So she did what every sensible woman does in moments of crisis. She made a list.

First up, some new clothes. Jeans, a decent pair of black trousers and maybe a pair of combats. Then a couple of cheap T-shirts, a jumper and a good jacket. She allocated a sum of money. Next, a small amount for make-up and some new face products and toiletries. Finally, a couple of things for the house, including paint for the front door and two windowboxes and a hanging basket, just in case she had to entertain any of her new friends.

She added material for curtains for the parlour, resolved to try and find a cheap mirror for over the fireplace and allowed 20 euro for some new plants. If she stuck carefully to her budget, she should still manage to save some for a rainy day. Not that she was planning any. And she was going to do a decent supermarket shop for once.

It was a great feeling. She cleaned the house with gusto, opening windows at the first hint of sunshine, bashing faded rugs and washing everything in sight.

In the supermarket she was less sure. Her eating habits had been screwed up for years. She couldn't really remember much about her mother's cooking, except jelly and ice-cream on Sundays and fish on Fridays. She could still smell the kippers, and it always reminded her just why she hated all types of seafood. Oh, and buns and a malt loaf on Saturday mornings, she'd never forget that. The memory made her want to lick a bowl all over again. It was funny that the loss of something so long ago still made her yearn.

Annie had never been a cook. After her mother's death, dinner for the men in the family became a nightmare. Her father helped in the early days, but drifted away quickly. Annie soon learned that a big pot of potatoes, as much meat as they could afford – sausages when they ran out – and beans or mushy peas went a long way. Biscuits and crisps were the only snacks in the house.

Then when she was in hospital, the smell of

cabbage and sprouts ensured a lifelong hatred of anything green and soggy. The chops were fatty and grey and she shuddered even all these years later. She remembered a tasteless, rubbery chicken curry and rice so watery it could have been pudding.

When she'd been at home recovering her father had developed a routine and it never altered. A small piece of roast on Sunday. Cold leftover meat on Monday. Mince for shepherd's pie on Tuesday. Sausages on Wednesday. A chop on Thursday if his budget allowed, otherwise tinned corned beef. Fish fingers, egg and chips on Friday and a take-away treat on Saturday.

Those years had had a dramatic effect on Annie's relationship with food. When she left hospital they'd cautioned her to eat a sensible diet, with lots of fresh fruit and raw or lightly cooked vegetables. She had every one of the 'you are what you eat' leaflets. Her father had scoffed at them and even after she'd left home Annie had never really made much of an effort, not really believing that it made any difference. Food didn't interest her and over the years she'd grown to loathe cooking. She wished she could afford to eat out more often but for that you needed money and friends or a date and all three had been scarce.

She knew she needed to experiment more and try out different tastes from other countries but, even in the restaurant when she could have any-thing she wanted, it tended to be steak, or pasta with a token salad which she rarely touched, finding the strong dressings too oily. She was always nervous about trying confit of duck or scallops or venison or other such exotica, afraid she wouldn't like them or worse, know how to eat them.

And no matter how hard she tried, vegetables always tasted of hospital.

Guilt was a great prompter, however, and now as she skated excitedly around Superquinn she resolved to make an effort. She started by swapping her usual white, wrapped loaf for a brown, nutty unwrapped model. Next she decided to buy fresh fruit, but ended up with only oranges and a tin of peaches in syrup. She substituted fresh mince for her usual frozen burgers but hadn't a clue what to put with it. Ditto with the chicken breast she determinedly threw in her trolley, instead of crunchy, coated chicken Kiev. A few E numbers and a dash of MSG were needed, she suspected, but these weren't instantly evident on the shelves. She dropped fizzy drinks altogether, but couldn't resist the usual supply of bikkies. Overall, she felt much healthier already.

*

Christina Marlowe was worried about Libby. Her daughter looked dreadful, thin and grey, which she knew was only to be expected, but it was her mood that was causing immediate concern. She was still at home, thankfully, but she spent her days in the bedroom, sitting by the window, staring into the distance for hours, only coming downstairs for cups of coffee and when forced to eat. She'd started smoking, a filthy and damaging habit that Christina had never been aware of.

It was only in the evenings, when Vera had gone and the sky turned to treacle, that Libby seemed to relax a bit. Darkness suited her. Christina had taken to lighting the fire in the bedroom, then drawing the curtains and opening a bottle of good wine for them both. They sat for long periods in silence but Christina was very used to her own company.

It was a week since the funeral and life had simply come to a halt for Libby. She got up late, watched TV but couldn't discuss a word of what she'd seen, only showered every second day and hadn't washed her hair once. Vera brought the post up to her room each morning with her breakfast tray. The food remained untouched; the huge mound of letters and cards were still unopened.

This evening, Christina set down a bottle and two glasses and went to sit beside her daughter on the comfy windowseat. It was pitch black outside but Libby's eyes searched the darkness, hunting for a clue in a landscape where nothing could be seen clearly.

It wasn't a typical mother and daughter pose. Christina felt the yawning gap and reached over and gently stroked her daughter's lifeless hair. There was no response for a moment and then the younger woman moved closer for warmth and succour.

'Tell me what you're thinking.' It was a regular request.

'I'm wondering where he is.' The subject matter was always the same.

'I feel he's up there, somewhere, watching over us.' It was the way she felt about her own husband.

'I want him back with me.'

'I know, darling.'

'I can't survive without him.' For the first time, despite what she'd said at the funeral, Christina saw a spark of anger in her daughter and decided it was better than the nothingness she'd come to expect.

'You know what he'd want.' She chose her words for impact. It worked.

Libby turned sharply. 'What about what I want? He went away. He knew how much I needed him and yet he left me.'

'It wasn't a choice he made.'

'Yes, it was.' She was like a truculent child.

'What would you say to him?'

'I'd shout at him. I'd hit him. I'd scream.' She paused and remembered their few fleeting rows. She wilted. 'But it wouldn't do any good, he'd only laugh at me. He always did when I lost my temper. He enjoyed thwarting me.' A ghost of a smile escaped at the happy memory and Christina clutched at the straw.

'I think it's time, darling, to start living again.'

'I can't.'

'You can. Just tiny steps. I'll be here and so will everyone else.'

'I want to die.' She turned and looked closely at her mother. 'I fantasize about it all the time, how

135

I'd do it, what the papers would say.' She looked almost elated.

'What about me, your friends, David's family? What do you think it would do to us if anything happened you?'

'Know something, Mum? I don't really care. I suppose that sounds selfish but it would be the answer to all my pain.'

'The hurt will lessen, I promise. And eventually you'll begin to look forward.'

'But I don't want to start again. My life was perfect. I had everything. I'll never have that now and besides, I'm nearly forty, I'll be on the scrap heap soon.'

'Nonsense, you're a beautiful young woman in her prime with a fantastic career and everything to live for.'

'No. I'm all alone and the fact is that I've never had to look after myself. I went from Daddy to David basically and I liked being protected.'

'You still have your friends.'

'Do I? I have lots of acquaintances, like Moya, that I used to call friends, but I only ever saw them as part of a couple and it was always very social, no deep conversations there.'

'What about Carrie?'

'Carrie's a dote but our lives have gone in opposite directions. Maybe if she lived closer, I'd meet her now and then but,' she shrugged, 'David was all I wanted really.'

'Well, at least make a start by returning a few calls.'

Christina knew that David's parents and brothers were concerned about her, as was John Simpson and a couple of David's other friends who telephoned or dropped by. Despite what Libby had said she knew Moya had called twice and Carrie had written and telephoned each day, urging her to visit.

'You know what, I'm not interested. Helen Radley mentioned a charity event the day of the funeral. Can you believe it? And that Selena is already trying to pump me for information on what I'm doing with the business. Did you hear what she said in that message she left yesterday? No, thank you.'

'Maybe you could start by having dinner with Charles and Monica before they go back home the day after tomorrow.' Christina ignored the violent shaking of the head beside her. 'They're worried about you. They need to know you're going to be OK.'

'I can't go out. I just can't face it.' She hadn't been outside in a week and her grey face reflected the lack of air and exercise.

'Well, how about we cook dinner for them here? We can both do it.'

'I can't cook any more.'

'Nonsense. Tell you what, I'll plan it, you just do one dish.'

'No.'

'I'm afraid I'm going to have to insist.'

Christina took the long pause and reluctant sigh as agreement. It was a start.

Chapter Fifteen

The recovery process hadn't even begun but at least she was up and washed and dressed and, most importantly, had been occupied for an hour or two. Christina was relieved and she tried to ignore the hollow eyes that watched her constantly but said nothing.

David's parents were shocked when they saw Libby, despite her mother's best efforts. She wore a simple black shift dress and her pale hair had been caught loosely back, but there were black circles around her dead eyes.

Dinner was quiet. Afterwards they had coffee and brandy in the drawing room.

Charles English sat beside Libby while the two mothers looked at happy family photos.

'Elizabeth, Monica and I are worried about you. Have you any plans?'

'No, I'm fine.'

'Would you consider coming back home with us for a while?'

'I don't know. I can't really make any arrangements yet. I'm just not up to it.'

'I understand. What about David's business? I met Alex O'Meara yesterday by chance. He seemed unsure. Have you spoken to him?'

'No.' Libby had completely forgotten that the chief financial officer had telephoned her yesterday. 'I'll call him next week.'

'Would you like me to stay on and see that things are ticking over, or will it run itself for the next few weeks, do you think?'

'I've no idea.' She meant it. 'I know nothing about David's business interests, really.'

'Neither do I, dear. But I can find out pretty quickly.'

'No, thank you, Charles. You go back home. I'll call John Simpson tomorrow. He'll know what to do.'

'What about your own work?'

She looked at him blankly. 'I haven't given it a thought. We're supposed to start shooting a new series soon.' She paused. 'Next Monday, in fact.' She was taken aback. 'I've no idea what's happening. I suppose they'll phone me one of these days. I really couldn't care less, to be honest.'

'I know how you feel, but you need to get going again.'

'You sound like Mum.'

'Well, you're almost my daughter too.' He looked sad. 'Don't forget that. We care about you very much.'

'I know.'

'You will keep in touch?' It had always been David who'd phoned before.

'I promise.'

They didn't stay late. Libby was glad to go back to the safety of her room, but sad to say goodbye to another link to her husband.

Next day she made her first decision and it took her mother completely by surprise. 'I think I'll go home, today.'

'Are you sure?'

'I have to do it some time.'

'Why don't I come with you and stay for a few days?'

'No, thanks all the same. Mrs O'C. will stay as long as I need her. I rang her just now so she's expecting me.'

Her mother seemed to understand. 'I'll let you go – on one condition.'

'What's that?'

'You promise to call me anytime you need me. Day or night. No shouldering this alone. OK?'

'OK.'

They drove home together early that evening. Everything looked exactly the same as her mother swept up the immaculate driveway.

'Where's his car?' Libby was anxious.

'I asked for it to be put into one of the garages.'

Libby bit her lip; she hadn't wanted David's things touched, yet knew her mother meant well.

Mrs O'Connell was out as soon as she heard the car. 'Let me take your bags.'

'I can manage, thanks.'

'George is doing the garden. He should have been finished by now.' The woman sniffed in the general direction of the elderly man whose life she made hell. 'I'll ask him to move to the back.'

'Honestly, it's fine. There's no need.' Libby sounded agitated.

'A cup of tea would be lovely,' said Christina, ever the peacemaker.

'I've lit the fire in the small sitting room. Everything's ready. I'll bring it right in.'

After tea, her mother left, sensing Libby wanted to be alone. She sat by the fire until it got dark, refusing all offers of food, flicking channels relentlessly, anything to avoid going upstairs to their room. She could hear her housekeeper still working and she glanced at the clock: it was almost eight.

'Mrs O'Connell . . .' The woman turned sharply as Libby entered the kitchen like a ghost in black. 'Please don't keep working. It's late.' The busy bee approach was intensely irritating to Libby and she knew her voice was unnecessarily sharp. 'I appreciate you staying for tonight but honestly, I'm fine, so go to your room or sit down and relax and watch some TV.' It was a vague attempt at friendliness, the most Libby could muster right now.

'Let me make you a sandwich, at least.' God, the woman never gave up. 'You haven't eaten anything.'

Libby poured herself a large glass of white wine

as the food was prepared. She barely thanked her housekeeper and returned to the sitting room, leaving the food untouched. She headed upstairs only when she could no longer avoid it.

David was everywhere. She touched his cufflinks still on the bedside locker, hugged his towel tightly to her face, ran her hands over his casual clothes, perfectly organized in the regimented closet, and smelt the cool, clean smell of him in his walk-in wardrobe. It was heaven: for a split second she almost didn't believe he was gone – then a raging torrent flooded her and she knew that this was what hell must be like. But it was a torment she was addicted to. She wandered around, smelling his soap and fingering his razor, wrapping herself in his bathrobe and sliding into his leather slippers as she'd watched him do so many nights after they'd made love. The wine dulled the pain slightly so she headed downstairs and fetched the bottle.

She didn't sleep for hours and when she did it was an unnatural slumber and she woke early, feeling thirsty and groggy. When Mrs O'Connell knocked gently Libby wanted to scream at her to leave her alone. Nothing on the beautifully prepared silver tray of warm croissants, fresh juice and sweet-smelling coffee was remotely tempting.

As it was Sunday she stayed in bed till lunchtime. Her mother stopped by and tried to persuade her to come for a walk, without success. Mrs O'Connell seemed to have fires burning in every room and the only time Libby relaxed even slightly was when the lamps were switched on and the heavy curtains drawn against the dull grey, but still too bright day. She refused a late lunch and sat by the fire with her mother, still wearing David's dressing-gown. They had coffee and toasted sandwiches and later Libby made hot whiskies without asking. Christina hoped she wasn't using alcohol as a crutch but wisely didn't mention it, thinking she'd probably be doing the same herself in her daughter's situation.

Next morning an exhausted Libby showered and dressed in a pair of black trousers and soft black sweater, catching her unruly mop in an equally unruly twist at the nape of her neck. She phoned John Simpson and he agreed to drop by on his way home that evening.

The only other call she had the energy to make was to Leo Morgan, her friend in RTE. She rang his mobile to avoid having to talk to his secretary.

'Leo, it's Libby.'

'Libby, I was wondering whether I should phone you today. How are you?'

She wanted to tell him, but it was too much to inflict even on an old friend.

'I'm OK.' They'd spoken the day of the funeral when he'd come back to the house for lunch.

'Where are you?'

'I just moved back home last night.'

'That must have been tough.'

You've no idea.

'Is anyone staying with you?'

'No – at least, Mrs O'Connell is sleeping over. My mother offered but I'm better off . . . I have to get used to it.'

'Don't try to take on too much, Libby. Would you like to have lunch?'

'Not yet, Leo. It's . . . too soon for me.'

'Of course, I understand. I could call round and see you. You could make me one of your glorious omelettes.'

She didn't want that, for some reason.

'Actually, I won't take up that much of your time,' she said. Leo knew a brush-off when he heard it. 'I just wondered if you knew what was happening with the show.'

'Well, I had a meeting with the production company a few days ago. Shooting was to begin today but I've told them to postpone it for a week, at least.'

She recoiled from even the thought of facing people in a week. 'I don't know if I'll be ready.'

'I understand. I simply couldn't put it off any longer because there's pressure on the editing and post-production studios at the other end. There are several options, though. Why don't you think about it for a day or two and I could drop by for a coffee, say, on Wednesday.'

She hadn't the energy to argue. 'OK, just call me an hour before you come.' Anything to get off the phone and back to her own private world.

John Simpson arrived about seven, clutching a huge bunch of white lilies and looking uncomfortable.

'Joan's idea,' he grimaced, referring to his secretary. 'I wasn't sure.'

'They're beautiful, thanks. I'll just get Mrs O'Connell to put them in water. She has food prepared for you, if you're hungry.'

'Are you eating?'

'I'll have a bite.' He knew she wouldn't.

'I'm famished and Anna's away, so I'd love something, if you're not too tired?' Anna, John's wife, was a psychologist and worked with a number of corporate clients, so travel was a major part of her job.

'What's she doing at the moment?' Libby asked. She hadn't had a chance to talk to her at the time of the funeral.

'Some big recruitment drive for one of the banks, she's involved in the assessment. She sends her love.'

Libby excused herself and gave the flowers to her housekeeper, who was delighted that someone was prepared to eat her food.

'Drink?' she asked on her return to the formal sitting room, which they rarely used. Mrs O'C. regarded John as important because he was a 'legal gentleman', so she'd prepared the room specially, stacking the fire with logs, plumping the cushions and lighting the lamps but leaving the curtains open. It was a magnificent room and David had loved it.

'I'd murder a G & T, thanks.'

Libby poured him a generous measure and one for herself.

'Will I set up the dining room?' a voice enquired from the doorway a little while later. Libby wished the older woman would stop fussing.

'No.' Her voice was sharp. 'No, thank you Mrs O'Connell. I think we'll just have a plate on our lap, if John doesn't mind?'

'Not at all, I'm easy.'

Soon Mrs O'Connell appeared with a tray for each of them – a slow-cooked chicken casserole with rice and salad. Her cooking was dead plain but very tasty, and John cleared his plate. Libby picked at hers and opened a bottle of wine.

'I'd better only have one glass, I'm driving. Thanks.' He accepted the crystal goblet and she sat down beside him, comfortable because he'd been so close to David, even though she'd never been on her own with him in the house before.

'John, I don't have any idea where to start with the business, the bank and so on. I don't even know if there's a will. I need help.'

'That's not a problem. I was going to talk to you about things anyway. As you know, I act for David's companies as well as for him personally, so that simplifies things.' There was a slight pause. 'Actually, he hadn't made a will, but that needn't necessarily be a problem.' He noticed Libby's reaction and kept going. 'It will just delay things, so don't go dwelling on it.'

Libby was shocked. 'But he always talked about sorting out his affairs when we married, I just assumed . . .'

'It's not uncommon. A lot of people mean to do

146

it but don't get round to it and he was under a lot of pressure most of the time. Don't worry about it. Look, I haven't been doing very much for him on the business front recently so I need to update myself. Why don't I sit down with Alex O'Meara next week and go through everything?'

'Alex did leave a message wanting to talk to me but I couldn't face it.'

'No problem, leave it all to me. It will take me a couple of weeks. I'll get a clearer picture of where things stand and then we can talk. By that stage you'll probably be feeling a bit stronger anyway. No need to take on too much just yet.'

He smiled at her and Libby was grateful for his friendship and easy sense of calm.

Chapter Sixteen

Leo Morgan called on Wednesday morning and he too was taken aback by the gaunt, lifeless woman who greeted him, still dressed in black. She shuffled around, with no energy or spark about her. Somehow, he'd felt she would have bounced back. Libby even seemed to have shrunk in stature, he noticed as she led the way to the small sitting room where coffee and scones, muffins and tea brack were waiting to tempt them. It seemed that Mrs O'Connell wasn't sleeping well either and was baking at all hours. Most of the food was thrown out or given to her own friends or the few visitors Libby allowed.

'How are you doing?' It was the question everyone asked.

'I'm surviving.' She gave him the ghost of a smile. 'How are things with you?'

'Fine. Busy. Lots happening in terms of a licence fee agreement.' He spoke for a while about the subject that occupied every senior broadcaster's waking moments.

'So, tell me about the show?' she asked during a break in conversation.

'Well, at the moment it's scheduled to start recording next week. That has to stay if we're to meet our proposed transmission slot. As I mentioned, though, there are a few options. One, we could cancel the run altogether, but we are already heavily committed in financial terms. Or, we could go ahead and do a shorter series, say six episodes. That would require a lesser commitment from you, although our cost per episode would increase dramatically, but let's leave that for the moment. Thirdly, we could bring in another presenter and use the basic idea but change the name, because it's already associated with you from the pre-publicity. If we did that we would, of course, do your series next year, and maybe even stretch the budget to go ahead with the original format, which I know was to travel to a different country for each show.'

'I thought that was agreed, anyway?'

'Well, it's certainly on the table but nothing's been signed yet.'

Libby was surprised that Melanie, her agent hadn't nailed that one by now. It was the only reason she had agreed to this current format. It just showed what taking your eye off the ball for a week or two could do.

'If I don't do it, who would you get?'

'There's a new young chef working in Children's

at the moment. We've been looking for something for her for a while now. We'd have to simplify the format because she doesn't have your experience and, of course, she wouldn't attract your audience, so the sponsor would have something to say about that. Also there are the ratings to consider. To be honest, it's not an option I want to pursue. I'm not sure she's ready for mainstream TV, although her slots have been working really well and she's a bright, appealing girl, but I may have to consider it because of the heavy financial losses we'd otherwise incur.' He hadn't taken his eyes off Libby as he spoke. They were old friends and he was determined not to put the gun to her head, despite the pressure on him. 'What are your thoughts?'

Her voice seemed to come from a long way away. 'I suppose I feel I should do it, but I'm not entirely happy with certain aspects of the series. If all this –' she spread her arms – 'hadn't happened, I'd have insisted on some changes. But I've always known that transmission slots and ratings are sacrosanct and the wonderful world of show business doesn't stop for anybody.'

'Libby, we've known each other too long and you know I'll do anything I can for you at this time. If you don't want to do it, I'll consult with you or Melanie all the way on what happens next. You're a big star and very important to us. I don't know enough about the detail of this current series but if you are unhappy then, speaking personally, I would advise you not to do it.' He smiled at her gently. 'Of course, I never said that.'

She gave a small grin back. 'Thanks, Leo, I know I can trust you. I don't know what it is, to be honest. It's most likely just me. Anyway, I have been thinking about it and it's probably best I do it. I can't sit around here any longer.' She didn't mention her demons. 'I have to face people some time. Also, I know the team will look after me.'

'Are you sure? Do you need another twenty-four hours?'

'No, I've been thinking about it on and off since we spoke on the phone. Besides, I'm incapable of sustained logic at the moment. It'll probably do me good to be occupied for the next few weeks.' Too selfish to seriously consider ending it all, she desperately wanted to keep busy until some of the grief lessened and the fear subsided.

He looked relieved, then sad. 'I think it probably will.'

'Although Leo, I'm not sure I'll be able for such a hectic schedule in the first week, so you're going to have to bear with me on that one. If I can't do it . . .'

'Don't worry. I'll keep in touch and liaise directly with Jeremy. Don't push yourself too far, just do what you can. If we only get nine or ten programmes, then so be it. I'll take responsibility for agreeing to it.'

'Thanks.'

'No problem. I have here the proposed schedule and the running orders for the first week. I haven't been involved so I know nothing about them really, but they'll obviously make sense to you. Would you like me to leave them?'

'Sure, then I can contact the team myself. There's no point in you being the go-between any longer.'

They chatted for a while and when Leo left Libby settled down at her desk and tried to concentrate. Her mind kept wandering, wishing for the impossible. At least the small amount of effort made her feel hungry for the first time in days so she prepared herself a ham sandwich in the spotless, lifeless kitchen and made a mental note to send Mrs O'C. home at the weekend. She poured herself a glass of white wine and returned to her desk to try and make sense of it all.

Her mother arrived, as usual, at around three-thirty and this time Libby allowed herself be persuaded to go for a walk. She pulled up the collar of her long black wool coat and wore her sunglasses, just in case she met anyone. They strolled around the beautiful Herbert Park and Libby thought of David chasing her here one day last summer. She knew it was always going to be like this. The faintest trace of warmth in the late afternoon sun was a promise of better days to come and Libby felt slightly more alive after feeling the fresh air in her lungs.

It took two days for Libby to pluck up the courage to phone the office. Her secretary didn't know what to say to her, so she talked about inconsequential things that needed attention, rabbiting on until Libby felt like screaming. When she managed to get a word in, she asked to be put through to Jeremy Scott-Thomas.

'How are you?' There it was again: why couldn't they all stop asking?

'Fine, thanks.' She wasn't in the mood for small talk. 'I presume Leo Morgan has been speaking to you?'

'Yes, I was going to call you today. Have you had a chance to look through everything?'

When they'd discussed it, Libby agreed to go in first thing on Monday morning to go through everything in detail and meet with the stylists. 'I don't want to go traipsing around the building, so perhaps you could set it all up so that they come to my office. I'll be there by ten.'

'Sure, no problem. You're happy that we do a technical run on Tuesday, then we have a day to get everything finally sorted, which gives you a breather and then we record on Thursday and Friday?'

'Fine.' Her response was vague. 'I may need some alterations to one or two of the outfits, by the way.'

He'd been warned of that already. 'I'll have two people on standby.'

Libby couldn't be bothered any more. She said a curt goodbye and as she hung up realized that her whole body was tense. She phoned her mother and put her off, not telling her that it was to be her first night alone. She simply couldn't take any more fussing.

A long, hot bath helped, filled with the wonderful aroma of essential oils and expensive muscle soak. The fire was roaring and a tray was waiting. She forced her reluctant housekeeper out the door at seven, assuring her she'd be all right. 'I'll see you on Monday, as usual.'

'I'd rather come tomorrow and Sunday.'

Not if my life depended on it. Libby didn't say it but her demeanour did. 'I promise I'll call you if I need you.'

'I don't like leaving you.'

Libby was getting tired of this. 'Mum is around and I have a list of people who've been ringing. I won't be short of help.'

She'd no intention of calling any of them. She wanted the weekend to herself to shut out the world and live in David's dressing-gown and not wash and spray herself with his cologne and try to get to grips with the dreaded week ahead. A bottle of good brandy helped.

Chapter Seventeen

Monday couldn't come fast enough for Annie. It was her first day in studio and she was excited and terrified in equal measure. She had only two scenes today and they were both short and she knew her own and everyone else's lines backwards. One was a small piece in the nightclub with a group of actors and the other a two-hander with Stephen Wilson, which she was looking forward to. Nothing too elaborate. She knew it had been planned this way to ease her in.

The week had been hectic but Annie was thriving on it. Her clothes had been chosen, her make-up eventually decided on by the theatrical chief make-up artist and, best of all, she had a fabulous new hairstyle.

Paul Hession had been brilliant. The whole ambience was amazing and the experience worlds away from her local 'ladies and gents hair salon' where old women gossiped under brightly painted helmets and embarrassed men buried their heads

155

in the racing pages. A head massage had almost left Annie unconscious and she'd emerged after three hours with a soft, sleek, shoulder-length style and subtle streaks in every shade of gold imaginable. Paul claimed to love her fiery auburn hair and refused to drastically alter it, to her initial dismay, but when he'd finished she was astonished at the difference. Even her eyes appeared a stronger shade of green. It made her feel sophisticated, which she knew she wasn't. And best of all it had cost her nothing.

The alarm went off at six-thirty, even though her call wasn't till eleven. Of course, she'd nothing to do because clothes and hair and make-up would all be taken care of. After an hour spent watching the paint-drying scenario that was breakfast telly, she dressed in her new black jeans and soft, pale blue sweater and headed out the door. She was miles too early, but at least now she knew her way around and didn't have to wait for someone to collect her. She smiled, remembering her first visit and the image it must have created. Today she walked jauntily up the long driveway and confidently strode through the car park towards the production offices of *Southside*, red-gold hair swinging.

As she came within sight of the main reception area a vaguely familiar, sleek black car eased itself into a reserved spot and Libby Marlowe hurriedly emerged. Annie slowed her steps so as not to catch up. She watched her idol move towards her and was shocked at her appearance. She looked thin and haggard and her voluptuousness seemed to have vanished, although the shapeless black coat probably had something to do with that. Her eyes were lined and puffy and even her make-up couldn't conceal the shadows. Noticing the younger woman, Libby pulled on her sunglasses and quickened her pace.

It was a strange experience. Annie had been thinking about her on and off for the past week, couldn't get her out of her head; she'd even considered writing a note to explain that she'd served David on the night of the tragedy and assure his wife that he'd seemed relaxed and happy. She dismissed the notion as that of a stalker but seeing Libby today, looking so vulnerable, Annie wondered for the first time about her supposed idyllic lifestyle.

Before she even knew what she was doing herself, Annie had closed the gap between them. 'Excuse me, I hope you don't mind if I—'

'I'm not signing anything today.'

'Oh, no I wasn't . . .' This was all going wrong very fast. Annie stepped in front of her idol, anxious to clear up any misunderstanding. 'I just wanted to tell you . . .'

'Please get out of my way. I'm late for a meeting.'

'I won't keep you a minute, I just thought you might want . . .' Annie's face was crimson. Libby's was ashen.

'If you try and keep me for even a second longer I'll call security and have you ejected from these premises.' Libby spat the words. 'How dare you upset me like this. Now, get out of my way immediately.'

Annie stepped back as if she'd been shot. 'Yes, of course, sorry. It's just that I met your husband on the night he—' But she was speaking to herself.

Libby was shaking as she sped through reception and found the sanctuary of her office, terrified in case anyone would stop her and she'd break down. How dare that awful woman approach her? She made up her mind to report the incident to security. As she entered the lavish production offices she knew so well, she kept her head bowed, not trusting herself to utter a greeting. If she had looked up she would have realized that everyone had suddenly busied themselves, wanting to give her space. No-one even tried to make eye contact.

Libby couldn't believe how scared she felt, coming back to work. If a tabloid photographer spotted her now, he'd have a field day. God, maybe that woman was from one of the tabloids. She picked up the phone in her office and called the head of security.

She relayed the incident and exaggerated it for effect.

'Don't worry, we'll track her down. If she was visiting then she'll have had to check in at reception. If she works here she'll have used her security pass to get past reception, so it will be on the main computer. What time was it exactly?'

'About five minutes ago.'

'Fine. Leave it with me. She won't bother you again. I'll pay her a visit myself. What did she look like, by the way?'

Libby told him what she could recall and hung up, feeling slightly mollified.

She was left alone for a good while, then Jeremy knocked gently and came in carrying a cup of herbal tea, her normal mid-morning refresher.

'Hi.'

'Hi.'

'How are you doing?'

'OK, thanks.'

'Good. Listen, as soon as you've had enough today, just say so. I can handle most of the stuff. We only need your input on a few things.'

'Fine.'

'Ready to face the first group?'

Libby nodded, looking anything but ready. She gave him a thin smile.

'I've kept all the meetings small and they've been warned not to raise anything that isn't essential so that should cut out a lot of the usual bullshit. And there'll be no moaning, at least, you can be sure of that.' He smiled at her kindly and she was grateful.

The first meeting was with the food stylists who took charge of all the recipes. As they shuffled in, nobody looked Libby directly in the eye. Everyone said good morning to her nose or her chin.

Jeremy ran the meeting with a rod of iron and it was over in a flash. Every time she made a suggestion, which wasn't often, someone offered to see to it. She was touched at the way they were minding her: before she would have taken it for granted. It was easier than she had imagined.

She didn't leave her office except to go to the loo and at twelve-thirty Eleanor her secretary offered to bring in lunch, sent by Jeremy after she'd refused his offer to go out to eat. 'Just a sandwich would be fine.'

'Any particular kind – ham, chicken, salad, toasted?' the young girl asked her breasts.

'A chicken salad on brown.'

A tray arrived with a sandwich, some fruit, a muffin and a small portion of cheese and biscuits and Eleanor had even managed to find a real cup for the coffee instead of the ubiquitous plastic beaker. Surprisingly, Libby was hungry, which pleased everyone in the outer office. They were monitoring her as if she were an invalid.

By four o'clock she was absolutely whacked. Jeremy walked her to her car, for protection, she suspected. He'd been horrified when she'd told him about the earlier incident and promised to lean on security as well.

'Take it easy tomorrow. We'll be working flat out. I'll only ring you in an emergency. If we need you at all it will only be for an hour.'

'Thank you. You've all been so kind. Will you tell them I really appreciate it?'

Libby wasn't known for saying thank you, but he knew it had been a tough day for her. She looked a bit tearful and her voice wobbled slightly.

He didn't quite know how to deal with a slightly emotional Libby, it was a new experience, so he simply said. 'Take care of yourself.'

'I'll try. Goodnight.'

Jeremy waited until she was moving off and then hurried back in to the warmth of the office, wishing he was closer to her.

Libby drove home without even the radio for company, wanting to stop off at one of her favourite shops, a gorgeous Italian deli in Ranelagh, but not having the courage.

The house was dark and uninviting. Mrs O'C. had left early to take one of her cats to the vet and she was glad, because the bleakness matched her mood. She pulled the curtains in the small sitting room, not bothering to put a match to the already set fire. In the kitchen she ignored the tempting tray of food and instead unwrapped a hunk of cheese and smothered some crusty bread with butter, eating as she went to pour herself a gin and tonic. A chocolate roulade that her mother had delivered she sliced and topped with cream. In the past few days she seemed to crave comfort in the form of sugary, fatty food, and solace and dullness in liquid form.

The television provided little relief and she was left with the cast of *Southside* for company, as yet another far-fetched plot was thrown at an unsuspecting public, or so she thought. Outside, the rain lashed matching her gloomy mood.

Annie was also enjoying the company of the *Southside* regulars, in the warm atmosphere of the local pub. They'd decided to celebrate Annie's first day and even though she'd been finished since three she was happy to hang about in the wings, watching and learning. They'd been drenched making a mad dash to the old world bar but the warmth of a real log fire and a round that comprised mainly hot rums and ports helped ease Annie's tension, which had nothing to do with her first two scenes. They'd been over in a flash. She hadn't fluffed once, and felt ready for anything – except the unexpected visit from the head of security to what was usually a closed set.

He'd called Annie aside, she'd turned purple in the face and hadn't been the same for the rest of the day.

'What a bitch that Libby Marlowe is.' Isobel couldn't believe her ears when Annie told her what it was about as they sat side by side in the pub. Suddenly everyone was listening and Annie was mortified all over again.

'What did he say?'

'He balled me out for daring to speak to her, basically. Said she'd been very upset. Threatened to contact Max about the incident. Oh God, I feel so stupid.'

'And when you explained, what then?' Mike Nichols wanted to know.

'Said he didn't care what information I had. Accused me of being insensitive, at best. Apparently it was her first day back and she was very shaken by the encounter.'

'Oh yeah, you really look like the sort of person who might have stabbed her with a screwdriver,' said one of the assistant floor managers.

'Don't worry, there's nothing he can do.' Mike Nichols shook his head in annoyance.

'God, I hope he *doesn't* write to Max.'

'I'll keep an ear open and if I hear anything in the office I'll let you know so that you can speak to Max yourself. Otherwise I'd forget about it. What a cow, eh?' Isobel's words started a flood of 'Libby legends', as one of the crew called them. Evidently the star wasn't popular.

'Oh, she's huge, the audience love her but she can be an absolute nightmare to work with. She's totally self-obsessed,' one of the cameramen told them and others followed with similar tales, none of which gave Annie any comfort whatsoever.

Several people came to say 'well done' to Annie, which helped a little. She knew the real challenge would come later in the week, but was satisfied with today's performance. The director had come on the floor especially to congratulate her and the girls in make-up, great for sharing confidences, assured her that other cast members thought she was doing really well. Thankfully, Susannah Browne, or Attila the Hun as Annie had secretly christened her, was nowhere to be seen today, although she'd left specific instructions regarding Annie's make-up. Janey, a small, plump girl from Scotland with a roguish twinkle, had read the notes, torn them up and smiled sweetly at Annie.

'Let's just play around with it a bit until we're both happy, shall we?' Annie knew she was being given special attention on her first day and was delighted that Janey seemed not to be in awe of the boss. It had been fun.

Max Donaldson joined them later. He handed Annie a hot rum and black and sat down beside her, taking a long, pleasurable gulp of his pint of Guinness.

'What's that stuff? It smells awful.'

Sipping the warm brew appreciatively, Annie was uneasy. 'I've never had it before but one of the gang suggested it and I was freezing so I'll try anything once.' She grinned nervously, hoping he wasn't going to say anything to spoil the feeling as the warm glow meandered through her body. Please God let him not mention this morning's incident, she prayed for the tenth time.

'Women are amazing. Men would never change their usual tipple on a whim.' Max seemed oblivious to her discomfort.

'But look what you're missing. It tastes even better than Ribena!'

'I'll risk missing that particular pleasure, thank you. How did you get on today?' he asked.

She knew he must have seen the takes: one of the others had told her that he had a monitor in his office and kept a constant eye on the floor, watching every scene he could.

'OK, I think. It was easier in one way because it was all over in a flash and I'd no time to be nervous, and yet harder to concentrate with the number of people on set. Theatre is much quieter generally.'

'Unless a bloody mobile rings in the middle of the performance, which is what happened last night when I was at a show. Idiots, I'd love to strangle them.' He grimaced and Annie giggled in spite of her nerves. He looked quite ferocious and it didn't suit him. 'But no, I understand what you mean. It can be really hard sometimes.'

'It's just all the hanging around, then bang, it's over. Still, I'm not complaining. Did you see anything?' She had to know.

'I did and you were great.'

'Thanks.'

'I'm looking forward to the more meaty scenes later in the week. But you seem to be settling in nicely, well done.'

They all had a natter and a great laugh for an hour or so before everyone piled into cars or taxis, complaining about the bitter wind and rain. Annie headed for the local bus stop.

'Which way are you going?' Mike Nichols asked and when she told him he offered to drop her home. 'I'm on my way to see my sister in Clontarf who's just had a baby, so it's on the way.'

They chatted like old friends and Annie was delighted to be warm and snug in the car. As she got out he reminded her again not to worry about anything. 'You won't hear any more about it, I'm sure,' he smiled reassuringly.

As Annie let herself into a freezing cold house, she felt warm and content and really glad not to be working tonight, but knew she'd have to be careful not to take advantage of Owen Kerrigan's kindness. She still needed that job.

Fish fingers, frozen chips and a big glass of milk provided sustenance. Annie vowed to try and eat less to keep the pounds off that television added. She settled down comfortably to read and laze, but her mind kept wandering back to that awful incident with Libby Marlowe. She wondered if she could somehow make amends to her hero, despite having been warned not to go anywhere near her in the future.

Chapter Eighteen

The first day of recording was a nightmare for Libby. Day one on a new series was always trying, and her own lack of energy and emptiness didn't help. They had taken over a stunning house on the outskirts of Dublin for the duration of the recording but it was freezing and the caterers hadn't turned up, neither of which helped anyone's mood.

Everything that could go wrong did. They were still putting the final touches to the kitchen and the noise added to Libby's headache. She started to rehearse a link, then stopped. 'I just cannot possibly work with that racket going on behind me.' She looked straight at the young carpenter who was brandishing a hammer in mid-air. He scurried off, puce.

And there was her look. Hair and make-up had tried their best, she knew, but nothing could hide the black crevices etched deep under her eyes, and a grey, pasty face and dull hair – despite intensive conditioning treatment – made things worse.

Libby got a fright when she saw herself in the cold, harsh, unforgiving lights of the make-up room. Nearly a month of the worst misery had taken its toll. Even her dramatic weight loss didn't help. The pounds seemed to have disappeared from her boobs and bum, which emphasized her lack of shape, but the piles of luscious cakes eaten as comfort over the past week had found refuge on her chin or around her middle. She felt ghastly.

She wasn't sure about the clothes either, even though they'd already agreed on them weeks before and everyone assured her they were to die for. The look was very modern and for the first time ever she felt like mutton dressed as lamb. The outfit chosen for this programme hung like a habit yet the skirt pinched her waist.

By the time they actually got around to recording, Libby was close to tears, feeling the director was so busy that he was paying no attention to how she looked. She caught sight of herself on a monitor. It was the final straw: she simply walked off the floor. The new hotshot followed her to a corner. 'I'm not happy with how I look and I feel no-one has been paying any attention to it.' She was way past trying to be nice. It was all going horribly wrong and she wanted someone to blame. 'And this mic is ruining the look of my shirt and I can't understand why it needs to be placed practically at my chin.' She shot a venomous glance at the new sound op who'd been slightly offhand with her earlier.

Jeremy Scott-Thomas was over in a flash.

'Why don't you go to your dressing room and I'll get someone to bring you tea while we have a look at your camera position.' Libby nodded abruptly and disappeared. She rang Melanie, who'd been in touch with her every day since the funeral.

'Mel, I'm not happy – this whole thing looks like an amateur production.' Melanie recognized the tone.

'Let me talk to Jeremy and I'll call you back, or I can come over?'

Libby had the sense to know she was being a bit unreasonable. 'Oh Mel, it's probably just me. I feel so awful, I look like a monster and I'm dying inside. I should never have agreed to do it. I can't cope.' She broke down. 'And everyone is being a bit horrible to me,' she added for effect, even though it was completely untrue.

Melanie had the distinct impression her client was losing the plot. She'd called Jeremy earlier in the day, to check on Libby and he'd assured her that they were all on their best behaviour and treating her with kid gloves.

'Stay there. I'm on my way.' As if she was going anywhere. Libby hadn't the strength even to talk so she ignored the knocking on her door, lay on the couch and closed her eyes.

She must have drifted off to sleep because Melanie's singsong high-pitched tones woke her.

'It's only me. Can I come in?' She had one of those PR girl voices and today it irritated Libby along with everything else. The younger girl was a tiny slip of a thing with eyes of steel and a manner that proclaimed loudly, 'Don't fuck with me.' Of course, when dealing with her most valuable client she was sweetness and light, always. She was half hidden behind an enormous bunch of flowers and Libby gave a weak smile in spite of herself.

'Now, I've spoken to Jeremy and he assures me they'll sort everything out. I've told him you're not feeling great so he's suggested they spend the rest of the afternoon getting everything sorted and you start for real in the morning. How does that sound? I can stay around here for as long as is necessary this evening, and I'll phone you if anything crops up.'

Libby nodded, picked up her bag and made a beeline for the door, not stopping to talk to anyone. Melanie walked her to her car. 'Go home and get a good night's sleep and I'll be here in the morning when you arrive. OK?'

'Thanks. I didn't think it would be so tough getting back into it again and I guess I don't have the strength I thought I did.'

The younger woman made soothing noises and assured her everything would be fine. As she watched Libby ease out into the traffic, she sighed wearily. This was going to be a tough few weeks.

Libby decided to stop off at her mother's, then changed her mind halfway there and turned for home. It was all she could manage these days. Mrs O'Connell wasn't expecting her and she was flustered, but Libby shrugged off offers of food and headed to her room, insisting the housekeeper leave at her usual time.

She removed the heavy, ageing make-up and lay on the bed, drifting off to sleep in minutes. When she woke it was dark outside and she changed into her robe and made her way wearily downstairs. Mrs O'Connell had been baking for the afternoon. Libby found a mouth-watering array of scones, malt loaf and a chocolate cake, some still warm. The smell of home baking lingered as Libby sat at the kitchen table and sampled a bit of everything. It was quiet as she poured rich coffee and hunted out home-made jam for the scones. That suited her. She wasn't up to idle chat tonight.

She poured a glass of wine but could find nothing of interest on any TV channel. Reluctantly, she decided to limit herself to two glasses in an effort to get a decent night's sleep and look half human for the next day.

When she woke it was bright. She'd slept through her alarm, so she showered quickly and made some coffee. It gave her no time to think. She phoned to let the studio know she was on her way. Being late on a recording day was a mortal sin and they'd already lost time yesterday because of her. She didn't want to get a bad name among production companies, so she made a big effort and arrived soon after her call time.

She was met by several wary faces and everyone was on their best behaviour, anxious to placate their star. Hair and make-up were particularly on the ball and she was pampered and preened for what seemed like hours. When she finally appeared on set they spent almost an hour on her lighting and camera positions and both Melanie and Jeremy were very much in evidence.

At last, the recording got under way. Scripts had been written for her and whereas normally she used them only as a guide, ad-libbing as she went, today she stuck fairly rigidly to the prepared material, trying to look lively and interested. But it was a surreal experience, as if she was far above it all, looking down on herself.

The day was long and arduous and they all pushed on relentlessly, as if sensing she might crack up again at any moment. Libby knew she simply had to get through this and so was calm and methodical, if somewhat lifeless. Her smiles were fake and her normal chirpy banter on camera had all but disappeared.

Even the recipes, carefully chosen, seemed to lack the vividness associated with her cooking and the stylists constantly hovered, ready to touch up everything before the close-ups were taken. Normally, Libby tried to avoid letting the experts loose on her food, preferring her dishes to look natural, even if the home-cooked appearance was carefully orchestrated and styled. Today they fussed around, adding glaze here and placing herbs there, polishing plates and asking for special lighting, and Libby let them.

It was seven-thirty by the time they had a full programme in the can. She was talked out and her face hurt from trying to look interested. The relief on set was tangible. The first one of a new format was always the killer: at least now they knew it could be done.

Libby got a round of applause as soon as she'd finished her final link. She ignored it and walked off and the set was de-rigged in record time, everyone in a rush to get to the pub for a drink to celebrate. Then it was home to bed and up early, ready to do it all again, even though the next day was Saturday. They were a programme behind and had to catch up but at least she had Sunday to look forward to and the prospect of a break had never seemed more welcome.

Libby was out of her clothes in record time, anxious to get away and be by herself. Melanie popped her head round the dressing-room door.

'Fancy a quick drink or a bite to eat on the way home?'

Libby couldn't imagine anything worse. 'Would you mind if I passed? I'm absolutely shattered.'

'No problem.' The younger woman walked with Libby towards her car.

'How did you think it looked?' Libby asked warily as she threw her bag in the boot.

That was a no-win question, Melanie knew, so she gave the standard PR answer. 'It's a very interesting concept, you were fantastic and by the time it's edited and all the music stings put in, I think it should do well in the ratings.'

'I'm still not convinced, but for the first time I don't really care. I just want to get it over with. By the way, thanks for being around today, it was great knowing you were keeping an eye on things.'

'No problem, do you want me around to-morrow as well?'

Libby was about to say no then changed her mind. Let them all earn their money. They made enough out of her.

'If you could, it would be terrific. Once I get tomorrow over with, I'll feel we're really up and running and besides, I'll have Sunday to recover.'

'Fine, I'll be here.' She smiled at a tired, worn Libby. 'Get some rest.'

'Thanks, Mel, you're a star.'

She looked forlorn as she pulled out into the line of traffic on a chilly, damp winter night, resolving to ring one of her favourite restaurants and get them to deliver spicy Indian food to her door, something she never did as a rule, preferring to cook from scratch herself. She also decided to open a good bottle of wine and to hell with the two glasses theory. She'd survived in spite of it all.

Mel waved, turned towards her own car and was on her mobile in a flash, searching for company and a very large G & T.

Chapter Nineteen

Annie was in love. She'd never had these feelings before but she recognized them from the movies and magazines she'd seen over the years. The signs were classic: a net of butterflies had camped out in a tree in her stomach and she had a permanent tight, hard knot to prove it. She'd been going around grinning at nothing for days and had sweaty palms and an overactive heartbeat every time she saw him.

'Him' was Marc Robinson, an actor in *Southside* whom she'd always thought was cute on screen but who was seriously gorgeous in real life. He was Australian and had been headhunted for the part of Alan, a dentist who'd moved to Dublin for the summer and decided to stay. In the show, he was currently setting up in practice and encouraging younger women to worry about their fillings and have regular check-ups. His character was definitely not the shy, retiring type and neither, it appeared, was he.

He was the healthiest-looking man she'd ever seen, all blond hair and blue eyes and a lean, tanned body, courtesy of life down under. He looked every inch the surfing dude but funnily enough the first time she'd laid eyes on him he'd been dressed in an expensive suit and it didn't look out of place.

He was one of the few actors she hadn't met during her initial stint on the show. It was love at first sight for Annie and suddenly she understood what made all the screen legends swoon. It put her previous romances firmly in the shade, not that there had been many. She'd lost her virginity to an actor she'd met on one of her first full-time productions. After a couple of weeks he confided in her that he thought he might be gay. Then there was a heterosexual hairdresser called Jonathan, whom Annie thought she was in love with but who was more in love with himself. She had a brief fling with a bus conductor she met in the gym, but he left her for a bodybuilder. After her illness there'd been a couple of snogs with actors and one with a stage manager, but none of them had developed and Annie had been more interested in getting on with her career than in having a serious relationship.

This however, was different. It happened one fairly ordinary day, as she sat on the side of the set, watching and picking up tips and waiting for her own recording, which was not scheduled for another two hours. As usual she was dressed and made up way too early. The girls in wardrobe and make-up were used to her by now and teased her about being too eager, but in reality they were impressed with her dedication. Few realized how important this was to her. Being part of a successful show, even for a while, made all her struggles worthwhile.

She sat quietly in a corner as the floor manager yelled the names of four actors needed into a portable handset, staging rushed around getting ready for a new scene and lighting and sound argued over positions. Her heart quickened even before she saw him, as if it knew he might be something special. Marc strolled in ahead of the others, chatting to Rhonda, a dark, attractive production assistant. Everyone greeted him warmly, as if pleased to see him and Annie noticed one of the camerawomen fixing her hair as soon as she saw him.

There was more than the usual banter as people took their places and waited for final checks. Annie simply couldn't take her eyes off him. He was divine – she had to stop herself staring and try to pretend nonchalance.

He grinned a lot and flirted outrageously, but in such a way that he got away with it. It was a lethal combination for the would-be star hovering in the wings.

Marc's scene was over in about twenty minutes and she saw him looking in her direction as he said goodbye to the floor manager. She became conscious of her tight black skirt and plunging, stretchy, see-through top. She busied herself with her script, but when she heard the Australian accent she knew it was directed at her.

'Hi, are you Bobby?'

She looked up at a pair of the bluest eyes, then plunged straight in and drowned. That was it. Everything started working faster: her blood was pumping at twice its normal speed and her heart was in danger of exploding.

'Yes, hi.' She stood up quickly, in case he moved away, and tried to think of anything at all to say. It didn't work. She sat down again, afraid she might swoon. God, if they were recording this it would make great TV, she thought, licking her dry lips.

He grinned and Annie turned purple. 'I wondered what you'd be like when I read the part. I'm Marc Robinson and as you probably saw I play Alan.'

'Yes, I was watching.' It came out like Donald Duck. He laughed and she cleared her throat. 'I'm eh, Annie, Annie Weller.'

It sounded nearly normal.

'Are you on next?'

'Eh, no, not for another couple of hours.'

'God but you're keen.' He grinned and she blushed again.

'Just trying to take it all in,' she stammered. 'I've never done television before.'

'Hey, only kidding. Fancy a coffee?' In his glorious Australian drawl it sounded more like 'fancy a ride?' and she wanted anything he was offering.

'I was just thinking of getting one,' she lied, jumping up again a touch too quickly.

'Great, let's go and you can tell me all about Annie Weller.' He flashed her a dazzling smile and she felt sick.

They had coffee in the canteen and it might as well have been the Ritz. She was so engrossed that the stage manager had to come looking for her for a final make-up check and she was mortified.

She learned that Marc was from Sydney, thirty-two years of age, single, had an apartment in Rathgar, an exclusive suburb of south Dublin. He had three sisters – one in London, one in New York and one, the baby, still at home.

He asked her about herself and she found little to tell; but she told him how her mother had died and was happy to talk about the men in her life. She didn't mention her health. Men were funny about breast cancer, she'd discovered from an actor years ago. She could still remember every word.

'I'm cured, and . . . still have my breasts. And . . . it's not as if I've got huge scars or anything.' She still got embarrassed just thinking about that encounter. He'd looked horrified for an instant and then almost immediately his look changed to pity and he made an excuse to leave shortly afterwards. She never heard from him again and was convinced he'd told the others in their circle. She imagined whispers and pitying looks. She'd made sure it never happened to her again.

Almost an hour later Annie and Marc said goodbye and he offered to buy her a pint some night, but didn't ask for her number.

'Sure, that'd be great.' She didn't want to sound too keen and anyway Mags, the stage manager, was loitering, having lost actresses to Marc Robinson many times in the past.

'Cute guy,' she said casually to Annie as they strolled down the corridor.

'He seems nice.' What an understatement.

'He's very nice but he seems to have a lot of girl-friends. Be careful. I think he has a—' Her pager went off and she was all business again within seconds. One of the actors had gone walkabout in the middle of a take. Mags left Annie to make her own way over and hurried off, ready to bawl someone out. Annie was surprised to find herself gutted by the casual statement. She didn't want Marc to have *any* women friends.

Don't be stupid, you've only just met him. He's a good-looking guy, of course he has girlfriends. Annie continued this train of thought right up until she stepped onto the studio floor, then forced all images of him from her mind, knowing that otherwise she'd never be able to concentrate.

She half hoped he might have stuck around for her scene, but he was nowhere in sight as she left the building, having casually checked out the green-room and the canteen just in case. Next day she found herself glancing at the recording schedule and was disappointed to see that he wasn't in any other scenes that week. She moped.

The following Saturday he was in rehearsal.

They had lunch together and she smiled a lot and was happy.

On Tuesday, after they'd both finished a big scene in the pub, where he had a lot to do and she virtually nothing, he suggested a pint in the local. Annie said a fervent prayer of thanks that she didn't have to work that night and was delighted she'd worn her new jacket. Her heart tumbled again when he mentioned a drink casually to some of the others and she struggled not to burst into tears when one or two of them decided to join them. Then it soared again an hour or two later when he offered her a lift home.

It was only nine-thirty and she sat chatting to him in the car for ages, afraid to ask him in for coffee in case he thought she was too keen. Five minutes later she couldn't resist it, despite worrying about her well-worn, tiny house and comparing it in her head to his luxury south Dublin pad. She was gutted when he declined, citing an early start as the reason.

'No problem, I'd better go in and get rid of all this make-up.' She did her best to sound breezy.

'I'll see you on Friday, I see we're in around the same time.' So he'd checked the schedule too.

'Friday is my last day.' Annie couldn't believe she might not see him again. It didn't bear thinking about.

'Well, let's hope it's not the last time I see you.' He leaned over and kissed her briefly and gently on the lips. She had to restrain herself from going straight in, tongues blazing.

'You're nice.'

'So are you.'

He winked at her. 'See you Friday.'

She had no option but to get out of the car and she couldn't think of a single witty goodnight.

Chapter Twenty

The next few days were a soufflé of joy and despair. Annie couldn't believe the best job she'd ever had was coming to an end. She agonized about whether or not her contract would be renewed and went from being cheerful and optimistic one minute to feeling flat and depressed the next. Added to this complicated emotional mixture were feelings of elation when she thought of Marc's kiss, immediately followed by a sense of impending doom when she realized she might not see him again after this week. Being in love was the pits.

She'd had to do some tough negotiation with Owen Kerrigan to get Friday night off, but she simply couldn't bear to run out of the studio on her last day and go straight back to her old, monotonous routine. This part had opened up a new world and in the space of a few short weeks she realized how hungry she was for a proper life.

She thought about it as she made her way to the

restaurant on Thursday evening, having spent the afternoon looking for something to wear for the following day.

Over the past few years, she'd been so grateful to be alive that she hadn't really questioned what sort of life she'd managed to carve out for herself. Thinking back on it, it was pretty grim, really. Eking out an existence, getting by from week to week, with a couple of tiny parts that didn't pay very well her only bright spot, it could hardly be called living. Only her fierce determination made it bearable at all. This chance had made her see things clearly and it wasn't a pretty picture. Working five nights a week and every weekend meant she had no social life, and lack of funds meant she had little control over other aspects of her life. It was depressing.

Now, however, it seemed to have shifted from dreary black and white to glorious Technicolor and Annie desperately didn't want to go back to grey and nondescript. As she changed into her work suit and tied her hair back in the ladies' loo she wondered how much it all had to do with Marc Robinson.

Friday came at last, another chance to shine. Annie chatted happily to Orla, one of the other young actresses with whom she shared a dressing room. She played the part of Beth, who worked on a till in the local supermarket. She was sassy and cute and seemed much younger than Annie, even though there was less than a year between them. In many ways Orla reminded Annie of the life she'd left behind, before the big C. It made her faintly nostalgic for her old innocence and that sense of being unstoppable.

'Are you on for a pint later? It's my last day.' She was a little nervous in case everyone would be rushing off for the weekend, although she knew most would be back at work the following morning for another round of rehearsals. It was just like a factory production line really, except that instead of packets of biscuits or jars of jam they churned out neatly packaged forty-minute television programmes to tempt the taste buds of the mind. And no matter what, it just kept on rolling.

Orla was making faces at herself in the mirror. She hated the overall and hairnet that made up her working clothes on the programme and they all teased her about it.

'Sure, I'm looking forward to it. I should be finished by lunchtime, but I'll meet you in the pub around six-thirty. I presume it's the local and not the social club here, which I cannot stand?' She added a bit more colour to her already scarlet lips.

'I'd say so. I'm not even sure that anyone else will be free.'

'Don't worry, there's always someone gasping for a pint on a Friday and anyway people will make the effort 'cause it's your last day.' She glanced up from pulling on her boots. 'Speaking of which, any news yet on whether you're coming back?'

Annie shook her head.

'Why don't you ask Max?'

'I haven't got the courage, to be honest.' Annie knew it sounded weak but she hated pushing herself forward where money and contracts were concerned. Her determination was channelled towards getting the parts, it was all that had ever driven her on. 'I think I'll just hold off for a while and see what happens.'

'You need an agent.' Orla was streetwise and not afraid to be upfront about it.

'I can't afford one.'

'You can't afford *not* to have one. This is a tough business.'

As they talked, Annie felt a bit flat again. She tried to pull herself together as she hung up the new slip dress she'd bought for tonight. It was longish and flimsy with a bra-type top with skinny little straps and a skirt that was sort of floaty. The tones were soft and spring-like and matched her colouring. Teamed with her only pair of flat boots, the dress looked casual and funky, if a little summery for the time of year. She'd need to wear her denim jacket with it. It had cost 70 euro in Oasis, a fortune as far as she was concerned. She'd bought it for Marc, really, but she wasn't admitting this to herself. It made her feel girly, something she definitely wasn't used to. But when he'd kissed her in the car that was exactly how she felt and she liked it.

The day flew and Annie's last scene was called and she was nervous because it would really stretch her ability and test her as an actor. It was the one where Ted Doran explains that he wants Bobby to work privately for him and Annie had given a lot of thought to how she should play it.

After two rehearsals they went for a take. Annie was nervous and felt she blew it. The director played it back for them and she felt even worse.

'How does Tim feel about it?' she asked the floor manager, hoping the director would ask for a second take.

'He's happy, if you are,' came back to Annie and her heart sank. She knew she could do better but time was always against them, especially at the end of the week. Her face must have given away her feelings because the young floor manager came over and spoke quietly to her. 'Tim wants to know if you'd like another go.'

'Oh, yes, please, if there's time. I felt I made an awful mess of that one.' Annie was hugely relieved.

'OK, folks, take two please.' He moved off to tell props to reset. Annie took a moment to think over the scene again.

This time her performance was completely different. She played it a bit more vulnerable to start, touching her low-cut blouse and fidgeting with the buttons as if to protect herself when Ted Doran made his offer, then reverting to the normal, harder Bobby, afraid he'd notice how unsure she really was. It was an important scene and she gave it everything. When it was over the floor manager moved off to a corner and spoke quietly into his headset, obviously talking to the director.

'Tim's coming on to the floor for a moment,' he announced to no-one in particular and Annie's heart sank. That meant a problem, usually, and Annie immediately assumed it was her. Tim Furlong was a small man who'd been directing drama for years, both in the UK and Ireland. He was very dramatic himself, a bit of a queen really, and he name-dropped all the time about the 'prima donnas' he'd had to put up with. Everyone liked him though, he was funny and sharp and sarcastic, and now he headed for Annie.

'Darling that was great but you're going to kill me because we had a problem with vision and I need another take. I'm really sorry about this.' He glanced at Stephen to include him. 'I've bawled out the relevant people and they've assured me this one will be fine. Could you bear to do it one more time?'

Annie didn't care how many times she had to do it as long as it wasn't her fault, and thankfully Stephen Wilson was fine about it as well.

Take three went OK, although Annie wasn't sure she'd captured the moment as successfully as she had in the previous take but when she saw it back she was pleased.

For a change this time everyone was happy and they all seemed genuinely sorry when she announced forlornly, 'That's my final scene.'

'Well, if they've any sense upstairs they'll bring you back quickly.' Ben, a shy, smiling cameraman, took off his headset and came over to shake her hand. 'It's been a pleasure working with you.'

Annie felt her face turn beetroot with pride. 'Hear hear!' one of the older stagehands shouted from the corner. Annie ran over and hugged the man, who'd been especially kind to her.

'Is this a private snogging session or can anyone join in?' a voice asked from the other side of the studio and Annie felt the familiar feeling in her tummy.

'Come on, gorgeous, I'll buy you a beer.' Marc Robinson was smiling at her warmly and she grinned back, delighted.

'Great, I need one after that.'

He put his arm around her casually as they strolled out towards the dressing rooms and Annie wanted to stay there, feeling safe and protected, for ever.

'I'll be five minutes,' she warned him as she rushed to change into her new clothes.

'Sure you don't want company?' He grinned and she laughed and ran away.

The pub was Friday evening rush hour busy but luckily a couple of other actors had snatched a big corner and Annie and Marc joined them.

'Hello, you two look very cosy.' Tessa Rowan who played Carla was smiling, but not with her eyes. Annie knew she was one of the prima donnas on the series. Nothing ever seemed to be right for her and she constantly criticized people but always behind their back. Annie was a bit afraid of her.

'Hey Tessa, you're just jealous,' Marc joked.

Annie suspected there was more than a grain of truth in his words.

'Don't flatter yourself,' the older woman said, still smiling. 'I only date men.'

'Ouch. Vicious.' Stephen Wilson had joined them. 'I think we should stay out of this one, Annie. Come on, I'll buy you a drink. Marc, pint of Guinness?'

'Cheers, mate.' He sat down beside the actress who'd been only half teasing and pinched her leg. 'I'm more of a man than you'll ever need.' It was all jokey banter but Annie sensed an undercurrent. She didn't like the crazy feelings it aroused either and the notion of scratching the older woman's eyes out was not one she'd experienced before. Tessa Rowan was in her early forties, and very glamorous, although she looked as if she tried a bit too hard. Annie knew she was jealous and didn't like the alien emotion one bit. Reluctantly she joined Stephen at the bar.

'Listen, I've really enjoyed working with you. I hope we get to do it again soon,' he said.

Annie nearly cried. 'So do I. You've no idea how much, and thanks for saying that, it means a lot.'

'You should ask Max what his plans for the character are. You deserve to know, before you take on other work.' Annie didn't want to tell him there was no other project on the horizon, so she just smiled weakly and shrugged.

'There he is now. Why don't you?' Annie froze when she saw the producer come in. 'I couldn't, honestly. I'm just not the type. Complete and utter coward where pushing myself forward is concerned, I'm afraid. I nearly told him I'd take the part for no pay, that's how bad I am,' she apologized.

'Then get yourself a good agent.'

'That's what Orla said earlier. I really will think about it.'

'It'll save you money in the long run. Trust me, I'm an actor.' He smiled as he handed her a glass of lager and they moved over to the by now fairly large group and sat down. Annie wanted to sit beside Marc but he was wedged in and she didn't have the nerve.

There was a great deal of banter going on. Annie smiled and said very little, simply happy to be part of it all.

As some of the crew joined them the circle widened and they broke into smaller groups. Everyone was relaxed and casual and Annie felt she had tried too hard. The outfit was just a bit too dressy for the local pub and she'd spent money she couldn't really afford on it, which was niggling away at her, especially as it looked as if she was going to be out of work for a while again.

'Annie, I'm off. I'll be in touch soon.' Max Donaldson put his hand on her shoulder and she jumped up, spilling her drink and liking the dress even less.

'I saw all your scenes today. It was your heaviest day so far, wasn't it?' She nodded and gulped the remainder of her drink, hoping he'd keep talking.

'Well, all I can say is, congratulations. You handled it very well. Your last scene was excellent and really worth doing those extra takes. You got it just right.'

Annie was beaming. She wanted to beg him to keep her on but would have settled for replying with even a hint of intelligence. As usual, nothing came.

'We have a major brainstorming session planned for the week after next with the writers, so I should know more after that.'

Annie knew they were fairly advanced with scripts and realized that even if they wanted her back it could be months away, which was very depressing. Now she did the best acting job Max had seen yet, smiled and said casually, 'I've really enjoyed it and it's a part I'd love to get my teeth into, but I know you've a lot of other options to consider. And thanks for taking a chance on me in the first place. You gave me my first break on TV and I'm very grateful.'

'Pleasure. Talk to you soon. And maybe you'd let the office know if you are taking on any long-term projects, just so we have your availability on file.'

'Sure.' Annie tried another casual smile, not wanting to tell him that her longest project to date had been joining the dole queue. 'I'll keep in touch with Isobel or Mike.'

'Great.' He looked around. 'Bye everyone, I'm off before you make me buy another round.' There was a general shouting of 'Skinflint' and 'Scrooge' as Annie consoled herself with the fact that at least Max was interested in knowing her availability.

'Well, what did the great white chief have to say?' Marc was beside her and she was happy again.

'Nothing much I'm afraid, but he did say he liked my stuff today, especially the last scene.'

'You were great, I was watching.' He made her feel she was the only woman in the room and she wanted to kiss him really badly.

'You would say that – anything for a drink.' She tried to lighten the mood before she grabbed him and stuck her tongue down his throat.

'You're right. I'll have a pint, thanks.'

'Bastard.'

'The women love it.'

'I'd say they do.'

'They just can't resist my charm.'

'Well, I think I can just about manage.' She grinned as she headed for the bar, glad he couldn't read her mind.

It was a happy two hours for Annie, especially as Marc didn't leave her side. At about eight-thirty he suggested they go for a Chinese.

They left to a chorus of slagging and taunts about Marc being 'a fast worker' and Annie was delighted: at least now people saw them as an item. Tessa Rowan urged Annie playfully to 'ask him all about his other women', but the catty remark went right over her head.

Chapter Twenty-One

Although she was starving, Annie hardly ate a thing. She was too nervous. Marc seemed to have no such feelings because he tucked in with gusto, demolishing half of her food as well. He kept her entertained with tales of his family in Australia and horror stories about various acting jobs. He seemed to want to keep it light and said little about himself. Annie wanted to know everything, but for now she had to content herself with the bits he was prepared to share. She wondered briefly if he was being deliberately cagey with her but dismissed the thought as the mad notion of someone who hadn't had a proper date in a very long time.

They laughed a lot and he teased her about being so eager and Annie wanted to tell him why this job was so important, but was afraid the big C would scare him off. She knew there would be time for all that later on, or at least she hoped so. He was addictive and she was fast becoming hooked.

As they headed for his car she realized she was a

bit tipsy, having polished off three glasses of wine, as well as the beers she'd had earlier. Marc had stopped after two because he was driving, and slagged her because she kept giggling. As they neared the car park he grabbed her hand and pulled her towards him, kissing her hard on the lips. If she was light-headed before, she was in orbit now and she kissed him back with real longing.

He was the first to break free and he grinned down at her. 'You're quite a kisser, Annie Weller.'

'You ain't seen nothing yet.' She couldn't believe she'd just said that. It was so naff.

When they reached her house he leaned over and kissed her again, and this time their passions rose in tandem. She wriggled her body as close to him as possible and wondered if he could feel her nipples hardening through the thin bra top of her dress.

He obviously could. He slid his hands up along her sides and then lightly over her breasts and she tried not to gasp as a warm feeling spread all over her body and lingered between her legs.

He moaned and tried to pull her even closer and she dragged him over to her seat and straddled him, not caring that they were in a car in a busy housing estate, parked under a street lamp. Annie couldn't believe she was being so eager – it was an odd feeling to want him so desperately and it made her feel vulnerable, although the alcohol was giving her courage.

'God, you feel gorgeous and you're driving me

mad,' Marc said softly as he licked her neck and shoulders expertly, pushing down the straps of her dress with his nose and kissing each bit of exposed skin. His hands were roaming over her bottom and he could feel the silky thong she wore. Annie had laughed hysterically when she'd put it on this morning and looked at herself in the mirror. It was a million miles away from the sensible faded white cotton knickers she normally wore and she would never have dreamed of buying it except that the shop assistant had insisted she get one, telling her firmly that ordinary pants would ruin the line of the dress. Annie thought she looked absolutely ridiculous with a piece of string between her buttocks. All day it had been uncomfortable but suddenly it was fantastic and made her feel like a real woman for the first time in years, instead of boring old reliable Annie.

Marc pressed her close to his dick and she knelt up so that he could feel her properly all over. He was feather-kissing her nipples through the thin material of her dress and she was dying for him to simply unzip her but she knew they couldn't possibly go that far in a car with the local kids playing nearby. The fogged-up windows helped their seclusion, but could just as easily give the game away.

He slipped his hand underneath the crotch of her thong and his breathing was heavy. She nearly died with the sheer, intense pleasure of it all, as feelings she'd never experienced before came bubbling to the surface. Yet something was holding her back, telling her she didn't want to have sex with him for the first time in a car – not with a perfectly good bed a few yards away.

Anyway, she thought as she struggled to clear her brain, she wanted to be sober when it happened and she didn't want him to think she was easy. Bit late for that now, she chided herself, sitting back down and leaning away from him slightly, against all her instincts.

He sensed something had changed. 'You're driving me mad, do you know that? I want you so badly.'

She laughed. She didn't know what to say.

'Can I come in?'

'Not tonight, I'd be asleep on you in five minutes.' When had she started lying so easily? And what was she doing, turning away the best thing that had happened to her in ages?

'I promise I've got something to keep you awake.'

She grinned, embarrassed and felt nervous all of a sudden, in case he went off her.

'I think we should wait a bit, you know.' It sounded lame even to her.

He took her hand and placed it over his crotch. She could feel him, rock hard. It caused the delicious, warm feeling to spread again. 'See what you've done to me. How can you be so cruel?' She knew he was only half teasing and she was mortified because it was all happening too quickly and she felt like a schoolgirl on her first date, instead of the sophisticated woman she suspected he thought she was.

'I've no heart. Anyway, I think you'll survive.' Please don't let him go off me for this. 'I'd better go in and make some black coffee.'

'I'll come with you.'

'You don't need black coffee. I'm the drunk here.' She laughed and he kissed her again and she went weak all over. The kiss lingered and this time he contented himself with running his fingers lightly up and down her arm and driving her mad with anticipation.

'You won't get away so easily next time.' He nibbled at her ear and ran his fingers along the nape of her neck and down to her breasts, but stopped short of touching them. It was a practised gesture, but to Annie it was heaven and hell all rolled into one excruciating pleasure.

'Next time I'll make you pay.'

'Promise?'

'Oh, I promise.'

'Good. I can't wait.'

He slapped her bottom playfully and she was relieved and happy as he disentangled himself and moved back to his own seat, but she let him go reluctantly.

'Thanks for a lovely night.' It was all she could think of.

'Let's do it again soon.'

'I'd like that.' She got out while she was still ahead.

'I'll give you a buzz over the weekend.'

'You don't have my number.'

'That's what programme call sheets are for.'

She grinned. 'Night-night.'

'Sleep well, you vixen. I'm off home to take a cold shower.'

'Enjoy yourself.' She waved as he turned the car and sped off into the black night. Annie hoped she hadn't made a big mistake, just because of some stupid, old-fashioned idea that he might go off her once he'd got what he wanted.

Chapter Twenty-Two

The days were crawling by for Libby and things seemed to be getting worse instead of better. The series was up and running but as each day passed she became more convinced than ever that the concept was wrong for her. She was too exhausted to worry much about it, though. Getting through the day was like tackling an enormous obstacle course and she spent her evenings eating and drinking and avoiding her mother as much as she could, insisting she was fine and using her workload as an excuse to avoid visits. She knew Christina had taken to popping round most days to chat to Mrs O'Connell. Between them they left enough food to feed a small army and Libby was eating most of it. It was very tough, and tough was taking its toll. And there was worse to come.

John Simpson had left several messages and when she could no longer put if off she shut herself into the small sitting room, pulled the blinds, poured herself a stiff drink and called him at home.

'John, I'm sorry not to have rung before now. I'm in the middle of the new series and it's about all I can manage at the moment.'

'That's OK, Libby. How are you?'

'Exhausted, emotional, stressed, run down and getting as fat as a pig.' She laughed to try and lighten her own mood.

'Well, the last one can't be bad. You were as thin as a whippet when I saw you recently.'

'In that case, you'll have difficulty recognizing me next time.' She was only half joking. 'My mother and Mrs O'Connell are determined to fatten me up and I seem to crave comfort in the form of food at the moment. Stuffing my face is about all I can manage these evenings. To think I used to be able to go to the gym after a day's work, and then party for Ireland.' Her laugh was not a happy sound.

'Don't be too hard on yourself, Libby. You're doing fine. Being back at work so soon is an enormous achievement. You're entitled to your rewards.'

'Yes, but not in the quantities I've been having them. And believe me, I wouldn't be back working except I wasn't really given much choice. The series was already too far advanced and it was either I do it or they get someone else.' She heard his intake of breath. 'No, I'm being unfair. They did offer to facilitate me but I needed to stop moping around, although now I'm not sure I made the right decision. Anyway, enough about me, it's more of the same boring old stuff. How are things with you?'

They made small talk for a couple of minutes and then he got to the point.

'Libby, I need to talk to you about the business.'

Her heart sank. She wasn't sure she could cope with anything else right now.

'Can't it wait?'

He hated doing this but she had to know.

'Not really. We need to sit down and go through a few things. There are some decisions to be made.'

'Can't Alex O'Meara take care of it, John? I don't think I can take on any more until we finish the series.'

'I think we need to talk first, then the three of us need to sit down together. Is there anyone else who could handle this for you?'

'No, unless David's father. He offered to come over and go through everything, but I don't think he's that well, and Monica has taken this whole thing so badly, I don't really want to call on him just now.'

'No, I don't think we should either.' He was at a loss, not wanting to push her yet needing to make some decisions.

'I'll tell you what, after this week I have a break in recording for two weeks. I do have a lot of setting up to do for the rest of the series, but at least it's only office based and I don't have to get dressed up and talk to morons all day. How about if we have dinner next week?'

It was the best he could hope for. 'Fine, Libby.

I'll fill you in as best I can then. Meanwhile, I'll keep working with Alex and we'll have as much as possible sorted out.'

'John, I'm not going to be much help to you, by the way. I know absolutely nothing about the business. I'd say the postboy knows more. David didn't discuss it at home, you know what he was like.'

'I do indeed.' Not for the first time recently, he wished he'd pushed a bit harder with his oldest friend. 'I think maybe we both let him away with too much, Libby.' He hadn't meant to voice his private thoughts and was almost relieved when she didn't seem to pick up on it.

'He was way too charming for his own good, you know that more than most, John. It meant he got away with murder. With me, he hardly ever discussed things, especially in the early days. And later, on the odd occasion he tried to my eyes glazed over within seconds.' She smiled a secret smile, remembering all the tactics she'd used to shut him up when he was having a rant about a client, or threatening to sack an employee. She sighed. 'He liked to do things his way most of the time and I just let him get on with it. The high-flying world of finance has always been as dull as ditchwater for me. I think I was only ever involved for a variety of complicated tax reasons, which I never understood anyway. Bit of a dunce about money I'm afraid, except when it comes to spending it.' She paused for a second, sensing he wasn't laughing with her.

'It's all right, though, isn't it? I mean, it's all turning over and everything?'

'Well, there are some complications.'

Libby didn't like the sound of his voice. He sounded much too like the solicitor he was, instead of good old reliable John. 'What sort of complications?'

He wasn't about to go into it now, late at night when she was tired and probably low. 'Don't worry about it for the moment. I'll explain it all next week. What day suits you?'

'Tuesday.' She had a sudden feeling she should see him as soon as possible.

'Tuesday's fine. Where would you like to go? The Grasshopper?' He could have bitten his tongue off as he realized that that was where David had been on the night of his heart attack. 'Oh, God, Libby, I'm so sorry. It completely slipped my mind. I'm an insensitive oaf. Please, forgive me.'

Her heart was pounding. She tried not to cry but the alcohol wasn't helping.

'It's OK, John, I know.'

'Jesus, Libby, I wouldn't upset you for the world, you know that. It was out before I could stop it. I'm sorry, I've been under a bit of pressure myself lately, not that that's any excuse . . .'

'John, shush, it's fine. How about you come here? I'll even cook myself.' She was trying to comfort him: cooking was the last thing she wanted to do. She just didn't want him worrying, he sounded weary enough already.

'Great. Thanks. I eat out too much as it is. And

Anna's never around to cook these days. The price of our glorified lifestyle, I suppose.' He sounded lonely.

'Pasta OK?' At least she could rustle up that with her eyes closed.

'Perfect. I'll be by on my way home about seven, if that suits?'

'Great, see you then.'

'Mind yourself, Libby. And I'm sorry again.'

'I've forgotten already. Bye.'

But she hadn't and that, coupled with whatever he had to discuss, sent her scurrying in the direction of the wine bottle, the only thing that numbed the feelings of pressure these nights.

Chapter Twenty-Three

Despite tossing and turning all night following their conversation, Libby put it out of her mind as the horror that was 'How to have people round without going round the bend' – thankfully a working title only – took hold again. She'd seen some of the rushes and had hated them with a passion, although everyone else, including Melanie, seemed to think they were fine. Libby wondered if she was going mad, and that seemed entirely possible too.

The much-needed break arrived at last and they set about planning the second half regardless, to keep up with the voracious appetite of 'the schedule'.

Tuesday came and Libby had almost forgotten about John until his secretary telephoned to confirm. She was devastated, having planned to spend the full day at home in front of the TV with only Terry, she of the chocolate orange fame, for company.

At four-thirty she threw herself into the shower, dressed in a long black wool skirt and soft cashmere sweater and added high-heeled boots to try and smarten herself up. She applied her make-up with care and left her blond hair loose, conscious that she hadn't seen John in several weeks and realizing that she was vain enough to want to look good for David's friend.

He arrived with more flowers.

'God, your secretary is definitely looking for Brownie points,' Libby said as she took the enormous bunch of red roses and dunked them in a basin. 'Come into the kitchen and I'll give you a glass of wine while I finish off supper.'

He watched her closely as he sat on a high stool and loosened his tie. She looked tired and drawn and her face was a bit puffy, he noticed with concern.

'So, how's the series progressing?'

'Do you know, I really have no idea. I think it's horrendous and everyone else thinks it's fine. And knowing me as you do at the moment, who would you believe?'

'Things still rough?'

'You've no idea.' All of a sudden a wave of sadness and hurt washed over her and the pain was physical and intense. 'I miss him so much. It hurts all day, every day.' She stopped stirring and bowed her head. Tears ran down her face, this time nothing to do with alcohol.

He wasn't sure what to do, but he sensed she needed something from him, so he came and stood behind her and rubbed her shoulders and put his head against hers. The gesture was too much. She turned and collapsed into his arms and buried her head and sobbed. It had been weeks overdue and it looked like it was going to last for months.

'Come on, sit down. Why didn't you call me?' Libby merely continued to sob so he took the spatula out of her hand and led her over to a nearby chair.

'It'll burn.'

'Don't worry, I'm not really hungry,' he said. It was a fib and she knew it.

'You're always hungry. Stop lying.' She gave a ghost of a smile and he tilted her head up.

'You'll get through this, I promise. You're a terrific girl, everyone thinks so. Look how much you've achieved yourself.' He was kicking himself for not checking in on her more regularly. Anna had warned him to keep an eye on her, but she was very good at avoiding him and his phone calls.

She wiped her streaked eyes on her sleeve, a gesture he wouldn't have associated with her, and got to her feet. 'I'm fine, honestly. I'll have this ready in a second. I don't know what came over me. I suppose it's because you knew him so well too.'

She was a sorrowful sight as she stirred and sniffled and John Simpson pitied her for the first time ever. She was hard to get to know and of all the words he'd have used to describe his feelings for her in the past, pity was never anywhere on the list.

She produced a big bowl of creamy pasta and a crunchy green salad, then topped up his glass and sat beside him at the kitchen table where they ate in relative peace. The tears had been a release of sorts.

'So, talk to me about the business,' she said as she led the way into the sitting room after they'd finished, coffee and wine glasses in hand.

He was reluctant now, didn't know where to start. 'There are things that we need to sort out,' he said finally.

'What sort of things? I told you already, John, you'll have to treat me like an imbecile as far as the business goes.'

'It's complicated.'

'Then you'd better start at the beginning.'

He didn't want to be here, having this conversation.

'The business was going through a tough time when David . . . went. Things hadn't been easy for him for a while.'

'But he never mentioned anything.' Libby was puzzled and guilty, knowing she wouldn't have encouraged David to talk to her about it.

'He didn't say anything to me either. In fact, he probably wouldn't have had to. It's just, the markets are all over the place at the moment, have been since nine-eleven, even though that now seems a long way off. I'm sure you know what's happened in the technology sector, and pharmaceuticals haven't fared much better. David had taken a lot of risks. Short term they weren't paying off, but knowing his ability to read the markets, they probably would have turned around.'

'So what are you saying?' She had a very uneasy feeling about this.

'He owed a lot of money. Ordinarily, it wouldn't have been a problem but now that . . . the situation's changed, the banks are beginning to accelerate their demands.'

'Well, pay them.' He wondered if she really believed it was that simple.

'We are, but in some cases we can't. It's either tied up or we simply don't have the cash.'

'But we have lots of money! There are accounts everywhere. I have a wallet full of gold cards.'

'Libby, we're talking big money, there's no way David had that kind of money stashed away.'

'How big?'

'Millions.'

'Millions?'

He nodded. He could have said more, but he wasn't prepared to put her through anything else tonight.

'So what do we do?' She swallowed hard, not sure she wanted to know.

'I don't know yet. Alex is still trying to sort it out. I've spoken to the banks, explained that I'm across it, bought us some time. We should know more by the end of the week.'

Libby stared at him, gulped her wine, bit her lip and reached in her bag for a cigarette, something she was doing more frequently these days.

'I didn't know you smoked.'

'I don't.'

He wasn't about to lecture her, although he wanted to. David would have.

'I only have one occasionally,' she lied because he looked so concerned.

'Libby, I'll try to sort it out for you, I promise. But I'm worried. And so is Alex, he's been shouldering it for weeks now.'

'But he's the chief financial officer, how could he have let this happen?' She needed someone to blame.

'David was the boss, Libby, you know that. He kept his deals very close to his chest. And he was very persuasive.' He shrugged. 'As long as he was in charge, it would have been OK. That's where his skills lay.'

She still couldn't take it in. 'But that's just it. He was one of the best business brains in the country, you've said so yourself many times. People, even politicians and other successful business people, came to him for advice. Look at that award he received, only a couple of months ago . . .' Her voice trailed off. 'How could he let this happen to me?'

'Libby, he didn't know he was going to . . . leave you, remember. He'd have sorted it out. It's what he did all the time.'

'Except there wasn't any more time.' The anger and bitterness were a first for her. They masked the pain and threatened to swallow her up. These feelings were scary enough, but the sudden realization that she might not be able to keep up the lifestyle he had built up for them both was absolutely terrifying. Her whole identity was tied up in this lavish house with its art and antiques. She needed her staff and her car and all her luxuries and in a couple of sentences John Simpson seemed to be trying to take them all away.

'How will this affect me?' Her tone was chilly and her words measured.

It was the question he'd hoped she wouldn't ask tonight. He paused. 'You were a partner in the business.' He spoke softly, hoping to ease the effect of his words. An icy hand gripped her heart.

'I know I was a partner. You drew up the documents after we were married. But I was a silent partner. I'd no idea what was going on, you of all people should realize that.'

'I know, Libby, I know.' He looked tormented and she felt sorry for doubting his intentions towards her. 'But the banks won't see it that way and that's what I'm worried about.'

He'd said enough, he couldn't face telling her straight out that she was now solely responsible for David's debts. Joint and several liability, they called it. He thought he'd made it all clear to her at the time, but maybe he'd been naïve or, even worse, negligent and she'd been starry-eyed and in love, and none of them ever thought David wouldn't be around for a very long time.

Libby jumped up and shook her head as if to rid it of nasties. 'John, I think I've had enough for one night, if you don't mind.' She was cold with him again and he wanted to reassure her but couldn't.

'Sure, and Libby, I'm sorry. I'd do anything not to have to tell you all this. I wish I could do something to make it easier.' He cleared his throat. 'Anyway, I'm working on it all week with Alex. Give me a bit more time and then the three of us will sit down.'

After he finished his coffee and drained his glass she saw him to the door and remained stiff as he hugged her.

'Try not to worry, OK?' It was a futile statement and both of them knew it.

She gave a half-smile but didn't trust herself to speak.

As soon as she shut the door she poured herself a balloon full of brandy and tried to work it out in her head. How could he do this to her? It was her favourite question now. This was a nightmare. The idea that she might lose everything was one from which she'd never recover. Tears ran down her face and she sat huddled in David's favourite chair and drank herself stupid and cursed him into hell.

Chapter Twenty-Four

Since the famous Friday night in the car, living had become a cocktail of pleasure and pain for Annie. Marc hadn't called over the weekend, hence the mind-numbing sensations of grief. She needed to talk it through with someone. She nearly rang Orla, her new friend from the show, but couldn't bear it. She squirmed every time she thought about exposing her childish emotions to someone who was almost a stranger. Discussing it with one of her other friends who didn't know him wasn't the same.

He finally rang on the Tuesday night while she was at work and the sensation she felt at the sound of his voice on her machine told her she had it bad. She replayed the delicious Aussie drawl a hundred times and sat on the floor in the draughty hall, drinking her cocoa, pressing rewind and feeling her heart soar. He did like her. He hadn't forgotten her. He really wanted to be with her. It was glorious.

She just about managed to hold off ringing him that night, mostly because it was after midnight when she got in, the restaurant having been jammed all evening. Also, she was slightly afraid he might not be alone so late at night, a thought that sent her mood crashing. Next morning she barely held on until the respectable hour of 9 a.m. – mid morning for her, as she'd been awake since six-thirty.

He obviously wasn't waiting for her call, judging by the fuzzy greeting.

'Hi there, it's Annie.'

'Hi Annie, how are you?'

'Great. Hope I didn't wake you?'

'You did, actually.'

'Oh.' The bald statement left her fumbling for something to say. The only thing that sprang to mind was a lie. 'Sorry, it's just that I'm on my way out and I thought I'd get you before I left for the day.'

'Are you always so cheerful in the mornings?' There was more than a hint of suggestion in the singsong drawl.

She laughed. 'Always.'

'Wow, now that could be our first row.'

'I don't fight.'

'Neither do I, come to think of it.'

'Another thing we have in common.' She sounded desperate, so she rushed on in there. 'How've you been?' She resisted asking about his weekend and why the hell he hadn't rung her as promised. Even she knew that that was seriously not cool.

'Fine. Busy. You?'

'Same. Working mostly.'

'Any news from the show?'

'Not yet.' It was her only gloomy thought. 'Max did say it would be after next week, when they had their brainstorming session.'

'Oh yeah, I remember. Well, how about a date this week then?'

Yes please, she wanted to say. 'Fine' was what came out.

'How about Friday?'

'I'm working.' She was gutted, but there was no way on earth she could ask any more favours of Owen Kerrigan at the moment. 'I'm free on Sunday night. How's that for you?'

'I've been invited to a barbecue, but hey, why don't you come along? It should be fun.'

'A barbecue, are you out of your tree? It's winter.'

'Ah, but you forget, my friends are nearly all from down under and it's summer over there, so unless it snows we eat out of doors.'

It wasn't quite what Annie had in mind but she desperately wanted to be with him. 'Great, what time?'

'I'll pick you up at five, OK?'

'I could meet you somewhere, if you like? In town maybe.'

'How old are you, fifteen?' He was teasing. 'Only teenagers meet in town. I'll collect you.'

She blushed, thinking how few dates she'd had over the years. Out of touch was just not in it.

'Do I have to ask your father's permission?'

'Idiot,' she laughed and it was OK.

'I'll see you on Sunday then.'

'Should I bring anything?'

'No, no worries. I'll pick up a case of beer on the way. See you about five.'

'OK, then.'

'Don't work too hard.'

'Don't sleep too long.'

'I'm awake just thinking about you.'

She was scarlet.

'Bye.'

'Bye, babe.' From him it sounded dreamy.

She bought some new underwear and threw out all her sensible cotton knickers in preparation. On Saturday she splashed out on a blow-dry, which she hoped would hold till the next day. It meant a night trying to sleep sitting up, but what the hell. Sunday saw her in her best jeans and a funky sweater. Her new jacket ensured she didn't catch her death but made her feel sensible, which she didn't like.

Marc looked even better than she'd remembered and his kiss made the wait almost worthwhile.

She closed the door and turned to lead him into the sitting-room, polished to within an inch of its life, but he grabbed her arm and swung her round to face him, then pulled her close and kissed her hard on the lips, pushing her mouth open with his. She inhaled the salty, outdoorsy smell of him and melted. He teased her with his tongue and she was immediately aroused, convinced she could have had an orgasm there and then with just a little more effort. This guy was dynamite and the effect he had on her was a disaster when it came to playing it cool. So she didn't. She simply wound her arms around his neck and arched her whole body and wished they were naked.

He was first to pull away. 'Let's go, I'm starving. But I'll definitely have more of that later.'

Annie grinned and picked up her bag and they headed off. The party was in full swing, in a modern townhouse belonging to another Australian couple whom Marc knew from Sydney. The music was blaring but the neighbours had been invited and there were plenty of cold beers and great smells. Annie was so happy to be with him, and to meet his friends, that she had a permanent grin on for hours, helped by the fact that he kept coming back to her and kissing her neck, or standing beside her and stroking her arm, or occasionally dragging her off to a corner and kissing her properly.

Everyone seemed really friendly. It was the kind of life Annie had missed out on for years and now she revelled in it.

'Is it only me or is it seriously freezing out here?' Annie turned and smiled.

'Hi, I'm Audrey, you must be Linda?' A small, curly-haired Australian greeted her warmly as she got herself another beer.

'No, I'm Annie.'

'Oh. Sorry, I . . . eh, must have got it wrong. I

was talking to someone earlier and eh . . . I thought they pointed you out as Linda. How are you anyway, Annie?'

'Hi, how are you?' Annie wasn't in the least put out, delighted to have someone new to talk to.

'Freezing. You?'

'Yep, it's cold all right. Only an Aussie would even attempt to eat outdoors in this weather, even though it's actually very mild for this time of year.

'Who did you come with?'

'Marc Robinson.' Annie nodded happily in his direction.

'Well, I gotta hand it to you, he's a good-looking guy.'

Annie was thrilled. 'We've only known each other a couple of weeks.'

'Well, knowing Marc as I do, I'd say he's keen. How did you two meet?'

'On the programme.'

'Oh, I'm sorry, I didn't recognize you. I normally get to see most of it.'

'Haven't been on yet. I've only just recorded my first four episodes.'

'Ah, that explains it. Well, I'll have to watch it now, keep an eye out for you. Who do you play?'

They chatted on and Marc came back and teased Audrey, whom he hadn't seen in ages but had once shared a house with. He kept his arm protectively around Annie and even kissed her in front of his old friend, who winked conspiratorially at her.

'You'll have to tell me your secret,' she laughed good-humouredly as someone dragged her off for a dance. Annie thought she saw her give Marc a questioning look but decided she was imagining it.

'What secret's that?' He put his two arms around her but held her away to study her face.

'Girl talk.' She tugged at his T-shirt and dragged him close until their faces were only inches apart. 'She's nice. She came over thinking I was someone else.'

'Oh?'

'Someone called Linda. Is there something you're not telling me?' Laughing, she poked him in the ribs, feeling tipsy.

'Ah, *Linda*, now there's a story.' He leaned over and kissed her full on.

'Thanks for bringing me. I'm having a great time.'

'I could eat you instead of dinner, you know.'

'With or without salt?'

They kissed again; it was one of those light easy ones that suddenly turns serious and Annie was sorry when someone called them to tell them food was being served.

The evening wore on and everybody mellowed. Some couples danced and some smooched and some smoked dope, while others sat around and talked and laughed. Any lingering warmth from the watery sun disappeared rapidly once darkness fell, so the patio heaters were turned on. Most of the revellers had given up and moved inside, although the doors remained open as a gesture to the few hardy bodies left.

Annie and Marc sat under a spreading orange

glow. They snogged until someone came and dragged them indoors for dessert, which they were already enjoying. Later, Annie saw him talking earnestly to Audrey and she watched him with a sense of ownership.

When the time came to leave Annie realized that they were both quite drunk. Marc abandoned his car and they grabbed a cab, and kissed passionately for most of the journey. Annie felt like a teenager as she adjusted her clothing when they pulled up outside her house.

'Next time, no alcohol for either of us. It gets in the way of things. Deal?' he asked as he walked her to the door.

'Deal.' Her heart was beating at twice its normal speed, knowing what he meant. 'When will I see you?' she asked, the drink giving her courage.

'What nights are you off?'

'Tuesday and Sunday.'

'Tuesday it is. I'll ring you tomorrow to make arrangements.'

'Sleep tight.'

'I'll be thinking of Tuesday. I won't be able to sleep.'

'You'd better. You'll need all your energy.' She could feel herself blush as she said it, but she didn't care.

One last passionate kiss and he was gone, smiling back over his shoulder as the taxi pulled away.

Chapter Twenty-Five

Tuesday couldn't come fast enough for Annie, although she really needed Monday to recover from the worst hangover she'd ever had. Work was hell, the smells from the kitchen made her nauseous and her head was killing her, despite half a packet of fizzy tablets that failed to live up to their claim.

Marc had rung as promised this time and when he suggested coming over to her place and bringing some Chinese food, she doubted they'd get around to eating it. Luckily, she slept soundly on Monday night and woke feeling fresh and tingly and nervous about the evening ahead. She cleaned the house again and changed the sheets, then she sprayed Febreze over everything and stuck air fresheners in all the rooms, so that the whole place smelt like a cheap hotel toilet.

In the local garage she bought flowers, popcorn and biscuits and threw in a bottle of not very convincing wine for good measure. Despite the deal with Marc she felt she might need at least one glass, for although she was high as a kite she was also nervous as a kitten.

Once again she wished for a much-needed bath, but settled on a long, weak shower then covered herself in the latest Intensive Care Body Lotion. She shaved and plucked and painted and put on her cheap sexy underwear and felt like a virgin. It had been so long that she was almost one anyway and she hugged herself in delicious anticipation as she played music before giving in and pouring herself a glass of wine. She'd had as much to drink since she met Marc as she'd had in the previous ten years, but it was a pleasant feeling as it hit the spot on an empty tummy. She contented herself with small invalid-like sips. There was no way she was getting drunk and missing a second of tonight.

She dressed in a pair of tight, plastic trousers that looked like leather and made her bum look round and sexy, then panicked and put on a long-sleeved jumper so it didn't look as if she was trying too hard.

By the time she heard the knock-knock she'd convinced herself that Marc wasn't coming. Her heart pounded as she let him in.

'Dinner, madam.'

'Smells gorgeous.' She could barely look at him, afraid her face gave everything away.

'So do you.' He kissed her, but only lightly, and followed her inside. 'Where's the candlelit table?'

She was flustered: she'd been so sure he wouldn't be interested in food.

'Two minutes.' She ran into the kitchen, grabbed plates and cutlery and kitchen towel to use as napkins, and reappeared almost immediately, with some matches in her mouth. He laughed.

'Are you sure you're not lying when you tell me you work in a restaurant, or do you always greet your customers like that?'

'Only the important ones,' she murmured through gritted teeth as she laid the coffee table in front of the fire and lit the candles she'd carefully placed 'casually' around the room. The fire was lighting and it looked cosy and much less ordinary than it did in daylight.

'Want to watch the show?' was not what she'd expected to hear.

'I'd love to,' was not what she'd expected to say back.

So they sat in the easy warmth of firelight and had their candlelight dinner and he roared with laughter as she gingerly produced the wine, but agreed to 'one glass only'. Annie didn't admit to already having had half a glass earlier. It was cosy and intimate and the best bit so far was being part of his world as they watched the programme. They exchanged stories; Marc was in several scenes, and she was so full of praise that he looked pleased. Afterwards he amused her by telling tales of catastrophes on set and she felt happy and said a quick but fervent prayer for it to continue.

They talked about the show and their careers for a long time. She was laughing at yet another of his stories, which she suspected were more than slightly exaggerated, when he caught her unawares by leaning over and kissing her fully open mouth, covering her lips with his and stifling her giggles.

In an instant the atmosphere changed and he pulled her to him and their kisses deepened.

'I want you to sit on me like you did the other night in the car.'

Without a word she did as he asked. Even through the fake leather and her underwear and his clothes she could still feel him.

He moved his hands all over her body, caressing her soft round bottom and eventually settling on the waistband of her trousers, running his finger along her waist until she was trembling with pleasure. She didn't know whether he was going up or down with his fingers and she wanted both. Slowly Marc unzipped her but did nothing else, just looked at the silky white lace thong, then ran his hands up her back and slid them around to her breasts. Cupping them, he stroked her nipples through the thin material. She knelt up so that her breasts were level with his mouth, but he declined her offer and simply continued to stroke them. His teasing worked. She was very aroused and had to stop herself from burying his head in her tits.

After a while he lifted up her jumper and she closed her eyes in pain as he slipped his hands underneath the satin and found what he was looking for. She pulled off the sweater herself when she could stand it no longer, amazed at her own desire, and he gave in very slowly to her unspoken demand that he kiss her nipples. When he did it was the most exquisite torture. As soon as he took his mouth away she tried to push him back again but he smiled lazily, as if knowing the effect he was having on her. He eased her off him, stretched her out on the couch and slowly undressed her, peeling the trousers from her overheated body. Annie could almost smell the burning rubber and when he removed her thong she was on fire anyway. He removed his clothes slowly, all the time watching her, and she was too aroused to be embarrassed.

Quickly, he bent over her and kissed her hard and slipped inside her expertly and she was surprised at the intensity of the sensation it evoked. She desperately wanted to come and yet didn't want it to end.

'You are gorgeous and I want to fuck you so much.'

He looked down at her with half-closed, darkened eyes and she arched her back so that she could feel him deeper inside. He shuddered and she gave a little groan.

'What would you like me to do?'

'Just don't stop.'

'Well, I might have to, otherwise it could all get too much for me.' He eased his penis out and paused to look down at her, then he plunged right back in again and she shuddered and he leaned over and cupped her breast in his hand and ran his fingers over her nipple, then he licked and teased and all the while she tried to push him deeper inside her.

'I think I'm going to have to give you what you want. I don't think I can wait much longer.' His eyes were closed and he was breathing heavily.

'You will use a condom?' It went straight from her head to her mouth and she was afraid that she'd spoilt the moment.

He looked annoyed for a fraction of a second and then she was sure she'd imagined it as he took a sachet from his trousers on the floor and gently eased the rubber over his penis, all the while watching her. She closed her eyes because it was so intimate, then writhed as he plunged back inside her.

She thought she might not be able to concentrate, afraid in case he was angry with her, but he kissed her hard and played with her breasts and within seconds they were like melons and she was breathing heavily again and so was he. They came together and he kept up the thrusting until she screamed and released years of pent-up frustration that had never managed to escape even when she masturbated.

'Was it OK for you?'

She nodded. 'You?'

'Oh yes. That was fantastic, although you sure can pick your moments.' She knew he was referring to the condom incident and she wanted to ask him about it but couldn't find the right words. He kissed her again and they lay together, with him still inside her, until his erection subsided.

'That was painful.' He stroked her stomach.

'In that case you won't want to do it again later.' She was teasing him and he smacked her bottom playfully.

'Don't get smart with me or I'll make you pay.'
He sat up and tidied himself and she did the same, feeling a bit vulnerable and embarrassed. Why were the moments afterwards always so awkward in the early stages, she wondered, reaching for her glass just to give herself something to do with her hands, now that they weren't exploring his body.

As they talked and joked some of the old ease returned and he put his arm around her and pulled her close to him.

'I suppose I should be making tracks soon.'

'Oh, I eh, thought you might stay.' It sounded insecure and possessive, she thought, mentally kicking herself.

'I'd love to.' He kissed her tenderly. 'But I'd better not. A huge bundle of scripts came in the door this morning and I really have to get on top of them tomorrow. I'm working on Thursday and then in again on Saturday for rehearsals and I'm way behind in the story.'

'No problem. I need a good night's sleep anyway.' She was a bit disappointed.

'What are you up to for the rest of the week?'

'Working most nights.' It sounded deadly boring and she tried to cover. 'I've got a few people to meet though, about some work in theatre.' She had an informal cup of coffee half arranged for Thursday with a production manager, an old acquaintance really, so it wasn't wholly a lie, she reasoned.

'Sounds great. And hopefully you'll hear from Max any day now.'

She couldn't tell him how much she was banking on it, it would make her seem way too desperate.

'I guess I'll just have to wait and see what happens there.'

'When are your episodes on, by the way?'

'Next week, I think.'

'Maybe we could watch your first one together?'

She sincerely hoped she'd see him before then, but wasn't about to ask, no matter how much she wanted to have another date nailed before he left.

'I'll call you later in the week.' Marc drained his glass and put paid to her current round of hopes and dreams.

'That'd be nice,' was the best she could muster.

She watched with just a hint of despair as he finished dressing. Stop being such a drag, she chided herself. It was so typical of her insecurity: just when she should be basking in the afterglow of perfect sex, she was already wondering if he was tired of her. What was it about some women that they constantly did this to themselves? She made a determined effort to tease him and look happy and by the time he'd left she was sure that everything was fine between them.

They were now a real couple, after all.

Chapter Twenty-Six

Time was passing slowly for Libby. It would have been easier if she'd been working, in some ways. Idle days meant too much time to think, and thinking led to tears and despair and comfort eating and liquid tranquillizers. She spent as little time as possible in the office. Seeing them all reminded her of the new series and she was now more convinced than ever that it was going to be a disaster. She was bolshy on the phone and insisted they fax or courier over papers. More often than not she didn't answer her mobile. She knew she was taking out her worry about the business and general unhappiness on her work, but she needed an outlet.

'She's impossible,' was the general consensus in the production office, even if they all felt guilty for thinking it. But they'd had enough of her constant rudeness and the way she barked instructions at whoever happened to answer the phone. The combination of Libby Marlowe and a series that some of them were secretly doubtful about was beginning to take its toll and Jeremy called a meeting one day in an effort to quash the barely simmering rebellion.

'We're really trying hard, Jeremy, honestly.'
　'She hates all the recipes.'
　'And the clothes.'
　'We can't get any answers to our queries.'
　'She isn't returning calls.'
　'My deadlines are fast approaching.'
　'She doesn't like any of the links, but won't give me any feedback.'

On and on it went and the producer knew the frustration had been building for weeks. But he also knew he had to defend her.

'Look, I appreciate what you're all saying, but for fuck's sake guys, the woman has just lost her husband in the cruellest way possible. He went out to dinner and never came home. How do you expect her to be?'

'We should have postponed, or got someone else,' one of the researchers, who'd been on the receiving end of yet another tongue-lashing that morning, murmured sullenly.

'Well, that's not an option now and we all have to do what we can to make it as easy as possible for her, and us, to get through the rest of the series.' Jeremy would not bad-mouth one of their most high-profile presenters: these things had a way of getting back to people. Dublin was just too small and the industry was incestuous.

'Here's what I'm proposing. Everyone give Rosa a list of queries they need answers to. I'll arrange a meeting with Libby and people can be at the other end of a phone line in case I need clarification. I'll go out to her house, if she'll buy it – that way she might be more relaxed. Meanwhile, I'd be very grateful if there was no more bitching. Let's just try to get through this and then I'll take you all out for a good night, OK?'

They liked Jeremy and that was the only reason he got away with it. Everyone had had enough.

'I may have to buy some more clothes. Some of the ones I've already altered will be a bit tight, I suspect, and I really don't want her trying on anything that's going to upset her further.' Eileen Waters blushed, knowing she had to let them know, yet feeling disloyal to Libby, whom she liked.

'Fine, do whatever you have to. Just talk to Phil about budget, we don't have a huge amount left to play with.' He knew he'd have to discuss the whole money thing again with Leo Morgan, but the older man had warned him to keep Libby happy. This was turning into his worst nightmare but he had to be very careful not to communicate his fears to the team or he knew the whole thing would unravel.

Later that day he rang Libby and tried to arrange a meeting. It was clear from her voice that she didn't want anyone to come to the house, which was fair enough.

'We have a few queries, nothing much.' He had a list as long as his arm and he was already mentally crossing several of them off as he spoke.

'I'll call in on Friday late afternoon.' Libby wanted to end the discussion.

'Fine, thanks.' He was relieved.

She hung up without a goodbye and wandered around the house and ended up in the kitchen as usual. Taking a plate of food to her desk, she began to sort through the latest pile that had been couriered over from her office. Most of the letters reached the wastepaper basket in record time, but one caused her heart to race.

It was from that awful woman who'd tried to accost her outside reception a while back. How dare she get in contact with her again? She scanned the contents and was just about to pick up the phone to complain to security once more when her eyes caught sight of the word 'husband'. Libby hung up and started to read the letter again, properly this time.

Annie was in the throes of a classic post-sex dilemma. The old warning about men not respecting you came back to haunt her, even though she knew it was a load of rubbish. A phone call would have helped greatly. She hovered around the house and practised the casual conversation she'd have with Marc if she ever plucked up the courage to ring him and end her misery.

'Hi, it's me.' Way too casual – what if he didn't have a clue who me was?

'Hello, it's Annie, just wondered if you fancied a pint at the weekend?' Too contrived.

'Marc, it's Annie Weller. Did you lose some money at my house the other night by any chance?' Wouldn't fool a simpleton, even.

There was nothing else to do but wait, given that she hadn't the courage, much less the panache, to carry off a casual 'how'ya, fancy a ride?' type conversation. Being in love wasn't much fun at the start.

Later, just as she was running out the door for chips, the phone rang. She pounced on it before the machine could. Her hello was loaded with anticipation.

'Hello, I wonder if I could speak to Annie Weller, please?'

'This is Annie.' It was delivered with caution. Where had she heard that warm, cultured voice before?

'Oh.' There was a pause, and she thought she sensed a slight reluctance. 'This is Libby Marlowe.'

If she'd said 'This is Mother Teresa' Annie couldn't have been more surprised. She'd written to her ages ago and had given up all hope of any feedback.

'Oh, Libby, hello.' She hadn't a clue what to say. Libby hated it when strangers called her by her first name.

'I just wanted you to know that I got your letter,' she said. Her voice seemed subdued and it sounded to Annie as if she was miles away.

'I hope you didn't mind me writing, it's just that I've been so upset in case you might have thought that I was pestering you in some way and I'd never . . .' Shut up Annie, she chided herself, you're waffling again.

'I wonder if we might meet for coffee, or a quick drink?' was the last thing she expected.

'Yes, of course, I'd be delighted to, but I have told you everything I know, I mean, just in case you think I've left anything out, that is—'

'What about next week?'

'Fine.'

'OK, I'll have my secretary call you to arrange it.'

'Great.'

'Bye for now then.' She was gone before Annie had a chance to try again. The call left Annie's head spinning, with delight at the prospect of finally meeting her idol and dread in case this was some sort of set-up. At least it stopped her thinking about Marc.

Of course, as soon as she stopped worrying, he showed her how the dating game was supposed to be played.

'Hi babe, what'ya up to?' The 'I've just shagged a Sheila' drawl sent shivers down her spine.

'Oh, hi. I've had a mad week, actually. How've you been?'

'Great. Busy. Fancy having lunch on Sunday?'

Lunch! She wanted dinner, a long, slow, romantic meal followed by even longer, slower, mind-blowing sex. She was disappointed so she lied to cover up.

'Yeah, great. I'm going out on Sunday night so that suits me fine.' She'd been practising that one all week and it still sounded stilted.

'Are you not working?'

'No, remember I said I was off Tuesday and Sunday?'

Obviously not.

'Well then, lunch it is, seeing that you're off out carousing later.' He didn't seem concerned. 'I'd love to try that new place in Temple Bar, beside the bank. How about I see you there at twelve-thirty? I'll bring all the papers.'

She knew where he meant, they'd discussed it the last night. 'OK, see you there,' she said. Did that mean they'd be back to one of their houses for the afternoon? She needed to know, although God knows she'd cleaned the place to within an inch of its life and the one bit of carpet was practically threadbare from hoovering. Paranoia was getting to her.

'Bye then, see you Sunday.'

'Bye.' There was a brief moment of anti-climax and then she was ecstatic. He'd called, he cared, he wanted to see her! It was all OK again. He hadn't gone off her, or lost her number. They were still an item. Life was bliss.

Chapter Twenty-Seven

As soon as she knew she'd be seeing Marc again, Annie came back to life. She sparkled, refusing to let the fact that it was only lunch dim her glow. Forcing the Libby Marlowe saga to the back of her mind, she bought herself a new T-shirt and a pair of combats, even though her bank balance was becoming increasingly frail. The trousers were hipsters, in a plum-coloured silky satin and the T-shirt was tight and stretchy.

As soon as she saw Marc, her stomach lurched.

'G'day, Annie, how's it going?' He gave her a bear hug.

'Fine, I'm starving.' She wasn't really but it sounded casual, she hoped. She looked at him impishly and he laughed.

'Well, I've just seen the eggs Benedict waft past my nose, along with a bagel with smoked salmon and cream cheese on top and they looked pretty good.' He handed her the menu.

'Glass of wine, or is it too early?'

'I'll have a glass of white, a sparkling water and a large orange juice, please.' He shook his head and grinned at her again.

'Yes, ma'am.'

She was determined to be the confident, chilled girl he already thought she was and so regaled him with stories about her life and her job at the restaurant. Then she wanted to know more about him.

'So, what have you been up to since I saw you last?'

'Not much, it's been all go on the work front. I was in most of yesterday and I've got a pretty hectic week lined up.'

'So, you haven't been out much?' she asked hopefully.

'Went for a few bevvies on Friday evening with the gang from work. Last night I went to a party and stayed far too late, so I'm a bit tired today.' He looked anything but and she wondered why he hadn't asked her – she could easily have gone after work. Quickly she dismissed the idea, determined not to become possessive. It didn't go with her new, ultra-cool persona.

After a feast of brunch-type dishes they went for a stroll. Occasionally Marc put a casual arm around her but never left it there long enough, and he didn't hold her hand as she would have liked.

'Want to come back to my place for a coffee?' She thought it sounded offhand enough, but the raspberry ripple streaks on her face might just have given away her real intentions.

'Sure, that'd be great. Let's go.'

This time there was no pretence. Once inside Annie's house, he slid his arms around her and turned her to face him. He kissed her thoroughly and she felt the now familiar sensation in her limbs.

'I've been thinking about you a lot since the other night.'

'Me too.'

'You're so warm and sexy and inviting. I want to eat you.'

'Come on.' She took his hand and led him upstairs to her tiny bedroom and pulled the curtains. The bright sunlight made it appear faded and tired. It didn't matter where they were, though, he had eyes only for her and this time they both peeled off their clothes and fell into bed. It was wild and carefree and she felt like the sexiest supermodel in the world as he kissed and caressed and teased and admired her.

'Oh, baby, I want you so badly. Look what you're doing to me.'

He took her hand and wrapped it around his penis, then guided her up and down.

'What would you like me to do?' She sounded short of breath.

'I'd like you to suck me.' He had arched his back and was leaning away from her, thrusting forward in rhythm with her stroking, so he didn't notice that Annie was a bit mortified. She knew that practically every teenager in Dublin had done this outside a college or even secondary school disco at some point. Blow jobs were *de rigueur* these days. But amazingly – apart from a few childish attempts – she'd never done it and wasn't sure she could. Now, wanting to please him more than anything, she bent her head slowly.

'Oh my God, that is so right, don't stop.' He was looking down at her and the sight seemed to turn him on more. 'Stroke it as well,' he murmured, guiding her hand again. So she did and although she knew the technique it felt awkward but she didn't have the courage to tell him, much less ask for help.

'That's it, harder, yes, don't stop, I'm almost there.' She had no idea what to do but luckily he was too far gone for it to make a difference. Precision timing, she thought gratefully.

'Yes, yes, yes, oh my God,' he was moaning and when he finally relaxed they both collapsed.

'That was fantastic, babe.' He leaned over and kissed her tenderly. 'Sorry for being a selfish bastard, but I was so horny that when you touched me I just couldn't wait any longer.' He was stroking her nipples and now he bent to kiss them. 'I'll make it up to you though, I promise.'

It took her a while to get into the mood after all the anxiety of the past few minutes but he was an expert: soon he was smiling down at her as she climaxed.

Afterwards, they lay together and chatted and kissed and she felt close to him until he announced,

'I'd better go and let you get ready for your night out.'

'Actually, it was cancelled at the last minute.' She knew she shouldn't have said it but she wanted him to stay, maybe even stay all night.

'Ah, that's a shame because I arranged to meet a friend in town.' She waited for him to ask her to join them but he simply got dressed and sat on the bed talking until she felt a bit too naked. Not really able to carry it off, she finally pulled on her old dressing-gown, which made her feel like his granny.

After he'd left, her day went surprisingly flat. Instead of feeling confident she felt more vulnerable than ever and cursed herself for not talking to him about it.

It was a balmy spring Sunday evening and she was uptight and tetchy. She knew her feelings were a combination of anxiety over Marc and a constant dread when faced with the thought of meeting Libby Marlowe, in case she was in trouble again. It had not been a good week.

Chapter Twenty-Eight

When Libby woke on Monday morning she felt heavy and groggy. It had been an indulgent few days without even a walk to clear her head. Now her limbs felt like lead and her back ached from loafing around. She knew she couldn't go on avoiding people, either. John Simpson and his wife had both left messages inviting her to dinner and her mother was about to arrive with a tent and camp on her doorstep.

She was also unsure what to do about that tiresome Weller woman. It had been a moment of madness ringing her in the first place. Her emotions had been softened by a couple of G&Ts and she'd regretted it ever since. She'd almost decided not to follow it up, sure she wouldn't find out anything more about her husband. And she certainly didn't need the hassle.

It seemed like no time at all till she was back in the dreaded mansion, giving useless tips and promising the perfect fluffy soufflé to go with the most delectable wines, selling a lifestyle that no longer sounded convincing, even to the woman who once lived it.

The second-last day was one of the worst Libby had had in a while and that was saying something. When she arrived in her dressing room there were no towels and her favourite blend of herbal tea was nowhere to be seen. Also, some of her things had been moved. She stormed out in search of the stage manager.

'Adrienne, someone's been in my dressing room.' The young woman was sneaking a fag in the tiny pantry they were using as a wash-up area. She was at a disadvantage and she didn't like it one bit.

'Oh, I checked your room earlier.' Her eyes darted about nervously. 'Everything was fine.'

'There are no towels and my herbal tea has gone missing. Did you leave the door unlocked?'

'No, of course not.' She looked sullen.

'Well, I am not staying there and I can't go on set until I'm ready so you'd better get your finger out and organize it properly.' Libby had a thumping headache and she was in no mood for this.

'Could you just get ready there and I'll sort it out while you're doing the first run-through?' Adrienne asked hopefully. It was the wrong thing to say.

'No, I could not and please put out that cigarette. It's affecting my voice. I want it sorted now.' Libby turned on her heel to go in search of Jeremy.

'For fuck's sake.' It was almost inaudible and on a good day, the old Libby might have been tempted to pretend she hadn't heard it. Not today. In fact, not any day now.

She swung round so fast it caused a gust of wind in the vicinity. 'How dare you,' she said in a dangerously low voice. 'How dare you use that language at me.' The normally brazen young woman looked furious, and mad as hell at being caught out. She hated giving that bitch the satisfaction. She backtracked fast. 'It wasn't at you, it was at myself . . . I was just—' But Libby had gone.

She was spitting fire by the time she met Jeremy, and the otherwise competent Adrienne was sent home. It was just the start. She glowered at the autocue operator several times over minor fluffs, then addressed the floor manager in a loud voice: 'If people—' she gestured in the direction of the cowering older woman – 'cannot keep up with me then I suggest we forget this way of doing links altogether. It's impossible.'

'Sorry, Libby, give me a moment please, I'll sort it out.' He spoke through clenched teeth. He was trying really hard with her, but he'd already had to bollock two charge hands this morning and thanks to her he now had a new stage manager with little or no experience. Also, his old friend Niall, a painter with twenty years' experience, was threatening to walk off after the star told him to get his brush off her worktop immediately or she would report the incident to the health inspector.

He held onto his temper now only by taking

several deep breaths like his wife had told him and thinking of the creamy pint or two he was going to sink at lunchtime. Tomorrow couldn't come fast enough for any of them. It was not a happy camp.

At last it was over and the prolonged, warm sighs of relief practically stripped the wallpaper. Libby had only just managed to hold on several times that day and the people around her had paid the price. You could almost smell the tension. She was barely on speaking terms with one of the make-up artists and the two lighting directors who alternated on the programme were about to be canonized.

'That woman is a cow. I'd say her husband killed himself to get away from her.' Troy, one of the trendy young lighting assistants, said what many were thinking, although it still startled one or two who heard. 'She just told me she had more lines on screen than she had in reality and asked me how I'd managed to actually make her look older than she really was. Sarcastic bitch. If she gave up her fancy dinners it might help, not to mention the sauce.'

'That's enough Troy. Cool it.' Roger Dolan, the senior lighting director, privately agreed with everything his young operator had said, but he needed to work for this production company again.

'Look at her, she's a lush if you ask me and her eyes *are* red and sunken – it's nothing to do with our lighting.'

'Get back to work. This is not a conversation we should be having.'

'Well, someone needed to say it.' The young man moved away, but not before he'd seen the sympathetic looks of some of his colleagues. He was sick and tired of prima donnas and Libby fucking Marlowe was the biggest one he'd come across in a long time. 'Fat cow,' he mumbled. Nobody was arguing.

It was after eight by the time they wrapped the following evening and there was none of the usual banter, no cries of 'Where's the champagne?' or 'Last one down to the pub buys the first round.' Jeremy was just about to offer to buy drinks in the local, when he realized that everyone had cleared off. No-one wanted to spend a minute more than they had to in the company of 'the bleedin' head-wrecker', as the postboy had christened Libby.

'A production crew not hanging around for free drink, that's a new one on me,' Jeremy remarked to Mel, the only other person left on set.

'That bad, eh?'

'Pretty much the worst atmosphere I've encountered in a long time.' Jeremy felt he had to be honest.

'She can be hard work at times.' It was out before Mel realized she was bitching about one of their top stars. 'Still, as you know, she's had a lot to cope with these last—'

'I know. Listen, do you fancy sneaking off for a

drink and a chat?' Jeremy had always liked the sassy, no-nonsense girl.

'Sure. I'd murder a G&T.' She smiled. This day was not turning out so bad after all.

'Fancy a drink, you two?' Libby was feeling generous now that it was over. Besides, she couldn't face going home alone tonight.

'Eh, not for me, thanks. I've another appointment later.' Mel had been babysitting her for weeks and she'd had enough.

'And I've just arranged to meet a mate.' Jeremy took his lead from her, although guilt was written all over his red face.

'Fine, I'll remember that.' Libby was furious. She turned on her heel and headed for her car.

'I'm not sure that was the right thing to do.' Jeremy whispered as soon as she was out of earshot.

'Me neither, but it's done now. Come on, and make mine a large one. We might be paying for this for a while.'

Nothing like this had ever happened to Libby before. Normally, people were queuing up to be seen in public with her. She stormed out of the car park and punched in a number on her mobile.

'Moya. It's Libby.'

'Libby darling, how are you? I was just thinking about you today. We're having a dinner party, as you can probably tell from the noise. Dreadful lot of rowdies in tonight, I'm afraid.'

'So I can hear.' Suddenly, Libby didn't know

why she'd phoned at this time of night. 'Listen Moya, we must do lunch.'

'Love to. I'll call you next week.'

'OK, bye.'

'Bye, darling.'

Next up she tried Carrie. Her machine was on. She wanted to scream. All she wanted was a drink and a bitch. Mind you, she'd have had to travel quite a distance for a drink with her old friend. She flung the phone away from her, determined not to go home alone again. There must be someone around to have a drink with – she was a star, for Christ's sake.

Chapter Twenty-Nine

Annie's evening had started off brilliantly. It was the night of her first TV appearance and Marc was calling to watch it with her.

She had decided to cook, then chickened out and begged one of the chefs in work to provide her with something simple, that she could pass off as her own. He laughed at her. 'Christ, girl, you really have it bad,' he teased in his singsong Cork accent and Annie punched him and looked sheepish. But it had worked and she now had a fragrant Thai green chicken curry that only needed to be reheated and she'd bought two sachets of boil-in-the-bag rice to be cooked in a stock of cinnamon, lemongrass and cardamom pods provided by her workmate. She'd no idea what they were but the chef had assured her they'd add flavour to the rice although she rightly guessed he hadn't been thinking about rice wearing a plastic mac. She'd bought some good naan bread in Marks & Sparks and splashed out on a bottle of horrendously expensive dessert wine.

A fire crackled merrily and candles and flowers once again added to the illusion of comfort.

Marc arrived with a bottle of Australian sparkling wine, which he assured her was as nice as French champagne. She didn't like to tell him she wouldn't be able to tell the difference anyway, but consoled herself that he seemed to like her simple, uncluttered lifestyle.

They drank a toast and Annie watched in mortification as the episode unfolded, seeing a character who was over-confident and tarty and a bit brazen, and a million miles away from the insecure girl who sat on a bockety sofa and pretended to take it all in her stride.

Marc was full of praise. 'That was cool, really convincing,' he said more than once and Annie basked in the warmth of his admiration. When it was over the phone kept ringing – her father first, saying how proud he was of her. Then a couple of neighbours who were absolutely starstruck, and lots of her new colleagues who had taken the trouble to get hold of her number to offer congratulations, including Stephen Wilson and Mike Nichols, and her friend Orla. Annie was delighted and when Marc finally reached over and took the phone off the hook she was surprised to find herself feeling a bit disappointed.

'I want you all to myself.' He kissed her, slipping his hand under her blouse.

'After dinner, you animal.' Annie was happy again. She jumped up and pretended to slap him as if he were a bold puppy. 'Down, boy.'

'I'm hungry, but not for food.' He grabbed her and as usual he won. They made love in front of the fire and she had heat marks like waffles all down one side of her body and didn't care. Afterwards as they chatted easily she thought what a perfect evening it had been so far.

Then Marc stood up and yawned and it all changed.

'Gotta go, babe, I'm wrecked.'

'But it's barely nine o'clock.' Annie thought she was hearing things. 'Besides, we haven't eaten yet.'

'I've got a really early start in the morning and you've worn me out, not to mention ruined my appetite.' He grinned, then leaned over and kissed her nose. 'I'll give you a call, OK?'

'Sure. But won't you at least stay and try some food?' Annie heard herself sounding pathetic.

'Would you mind if I passed? All that wine's gone to my head.'

'Well eat something then, it'll help sober—'

'Stop playing Mummy,' he teased but Annie didn't like the tone. Two minutes later he was gone. Even with two glasses of wine on board she knew something was wrong and all at once her whole night went pear-shaped. The phone rang. She almost didn't answer it but now she needed the praise and attention.

She nearly passed out when she heard who it was and within fifteen minutes she was on her way to have a drink with Libby Marlowe, her torment forgotten in a new flurry of anxiety.

* * *

Libby entered the social club with all the enthusiasm of a Crufts champion poodle being taken to a local dog pound. It was not the sort of place she usually frequented but Annie had suggested it and she was heading back to her office anyway, to dump the files that she hoped not to see for a very long time. Annie spotted her immediately, as did everyone else.

It was hard not to, really. She wore soft black suede over-the-knee boots and a short tweed skirt. An oversized jumper and funky tights made the skirt look even shorter and her legs look like polished liquorice. It wasn't her normal attire, it was an outfit that was left over from filming, and she'd changed into it just to annoy someone, another petty attempt to get back at them all for putting her through the most horrendous few days. Her blond hair was loose and tossed and her make-up flawless though heavy; as she got closer Annie noticed that her face was tired and a bit bloated and her eyes were dull. Still, Annie felt like her frumpy, much older sister.

Although journalists and roadies mixed with actors and presenters most evenings here, Libby was not a regular and many were curious enough about this particular star to cast covert glances in her direction. Annie stood up nervously and waved, in case Libby didn't remember what she looked like.

'Hi.'

'Hello.' Libby held out her hand. It seemed rather formal to Annie, who immediately became more nervous. At least the two glasses of wine helped.

'Evening, Miss Marlowe.' The barman was over in an instant, wiping imaginary dust from the table. He ignored Annie. 'What can I get you to drink?'

'Do you have a dry white wine?'

'We certainly do. Chardonnay OK?'

'Actually, perhaps I'll have a G&T.'

'Glass of red wine for me,' Annie threw in quickly, in case he walked off. 'I've already had two,' she apologized, fearing she might stink of alcohol. 'It was my first appearance on TV tonight,' she explained quickly.

'Oh yes, you're in – what's it called?'

'*Southside*.'

'That's it. So you've just started, then?'

'Yes, I've done four episodes and now I'm waiting to hear if they'll want me back.' She looked excited and worried at the same time. Libby remembered her own early career and knew exactly how she felt.

'That must be very tough?'

'It is.' Annie could cope with anything but kindness after the disaster with Marc. The barman appeared with their drinks and she rushed to pay for them but Libby insisted and when she settled down again she noticed that Annie was on the verge of tears. It was exactly the way she'd felt herself all day. In spite of her natural reserve and sense of superiority she was drawn towards the younger woman and besides, she felt guilty that she was using her in an effort to avoid going home without having a good bitch about the series with someone. In an instant they were off, both needing to offload a huge amount at exactly the same time in their vastly different lives. The result was that they bonded in a way that left Annie elated and Libby startled.

Chapter Thirty

Next morning Annie was still on a high. She couldn't believe how well she'd got on with someone she'd admired for so long. It was fate, Annie decided, because initially she'd sensed a reluctance on Libby's part, an animosity almost. It had been a slow burn. Then suddenly they were laughing and telling each other the most intimate things. Maybe it was because of her husband, Annie thought now. Libby had wanted to know every detail of that last evening and Annie wished she had more to tell. She could still see the exquisite, porcelain, childlike face lapping up every morsel of information and in return Libby had told Annie how awful it had been, as if sensing that she would understand. And she did, and in the talking and telling of secrets all of Annie's fears about Marc had melted away.

Contentedly she strolled down to the shops as soon as she was washed and dressed and was amazed and delighted to find she had become a local celebrity overnight. Even the usually cool teenage boys shouted some filthy, if encouraging, remarks about her performance. And the local shopkeeper, who had never delivered a free smile with the morning paper in her life, beamed as she handed Annie her change. 'I suppose we'll be reading about you in there next.'

'You never know.'

'Well, don't forget us when you're famous.'

'I don't think I'll be worrying about that for a while yet, Mrs O'Brien.' Annie had always thought the woman was deaf and dumb.

When she got back there were two messages, the first from her brother Greg, saying how much he'd enjoyed seeing her on the show. Annie was amazed, he was so flaky she couldn't imagine him even remembering her number. The second was from Max Donaldson, asking her to call him at the office. She knew it was probably just a call to say well done, but she was still nervous.

'Annie, how are you? Thanks for getting back to me.'

'I'm fine, Max.' She was curt in an effort not to prolong the agony.

'Listen, first of all, well done on last night's performance. How did you feel seeing it on transmission?'

'Nervous, excited, scared. It was a very odd feeling looking at it from a distance. I suppose I felt I could do much better, but overall, given that it was my first time, I was pleased enough.'

'Well, we've had a terrific reaction already and

we did show it to a few people last week. The feedback has been very positive. So don't be too hard on yourself.'

'Thanks, Max, that's good to hear.'

'So, would you like to come back to us?'

Annie heard it but wasn't quite sure. Her heart had heard it too, apparently, and was getting quite excited, thumping with the strength of an overdue baby.

'You know I would.'

'Well then, we need to sit down and talk. Could you pop in at some stage? I'd like to fill you in a bit about where we see the character going. Dave Gordon should probably sit in on part of it, as well,' he said, half to himself, referring to the script editor. Anne could hear him scribbling.

'Sure, I'm free all day today.'

'Great. Say three o'clock then. Just hang on. I see Dave in the outside office. Let me just make sure he's free too.'

Seconds later it was arranged and Annie couldn't believe her luck as she put down the phone. Her instinct was to ring Marc, but she knew he was in studio most of the day, so she'd just have to wait till tonight.

It took her hours to get ready yet when she emerged it seemed as if she hadn't made any particular effort. She looked just like any other student really, if a bit older – hair in two little plaits, make-up so light it was almost non-existent and the ubiquitous jeans, T-shirt and Michelin man jacket. She felt better than any of them though, as she strolled along, bag swinging, hair bobbing, mouth in a permanent grin.

Everyone greeted her warmly in the busy hubbub that was *Southside* and Max and Dave took her to the conference room. Annie felt nervous, afraid it mightn't turn out as well as she'd been dreaming about on the bus.

'Annie, I suppose the first thing we should discuss is where the character is going, which is why I wanted Dave to sit in on this part of the meeting. We've more or less decided that we want her to have a major storyline, which hasn't been completely cast in stone, because we want your input.'

They talked at length and Annie was in her element. Bobby was about to become embroiled in a very seedy world indeed. It would all go horribly wrong of course, as it always does in soaps, and the outcome was to be a pregnancy and a heart-breaking decision.

'We're toying with an abortion and an attempted suicide, or an adoption forced on her by the man involved, or a handicapped baby which she then abandons. We haven't got much further and everyone has different ideas, which is why we wanted your input.' It was every budding actress's dream scenario.

Annie didn't know where to start and rightly took notes, said very little and asked for a couple of days. Her initial instinct was that Bobby would never abandon a baby, but she wondered aloud if that were true. Dave Gordon was insistent that it was a possibility.

'Make no mistake about it, Annie, she's a tough cookie. This business will mean money, opportunities and a chance she's never had. Also the relationship with the businessman will probably give her ideas above her station. A baby definitely won't feature in her plans.'

Annie listened carefully and wanted to think about it all. Both men agreed and suggested a meeting later in the week with the scriptwriters and storyline editors.

'So, now that you know a bit more, how do you feel?'

'I'm thrilled. It's a fantastic role to get my teeth into. I just hope I can do it justice.'

'It'll be a tough one to play, physically very demanding and at times draining. It's going to take a lot out of you.'

'I'm ready for it, I've been waiting for this for years.'

'You need to go and see the research team. Paula Hannigan has been doing some work on the story and can arrange for you to talk to some women's groups etc.'

'Great. I can't wait to get stuck in.'

They chatted some more, then Dave Gordon left and Max got down to the contract.

'What we're offering is a twelve-month contract with a guarantee of thirty episodes, minimum. Maybe more. It will commit you to us almost exclusively, although we would try to facilitate other work if you really wanted to do, say, theatre or something. Now, I know you do some other work in the evenings and that might be difficult for us to accommodate on a long-term basis. Is it important to you?'

'No, although I'd have to give them plenty of time to replace me. They've been very good to me and I don't like letting them down.'

'That's no problem. It will be weeks before this story takes off and even then we can cope for a while. It's just going to be hard when we get into the nitty-gritty of the story.'

'Yes, I understand. I'll talk to them tomorrow evening.'

'And what about an agent, or do you want to handle the negotiations yourself?'

Annie realized later she must have looked terrified because Max looked rueful and put down his pen.

'Annie, I shouldn't really be saying this, but I think it might be time to get someone to look after your affairs. There are going to be lots of offers coming your way if this takes off and even now, you need someone to represent your interests when talking to me. I'm not sure you'll be tough enough and I couldn't live with myself if I didn't say it.'

'Thanks, I really appreciate it. Can I think about that as well for a day or so?'

'Sure. Look, here's the business card of an agent we deal with regularly. She might be too busy to take you on, but she's good, one of the best in the business. Tough. Hard as nails but gets the results for her clients. I'll probably rue the day I ever introduced you.' He smiled and Annie laughed. 'You should probably shop around anyway. It's an important relationship. Most of the actors can give you some more contacts. It's a personal choice and one you have to be happy with.'

It was almost five by the time they said goodbye, Annie armed with masses of paperwork: schedules, scripts and a million notes. She felt a bit self-conscious as she slipped into the studio to see who was there, secretly hoping to bump into Marc and tell him her news. It was humungous, better than her wildest dreams and she wanted to share it with her boyfriend. She would have to ring Libby later too, she thought happily, hugging the thought of her new friend to her like a hot water bottle in a freezing winter bed. They'd exchanged numbers when they left the social club, hours later than either of them had planned.

As it happened, there were only two actors involved in the remaining scenes of the day in studio, and Annie didn't know either of them very well. They were older and a bit reserved, although they greeted her warmly and asked if she was coming back. The stagehands were delighted to see her and started slagging her at once. Annie felt as if she'd come home.

She left at around six and was making her way out of the building when Orla came tumbling down the corridor, waving.

'Annie, I heard you were in. Fancy a pint in the club?'

Annie could have hugged her, it was exactly what she needed.

'There's a gang there I think. It's Tessa's birthday so she's lording it over us, as if she needed an excuse.' They laughed and walked out together after Orla had collected her things. Annie told her about the meeting with Max.

'Oh my God, that is absolutely brilliant! I'm so pleased for you.'

Annie was thrilled, because they hadn't been that close but Orla seemed genuinely happy. Since last night she was measuring all closeness on the Marlowe-Richter scale.

'You have to get an agent.'

'That's more or less what Max said. He gave me the name of someone called Susi Carolan. Do you know her?'

'Everyone knows her. I've never really liked her, to be honest. But it's up to you. I'll give you the name of mine as well.'

They joined a group of other actors. Annie felt relaxed and happy, if a bit disappointed that Marc wasn't among them.

Stephen Wilson insisted on buying Annie the first drink, saying how pleased he was that she was back 'in the family'.

An hour later, buoyed with a new sense of confidence, she was considering phoning Marc from the payphone outside the door. She decided to go to the bar and order a round, then slip out unnoticed. Maybe he'd join them later and even if he couldn't she badly wanted to talk to him.

As she pushed open the swing doors she literally walked straight into him.

'Hi.' She couldn't believe her luck – this day would take some beating.

'Annie, hi there.' He looked very surprised.

'I was just on my way—'

'Annie, this is Linda. Linda, Annie Weller, who plays Bobby.'

She looked from one to the other, sure she was missing something here.

'Hi, Annie, nice to meet you.' Linda had the faintest Australian accent but it was well hidden under an upper-class British one.

'Hi. You too.' She waited for Marc to explain.

'Well, don't let us keep you. See you back inside. OK?'

In an instant they'd gone and Annie walked in a daze to the phone, before realizing that she had no need for it now. She stood looking at it, not sure what to do, heart thumping, head not thinking clearly.

Eventually, she made for the ladies, locked herself in a cubicle and sat on the seat. She had a bad feeling about this one.

Chapter Thirty-One

Ten agonizing minutes later she knew it could only mean one thing. Linda wasn't his sister, or an Aussie relative or a new member of the cast. They'd looked easy and relaxed together. But why would he do that? Go out with someone else and not tell her first. She'd worried that it was too good to be true, but he'd seemed so into her.

She had to see more for herself, so she made her way back to the bar, eyes just a touch too bright. The barman laughed at her when she asked for her drinks. 'That lot are practically finished the round. Where've you been? The Guinness was going flat and they were starting to riot.' He took the money and shook his head. 'Actors, all the same, away with the fairies.' He was grinning as he handed over the change.

Orla made room as Annie approached. 'Where did you go? I was about to call the police. I've just been telling Marc your news.'

'Yeah, well done, mate. Terrific.' He raised his

glass and smiled at her as if they were just that. Mates. Annie felt the first trickle of anger but it had nowhere to go. She simply wasn't used to dealing with such an emotion, she'd suppressed it all her life.

Orla resumed her earlier conversation, regaling Annie with stories of her latest lover. Annie listened and nodded and as soon as there was a break in the chat, asked casually, 'Who's that with Marc?'

'Linda, his girlfriend.' In three little words, and not the three she'd been secretly hoping for, it was over.

'Is she Australian?'

'English. Wealthy. An engineer or something, although she doesn't look as if she gets her hands dirty much.'

'How long have they been an item?' It was torture but she had to know.

'Yonks. They met in Australia when she was just out of college. I'd say she's expecting the ring any day but my guess is she'll be waiting. Our Marc likes his freedom.'

'What do you mean?'

'He doesn't parade her in public too often. Mostly because there's always someone around he's been more than friends with. Although he's probably safe enough here. Most of the cast know what he's like and we usually warn the new ones.'

'But . . .' Annie couldn't believe it, 'I thought you all liked him?'

'We love him, he's a dote. Just wouldn't want to take him seriously, that's all. Marc fancies himself more than any of us could, anyway.'

So that was it. Her fledgling, blossoming, heart-stopping romance was over.

'Sure, didn't he even try it on with you that first night?' Orla poked her in the ribs and Annie almost burst into tears.

'Hey, you and he went off for a meal, didn't you?' She was teasing and laughing as she whispered the words, all nudge nudge, wink wink. Suddenly, she looked at Annie. 'What's wrong? You've gone all funny.' She was concerned. 'What! I was only teasing, honest.' Something told her this wasn't right. 'Annie, what is it?' she tried again through clenched teeth, staring at her new friend. A thought occurred to her and she could have kicked herself.

'Annie, you didn't, you weren't . . . Oh my God, you were.'

Annie knew she had to pull herself together fast. 'No, of course not, silly.' The younger girl wasn't convinced. 'We had a bit of a snog, that's all.' It was one of her best performances but she knew she had to lie to get the other girl off her back. 'I suppose, though, I thought he was cute and you know yourself, I kind of hoped . . .'

'Oh, you're not alone. I think we've all been there. He's very cute and an outrageous flirt.' Orla was relieved and, Annie thought, seemed to buy her explanation.

'But if you're tempted again, just remember that

Linda's not going anywhere. In fact, I think she moved into his apartment recently.'

It was the ultimate humiliation. Everything fell into place. His reluctance to let her visit, despite being a great cook and her hinting more than once. The way he never called her at night. His lack of affection in public places. The fact that he was always rushing home early. What a complete and utter idiot she'd been.

Annie kept a smile pasted to her face and was immensely relieved when Mike Nichols offered her a lift home at about nine. 'I'm off over to my sister's again so I'm more or less passing your door.' She stood up with alacrity, almost toppling the entire table.

'Thanks, Mike, that would be great.' She was feeling a little bit drunk and a big bit stupid and she left without really looking in Marc's direction.

If Mike noticed her lack of chatter he was polite enough about it. 'I must say I'm delighted about your part. You really deserve it. You put an awful lot of work into those first episodes.'

'Thanks. You've no idea what it means to be able to get my teeth into something at last.' She hoped she wasn't giving away too much about how desperate she was, but he'd always seemed like a friend. 'It's all thanks to you.'

'Nonsense, it would have happened to you anyway. If not on this then on something else. You can't keep talent down.' He grinned. After an eternity he dropped her off and she scurried inside and made a cup of cocoa and sat, curled up in the drab, chilly little room in the dark.

No matter how much she tried to reason it out in her head, it seemed inexcusable that Marc hadn't told her that he had a girlfriend. Unless she'd read way too much into what they'd had? It was all such a muddle. Maybe her lack of experience with men was the real problem. What would Orla have done? Probably had a fling and then moved on. Orla was the type of girl she herself might have been if her mother's death and her illness between them hadn't robbed her of every shred of both carelessness and security. It made for a curious combination and Annie knew she needed to toughen up if she was to survive bumping into him all the time on the show.

No matter how much she wanted to blame Marc for what had happened, she secretly felt she deserved it. She'd been stupid to think a man like him could ever really have fallen for a woman like her.

She thought of ringing Libby, but was reluctant to risk pissing off her brand new friend by seeming over-keen, especially while she was feeling mopey like this.

Chapter Thirty-Two

The next few days passed slowly and even though Annie was busy, she was lonelier than she'd been in a long time. But as usual she simply accepted her lot, was thankful for the huge break she'd been given, and worked harder than the entire cast of *Southside* put together. After a while it worked and she stopped thinking about Marc all the time. She even convinced herself she couldn't be missing what she'd never really had.

The role of Bobby was turning out to be amazing. The scripts were better than she could ever have hoped for and the papers were beginning to pick up on the character. The TV Press Office was starting to get requests for information and photos of Annie. She was somewhat taken aback and tried to avoid the publicity as much as possible. The now permanently beaming Madge O'Brien had shown her an article entitled 'Southside's Sexy Stunners' and Annie could hardly believe her photo was featured. She bought the paper quickly because she was embarrassed. Later she was startled to read that the 'gutsy, streetwise Bobby' was played by 'sex siren Annie Weller' who was supposedly 'driving the viewers wild' and 'sending the ratings soaring'. She laughed at the ridiculousness of it and hoped that her father hadn't seen it.

But it was good for her fragile ego and childishly she wished that Marc would be jealous as hell. She hadn't heard from him except for a message on her answering machine the evening after the disastrous pub encounter, left when he knew she'd be at work, she suspected. It was bright and chirpy, hoping she was OK about things and suggesting a pint the following week. Annie was still clinging to the hope that maybe it had all been a mistake so she rang him back straight away, but got his answering service. After two or three days of her calls being diverted she came to the inevitable conclusion that he was avoiding her, so she left a cheerful message suggesting that if he wanted to make it up to her he could cook her dinner at his apartment, as promised. He never phoned back and she hated that it mattered.

She moped around for a while, then put him firmly out of her head and got on with things, as she always did. Something else was playing on her mind these days anyway – she really wanted to see Libby Marlowe again and wasn't entirely sure why. There'd been a connection between them, she was certain of that. They'd laughed easily together and had told each other a lot of intimate details for a first meeting. Annie worried that she was simply star struck, but Libby had seemed really nice, once she'd thawed out a bit. Perhaps it was the completely contrasting lives they led that made them trust each other: since they moved in such different circles maybe each thought it unlikely that the other would ever meet anyone they knew. Whatever it was, it had left a niggling gap in Annie's life.

It helped that she was busy with the project of her dreams and by the time she went back into studio Marc wasn't on any of the schedules, and that helped a lot too. On the work front everything was great. She'd taken Max's advice and phoned the agent he'd recommended. She hit it off with Susi Carolan at once and the glamorous fifty-something agreed to represent her. She had negotiated a deal that left Annie reeling.

Suddenly, money wasn't a problem any more and she was able to give up her job in the Grasshopper and not worry. Owen Kerrigan was sorry to lose her but understood her predicament and made her promise to visit them when she was seriously famous.

For the first time in years Annie could relax about her finances and was astonished to realize that she would soon be able to afford the down payment on a one-bedroomed apartment she'd seen advertised in a really upmarket location close to the production company, a complex that boasted a swimming pool and leisure centre in its massive manicured grounds. Securing the mortgage might not be so easy with only a year's contract, she reckoned, so she decided to do nothing for a few months, just in case it all went belly-up. She was not about to tempt fate, not with her track record.

For the moment, life was very good and if she sometimes ached for the closeness of a best friend or the intimacy of a relationship she was enough of a realist to know that nobody had it all, and was content. Her wish list was simple – a tiny place of her own and maybe a small, second-hand car and, if she was lucky, a few bob in a savings account for the proverbial rainy day. Meanwhile, nothing changed. She continued to live as frugally as she always had and still spent the long, weekend nights eating popcorn and crisps and curled up with only her scripts for company, a lifestyle vastly different from that of the character she portrayed.

When she read one of the new episodes, tucked up in bed early on a Saturday evening, exhausted from a full day's rehearsals, she couldn't believe what she saw on the pages.

Bobby was to have a fling with Alan, Marc Robinson's character. It was a minor storyline, as far as she could tell, but she read on with a great deal of trepidation. Bobby was having her teeth cleaned – a bit unusual for a prostitute, she thought, but then she recalled that several of the 'girls' she'd spoken to during her research had told her they were paranoid about personal hygiene, mainly because they felt dirty all of the time while they worked. The suave dentist Alan chatted up Bobby, who fell hard for his charms, unable to believe her luck. It wasn't written down anywhere but Annie suspected that Bobby would get completely carried away with the possible fairytale ending and see Alan as the answer to her prayers. After a lot of flirting they arranged to meet for a drink and Bobby appeared to be building it all into something much more. Later, when Alan brings her to dinner in a fancy restaurant and treats her like a lady, she is happier than she's ever been, turning it all into *Pretty Woman 2* in her head. Very hard to play anyway, Annie thought as she read between the lines; with the added complication of their real-life situation, she hadn't a clue how the hell she would handle it.

Fortunately, it all appeared to come to a head quickly because when Alan took Bobby home after buying her dinner, he assumed she was dessert.

Annie studied the script carefully, trying not to panic. She contemplated ringing Max to explain why she couldn't do it, but hadn't the courage, then eventually decided to sleep on it but didn't manage to grab much shut-eye. The following day she went for a long walk and wished she had someone to talk it over with. Briefly she toyed with the idea of ringing Orla, with whom she'd had one or two nights out, but her natural reserve wouldn't let her easily reveal her inner turmoil, especially not as Orla and Marc were so friendly.

She really wished she could talk to Libby about it, but her bright and breezy e-mail hadn't elicited any response so far.

In the end, she decided to treat Marc as she would any other actor, and it worked at first. On the rehearsal day she was a bag of nerves and when he waltzed casually into studio she felt very uncomfortable. He clearly wasn't, greeting her exactly as he did the other members of the cast.

Fortunately, it was Tim Furlong's week as director. He took control and talked both actors through the storyline. As they rehearsed, Annie felt stiff and awkward and Tim assumed she was nervous and guided her lightly through it.

Judging by his reaction, he wasn't exactly delirious about her performance. Annie fretted but needn't have worried, because he was experienced enough to know that scenes like this could be awkward, until the actors got into rehearse/record mode. He trusted Annie: everything he'd seen of her on screen so far had been natural and not in the least contrived. He did, however, mention his concerns to Max on the Monday morning.

'I'm a bit worried about Annie. She seemed very wooden in rehearsals on Saturday, during the scenes with Marc Robinson. Would you keep your eye on them when we're recording, just in case?'

If the executive producer was surprised, he didn't show it. 'Sure, I'll pop down for the initial rehearsal and then watch the take on the monitor.

Do you think I should have a word with her in advance?'

Tim was anxious not to upset either actor. 'No, no, I think it will be fine. It's not a very big story-line and it's a difficult one to play on TV, 'cause there's so little written. It's all in the performance and it's hard to get that in a cold, bright, half-empty studio with a bored crew looking on. I think it will be all right on the night.'

Chapter Thirty-Three

It was the day of reckoning for Libby. John and Alex were coming over, after a very tense phone call in which she had used every possible tactic to avoid getting involved in the business. She was dreading the meeting. Carrie had been surprised when she'd rung out of the blue, sounding a bit lost, most unusual for the confident celebrity she knew. Libby tried to tell her some of the details, but the kids kept interrupting and she didn't get very far. Their conversation ended with Carrie promising to ring her over the weekend, when her husband was around, for a proper chat. Libby felt restless. She picked up the phone twice to call Annie Weller, but didn't know her well enough to trust her with worries about David's business that she hadn't fully thought out herself.

She dressed in black and applied a lorryload of make-up: heavy foundation and highlighter and blusher and powder and blood-red lipstick. Her freshly washed hair was left unattended and she added some jewellery in an effort to look glamorous.

Alex O'Meara was visibly shocked when he saw her, John less so because he'd been to the house several times. She looked tired and grey and bloated, with sunken eyes. The extra weight made her look older and the financial whizkid couldn't believe she was the same woman he'd fantasized about many times over dinner with David.

Her housekeeper had set up the formal dining table and Libby had prepared a huge bowl of rich pasta with gorgonzola and broccoli, which the two men tucked into with gusto, refusing her offer of wine. Reluctantly, she stuck to mineral water herself.

The details, when they emerged, were worse than she had expected, even though several late-night phones calls with John while she'd been working on the series should have prepared her.

'The basic problem is that David invested heavily in the American market and it took a sharp downturn post nine-eleven, which of course no-one could have predicted.' Alex O'Meara tried to keep it as simple as possible. 'When the market plummeted, he didn't react as I expected. He had a brilliant business brain, yet he seemed thrown in this instance and instead of waiting to see what happened, he began investing on his own account, and borrowing heavily, in order to put money into telecommunications and technology shares and other high-risk stocks.'

'Why do you think he panicked? That doesn't sound like him.' Libby didn't miss the glance that passed between the two men. 'What? Tell me.'

It was John who sighed and eventually spoke. 'Libby, I need you to understand that this next bit is off the record, because I have no proof of it.' She barely nodded, the sense of impending doom descending immediately.

'There is a possibility he may have been using client money to fund part of his investments and of course these funds should never be touched for this purpose. Now, this is not something I would ever say in public, nor is it something that should ever be repeated outside this room. It's based on a hunch I had at the time and a couple of conversations that Alex had with him, although it was never formally discussed.'

Libby looked from John to Alex. 'Is this what you believe too?'

He nodded.

'The most important thing though, Libby, is that all client money is safe. I'm merely speculating to let you know why I think he reacted as he did and then borrowed so heavily later.' He paused, glancing at her to make sure he wasn't going too fast. She seemed calm and icy.

'Libby, he'd always taken risks with his own money,' he said, anxious to make her understand, 'and in fact, even at the worst moments his investments were performing less badly at a time when others were losing their shirts. The banks trusted him. Of course, he gave them a personal guarantee backed by his own assets.'

'And now?'

Alex O'Meara rowed in to help his friend. 'The problem is that his expertise was the business. He'd have sorted this problem out by now, turned things around as he always did.'

She let the silence hang.

'The problem is he died.' If it sounded cold and clinical it was because that was how she felt. 'So what's next?'

'Now the banks are accelerating their demands for money.'

'And because I'm a partner I'm liable for his debts, even though I knew nothing about them?'

Alex's sigh was ragged. 'Yes.'

'Can they go after my personal assets?'

Another frown, followed by a reluctant nod.

'Even my own business account?'

'No, that should be safe.' Alex looked upset, in spite of delivering the only bit of good news today.

'Well, I suppose that's something.' She stood up in order to clear her fuzzy head. 'Is there any way the three of us can turn this around in the way that David might have?'

'No.' They were quick to say this.

'Not even if we hire a star trader from New York or somewhere?'

'I wish I could be more optimistic, but I don't think it's the thing to do.' John again, trying to let her down gently.

'So what are our options?'

'Well, we could liquidate the company, appoint a receiver and take it from there. Or we try and come up with the money, pay off the banks and simply close the company on the basis that he was the entire operation.'

'How long have we got?' She really didn't want to know the answer but felt she had to say something.

'We need to act fast, Libby. Apart from the mounting pressure from the banks to know what's happening, interest is accruing daily, our overheads are considerable and we're not trading.'

Libby drained her glass of water and decided she needed something stronger. They all did. The two men opted for a whiskey and Libby joined them, taking her tumbler over to the window and cradling it as she stared into the gloomy blackness, seeking a solution.

The mellowness had a calming effect and she took several more gulps in an effort to gain the oblivion she craved. Without warning, the irony of her situation hit home and with it came a cold fury.

Here she was, standing in her magnificent home, gazing out at a garden that had left many photographers speechless, drinking God knows how many years old whiskey out of a hand-blown crystal tumbler and the truth was she couldn't afford any of it. It was a tribute to the craftsmen involved that the glass didn't smash as her hand strangled its generous base.

The explosion had been building for a while.

'I can't bear this any more.' She spun round to face David's two closest friends. Telling them was the next-best thing. 'He put our whole lives at risk. Our lovely home, our investments, all of our assets, everything. Even if he was still around we could still have lost every single thing we'd worked for. And he never once asked for my opinion on what he was doing, even though I was supposed to be his business partner.' Her eyes were full of bitterness and her voice was rising despite her usual iron control. 'And as if that wasn't enough of a betrayal he fucking well died and left me to face the music.' She was sobbing with frustration. 'He's ruined my life and he didn't even ask if he could.' Her eyes were slits.

'I hate him.' She only knew she'd thrown the glass when the fire spat viciously as the alcohol ignited and she heard the musical smashing of expensive crystal.

Neither man knew how to deal with the outburst. They looked horrified, scared of the raw emotion running riot in the room. This was not a normal business meeting. John wanted to go to her but the look in her eyes stalled him. Alex simply didn't want to be there. As quick as it erupted, the explosion was over and the silence that followed was deafening.

'I'd like to be left alone to think this thing through, if you don't mind. I'll call you in the morning.' Libby didn't look at either of them.

'Of course.' John was first up. 'You will ring me later tonight though, if you need to talk it through further?'

She nodded.

'Are you sure you're OK?' He had to ask. Another slight nod was the only recognition.

'Want me to fetch a dustpan?'

'No.' It was unequivocal. She rose silently, ending the meeting that had changed her life. The last thing she wanted now was anyone trying to smooth it all over.

They followed her to the door, both sorry to be leaving her but anxious to be away.

Chapter Thirty-Four

Her reason for wanting rid of them was quite simple really. She wanted to drink herself into oblivion and put off making a decision for another day. Only it wasn't working this evening. She headed for her room, glad Mrs O'C. was away until lunchtime tomorrow visiting a sick relative.

Lying on the bed drinking, Libby noted that the sedative wasn't doing its job. She struggled to simply go with the flow and imagine a different life for herself, but her mind was too active and the enormity of what might happen to her was not easily put to sleep. Getting out of bed, she opened a notebook and wrote down all the options, a trick her father had taught her when she was growing up. The only real answer had been evident to her all day but her still fragile brain wasn't yet ready. She tried to magic her husband back to sort it out, wandering through his closets and touching his things, feeling desperate and spinning out of control.

Looking at a photo of the two of them taken on holiday only weeks before he died brought some of the earlier anger back. She hated it that he'd known then that they could lose everything. It was another betrayal. She opened one of the bedroom windows and flung the smiling couple into oblivion. A few of his favourite things followed. She emptied the closets, dancing on his Italian designer suits and kicking his handmade shoes around the room. She crushed his carefully laundered shirts with her hands. He would have hated the intrusion and she hoped he was hating it now.

She wished she had the courage to cause serious damage. Overall, it was a pathetic effort and she collapsed on the bed, wondering why she still wanted to hurt him while still wanting him so badly. Eventually, she dozed, but all her resting thoughts were of a man who'd made her so happy and now the good times they'd shared haunted her.

Later she made coffee and wandered through the house that was no longer hers, touching the pieces that had made up a perfect life.

The phone rang. Few people had access to her home number so she guessed it would be John, checking up on her. Unusually, there was no caller ID but at least that meant it wasn't her mother, whom David had keyed in as 'Mum', encased in a computerized heart, much to her annoyance. It all seemed so long ago now.

'Hello.' She immediately regretted her foolish impulse.

'Hello Libby?'

'Yes?'

'Hi, it's Annie here – Annie Weller.'

Libby could have kicked herself. 'Oh Annie, hi how are you?' She didn't really care.

'I'm fine, thanks. Listen, I didn't mean to bother you, I just rang to say hello and see how you were doing and to say thanks for the other night. I really enjoyed it.'

'Me too. Em . . . could I give you a ring back tomorrow?'

'Oh, yes, of course, whenever. I was just sitting here reading and you came into my mind without warning and I couldn't stop thinking about you. I've no idea why. Please . . . go. Sorry again for disturbing you. And hopefully, I'll talk to you soon.' She was getting ready to hang up and berate herself when she heard the cry for help buried in a casual, ultra-cool tone.

'I'm just making a decision about whether I should sell the house.' She might as well have said she was baking a cake, if you took it at face value. But Annie knew, and she didn't know how she knew. 'I see.'

'It's too big for me really and I don't need it any more.'

'It's a tough decision.'

'Actually, I don't think I've any choice.'

'Is there anything I can do?'

'Not really.'

'Well, just take your time.'

'I keep wondering what he would have done.'

'He'd have weighed up all the options carefully, I'm sure.'

'That's just it. He left me with no options. And I loved him so much, you know. I never imagined my life without him.'

'You couldn't have.'

'And now, it's all gone . . . and I hate him for it. And I hate myself for hating him.'

'It's been a very tough time for you.' It wasn't what Annie said, it was the complete lack of blame. It proved to be Libby's unravelling. Slowly, it all came out and she talked and cried and talked some more and Annie said nothing and yet she said everything. It had always been her strong point, it was just that she never had anyone to share it with.

'I sound like a spoilt brat, don't I?' Libby asked after one long, particularly selfish rant.

'No, you sound normal.' Annie was sad but smiling.

'I haven't even asked how you are.'

'I'm fine. Listen, would you like to come round for breakfast tomorrow? I can't cook, but my toast is impressive.'

Libby never expected she'd like anything so much. 'Yes I would, thank you.'

Annie gave her the address and Libby promised to be there early, then she hung up, cleaned her teeth and climbed wearily onto his side of the bed and tossed and turned for hours. Somewhere around 3 a.m. she finally made a decision and then made up with him.

Chapter Thirty-Five

Next morning Annie was nervous. It had seemed like a good idea to invite her new friend round for breakfast, but this was no ordinary penniless actor. She rose at six and dashed around, tidying and plumping and rearranging. At bang on eight she was skidding around the shelves of the local shop, buying healthy brown bread and real butter and jam and a load of fresh oranges for juice.

Libby too had woken early, her first morning without a hangover in a long time. Her eyes were sore and she was tired but she felt calm.

She arrived at Annie's shortly after nine, and seeing where she lived put Libby's financial problems into perspective. The identical, solidly built houses were well cared for but the area was full of litter and the overall palette was grey, despite the multicoloured doors and facia boards. The only green space for miles around had a burnt-out car as its centrepiece. Even at this hour there were kids whistling at the car and she clutched her handbag tightly, wondering why they weren't at school.

'Hi.' Annie had obviously been watching out for her.

'Hi.' Libby held out a bakery bag. 'It was the only place open.' She hesitated. 'Is it OK to leave my car there? If I don't ask I'll only spend the time fretting,' she apologized.

Annie grinned. 'Yes, don't worry. Everyone will know I've got a posh friend visiting and the kids on the corner will keep an eye on your car. Now that I'm on TV they keep expecting the stretch limos to arrive but you're the only likely famous visitor, I'm afraid. Don't be surprised if you get asked for your autograph on the way out. They sell them round here.'

Inside, the tiny house was immaculate. The kitchen was Formica city but the table was set with a white cloth and fresh flowers.

'You shouldn't have gone to so much trouble.'

'Wait till you see what I can do to healthy brown bread. I'm a bit mortified, to be honest. I'd forgotten you were a chef when I invited you.'

'This looks lovely. Tea and toast is all I ever eat in the mornings.'

'Well, I have managed to squeeze some fresh orange juice by hand.' Annie passed her a glass and then fussed around. 'So, how did you feel afterwards last night?'

'Worse and then better, actually. I made an awful

mess of the bedroom, I'm afraid. Took my anger out on some of David's things.'

'You don't seem like the tin of paint and scissors type.' Annie's smile was tentative.

'No.'

They talked for over an hour and Libby clarified it all in her own head by sharing it. Annie contributed only occasionally and when she did it was short and concise and encouraging.

'That's it, enough. I'm bored with me. Tell me what's been happening to you.'

'Well, it's all over with Marc.'

'Oh no. Why?'

'He forgot to tell me about his regular girl-friend.' Annie filled her in.

Libby was amazed that he was so brazen about it all.

'Are you all right?'

'I would be if I didn't have to do a big kissy scene with him.'

'What! When?'

'Tomorrow.' It took Libby's mind off her own problems and she insisted on reading the script, so that she'd have a feel for what Annie had to do.

'This is going to be tough.'

'I know, I'm really nervous.'

'Just keep thinking of what a bastard he is. That'll keep the nerves under control. And phone me immediately afterwards.'

They refilled the teapot several times until at last Libby left, reluctantly.

'Want me to come and help you clear up the

bomb-site?' she asked as she walked Libby to her car.

'Would you?'

'Sure. Now?'

'Can you afford the time?'

'Yep, give me two minutes to lock up and grab my coat.'

It was a simple enough gesture but Libby wasn't used to such generosity when the giver wasn't looking for anything back.

When they pulled up at the house Annie was afraid to comment, in case she appeared gauche. She had never seen anything so beautiful – the sweeping driveway, the colour, the proportions, and most of all the space.

'I am so glad I invited you to visit me before I saw this, otherwise you wouldn't have got within a ten-mile radius of my place,' Annie told her, deciding she had to say something.

'It is beautiful but a house is only a box, that's what one of my friends' mothers used to say. It's the people who make it special. Anyway, it's not mine any more.' Annie looked at her friend but she seemed not to mind.

'Ready to face the mess?'

'Hand me the Marigolds.'

Annie had to stop saying 'wow' after a while but was having difficulty keeping her mouth from dropping open. Every room she saw was exquisite. There were magnificent antiques and glorious paintings but it was all understated and warm and homely.

They worked for an hour or so and bagged all David's clothes for charity. Libby rescued what she could from the garden. The picture she liked so much was nowhere to be seen though and she was sorry she'd been so hasty.

'Lunch?' Libby asked eventually. 'Have you time? I could rustle up some pasta very quickly.'

'Sure.' Annie followed Libby to the kitchen, squirming again at the thought of her own pathetic excuse for a breakfast table.

'Glass of wine?'

'Eh, sure. Thanks.' Annie never drank wine during the day. It didn't feel right somehow.

'Actually, I think I'll just have water.' Libby made another decision, but didn't like admitting why. 'I've . . . been drinking . . . a lot lately.'

'Know something, I'd rather have a glass of milk. I was just trying to be posh.' They both laughed at their insecurities.

When Libby returned from dropping Annie home, she decided to act before she could change her mind.

'I'm selling the house and most of the contents,' she announced baldly to John Simpson on the phone, as soon as the pleasantries were out of the way.

He sighed, sorry and relieved in equal measure.

'I've gone through it time and time again since yesterday and it's the only way I can see to pay off the debts and then close the company, without going into liquidation and damaging David's good name.' She didn't yet fully understand why she wanted to preserve it really, perhaps out of a sense of duty, or maybe to protect herself.

'Are you sure you want to do this? Remember the family home is sacred in law, I'm not sure there's a court in the country that would force you to sell it,' John Simpson felt honour bound to advise her.

'That's just it. I don't want to end up in court. The media would have a field day. I'm not sure I'd survive it right now. If we sell the house and the paintings, say, it should cover our existing loans, right?'

'Let me get Alex on a conference call.' When he explained Libby's decision briefly the accountant was clear.

'Yes, the mortgage on the house is comparatively small and it should fetch more than two million euro at auction, maybe more. I'd have to get the contents valued but I'd guess, from the insurance valuations I do have, that we're talking at least another two million there.'

'And you're sure that would clear everything, and we could simply close down the business because he's no longer here to run it?'

Both men agreed and Libby didn't waste any more of their time. She knew what she had to do.

'OK, let's do it. I'll have to spend some money getting the gardens tidied up and the kitchen and bathroom upstairs probably need a coat of paint, but apart from that, it's ready. Give me a couple of weeks.'

'Where will you go?'

'I'll buy something smaller, or rent for a while. Anything to avoid going home to my mother.' They knew she was serious and marvelled at her sense of calm. The truth was she just didn't care very much about anything, she was simply determined to try and move forward and stay sane.

'Libby, I think you should take your time over this. It's a big decision.' John Simpson felt responsible for her.

'Is there any other way to avoid a media frenzy?'

'Probably not.'

'Then I've no choice, have I? I was such an innocent, really.' She said it more to herself. 'All those papers I signed, never knowing that if anything happened to him all the responsibility would fall to me.'

There was no answer and John Simpson felt guilty for the umpteenth time that he hadn't kept a closer eye on things.

'You know they can't touch any of your personal accounts?' Alex asked again.

She mumbled something, too angry even to be thankful that she'd earned a decent income all these years. Libby had money, but nowhere near enough to keep her in the style to which she had so easily become accustomed. She'd grown used to the very best money could buy over the years with David, couldn't even remember the last time she'd checked any of her accounts, or paid her own Visa bill, or for her holidays, or her car or household expenses. She merely used her personal account for bits and pieces, the odd face cream or massage: everything else had been paid for by him.

When they hung up she wandered into his favourite room and cursed him but it was a very lukewarm rant.

Next she sat down and made a list, her first real plan since David's death. The most immediate conversation she needed to have was with her housekeeper. She waited until the woman was getting ready to leave for the day.

'Mrs O'Connell, there's something I need to talk to you about and I wanted to tell you before you go off on holiday on Friday.'

'What is it?'

'I'm afraid I'm going to sell the house.'

'I see.' There was no shock or surprise on the worried face, just acceptance and resignation.

'It will probably all take months, but I need to let you know so that you can start thinking about another job.'

'Where will you live?'

'I'll buy an apartment, or a smaller house. This place is just too big for me now, and too expensive to run.'

'Will you not need me?'

Libby wasn't about to tell her that she might not be able to afford her. 'It wouldn't be fair to you. I might only need someone for a day or two a week, it depends on the type of place I buy. I may even stay with Mum for a while,' she lied easily.

'I've worked all my life for Mr English's family. I'd be happy to help you in any way I can.'

'Well look, it's a long way away. Meanwhile, you take your leave as normal and have a think about things. We can discuss it further at a later stage.'

The housekeeper knew she was dismissed.

Libby handed her an envelope with five hundred euros in it. 'I don't know what David usually paid you as a bonus, but I hope you'll accept this from me, for your holidays.'

'Thank you.' Her wages were paid directly into her account from David's company each month and Libby hoped she wouldn't be too disappointed at the relatively small gratuity.

'I wonder, before you go away, if you could arrange for George to spend a few weeks tidying up the gardens. I've neglected them badly, I'm afraid.' She sounded as if she usually did the work herself, whereas 'neglecting them' simply meant that she couldn't bear George cornering her every time she appeared, so she'd told the housekeeper not to have him around.

'George hasn't been well lately, but he's given me the name of a good person who's looking for work. He comes highly recommended.'

'Fine, fine, perhaps you'd get him to start on Monday if possible.'

'I'll do that.'

'Thanks. And would you mind ringing the decorator and see how soon they could call and have a look around and decide what rooms need freshening up and give me a date when they can start.'

'I will.'

'Thank you. And I'm sorry it's come to this. I hope you understand.' The older woman nodded.

'Well then, I'll see you tomorrow as usual.' Libby smiled and disappeared, badly needing to be alone. She had a splitting headache. Refusing to give in just yet, she headed for her study with just one more job to do.

'Hello Mum, it's me.'

'Elizabeth, darling, how nice to hear you.' Things had been strained between them lately; all the warmth and easiness had gone from their relationship.

Now they chatted about nothing for a while, until Libby baldly announced, 'I've decided to sell the house, by the way.'

Christina Marlowe was speechless.

'I don't understand . . .'

'I've talked it over with John and Alex and it makes sense. It's too big for me now and besides, I need to start again.' Libby hoped she sounded convincing.

'I understand that but, Libby, you love that house.'

'Things have changed. Anyway . . .' she now wanted out of this, 'I won't be doing anything just yet. I'll keep you informed.'

'Why don't you come over for supper tonight?'

Not a chance, Libby wasn't that much of a glutton for punishment. 'No thanks, I'm rather tired. It's been a long day. I'm going to have a bath and go to bed.'

'Well, why don't I pop over to you and bring something with me? I have a delicious chicken casserole that Vera made this afternoon and I could bring—'

'No thanks, Mum. I've already eaten.' She was getting quite good at this. 'Look, I'll talk to you later in the week, I'll phone you and we'll have lunch.'

There was nothing left to say. Christina knew her daughter wouldn't discuss it any further. She said good night and hung up and wondered whether to ring John Simpson or Charles English or both.

Libby heard the front door click just as she replaced the receiver and with a huge sigh of relief she kicked off her shoes and slowly rotated her head in circles in an effort to ease the tension.

Chapter Thirty-Six

The dreaded day had come for Annie. At the studio she got dressed and made up, then sat in her dressing room, thinking. She knew exactly how to play the scene: the problem was, could she carry it off without going overboard? It was a very fine line, especially given their history. She felt tense and her back ached.

The first few takes went well and she relaxed slightly. The scenes in the restaurant, where Alan treats Bobby to an expensive meal, were not being shot until the following week, on location in a city café, so it meant that they had to go straight to the big one, where he takes her home and expects sex. It was the final scene in the episode and in the script Alan slaps Bobby and walks out, leaving her alone and vulnerable. Tim Furlong had talked through several ways of playing the scene with both actors and eventually they'd agreed that Alan would begin to unbutton Bobby's blouse playfully and that she'd refuse, flattered but not wanting him to think she was easy. A well-written one-liner meant she would realize straight away that he already knew exactly what Bobby really was.

Marc was clearly fine about it all, even teasing Annie about the slap, acting as if they'd never been close. 'I don't want to go in too hard, in case I break your jaw.' He was all smiles, safely surrounded by other cast and crew. For the first time his accent irritated her.

'Just do it as if you were doing it for real. I'll be fine, but save it for the take, OK?'

'Of course.' Now he was the one to sound irritated.

Just before the scene Max knocked on the door of her dressing room.

'Sure you're OK about the next one?'

'Yeah, it's just a difficult one to get right . . . you know.'

'Well, as I see it she has great hopes for this relationship, which we all know is ridiculous, but she's been through a lot lately and I think she sees him as a bit of a saviour. When it becomes obvious that he's only being nice to her for sex, and that he knows exactly what kind of girl she is, she's devastated. I think she would see what happens as the end of a dream, really, because if he knows then so do all the other men around, and that means her options are seriously limited.'

Annie listened, knowing suddenly that she'd been resisting appearing too vulnerable, because of what had happened between them personally.

Now she saw that that was exactly how she had to play it and it turned the whole scene around for her.

'I also think you need to see this as one of the reasons she becomes so hard-nosed on the outside, yet much more fucked up on the inside later on, why she gets involved in drugs and puts up with beatings and general abuse from men. It's because deep down she feels useless, has done since she was a child, and this episode with Alan finally finishes her off. So there's an awful lot going on under the surface that the viewers have yet to discover about her, and this is your big opportunity to reveal all her hopes and fears, without really doing a thing. Do you understand that? It's all built into her expectations for this relationship and her devastation when she turns out to be wrong, culminating in her ultimate humiliation when he slaps her. Also, you should know that it's the first time the viewers will see Alan as having a bit of a nasty streak, and I think we're going to take that further, depending on how this goes.'

It all made much more sense and really helped Annie understand what she had to do.

Just before they went for a take Tim checked that both actors were happy. Marc and Annie nodded. 'Tim, I've probably only got one take in me for this one, so I'd really appreciate if we could make this the one, barring an emergency.' Annie felt compelled to say it but still the request sat uneasily on her lips. She wasn't used to being demanding.

'Absolutely, I understand.' She could already hear the floor manager telling all the seniors that this was a one-take scene. She really felt she could only give it her all once.

'Remember, don't hold back on the slap,' she reminded Marc and he nodded and looked away quickly, as if sensing her vulnerability already.

When they finally went for it she became putty in his hands, all girly and giggly, and when his motives became clear her huge eyes said what she couldn't. She kept them glued to his face, pleading with her look, not wanting to believe that he was the same as all the others. When he sneered at her and called her a prick-tease it was shocking coming from the middle-class mouth that had once caressed every inch of her body in real life. All the edges became blurred for her as an actress and when he slapped her across the face it was the final humiliation for Annie as well as Bobby. Her jaw stung and her eyes filled up. When he left with a last look of contempt on his face she sank onto the chair and pulled her blouse together and touched the side of her face, biting her lip as the tears trickled out unannounced.

It seemed an age until the director called 'cut' and Annie experienced her first round of applause in a TV studio. Everyone working on the scene had watched it very carefully and knew she'd given it everything. The crying was a bonus they hadn't expected: the audience would identify with it and like Bobby even more. They'd finished on a big close-up of her stroking her supposedly bruised

301

face – a perfect end to an episode filled with real drama. It was television at its most powerful.

'That was brilliant, Annie, really well done.' Tim Furlong was beaming. 'What a performance, you were fantastic. Check it please folks, before anyone moves.'

'Great stuff, Annie, you all right?' Max came over and she nodded, not trusting herself to speak. Sensing something in her, he gave her a hug and she was able to smile even though she badly wanted to bawl.

'That is going to be one of those great TV moments, I can tell you, you were terrific. Well done you too, Marc. You sparked off each other brilliantly.'

'Well, we get on well together and it came across. I hope I didn't hurt you, though.' He was all fake concern, Annie thought uncharitably, thinking he looked remarkably relaxed and unfazed. She wondered if her pleading eyes had unhinged him but if they had he was a very good actor indeed.

She was emotionally and physically drained and grateful it was her last scene of the day. As she strolled out into the daylight she bumped into Mike Nichols.

'There you are, I was hoping I hadn't missed you. I believe it went fantastically well.'

'I think it went OK, yeah.' His unfailing kindness made Annie want to burst into tears for the second time in minutes. She swallowed a giant boulder in her throat and felt very sad.

'Are *you* OK?'

'It's just that I still think I'm Bobby, I guess.' She grinned at him. 'Stupid, isn't it? I'll be fine in a few minutes.'

'Fancy a drink and you can tell me all about it?'

She glanced at her watch. It was almost five o'clock. 'Are you not on till seven-thirty?'

'Officially yes, but I could say you needed to unwind a bit.'

'No way, I'm not getting into trouble. Max has already been babysitting me this afternoon.'

'OK, then. Officially, I need to discuss something in the next batch of storylines. I'm not sure you understand where Bobby is going.' He was grinning at her and she was grateful.

'Actually, I'd murder a glass of cold beer and a toasted ham sandwich. Even a plastic one would be great.'

'I'll bet you haven't eaten all day. Stay there, don't move. I'll get my keys.'

She did as she was told and Mike was back in an instant. They went to a quiet pub in the neighbourhood where they sat in a corner and ate thick-cut toasties with real ham and sipped their drinks. Annie relaxed. It was exactly what the doctor ordered.

'Come on, I'll do my last good deed for the day and drop you home.' He smiled at her after she'd yawned for the second time in five minutes. 'I know when my company is sending women to sleep.'

'Honestly, it's nothing to do with you. I haven't been sleeping well these past few nights. I've been thinking too much about today.'

'Well, from what you've said I can't wait to see it.'

As they strolled to his car, Mike asked, 'Where did Marc go afterwards? Usually, he'd be the one dragging everyone off for a pint.'

'I think he had another scene to do.' She was glad he hadn't joined them.

'You're right, he did have another one in the pub, the last of the day. Well, I'd say he's feeling pleased with himself too.'

Marc hadn't given anything away to Annie, simply strolled off chatting to Max, without even saying goodbye. In one sense, his apparent indifference was easier for Annie to handle. When she'd looked into his eyes as Bobby, pleading with him to like her for herself and not simply as a prostitute, she felt she'd exposed all her own feelings of hurt because he'd used her and gone home to his real girlfriend.

Amazingly, when she phoned Libby and blurted it all out, the other woman understood perfectly. They teased it out for ages and Annie felt in much better shape emotionally.

Chapter Thirty-Seven

Libby was awoken very early on Monday morning by voices underneath her window. She was groggy, having taken a sleeping tablet to avoid another night thinking, and now she lay still, slightly disoriented, trying to imagine what could be happening.

Eventually, heart beating faster than normal, she padded over to the window and looked gingerly outside, not sure what to expect. She heard what sounded like a radio but couldn't see anyone. It took a moment or two to realize the sounds were of someone digging. Of course, bloody George was coming today. How dare he start working directly underneath her window? He knew exactly where she slept.

Furious, she pulled on her dressing-gown and glided downstairs as if on a skateboard, glancing at her watch to discover that it was barely 7 a.m. She desperately wanted some juice or water but she needed to give the man a piece of her mind first.

The absolute cheek of him! He'd always irritated her but now it was bordering on nuisance.

She unlocked one of the french doors at the side of the house and bulldozed out, pushing her hair from her face and wondering if she should have dressed first, to give her more authority. Not worth it for George, she decided. Anyway, she was heading straight back to bed.

She rounded the corner at breakneck speed and was in full flow before she realized the man was a stranger.

'What on earth do you think you're doing at this time of morning, George, you know I don't like to be disturbed and turn that—' She screeched to a halt and looked down at an unruly mop of long, dark hair that in no way resembled George's shiny, bald patch.

'Who the hell are you?'

A pair of chocolatey eyes looked up at her. The man put down the small hand trowel he'd been using.

'I'm the gardener,' he said. His voice was soothing, like a honey and lemon drink on a sore throat. Unfortunately, she wasn't soothable.

'Well, that much I gathered. How did you get in?'

'Your housekeeper gave me keys to the side gate.'

'When?'

'When I met her on Friday and agreed to do this job.'

'She didn't mention any of this to me.'

He raised his dark eyebrows very slightly and looked at her for a moment. 'I'm sorry, but I hardly think that's my fault.' He said it in such a reasonable tone of voice that it was impossible to take offence.

'You're the person who's going to tidy up the gardens?' In the midst of the fog that was Libby's brain, a faint recollection was dawning.

'That's right.'

Libby badly wanted to tell him to take his awful, plastic, tinny radio and scoot, but she knew she needed this job done before she could put the house on the market.

She took a deep breath and mustered her full height, holding her hair back with one hand so that she could give him the benefit of a glare that had sent many a TV technician running for cover. Her state of undress and general dishevelment detracted from the iron maiden image somewhat but she was too angry and too dehydrated to notice. Her mouth tasted sour and she ran her tongue over her teeth and stepped back to avoid him sampling her stale breath.

'Fine,' she spat, annoyed and frustrated at herself as well as him, but that—' she jerked upwards in a vaguely two-fingered gesture – 'is where I sleep and I do not want to be disturbed at any time. Do you understand?'

'Perfectly.' It was just a bit too laid back for her liking and the faintest hint of a smile convinced her the man thought she was bonkers.

'And if you wouldn't mind turning off that

radio, I'd appreciate it.' The tone was milder, but she was determined not to give him an inch.

Without a word he leaned over and pressed a button and the drone of early morning fake chirpiness that passed for commercial radio ceased. He resumed his work with hardly a shift of his body, this time weeding with his hands so that she couldn't complain.

She turned on her heel then spun back around. 'Do you have to start so early? Nine-thirty would suit me better.'

'I was told you wanted this done urgently.' How the hell did a gardener get an educated accent? she thought. 'There's a lot to do. I can start at eleven if you like, but I won't guarantee I'll finish on the date I agreed with your housekeeper. And I'm afraid I have another job waiting, so I can't stay here any longer.' Again the manner was mild but the tone was confident, and just a teeny bit too cocky for her liking. Libby was used to her workmen being in awe of her and very subservient and this one definitely didn't fit the bill. She knew he'd won in this instance anyway, and she took even more of a dislike to him, storming off in the direction she'd come, sensing he'd be smirking. As she turned the corner she glanced back and saw he was deep in concentration, pruning away some tangled bindweed from a delicate flower, incident clearly forgotten.

Back in the kitchen she poured juice and water, made coffee and took a tray back to bed. Her head throbbed and as she searched in the bathroom cabinet for some relief she looked in the mirror and saw a mass of hair that needed washing and a lined, grey face. It was not pretty and just for a moment the old Libby wished she had died along with her husband, before the newer, determined model took over. She opened the shower door, turned on the jets fully and abandoned the notion of a lie-in.

She was agitated as she dried her hair so she lay on the bed for a few minutes and flicked channels and realized again why she hated morning TV. All those fresh-faced, cheesy weathergirls who loved reminding people to stay in bed unless they absolutely had to travel, even though they'd been up since five and looked fit to burst with energy and general bonhomie. And then there was the endless round of female newsreaders who could make a story on the Middle East sound sexy with their pouting, collagen-injected, blubber lips. They made her want to throw up, because unknowingly they made her feel inadequate, like being caught in your PJs at lunchtime by a slinky, polished neighbour on her way home from the gym. It never occurred to Libby that she must have aroused those same feelings in others many times. And why did all the shows talk about revolutionary new diets and miracle face creams and cellulite and fake tans, as if there was nothing else to life? She felt like smashing the screen.

Grumbling, she pushed back the duvet for a

second time that morning and faced the day, even though it was not yet eight o'clock and her dull, groggy head needed at least another two hours of oblivion.

Toast and muesli and full cream yoghurt helped, and she plodded around the kitchen still plotting revenge. He was certainly not getting the traditional coffee and scones with jam and cream for elevenses, as she was sure he had with Mrs O'C. when he'd called the first time. The woman loved feeding workmen or 'real men', as she annoyingly referred to her favourites, going all girly. Ugh. Libby had never got used to finding strangers sitting scoffing a banquet in her kitchen, spreading home-made jam and clotted cream on plump scones and staring at her endlessly as soon as they realized who she was. Well, this one could starve.

An hour and a half later she emerged dressed in black leather and wearing dark glasses, hair and make-up immaculate, and revved up and shot past him in her shiny motor, feeling very pleased with herself in a childish way. She had nowhere to go, really, but she did a few bits and pieces and when she returned he was sitting on a corner of the lawn with a flask and food spread out like a picnic. Instantly, her annoyance returned and she wanted to stop and roll down the window and ask him not to eat in full view of visitors.

As soon as he saw her he leaned over and turned off the radio and that irritated her even more. She screeched to a halt, skidded and gave herself a fright, then tried to look nonchalant, but he was reading and didn't even glance in her direction.

Next morning she woke early, much to her annoyance, and this time there were no intrusive sounds to blame it on. When she peeped out the new gardener was still kneeling in a corner, as if he'd never gone home and this time he was wearing a tiny earpiece, his way of getting his fix of trash, she thought nastily.

By lunchtime Libby was feeling she'd gone over the top the previous morning. He was doing an amazing job, the place was starting to look really cared for and he was even replanting some of the large old urns, badly neglected since the early spring bulbs had faded.

At about one she crossed the gravel area, heels scrunching. Again he was bent down, trowel in hand, and didn't turn around as she approached.

'I've made some soup and a panini, if you're hungry.' She wondered if he'd know what a panini was. No reply. She coughed. Still nothing. She tried again, tipping him on the shoulder and causing him to turn his head sharply in her direction but still he did not stand up. She towered over him and immediately felt the full weight of her double chin as she looked down on him. Quickly she straightened up and ended up making her offer to the beech tree.

'I've made some lunch if you'd like to come into the kitchen.' Her tone was cool; she wanted to keep him at a distance yet didn't want him bad-mouthing her down at his local.

He took the earpiece out and shook his head.

'Thank you but I have my lunch with me.'

Didn't he know she was an internationally renowned chef? 'Can't you eat that later? It's all ready inside.'

'No really, I prefer to eat outdoors when I can, but thank you anyway.' He was determined to make her grovel. Well, he could rot.

'Fine, suit yourself,' she said airily and disappeared in a waft of DKNY's latest offering.

She sat in the kitchen and ate all the lunch herself and when she glanced out he was sitting on a stone, eating and staring around the garden. He looked relaxed and content and she envied him his utter self-containment.

Chapter Thirty-Eight

For some reason the gardener's calm self-assurance unnerved Libby and made her want to find out more about him. To do this she reckoned she first had to make her peace with him, and admitting she might have been wrong had never come easy to her. She thought about it that afternoon. She was making heavy work of a voiceover script when her phone rang. The interruption was welcome and the caller doubly so.

'Libby, hi, it's me.'

'Annie, hi.' She recognized the voice at once now, they'd spent so many hours on the phone to each other recently.

'Any news?'

'No. I'm getting nowhere fast today, I'm hot and sticky and I've got the gardener from hell outside.'

'Worse than George?' Even Annie had heard the legendary tales.

'No, actually, he's great in that way, just a bit too smart-assed for me.'

'I'll bet you could make mincemeat out of him,' Annie teased.

'Believe me, I've tried. He's bulletproof.'

'Well, if he's a good worker then go make your peace with him because you might need him very soon if you find your dream cottage. They always have overgrown gardens in the movies.'

Libby laughed and knew she was right.

'Any chance of a coffee? I'm just finishing for the day and I could walk around to your place.'

'Yes, please, I need someone to pull me out of my dark mood.'

'Maybe you could start by not wearing black all the time.' It was so unlike Annie to even suggest she do something that Libby responded immediately.

'Maybe you're right. I'll start tomorrow.'

'Great, see you in half an hour for that caffeine hit. Now, go grovel on the gravel.' Libby laughed. Annie always cheered her up.

It was a glorious summer's day and she felt heavy and frumpy as she made her way to where he was working, kneeling as usual. He wore faded jeans and a white cotton shirt, sleeves rolled up. An impractical choice for a working man, she thought.

'How's it all going?'

If he was surprised he gave no sign. 'Fine, thanks.'

'You've made big changes already. I hadn't realized how we'd let things go.'

He nodded, then shifted around and continued

working. 'A few more days should see a big difference.' Libby was dismissed. She resisted the urge to simply walk away. There was something about him, an intriguing take it or leave it attitude. Nothing for it but to plunge straight in; she wasn't used to being at a disadvantage, and certainly not with an employee.

'Look, I eh, think I may have over-reacted yesterday morning when I first met you. I've been under a lot of stress lately and I took it out on you.' She didn't smile, not wanting him to think she was grovelling. If he'd known her he'd have realized she was nervous by the way she pushed her hair behind her ear and licked her lip.

'No problem, I'll be out of your way as soon as I can.' It was odd that he made no effort to engage her in conversation the way most people did.

'There's no hurry.' She didn't know what else to say.

The silence stretched between them, leaving her no option but to try again. 'I was rude, I hope you'll forgive me.' It sounded stiff and formal and she didn't look at him.

'Forget it. We all have our moments. I know I sure do.' He gave her a distracted smile, as if remembering something, and it annoyed her. She was used to being the centre of attention. The memory softened his face and it unsettled her further.

'Right then.' Libby was all business again. 'I'd better get back to work. If you need anything please let me know.'

'Will do.'

She walked slowly away and had the distinct impression that he saw her as a spoilt, rich bitch wife and she was sorry, even though he wasn't the sort of person she'd normally worry about for even a second.

Annie arrived, a bundle of energy in a bright red dress. 'I just saw him. He's gorgeous. Tall or small?'

'Do you know, I don't know. I've never seen him standing up.'

For some reason that sent them both into fits of laughter. It was one of the things Libby liked best about their friendship. As they drank a pot of coffee, they gave the stranger a character.

He was nowhere to be seen as she left to drop off some notes and recipes to the office and he was gone when she arrived home at seven. She was disappointed and didn't know why. His tools had been cleaned and they stood neatly in a corner: she liked knowing he'd be back.

Next morning she was up early and made a decision. No more black. It was too hot and ageing and morbid. Annie was right. She showered and put on a simple cotton dress that had cost a fortune, and left her hair loose. The gardener was nowhere to be seen all morning and when she eventually spotted him he was, as usual, on his knees in a far corner of the front lawn. She had no excuse to go anywhere near him.

Her mother arrived unannounced at lunchtime

and was delighted to see that Libby had shed her black clothes, although wisely she said no such thing. They were sitting in the conservatory when she suddenly announced, 'There's a man in the garden.'

'He's the gardener.'

'Where's George?'

'Not feeling well, as far as I know. Tea or coffee?'

'Coffee please, black. What's his name?'

'I've no idea. I was a bit rude to him when he arrived so we're not exactly on speaking terms. I know I should be grateful he's not a pest like George. Constant talkers irritate me no end and I can't pretend otherwise.'

Christina knew her daughter could be a battle-axe to work for, so she tactfully changed the subject, quickly losing interest in the workman.

In the early evening Libby was cooking, feeling more relaxed than she had for a long time. When she looked outside it was raining and he was sitting on his hunkers under a tree. Without thinking, she went out. 'Won't you please come into the kitchen and shelter. You'll get soaked.' He was wearing a light-blue cotton shirt and the pale sky colour emphasized his tanned, sallow skin. He looked completely unfazed by the downpour and didn't appear to have a coat or jacket.

'It's only a shower. I'm fine, thanks.'

'Not if you look over there.' She pointed to the pewter sky.

'I'm almost finished for the day anyway.'

'Have you a car?'

'Not here. I prefer to walk when I can.'

'Well, you can't walk home in this. Where do you live?'

'Not too far away. Don't worry, I'm used to it, although they didn't predict this on the early morning forecast.' That lazy smile was there again, and so was that uncomfortable feeling in Libby's stomach.

'Please. At least have a coffee until it clears. I'm cooking, so you're not disturbing me.'

He looked up at her for a moment but didn't move, then he seemed to make a decision.

'OK, thanks, a coffee would be great.' When he stood up, she was taken aback. He was tall – taller than her, and she was in heels – and the whole package was quite striking, if you liked the rugged, outdoor look. A bit unsophisticated perhaps, she thought, wanting to keep him at a distance. She was dying to tell Annie he had legs.

She led the way to the kitchen. 'Tea or coffee?'

'Coffee, black, no sugar.' He didn't look at all ill at ease. She remembered he'd been here before with her housekeeper.

'Is there somewhere I can wash my hands?'

'Yes, of course. Through there, second on the right.'

Libby set the table with silver cutlery and china cups, her everyday stuff, then thought he might prefer a mug.

When he returned he looked as if he'd splashed

his face with icy water: he was young and healthy and fit and she felt old and out of condition and fat.

'Please, sit down. Would you like something to eat?'

'No, coffee's fine. I'll cook when I get home.'

'You like to cook?'

'Yes, I suppose I do. Do you?'

She was amused. 'Sometimes. When I'm relaxed.'

'Well, it smells good. I don't think I could compete.'

'What sort of things do you cook?' She poured coffee and left a plate of goodies close by.

'Pasta, chicken, fish. Nothing too complicated.'

She wondered about a series aimed at men like him, hard-working labourers who probably wouldn't know one end of a stick of lemongrass from the other.

'Oh, and I like to try Thai when I can get the ingredients.' He smiled, scotching another of her theories. 'Do you cook a lot?'

'All the time.' He obviously didn't recognize her or else he was a very good actor.

'It's not much fun cooking for one. I like to have people round when I can, rope them in as well.' He stretched his long legs and looked perfectly at home. 'I suppose you have a family to cater for?'

She was taken aback. Surely Mrs O'C. had filled him in? She must have warned him. His remark threw her and she kept her back turned. 'No, actually. Still, I don't mind.' She paused in her stirring. 'You know something, I'm just about to have a glass of wine. Would you care to join me?' She was unsure of herself; it sounded like a very formal conversation to be having with a workman.

'No thanks.'

'Sure?' She took a heavy crystal goblet from the shelf and poured a generous glass of chilled Mâcon-Lugny.

'I don't really drink much, to be honest,' he said.

Libby took a gulp and tried to relax. He seemed content to sip his coffee and watch her cook, while the rain lashed at the window and the room filled with the comfortable sounds of sizzling and stirring.

She didn't know where the offer came from, but she found herself asking, 'Would you like to stay for supper? I've made risotto and, as usual, I've cooked enough to feed an army. It will only get thrown out.'

He hesitated for a split second and she wondered if he felt obliged, but he seemed relaxed enough.

'Fine, if you're sure.'

Surprised at herself, Libby went to set up the table in the conservatory. He jumped up. 'Can I help?'

'No thanks, it won't take a minute.' She felt him close behind her.

'Please don't go to any trouble. I'm happy to eat here in the kitchen. It's cosy and it's where I usually eat at home. No dining room, I'm afraid.' There it was, the self-deprecating smile again.

She realized he probably felt uncomfortable at a formal sitting so she hastily agreed.

He took the plates from her and cleared away the coffee and set up for dinner as if he'd lived there for ever.

Libby burst out laughing. 'I've just realized I don't even know your name.'

'Oh. Sorry. Andrew Harrington.' He held out his hand.

'Elizabeth Marlowe.' She hadn't called herself that since first class. They shook hands; she liked his touch, he felt smooth and safe and not rough and weathered as she'd imagined. When she took her hand away she felt a slight prickly sensation and she rubbed it against her leg.

'Do your friends call you Andrew or Andy?'

'Only my folks call me Andrew all the time. My friends call me both, and much worse. I used to hate Andrew when I was young but I've more or less grown into it.'

'My mother calls me Elizabeth, everyone else knows me as Libby.' She waited for recognition but none came. He just nodded.

'I like Libby, it's sort of . . . mischievous.' It was a word never applied to her before.

She put the shiny copper pan of artichoke risotto in the centre of the table and added some parmesan and a grater, a huge stainless steel pepper mill and some good ciabatta bread on a board. A herb salad was the only accompaniment.

'Sure about the wine?' she offered as she topped up her own.

'Just water, thanks. I have a lot to do tomorrow.'

'How long have you been doing this kind of work?'

'Nearly a year now.'

'I'd say it's hard. What did you do before?'

'It's a long story and I'd only bore you to death. And you're right, it is hard sometimes, but I love it. The early mornings are best, the smells and the air and the peace, although the balmy evenings, with the scent of jasmine and honeysuckle, are quite alluring too.'

Libby had the grace to blush. 'Well, I'm not really a morning person, never have been.' She looked to see if he was laughing but he was absorbed in his food.

'You should give it a try. There's not much to beat walking in your bare feet on the grass on a summer's morning.' She couldn't ever remember doing that and he looked at her without a trace of envy. 'You're lucky having such a beautiful space in the city.'

'Actually, it's about to go up for sale.' He didn't ask any questions. That reminded her of Annie, and she was drawn to his easy acceptance of situations. Most people wanted a lot of information about her.

She was just about to tell him more about the house and then wasn't sure, so she changed the subject and they chatted on. She didn't get to know much about him, although she told him about her parents' modern house and striking gardens and he seemed interested.

He left about eight and apologized for yawning.

'That food finished me off. I'll be in bed by nine-thirty.'

There was something odd about him. She couldn't put her finger on it. Why wasn't he going clubbing or – what was that much-loved phrase? – 'down the pub'? He was younger than her, early thirties she guessed, and he wasn't married, otherwise he wouldn't have mentioned cooking for one. She was certain he didn't spend his evenings going to bed at nine-thirty.

The rain had stopped. Andrew breathed in heavily as he stepped out into the garden and thanked her for supper. She wanted to walk with him and that surprised her so she hung back, flustered. He didn't seem to notice, simply said goodnight and strolled down the driveway.

And when he turned and waved casually she felt he knew she was watching him. She felt foolish, and quickly went inside.

Chapter Thirty-Nine

Friday was looming large on Libby's horizon and she doubted anyone would remember. It would be six months since David's death and she'd been thinking about him all week, dreading the anniversary the following day. Today had been particularly bad and by five she couldn't take it any longer so she poured herself a large glass of wine and wandered around the house, stopping at various windows and watching Andrew Harrington.

As the alcohol took effect she began to fantasize about him, wondering what it would be like to have an affair with the gardener, fancying herself as a modern-day Lady Chatterley. She giggled, then sat in a chair and pretended to be absorbed in something as she watched him move around, confident, assured, relaxed. At one point he stood up, arched his back and stretched his shoulders. He looked very alive and rugged and she thought about having sex with him. It aroused feelings she never thought she'd have again. The feelings unnerved her and she rang Annie.

'I'm in need of help. The gardener is beginning to look very attractive.'

'Well, he is cute, you're not wrong there, but I'd say you need to get out more.' It was a joke but they both knew that Libby hadn't been anywhere socially since David had died.

'Yeah. It'll be six months tomorrow.'

'I knew that, I was going to phone you anyway. It'll be hard. Anniversaries are always tough. How are you doing?'

'Not so good today. Did you really remember?'

'Yes.'

'Thanks. That means a lot.' The chat helped and they planned a walk at the weekend because Annie was on location for twelve hours the following day.

Later, Libby contemplated making an excuse to go outside and talk to Andrew, just so she could explore her feelings; then she felt guilty and stupid and busied herself in the study. When she looked again, he'd gone. As the evening wore on she became more morbid and later more self-critical and the feelings made her drink faster in an effort to reach the much safer, numb place in her head that seemed the only way to ease the discomfort. She went to bed early and slept soundly for a few hours. Then she woke thirsty and groggy, and lay wide awake and thought about the day six months earlier when her world had changed for ever. Today was not going to be easy.

* * *

She was up and dressed and walking in the garden on her third cup of coffee, still feeling dreadful, when Andrew arrived at seven-thirty. She was back in black.

'You're late.' It felt odd to be joking with him and she was glad he hadn't caught her in her bare feet on the grass. She'd been tempted to try it out but it felt disloyal on this of all days.

'I had a lie-in till six-thirty seeing as it's Friday.' He had just showered and his hair was wet. His skin glowed and his shirt and trainers looked too good for the job he was doing. Even his watch looked expensive but Libby couldn't get close enough to inspect it. As he rolled up his sleeves he slipped it into his pocket and she had the feeling he was hiding something.

'You're up early.'

'Couldn't sleep.'

'How come?' He looked interested but not nosy and she wanted to tell him.

'My husband ... died ... a couple of months ago – six months ago today, in fact. It's been looming all week. Last night it finally hit home.' Saying it aloud calmed her and she even managed a tiny smile. 'Sorry to dump that on you before breakfast. I'm not usually so ... forward with people I ... don't know very well.'

He looked at her for a long time. 'That must have been very tough.'

'It was.'

'Was it sudden?'

She nodded. 'Very. He went out to dinner and never came home. Heart attack.' The memories washed over her and she bit her lip.

He took a clean, white handkerchief from his pocket – another surprise – and she took it even though she didn't need it.

'That's a lot to have to deal with.'

She rubbed her forehead tiredly. 'I'm not dealing with it, that's the trouble. Big coward, really.'

'I think anyone would be frightened of the future if that happened.'

'Thanks.' She smiled. There was nothing else to say and she liked it that he didn't feel the need to make small talk all the time.

'Cup of coffee?'

'I shouldn't, I'm late already, but if you're making one, it seems too good a morning not to sit and admire it for a few minutes.'

She was glad he'd accepted. A few minutes later she returned with a tray of freshly brewed coffee and a plate of scones she'd defrosted and heated. Andrew was already working but stopped when he saw her and took the tray and put it down on the grass. He eased himself down and stretched his arms.

'I'm not usually so lazy,' he said. 'I didn't get a run in this morning so I'm only half awake.'

'I'd say you're a very boring person to be in a relationship with.'

'How d'ya mean?'

'You'd make someone feel very inadequate, all this early to bed and early to rise nonsense.'

'Well, you know what they say.' He quoted the old proverb and she grinned at him. 'Yeah right, and boring as hell.'

'Thanks.'

'I didn't mean *you* are.' She laughed. 'I could do with some of that discipline myself, I can tell you.'

'You should try it, it works. You'll feel great.'

'I'd settle for drinking a bit less.' She didn't know where that remark had come from.

'Are you drinking a lot?' He didn't sound even vaguely shocked or judgmental.

'I was, then I wasn't, but now I am again. It numbs the pain.'

He seemed to understand.

Libby felt uncomfortable and changed the subject. 'So, what are your plans for the weekend?'

'Nothing much. I'm going sailing on Sunday, weather permitting. I'll probably go and see my folks at some stage. All very dull.'

'Do you have a partner?'

He didn't seem surprised at the question, although she was.

'Not at the moment,' he told her.

'Sounds like a story there. I'm sorry, I didn't mean to pry.'

'It's OK. I was in a relationship for a couple of years. It wasn't right. Simple as that.'

'Did you get hurt?'

'Not in the way I think you mean, but I don't think you ever really emerge unscathed from an important relationship. It leaves a mark.'

'I really only had one significant one and that

was with my husband. It was love at first sight and it was . . .' she paused and couldn't find the word: 'Magic, I suppose.'

'You're lucky to have had it.'

'I guess I am. I miss him so much.' She looked away.

'There hasn't been anyone else since?'

She wanted to laugh out loud but it would have been a grotesque sound. It was such a male question. 'Are you mad? You're practically the only stranger I've spoken to.' She shook her head. 'There'll never be anyone else. He was an impossible act to follow.'

Andrew said nothing. She was glad he didn't offer any of the usual clichés. He simply buttered a scone and she drank her coffee and the sun was warm on her neck and she didn't want to leave when it was over.

The day passed with few interruptions. Annie sent her a beautiful bunch of white lilies, and rang during her lunch break. She thought that her mother, or Carrie, might have remembered, but it wasn't really any anniversary. She kept busy and tried not to think of the evening stretching ahead; she wished Annie had been free.

Libby buried herself in yet another of the much loathed voiceover scripts and it was six-thirty before she realized she was hungry. She had only another hour or so to do, so she headed for the kitchen and a spot of caffeine. A tap on the side door startled her, before she realized it must be Andrew.

He stood there with a huge handful of flowers from the garden. In any other man's arms they would have looked sissyish but in his they seemed perfectly natural. 'I'm just off. I don't like to cut flowers much but there's so many and I thought you might like them, especially today.'

'Come in. They're beautiful. I've never even noticed half of them, can you believe it.' She felt like an oddity. 'What sort of woman am I that I pass these every day and don't notice the colours or the scent?' She sniffed them deeply. 'They're exquisite.'

'Most people are so busy they take them for granted. And your garden is vast. But you're right, they are absolutely stunning.'

She got a huge crystal bowl, filled it with water and arranged them as he watched. There were still masses over.

'Got any more of those?'

'Eh, yes, in the sitting room.'

He came back with two tall hand-blown vases and plonked two big bunches into them: somehow they looked arranged, as garden flowers always seem to. 'Right then, I'll leave you to it.' He made for the door. 'What are your plans for the evening?'

Libby was embarrassed and began to lie, then stopped. 'None really. Watch some TV, I suppose.' It sounded pathetic.

'Have you reminded any of your friends of the date?'

'My friend Annie is working this evening, but

she rang me earlier.' Libby liked talking about her. 'Actually, I . . . don't really have a large circle of close friends. I thought I had lots when David was alive but now I realize they were more social acquaintances. My friend Carrie from school moved away and now she lives in the country with masses of dogs and children, so we don't get to see each other as often as I'd like.'

'Would you like to have dinner with me, perhaps?'

It sounded oddly formal and a little old-fashioned but it was a life-saver. 'I'd love to. Why don't I cook something?'

'No, that's the only condition.'

'What do you mean?'

'I don't think it's a night for cooking. Give me an hour and I'll shower and change and bring you for some of the best pasta you've ever tasted.' She doubted that but it sounded like the most fabulous idea in the world.

'OK.'

'Fine.' He opened and closed the door and she wondered for just a second if she'd been drinking and fantasizing again.

Chapter Forty

Libby cheated slightly on what should definitely have been a solid black day. After a quick shower she put on a black pinstripe suit with a black and cream Lycra top. It looked completely wrong, way too formal, so she cheated further and changed into a little white strappy T-shirt and topped it with a white stretchy blouse. Black hipster jeans with high boots offered the only mark of respect for the date, combined with a chunky low-slung belt she'd seen on Naomi Campbell and just had to have on her last visit to New York.

She did her make-up lightly, then caught sight of herself in the mirror: she was shocked to see the first spark of anything on her face for months. She felt like a traitor and the tears, never far from the surface, were a damp, salty aperitif. Here she was, feeling a sense of anticipation for the first time in six months, and it would have been so much better if it could have been with her much-loved husband, instead of a stranger who was taking pity on her. The reality of what now made her happy made her sad.

After a minute or two she returned to the mirror and tried to cool her swollen, red rims with eye-drops. Then she re-did her make-up.

She asked for God's help in a mumbled child-hood rhyme and felt somewhat better after the tears. The bell at the gate jolted her back to reality.

'Hi, it's Andrew.'

'Come in.'

She watched as a car made its way slowly up the driveway as if unsure of its welcome. It was a modest family saloon, and although new, not at all what she'd expected a boy racer to be driving.

She let herself out by the side door, where they always managed to meet. He got out and greeted her.

'You can change your mind about going out, you know. I won't be upset although it is the first time I've worn a suit all week and it seems a shame not to spill something on it, as I always seem to do when I eat Italian.'

She laughed, liking the image.

'I'm fine, thanks. Will we go?'

Andrew held the door open and waited until she was inside, another unexpected gesture. As he got in beside her she smelt the cool, clean smell of him and was nervous. He negotiated the sweeping driveway and she glanced across. His suit was far too expensive – black, beautiful fabric, exquisitely tailored. He wore an open-neck pale shirt and he'd washed his hair again. She wanted to touch it and the sensation worried her. She felt like a traitor.

'Where are we going?' she asked quickly.

'Wait and see. As long as you're not pretending to like Italian all will be fine.'

'I love Italian.'

'Good. Then sit back, relax and enjoy the ride.' He flicked a control on the steering wheel and the sound of Rachmaninov filled the space; he flicked again and something more contemporary took over. It was equally soothing and Libby wondered if the classical stuff had been an irritating glitch on the radio tuner. He didn't seem like the piano concerto type.

He drove along the coast towards Sandycove, where he pulled into a tiny side street and found a space easily.

'This is it?' She couldn't see a restaurant nearby.

'Try not to sniff, please. It's very off-putting.' Libby was mortified and then realized he was teasing her.

They went into what looked like a disused building, with no sign outside. As soon as the door opened the noise and the smell hit her and she stepped back as if she'd been cattle-prodded. There had been no hint of the vibrancy within.

'I forgot to mention the noise. I promise it won't be too bad.'

The building was obviously a converted warehouse and the original stone and brickwork exposed. There were lots of nooks and crannies and bottles of olive oil and balsamic vinegar on shelves and huge sacks of strong flour and polenta and pasta stacked around the floor. Bunches of garlic and dried chillies hung from the beams, and tins of tomatoes and jars of passata were stashed in little alcoves. Fresh herbs grew in pots; as they were shown to a table they brushed past thyme and coriander. The smell mingled with warm bread and something pungent like olives or anchovies. The music was pumping so hard that the walls were almost vibrating. Libby had never been anywhere like it in her life.

The waiters all wore Day-Glo orange boiler suits. One of them, tall and very black, sauntered over and smiled at them in a manner so relaxed he might as well have lit up a joint at the table.

'Hey, you guys. The specials tonight are skewered scallops with prosciutto and a warm basil dressing and eh, let's see, ricotta, spinach and egg ravioli. And if you'd like a starter we have a gorgeous tomato, red pepper and pesto soufflé. Otherwise it's all here.' He put what looked like plastic blackboards in front of each of them. 'Now, can I get you folks a drink?'

'I think I'll have a beer to start. Libby?'

'Beer is fine.' She couldn't remember the last time she'd had it. As the waiter departed, Andrew leaned across and grinned at her. 'What I really want is some of whatever he's on.'

'I was just thinking the same thing myself. How on earth did you find this place? It's a hoot.'

'I know. It always cheers me up. The atmosphere is crazy but the little nooks mean you can actually talk in peace. Most of the noise is coming from the bar over in the far corner and by the time it really hots up we'll be safely tucked up in bed.' He realized what he'd said and grinned and looked sheepish just as the drinks arrived. 'That came out not quite as I'd intended. Sorry. I hope you understood what I meant.' That politeness again: it seemed at odds with the rest of him.

'That's a relief.' It sounded like an insult and she immediately tried to rescue it. 'At least I—'

'Let's abandon this one, I don't think either of us is going to win.'

'Agreed.' She gulped her drink and looked around. The crowd were mainly twenty- and thirty-somethings, all ultra cool. 'Tell me when you first came here.'

'I've been coming here for years, on and off and I still don't know a soul. The staff changes every month, I'd say. The current trend is for very dark skins. I don't know if that means another new owner. Still, the food is consistently good, although you may disagree. I'd say you're an expert.' He was teasing her again.

'I doubt it. I haven't been out in so long I'll probably be hard pushed to order.'

'OK, I can solve that.' He took the menu from her hands and closed it. 'Trust me, I've tasted it all. Only decision you have to make is – red or white?'

'Will you be joining me?' She was intrigued that he took control so easily.

'Yep, I'll have a glass, two at most because I'm driving, but you're under no such pressure.'

She was glad he obviously didn't mind the fact that she might be an alcoholic and was prepared to take a chance on not having to carry her out later.

'You order, to go with the food. I don't care.'

It was all so relaxed, so informal, so different from the starched napkins and over-anxious waiters Libby was used to that she decided to just go with it and be glad that she wasn't home alone tonight.

They had a big bowl of crab linguine with chilli and garlic and herbs, tossed in a fruity extra-virgin olive oil and it was delicious. To follow they had rabbit, of all things. It seemed to have been slow cooked in wine with mushrooms and lots of wild garlic and was served with a peppery rocket and herb salad. A tangy balsamic dressing came on the side. Rough bread was offered to mop up and they took full advantage and even managed a portion of cassata and a helping of berries with a hot sauce laced with amaretto and served with a bowl of something that definitely had mascarpone cheese added.

Good coffee and an offer of free zambuccas followed.

'Well, does the food meet with your approval?'

'Everything was absolutely delicious. The flavours seemed to work so well and yet are so uncomplicated.' She didn't know it but her passion for food shone in her eyes. 'I just love simple food using good ingredients, it comes through all the time, especially when they use stuff that's in season. It's a winning combination.'

'You really do know your food.'

'Just as well. It's what I do for a living.'

He looked puzzled. 'What do you mean?'

'I'm a chef.'

'A chef?' It was the first time he'd shown any sense of disbelief since they'd met.

'You seem surprised.'

'No, it's just that you look too . . .'

'Too what? Old? Wealthy? Refined?'

He seemed a bit ruffled.

'I was going to say chilled, actually.' It was her own prejudices coming out and now it was her turn to be ruffled.

'Sorry. That was just my insecurity.'

'So you work in a restaurant?'

'No. Although I did, years ago, when I was training. Now I write books and do . . . some TV.'

'You're a celebrity?' He sounded like a little boy meeting his favourite pop star and she laughed.

'I suppose I am.'

'How come I've never seen you?'

'You said yourself you don't watch TV.'

'That's true. But I do read the newspapers. I should have recognized your name. Although the cookery pages aren't really my thing.'

She didn't like to tell him that she featured more often in the gossip columns, something he obviously had no time for either. A couple at the next table were staring at her and she found herself hoping there were no photographers around, a thought that had only now occurred to her. What on earth was she thinking of, being seen in public with a man so soon? And her gardener, to boot. The tabloids would love that one.

'Well, I don't feature that often so you're forgiven.' She yawned. 'I suppose I'd better get home. It's late.' She felt uncomfortable now and her anxiety spoiled the moment. 'I insist on paying, by the way, to say thanks for helping take my mind off the day.'

Now it was his turn to look uncomfortable. 'I invited you,' he said simply in a tone that brooked no argument. He signalled to the waiter and they left within a few minutes. He paid in cash, she noticed, and hoped it hadn't cost him an entire week's wages.

Libby moved ahead of him quickly as they left. He sensed her mood had changed and didn't understand it.

'Are you OK?' He seemed to ask that often now, she thought, yet they barely knew each other.

'I'm fine. Thank you so much, I really enjoyed it.'

'It's just, your mood changed towards the end. Did I say something to upset you?'

'No, I just felt a bit awkward.' She didn't know if she wanted to say it.

'Why?'

'Some people at the next table were staring. It unsettled me.' Sensing he'd misunderstood, she said, 'It wasn't anything to do with you.'

'I see.' He didn't sound convinced and they drove in silence until they got to her gate. Libby got out to punch in the code. 'I can walk from here,' she told him.

'I'll see you to the door.'

She got back into the car and he dropped her at the spot where he'd picked her up earlier. Now she wondered how she'd managed to put a damper on the nicest evening she'd had in months.

'I had a good time tonight, really, it was important. I'm sorry if I went a bit quiet. I think I'm just constantly moody these days. I let things get on top of me that shouldn't matter.'

'I understand how tough it must be for you.' Andrew's body relaxed and he smiled. Libby felt the now-familiar feeling and had a mad desire to touch him. Quickly she jumped out of the car.

'Goodnight.'

'Sleep well.' He spoke softly as if he'd read her mind and she turned purple, but it was dark so he couldn't possibly have noticed, she consoled herself later.

Chapter Forty-One

The summer had been good to Annie, so far. She'd worked hard, walked a lot, slept well and tried to eat better and she looked tanned and fit and healthy as a result. Having a 'proper' job had given her a new confidence and having some money had certainly helped too. Best of all was the warm, wanted feeling a 'best friend' gave her.

When the famous slapping episode was aired, the ratings were the highest of the year so far. Libby watched it with her and burst into tears. Max held drinks in the office to celebrate and made special mention of Annie in his speech. Everyone clapped and she was delighted and mortified in equal measure. Many colleagues she'd never even met came up to her to offer congratulations and she really felt part of it all at last. Finally she could stop pinching herself.

Even Marc's presence didn't bother her as much, although she flinched when she saw him put his arm around one of the extras, a real-life Barbie, all blond curls and big boobs and legs. Her skirt was about the same size as the doll's, Annie thought nastily. Orla caught her looking and suggested they go for a pizza.

Several of the cast and most of the crew decided to join them and it was a lively gang indeed that waved Annie off on the nite-link bus at about 1 a.m. They'd tried to persuade her to take a taxi, insisting that she was too famous to travel on the bus, and she laughed and accused them of being 'drunken, snobbish louts'. It was a fun evening and the scariest – and probably best – part of it all, she now admitted to herself, was what Max had told her. He had two bits of news. The first was that *The Late Late Show* wanted her to appear as a guest the following Friday.

'Why me?' Annie couldn't believe it.

'Why not you? There's been a huge reaction to your portrayal of the character and apparently viewers want to know all about you personally.' This made Annie very uncomfortable.

'Oh Max, I'm not sure. There's nothing to tell, really. Besides, I'd be so nervous talking about myself that I'd be sure to blow it and let you down.'

'Nonsense, you'll be great.'

'I've nothing to wear.'

'Well, it's a gig, you know. Talk to wardrobe. Tell them I said to get you something gorgeous. After all, you're promoting the show. I don't want you out of pocket.' He grinned at her. 'We'll arrange a wedding or something equally glamorous for Bobby to attend at some stage in the future. We'll find some use for a classy outfit.'

'Not judging by what she normally considers tasteful, you won't. It has to have Lycra, satin, cheap lace and a bit of ribbon thrown in for good measure, and that's only the bra.'

They laughed and she knew she had to do it.

'Besides, it's a powerful programme. It will be very good for Annie Weller's profile too, you know.'

'I know.' She sounded rueful. 'Sorry to be a bore.'

'You're a funny one sometimes.' Max put his arm around her in a fatherly gesture. 'I wish there were more like you, not a trace of ego. They should bottle you.'

Eventually she'd agreed that she'd talk to the researcher and at least find out more, but hadn't told any of the others. It was a gig many of them would kill for. Most actors loved promoting themselves. Annie hated it.

'I also have some other news.'

'No, enough is enough.' She was laughing.

'It's good, I promise.'

'Go on.'

'In fact, it's very good.'

'Now you have me curious.'

'Maybe I'll leave it for another day.'

'Not unless you want to go home with a black eye.'

'OK.' He smiled down at her. 'Try this for size. You've been nominated for best newcomer at the drama awards next month.'

If he'd told her she was taking a shuttle to Mars in a future episode she couldn't have been more surprised.

'You're joking.'

'I'm not.'

Annie was speechless. 'Where? . . . When?'

'I just got the call this afternoon. I was going to announce it but I decided you might faint on me.'

'Faint? Nothing so mundane. I'd have burst into tears and then collapsed at your feet and licked them, then run round the complex screaming hysterically. Believe me, by the end of it you'd have been praying for a faint.' She was laughing again. 'I can't believe it. You're not joking by any chance?'

He grinned back. 'No, Annie, I'm not joking. Are you pleased?'

'Pleased doesn't go anywhere near it. I am over the moon. My God, I can hardly take it in. You *are* sure?'

'I'm sure.'

'What does it mean?'

'Well, the ceremony is in Dublin this year so you don't get to travel, unfortunately. But it's big, in fact it's huge. I've never known it to happen so quickly before. Usually, they wait to see how an actress develops. But we sent in all your upcoming stuff and they included you. I reckon it was the scene with Marc that swung it.'

She shook her head in disbelief. 'What happens next?'

'The Press Office will do a release this week.

The Late Late Show got wind of it, that's one of the reasons they want you so soon. You're up against stiff competition this year. As you know, the awards cover England, Ireland, Scotland and Wales and there's some good stuff out there, so don't pin your hopes on winning. But it is one hell of an achievement to be nominated in your first year.'

'Listen, I know I won't win. But just to be nominated, I mean, it's like the Oscars of the TV world.'

'You deserve it, even if I am biased.' He shooed her away. 'Go tell.'

'No, not tonight. I don't want to hog the limelight. Anyway, I don't think I'd convince anyone because I'm still sure I'm dreaming.'

'I promise you, you're not. The papers will have it in a day or two anyway, so don't be coy.'

'I still need to get used to it myself. I won't be able to eat a bite now, you've ruined my appetite.'

Max sent her off. The rest of the night passed in a dream and she wanted to hug herself with joy every time she remembered. She couldn't wait to tell Libby, in fact she resolved to text her as soon as she got home. It was a habit they'd got into lately whenever one of them had news and was a good way of checking if the other was awake. They invariably ended up talking for hours in the middle of the night.

Annie thought about it again now as the bus pulled into the green at the other side of her estate. It wasn't her usual route because she was normally in bed long before the first nite-link driver came on duty, but it left her only minutes from home. She was still cocooned in a warm glow, so the fresh air was a relief.

She swung her bag and clip-clopped happily along the edge of the green, daydreaming in the dark, her thoughts a vibrant, heady mix. She was wondering about her dress for the night and imagining her father's pride. She had a nostalgic but not unpleasant longing for her mother and her mind was busy planning a pink and rosy future.

Afterwards, she couldn't remember when she first heard the rustle in the bushes behind, or the almost silent padding footsteps. She listened, half cocking her ear: was it her imagination? Much later, she would recall the exact moment she heard the laboured, heavy breathing.

Her first instinct was to stop dead and turn around. This was immediately followed by a desire to run, but she settled for quickening her step. In any event it wouldn't have mattered: within seconds she felt a hand across her mouth and her thoughts were viciously interrupted.

She was aware of the smell of cheap aftershave as he swung her round and whispered, 'Don't try to scream.'

The man was tall and wore a suit, which confused her and made her think her flailing body was over-reacting. Then she noticed it was a shiny suit. A shiny, grey, cheap suit and it smelt of cigarettes. He looked chillingly normal, though, dull greasy hair, slightly unshaven, sort of clean-living, as if he'd made a bit of an effort. But her abiding memory would always be stale smoke and cheap scent. And later alcohol and sweat.

He dragged her over to the bushes and shoved her to the ground. She was terrified but outwardly calm. And cold.

'Please, don't hurt me. I don't have much money but take what you want. My bag is over there—' she pointed vaguely in the direction of the path she'd been forced off, her breath coming in short gasps.

She didn't understand the shortness of breath, until she felt the pressure like a brick on her chest and realized she was struggling in a grip that threatened to cut off the air to her lungs. 'Please, I can't breathe.' She was getting slightly panicky: something told her she had to keep control.

'I don't want your money, Bobby. I should be paying you. Isn't that what usually happens?' His voice sounded hollow, his words slightly slurred.

She was concentrating hard on the details of his face, in order to convince herself she'd need to remember it for the police later. She had to believe in a future. It took a second to realize what he'd called her. It jolted her back to what was posing as reality.

'I'm not Bobby. I'm Annie.' Now calm again, she raised her body as much as she could, to sound more in control.

'I know who you are. I've watched your carry-on every night.' His words registered with chilling clarity. 'You're a whore and I'm going to teach you a lesson.'

347

He slapped Annie hard on the face and she fell back, hitting her head and suddenly struggling to keep him in focus. She knew she had to. If she lost consciousness she felt sure he would kill her.

He was straddling her. In slow motion she looked up and blinked and saw him silhouetted against an inky, starry, lovers' sky, as he unbuckled his belt and opened his fly. Her fear turned to sweat, which trickled down her spine and tickled her. He leaned over, ripped open her jacket and tore at her blouse and bra, exposing her breasts.

'You've been asking for it, teasing all the men, you bitch.' He spat on her and the contempt in the spewing saliva was somehow worse than what had gone before. His breathing was heavier now and he was closer. She could see the stubble glistening on his chin and the alcohol and sickly sweet aftershave made her gag. She'd often wondered what she'd do in this situation, like most women, but logical thoughts were easy in the cosy warmth of her bed or when listening to crime statistics or watching a police drama. How stupidly innocent it had been to decide that she'd kick and scream and tear his eyes out. Nobody had warned her about the paralysis that gripped every muscle.

He took a clean, shiny, innocent-looking Swiss army knife out of his pocket and held it near her neck. His breath was rancid. 'I'll fucking kill you if you make a sound,' he said smoothly, as if telling her the time. She looked up at him, feeling his body pinning her to the ground; yet on another level she seemed to be floating above it all, looking down on him.

With the knife in his right hand he reached over and yanked up her skirt with his left. Annie heard his laugh from a long way away as he gazed down at her childish white cotton pants. Later she thought it was probably the filthy, rasping laugh that finally galvanized her.

'Bitch. Innocent-looking whore, I'm going to—' She rammed her knee into his groin and he was momentarily stunned. Straightening her lower limbs, she forced her foot between his legs. It was as savage a contact as she could manage from her weakened position and was delivered with every ounce of strength she had. If he came close again, she knew she was in real trouble. Annie had only one scream in her. It was raw and strangled and seemed to come from very far away. When she saw him lunge at her with the knife she gave in immediately and was silent and flaccid. It was eerily calm for a split second.

'Hey missus, you OK?' She didn't connect the voice to a human until she heard the footsteps and felt her attacker stiffen.

In a flash he was off her and two teenagers took his place, staring down at her.

'What's going on?' one of them asked. She couldn't answer. 'Jaysus, Micko. Fuck, he was trying to bleedin' rape her.' It was a tough little gurrier of about fourteen. He looked as if he was going to cry.

'Get him!' screamed his pal, who had watched far too many over-eighteen videos while his mother was in the pub. They tore off and left Annie lying in the bushes, with her bruised face and bloody head and throbbing, exposed body.

One of them was back in an instant, having realized his priorities were not those of a cop. 'Are you OK?' He was looking at her in a very odd way.

She nodded, afraid. A tear trickled out, not because she was feeling sorry for herself – that was a luxury she couldn't yet afford – but because she knew she didn't have the energy to fight again and that gave him power over her. He took off his coat and an icy panic seeped through her.

It was only when he flung a big padded jacket over her that she realized his look was that of an embarrassed teenager.

'Thank you. Thank you so much.'

'Fuck, I'm just glad we came over, we thought you were only bleedin' messin' there for a minute. Me mate was afraid you'd kill us for interruptin' your . . .' He struggled to be polite. 'Your, eh, snoggin' session.'

'He jumped on me. I . . . I just got off the bus. I didn't hear him until he grabbed me from behind.'

'Don't worry. Seamo's fast. He'll get him and he's goin' to call the cops if he has enough credit. Here, Jaysus, sorry, I didn't realize, you're freezin'.' He was pulling off his jumper and winding it around her like a ball of wool. His kindness was the final straw. Annie felt her stomach heave and she was sweating and vomiting and shivering; it felt as if she was having some sort of fit.

'Jaysus, missus,' he stuttered his catchphrase again. 'Will ye stop it, you're freakin' me out.' The boy stood up and looked around as if contemplating making a run for it. But he didn't move and she was glad of his company.

'There's a car just pulled up over there. Hang on.' He was straining to see what was happening.

'Here's the pigs, eh ... I mean police.' It was probably his first ever sigh of relief at this particular intrusion, cops weren't exactly welcome where he came from.

'Over here! She's OK.' He looked down at her and murmured an unconvincing 'At least I bleedin' well hope so'.

Within seconds the place was like a film set. Lights blinded her and soothing words and kind gestures finally proved her undoing. She sobbed like an infant as she was led to the waiting car.

Chapter Forty-Two

Dawn was breaking in a pearly pink, cotton wool sky as the police car slithered gently to a halt, the driver afraid of hurting her further.

Garda John Reynolds skidded out before it had fully stopped, anxious to treat this woman like a lady to try and make up for the monster who hadn't. He held the door open and she inched sorely along the back seat, helped by a shiny, red-faced ban garda called Geraldine Cassidy who'd stayed by her side all night.

Momentarily faltering as she put her foot to the ground she was startled by her frailty as she limped like a ninety-year-old towards her front door.

'Give me your keys and let's get you inside for a nice cup of tea,' John Reynolds said. She'd had enough caffeine in the last few hours to keep Mr Tetley in business for a decade, but as usual Annie couldn't bear to rebuff a kindness.

'Thank you.' She handed him her handbag, unable to go about the menial task of locating her keys. He rooted around self-consciously and within seconds they were inside. The sight of familiar surroundings made her tearful all over again.

'Why don't you get out of those clothes and into your dressing-gown?' Geraldine asked kindly as John Reynolds battled with her electric fire and she headed for the kitchen.

'Would you rather a drink, brandy or something?' he asked because she was shaking so much.

'I don't have anything.' It was another pathetic reason for tears. He reacted by jumping to his feet.

'I'll be back in a second. Get changed,' he ordered in a gruff, country tone and she surprised both of them by obeying.

Twenty minutes later the three of them sat like tinkers around a campfire, Annie cradling a brandy balloon as if it were a lifeline. The useless electric logs flickered and cast a cheery glow but didn't deliver on their promise of warmth.

'Thank you.'

'You're more than welcome.' John Reynolds smiled at her and she felt safe. 'Is there anyone who could come and stay with you for a few days?' Annie shook her head, making no effort to hide her isolation.

'Family maybe, or a friend?' Geraldine was gently insistent.

'Only my father, and he's elderly, he wouldn't be able for all this.'

'Brothers or sisters?'

'They all live away from home. But I can ring my friend Libby later. I could go and stay with her, although I think I should try and stay here and get used to it.'

'Who's your friend Libby, then?'

'Libby Marlowe, she's a chef.' Annie gave a little smile.

'I know her, I met her the night her husband died.' Annie was startled out of her wanderings. John Reynolds was intrigued that they were friends. Libby Marlowe didn't seem her type. But he'd liked her just as he liked Annie now. They shared the same sense of vulnerability, which was rare yet very appealing, although the celebrity chef was, outwardly at least, a much less likely candidate for his protectiveness.

'Well, don't worry.' He was good at adapting to any situation. 'If you do stay here you can sleep soundly, we'll be watching the house all night.'

It was a lie, but a necessary one.

'What about tomorrow night?' It was an obvious question.

'I'll talk to the Super. We'll keep an eye on you and anyway, the man's unlikely to come anywhere near you again.'

'He must have been following me.' She'd told them the chilling details down at the station.

'Yes, well, he's sick and he won't get anywhere near you again.'

'Promise?' It was a pathetic plea.

'I promise.' He ignored the slight intake of breath from his colleague.

Annie relaxed for the first time. It was worth the fib. 'I'll leave you all our numbers.' He jotted them down and added his mobile number, a definite no-no, according to the Garda training manual. Quickly he folded the note, wanting to avoid another frowning glance from his partner, and thrust it in Annie's direction. He'd already offered too much.

It was an innocent, early summer's morning when they finally went and she sat huddled by the fire and tried not to panic.

She wanted to talk to Libby but was ashamed to tell her what had happened. She felt dirty. Finally, need won.

'Hello,' a sleepy voice answered on the third ring.

'Libby, it's me.'

'Annie?'

'Yeah, hi. Sorry, did I wake you?'

'Yes . . . no, it's all right. Is everything OK?'

'Not really.'

'Annie, what is it?' Libby was awake now.

'I . . . was . . . attacked . . . on the . . . way home. A man . . . jumped on me and . . .'

'Annie, listen to me. Where are you?'

'I'm at home.'

'Are you OK?'

'Yes . . . I think so.'

'Is there anyone with you?'

'No.'

'Stay where you are. Don't move. I'll be there in a flash.'

'No, honestly, I'm—' She heard the click and was still sitting there with the phone in her hand when the doorbell went twenty minutes later.

Libby had to bite back the tears when she saw her friend. Then she grabbed her and held her tight for ages.

'Oh Annie.' They both had a good cry.

'Tell me what happened?'

'It was awful.'

Libby cradled her like a baby and then made strong tea and laced it with some of the brandy and they sat for hours and talked through every second of the horror until Annie had cried it all out of her system, for the moment at least.

Chapter Forty-Three

The police, with Annie's permission, had contacted
Max Donaldson next morning. Max decided that
this wasn't the time for a phone call. He waited till
mid-afternoon before ringing the doorbell of the
spotless little house.

Annie hadn't really slept, although Libby had
tucked her up on the couch with pillows and a hot
water bottle, then slipped out to the shops for
supplies. She stood up immediately on hearing the
bell, then froze when she realized that it could be
him, looking for her again. Perhaps he'd followed
them home? Glancing out the window she saw a
strange car, and what little common sense she had
left told her he wasn't likely to visit her in broad
daylight in a shiny new BMW.

When Max saw her his TV-hardened heart
shrivelled.

'Annie, I am so sorry.' Her swollen face and eyes
were the last straw.

'Come in,' she said. She was past caring what he thought of her surroundings. 'Can I get you a cup of tea?'

He nodded absently, shocked at the change in the bright, lively girl he'd waved off less than twenty-four hours before and very unsure how to confront it.

Libby tiptoed in the door in case Annie was asleep, laden down with grocery bags.

'Oh, I'm sorry, I didn't realize you had company, although I noticed the car,' she said.

'The neighbours will really think I've made it, with those two machines parked outside.' Annie was trying to lighten the situation.

'Hello, Libby Marlowe.' She held out her hand. He knew who she was, of course.

'Max Donaldson. Annie, will I come back later?'

'No, no. Libby's my friend.'

'Actually, Max, it would help me if you were going to be here for a while. I need to slip home and get a change of clothes.'

'You go, please.' Annie jumped up. 'I'll ring you later.'

'I'm not going anywhere. I'm staying here tonight or you're coming to me, OK? I won't be long. Nice to meet you, Max.'

'You too.' He was surprised by her easy manner; he'd heard stories like everyone else. Just shows you, he thought now.

When Libby left, Annie poured it all out again and the details shocked Max further. The police information had been sketchy.

'Are you sure, Annie? He definitely called you Bobby?'

She nodded, not wanting to deal with it either. 'He said he'd watched me ... teasing the men, night after night. Said he was going to teach me a lesson.'

It was his worst nightmare and a situation he'd never had to handle on any of his training courses. 'OK Annie, look, our priority is you,' he assured her. 'If you want to stop playing the part right now I'll work something out. I just want you to know how sorry I am. I wish it hadn't happened. I've never heard of anything like this before, so I'm unsure of myself, but you are the main concern here. I promise we won't desert you.' He smiled weakly and his presence helped where his words couldn't reach.

'I can't do the *Late Late*, you understand?' Right now she couldn't imagine ever facing anyone again, let alone an audience of almost a million.

'Of course. I'll handle it, you just concentrate on getting well.'

That was the problem. She wasn't sick, except in her head.

'I'm OK really. I am so grateful that it didn't ... that nothing happened. But, I have to rethink things. I'm not sure I can go on playing the part. The thought that he's still out there, that there are others who might see me like that ... or think it's real ... or ...'

He made no effort to argue, only to soothe. 'I

understand. But do nothing for the immediate future. When are you due in again?'

'Not until the week after next, but I'm in every programme on air for the rest of this week and that scares me a bit.' He had forgotten that.

'Let me think about things. I'm not promising anything. It could be a huge undertaking to try and edit you out. I simply don't know if it's even possible with the storyline. But give me the rest of the day to view them and talk to the writers, OK?'

'I know you can't simply stop showing the programme. I wouldn't want that. It just . . . makes me nervous.'

They talked for over an hour and Max left as soon as Libby returned. He promised to call her next morning. That evening's programme had very little of Bobby in it but Annie watched her every movement on screen and wondered if the man was watching it too. Libby sat with her and rubbed her hand when she looked scared.

She hardly slept again that night, despite lashings of cocoa from Nurse Libby, who insisted on sleeping over, and a reassuring phone call from Garda Reynolds. Her dreams were all of monsters wearing shiny suits.

Next morning, Max telephoned as promised.

'Annie, I've had a look at the rest of the episodes. I think they're OK, to be honest. There's nothing graphic that I can see. How did you feel about last night?'

'Fine. Listen, Max it's all right, I know I'm just being paranoid.' It was hard to explain it to him. She didn't want that monster leering at her, even if only on TV. She didn't want him even to see her at all and think his filthy thoughts and possibly plan further revenge. It didn't make sense, yet she knew Max would understand.

'There's virtually nothing in there that should worry you, I promise. I was able to edit you out of one scene early and presentation are going to run a promo at the end to make up the time.'

She thanked him and he mentioned that a few people wanted to know if they could visit her. Annie felt she couldn't face anyone yet so she fobbed him off, saying she'd lots of visitors. In the office Mike Nichols was worried about her and organized two huge bunches of flowers to be delivered to her home, one from the cast and another from the crew.

That evening it all got on top of her again and she cried a bit, but found it brought no relief. Libby had gone to drop stuff off at the office and Annie hated being alone. She was sitting curled up like a kitten, shivering, convinced she was going mad, when the doorbell rang.

She broke out in a cold sweat and huddled up, terrified, sure he'd found her again.

After what seemed like hours the knocking stopped but she didn't hear a car drive off and that frightened her even more. She knew none of her neighbours would just drop by; they were used to her working odd hours and respected her privacy.

The phone rang and she jumped on it, grateful for any contact with normality.

'Annie, it's John Reynolds. I'm outside your door. I've been knocking for ages.'

'Oh thank God.' She dropped the phone and ran to the door in case he left. He got out of the car and came quickly up the path.

'Is anything wrong?' She looked as if she'd seen a ghost.

Annie felt her lower lip give way. She walked into the living room ahead of him to avoid crying all over his uniform again.

'What is it?' She shook her head.

'Please, tell me. We can help you.'

'No-one can help me.' Suddenly she was angry with the whole world, everyone pretending they could make it better.

He got up and made two strong cups of tea. They drank it and he promised they were doing all they could to catch her attacker.

Shortly after he'd left, Libby returned and the anger that had been brewing all day finally erupted like hot froth from a cappuccino machine.

'*Why* does this keep happening to me?' She glared with wild eyes at Libby, who didn't understand the question. 'When am I ever going to get a break? I've never done anything wrong, never hurt anyone and yet I keep getting all this shit thrown at me.'

'What else has happened to you?' Libby only knew bits and pieces of Annie's life, she realized.

So far in their friendship it had all been about her. 'Tell me everything. I want to know it all.'

'You name it, I've had it happen to me. When I was ten my mother died and I was left to look after them all. I wasn't able to be a kid any longer. I needed my mother more than any of them, they were boys, they had each other. I had no-one.'

Libby looked at Annie and saw the face of the abandoned child she'd been, and it nearly broke her heart.

'I'd no-one to talk to when my period came, I had to go to the library and buy a book. I was too scared to go to the chemist so I used to sneak out old towels and cut them up every month.' She felt no embarrassment at telling Libby these intimate details, had no idea she even still remembered the minutiae. And once the floodgates opened and the memories started to emerge they were like a torrential downpour. 'I never got the chance to go to college, never had anyone to buy me nice clothes, no-one to share things with. Then, when I eventually plucked up the courage to leave home it was a huge struggle. I'd no money, no job and nowhere to live. All I had was my dream of being an actress. And just when things started to turn round for me, I got cancer.' Libby reached out and cradled her like an infant.

'Oh, Annie, my poor baby.' It felt funny being in this role; Libby was used to being the protected one.

'Even then, I never felt sorry for myself. I just accepted it and got on with life. It was hell. I was so lonely. But I got through it and I started again and the struggle was harder and then I got the biggest break of my life.' She looked at Libby, tears streaming down her face. 'And now it's all ruined again. I can't do it any more and it's something I wanted more than all the other things put together. He ruined it!' She jumped up and wanted to lash out but there was no-one. 'He ruined everything.'

Libby put her arms around her but she punched and kicked and screamed and Libby held her friend and let her.

'I hate him. He's fucked up my life. And I hate God for doing all this to me. I can't take any more of this shit. And the fucking police are useless for not catching him . . .'

On and on it went and the words got louder and her face became purple and distorted and she pummelled as hard as she could.

Like all explosions, it fizzled out at last. Annie sank to the floor and Libby went with her, and she cried it all out of her system and they grew closer than most friends do in a lifetime.

After a while it was gone and she sobbed quietly for all that had been taken away the other night and Libby picked her up and carried her to the bockety old sofa and put her down and covered her with blankets and sat with her until the room became dark and chilly.

'I'm sorry, I must have dozed off.' Annie woke abruptly and looked at Libby as if she'd been dreaming and she shushed and reassured her.

'Would you like a cup of tea?'

'I'd like another brandy like I had last night.'

'At your service. And then I'm cooking you some real food. I can't believe the number of tins and jars you've got in here.'

'I told you I can't cook. I wasn't lying.' Libby heard the first touch of lightness in her voice.

'Well, it's all fresh food for you from now on, so you might as well give in gracefully. Your diet is a disgrace.'

Annie smiled weakly. 'I don't know where that all came from . . . earlier. I . . . I didn't mean to hurt you, you must be black and blue. I'm not usually so . . .'

Libby shushed her. 'Sounds like you needed it. I'm sorry you've had to put up with so much. It doesn't seem fair.' It had been a sharp lesson for Libby too.

'You'd think I'd be used to it by now. That's what annoys me most. I guess that when I got the part, I started to believe the hype. I thought the past was all behind me and I fell into thinking that life was going to be good. What an idiot, eh?'

'Annie, don't let this ruin your life.'

'It already has.'

'No it hasn't.'

She shook her head. 'The dream is over.'

'Why?'

' 'Cause I can't go on with it.'

'With what?'

'This part. Bobby. I'm not prepared to be her any more. And if I'm honest, I know giving up

365

now represents the end of the line for me as an actress. It's time to quit dreaming.'

'But why on earth would anyone give up on their dreams? Especially as you've just started to make the biggest dream of all come true.'

'He ruined it all.'

'Annie, he'll only ruin it if you let him. The police will get him eventually and in the meantime, all you have to do is not take any chances.'

Annie looked at Libby as if she'd dropped out of the sky. 'Take a chance. What planet are you from? I'll never go out again on my own, for God's sake.'

'You will.'

She shook her head sadly. 'I can't. I couldn't even answer the door in my own house. I'm petrified all of the time.'

'That'll pass, I promise.'

'No it won't.' She was angry again. 'You don't know what it's like. I can still see him, still smell him, still feel him all over me. And nothing you say will ever change that.'

Chapter Forty-Four

When Libby left the next morning Annie scrubbed herself clean – again. Soap was no good. She still felt dirty. This time she filled a small bowl with washing-up liquid and added a few drops of bleach, then she dipped her sponge into it and scrubbed her body until she smelt like a swimming pool. Her skin was red raw when she finished towelling herself dry and she made cocoa and went back to bed. This time she slept for a full two hours as exhaustion finally took over from fear.

As soon as she opened her eyes the memories came storming back, but she lay there and let them wash over her and slowly admitted that last night had helped and it didn't feel as bad this morning.

Her skin felt scratchy and rough, as if someone had used sandpaper all over her body and a faint school toilet smell still lingered. She got up and made tea. Around lunchtime, the phone rang.

'Annie, it's John Reynolds here. I just wondered how you were feeling.'

'Better, actually.' He was so nice, always calling and checking in. 'Are you on duty still?' She knew he had been on nights, so was surprised that he'd still be working at this time of day.

'No, I'm at home.' He sounded as if he'd been caught out. 'I . . . eh, just wanted to make sure you were OK before I headed off to bed.'

His kindness touched her more than he realized. Then her doorbell went.

'Oh, could you hang on, there's someone at the door . . .' She opened it without thinking, which pleased her later when she remembered.

'Delivery for Annie Weller.' The middle-aged man was hidden behind two enormous bunches of flowers. Annie was astonished.

She read the cards aloud to John Reynolds and he was delighted. 'There you are, you can't give up when all those people care about you,' he said.

They chatted for a while. The kind gestures had helped Annie feel less sorry for herself and she sat on the sofa, surrounded by masses of colour and thought about it all again.

It was three-thirty before she dressed in leggings and an old sweater, brushed her teeth and tied her hair back and splashed her face with cold water. She resumed her position on the couch, which was where Libby found her later.

'You're dressed – good girl.'

'You sound like my mammy.'

'Well, I feel old enough today.' She looked around. 'Where did all these amazing flowers come from?'

'Friends. I guess I have a few after all.' She was chuffed to bits as Libby hugged her.

'And you have me, don't forget that.'

'You're my best friend.' Annie smiled without a trace of embarrassment.

Hours later, as they tucked into a gorgeous chicken dish that Libby had thrown together, the phone rang and it was her father, wondering why he hadn't heard from her for a couple of days. Annie made an excuse but was glad that he'd been worried about her.

Ten minutes later it rang again and this time she recognized the accent.

'I'm getting great service from the Garda Siochána today,' she teased him. 'Two phone calls from you and one of your colleagues called in earlier.'

'So I hear. Well, it's not every day we have a major celebrity on our hands. Wouldn't want you complaining to the media about us.'

He was pleased to hear her laugh. 'I'm just checking in. I'm on my rounds,' he said. 'Is there anything you need?'

'No, I'm fine, thanks. Everyone is being great. I feel well and truly spoilt.' She smiled at Libby.

'You deserve it.'

'Thanks. Anyway, the neighbours will think I've finally taken to drugs if any more squad cars are seen outside my door.'

He promised to call the following day and when she hung up Libby was watching her carefully.

'I don't want you to give up.'

Annie was about to say that she already had, but what came out was 'I'll try.'

'Good girl. Do it for me.' She was satisfied for now.

'But I'm warning you, if life throws one more heap of shit in my direction, don't you come near me, or this time I'll really break a few of your ribs.'

'Why me? What did I do to deserve such venom?' Libby wasn't in the least put out.

'Because I wouldn't be doing this if it wasn't for you. I have to get you to go home somehow.' She was smiling, but suddenly she looked scared again. 'Please God, let them get him soon.'

'They will. But for now, I want you to ring me if you get scared at any time, OK? Day or night.'

Annie looked thoughtful for ages and Libby was content to sit quietly. 'I was asked to do *The Late Late Show*,' she said at last.

'Really. When? Why?'

'Because of the part. And also because I've been nominated in the Best Newcomer category in the Drama Awards next month.'

'What? How come you never said that before now?'

'I just heard the night of the . . . thing. I've only really thought about it now.'

'That is amazing. And you were going to give up. Well, that settles it, you can't.'

'You are so bossy.'

'Annie, I know very little about drama and acting, but I do know that just being nominated

370

for an award of this stature could change your career. Even the publicity could change things for you. This is huge.'

Annie nodded but said nothing.

'So get out there and start living again.'

It was the hardest time for her to start again. Getting back on her feet after the cancer had been a piece of piss compared to this. But Libby had convinced her she had to try one more time. She took a deep breath.

'Maybe I will do the show, after all. But I wouldn't want to mention this, you know . . .'

'Then you shouldn't. But remember, that's how men like him survive. Because women are afraid.' She felt she'd pushed her enough. 'Anyway, you'll do the right thing, I know you will.'

Chapter Forty-Five

Libby had eventually returned home and Annie had even come to stay for a day or two. Things were slowly returning to normal but Libby was feeling tetchy. There were many reasons why. Andrew Harrington was finishing work tomorrow and it bothered her. They'd taken to having cups of teas and long chats, and he'd been great when Annie was there. They got on like a house on fire and her friend had even told him what had happened, which surprised Libby.

'I really like him, you know. There's something about him,' Annie casually mentioned as she stacked the dishwasher.

'So do I.'

'*Like* like, or just like?'

'I don't know.'

'Well, don't be afraid if you really like him.'

Libby just nodded and Annie knew when to quit. 'I'll say just one more thing.'

'Have I ever been able to stop you?'

'If he's a gardener then I'm Dame Edna Everage.'

'Why do you say that?'

'He's too . . . everything. Too well spoken, too well dressed. Look at his hands, for instance. They're not the hands of a manual labourer.'

'I know exactly what you mean. But why would he pretend? That's not normal. And he does know a lot about horticulture, he's always blinding me with Latin names.'

'I dunno. We all have our secrets. Look at the pair of us. Who the hell are we to comment on normal?'

Libby pushed him to the back of her mind now and sat at her desk, determined at last to finish going through her stuff. She was still getting letters of sympathy and it was draining, having to respond to each one, but in the past few weeks she'd managed to get on top of most things. She also wanted to spend as much time as possible with Annie and she, in turn, was helping her clear the house. It was their own private unspoken pact, to each help the other move on.

A major source of angst was her mother, with David's father hot on her tail. They were not happy about the house being sold, in varying degrees. Christina Marlowe was furious. Charles English was worried. Libby refused to discuss it with either of them, anxious not to let her secret out. Keeping it to herself was the only way to avoid leaks, although not involving her mother and her father-in-law was proving tiresome. They were not easily put off.

She'd had a huge argument with the estate agents this afternoon as well, and it was all adding to the tension in her neck and shoulders. They wanted to advertise the house and have two viewings a week. John Simpson, who'd been handling it, seemed to agree with them. She was adamant there would be no punters traipsing around her home and told the managing director, who'd been a business associate of David's for years, in no uncertain terms.

'I don't want any open viewings. There'd be journalists, photographers, God knows who else, swarming all over the place.'

'Libby, I understand your concerns. But we'd get names and addresses and phone numbers of everyone who came through the door.' Dan Jordan was making every effort to keep her sweet. For her part she marvelled at his naïvety and wondered how these people got to where they did in business. She'd had enough.

'Dan, are you insane? We're talking tabloid journalists. They'd eat up your little minions for breakfast. No. No. No. I do not want the house advertised in the papers. I will not have a sign put up. You have enough wealthy clients to get word about discreetly that the house is for sale.'

'But we'd get a much better price at auction.'

'Frankly, I don't care. It's been valued. You and I both know what it's worth. Sell it privately, Dan and furthermore I will hold you personally responsible for every single person who walks through this door, even by appointment.'

That was the end of it and she hung up feeling stressed and thankful for all that David had taught her. She knew how to hold her own in these situations.

Even thinking about it now made Libby anxious. She needed a drink but she wasn't going there. Failing that, she needed to get out for a while. Glancing at the table she saw a copy of her latest book that she'd left out weeks before, to give to that garda who'd helped her on the night of David's death. For some reason he'd stayed in her mind, so she picked up the telephone to enquire if he was on duty. He was.

She let down the roof of the car and swung out into the traffic, feeling the warmth and the summer wind in her hair. It was not something she normally did, it made her feel exposed and vulnerable, in spite of her dark glasses. All these back to nature conversations with her gardener must be getting to her.

She pulled into the garda station and made her way to the public counter, hesitating as she entered. It was not the sort of place she was used to visiting and she was surprised that it was old and dingy.

'I'm looking for Garda Reynolds.' Her voice held an authority that people rarely argued with.

'Just a moment.'

In a minute he walked into the room and smiled at her. The junior had obviously recognized her.

'Miss Marlowe, hello. What can I do for you?'

She took off her glasses. 'I just wanted to thank you for being so kind to me the night of my husband's death. I'm sorry it's taken me so long to call.'

If he was surprised it didn't show.

'I was glad to be able to help. I'm very sorry we had to meet under such circumstances.' At that moment a drunk smashed through the door and lurched at them. Libby recoiled.

'Where's the fucking cops when you need them?' He hiccupped and stared at Libby.

'Fine-looking woman y'are, missus. Are they givin' ye grief?'

Libby was taken aback and John Reynolds moved quickly.

'Miss Marlowe, please come this way.' He ushered her into a small side room and summoned a colleague to deal with the man, who was still shouting at Libby. 'Hey, are you dat one off the telly?' And when he got no response, 'Fuckin' stuck-up bitch.'

'Sorry about that. Can I get you a coffee?'

'No, thank you.' She was suddenly awkward, unsure why she hadn't just posted a note. She thought it was because she wanted to see him again, to remind herself of that night. She was afraid she was forgetting.

She thrust a card into his hands. 'You were very kind to me at a very difficult time and it helped me a lot.' She hoped he didn't think it was money. This was all getting too complicated. 'I

wanted to give you this book – for your mother.'
She was uneasy. 'You mentioned she was a fan, I
think.'

He looked really touched.

'She is. A huge fan. This will be very important
to her.' He smiled shyly. 'She still asks me about
you. I think she worries.'

'Well, tell her I have a new series starting in a
couple of weeks and I'm fine. Should I sign the
book for her?'

'Yes, please.' He took out a pen.

'What's her name?'

'Martha.'

Libby wrote a note on the inside page and
handed it to him.

'Thank you. I appreciate it.' If he'd been wearing one, she felt sure he'd have tipped his hat. It
was that old-world courtesy again that she remembered so well, and it was endearing.

'Pleasure.' There was nothing else to say.

'I'd best be going.'

He saw her to the door. 'I believe you're a friend
of Annie Weller's?'

'You know Annie?'

'Yes. I only met her recently.' He didn't want to
give away any confidential information, unsure
how much she knew.

'You know then about what happened to her?'

'Yes. I was on duty that night.'

'Are you the person who's been so kind to her?'

He blushed. 'One of them, anyway.'

'Of course, she mentioned Garda Reynolds. I

377

just never made the connection.' She was silent for a moment. 'Please find him quickly. I couldn't bear it if anything else bad happened to her.'

'We're doing all we can, believe me. And meanwhile, I'm keeping a good eye on her neighbourhood.'

They said goodbye and Libby left a message on her friend's answering machine. 'Annie, it's me. I just met Garda Reynolds. You never told me he fancies you. So don't you dare lecture me again about my gardener. Hey, on second thoughts, maybe we could double-date.' Smiling at the thought of a date with Andrew, she hung up.

At home, she felt restless and poured herself a glass of wine. She thought about Andrew once more.

They'd become close since the night of the restaurant, in spite of her half-hearted attempts to keep him at bay. And he hadn't really pursued it: the string that seemed to bind them together was tugged at by her, mostly. She'd taken to inviting him in for coffee, or going out to eat with him at lunchtime. His calmness and sense of being at ease with life was like a drug she'd become addicted to. He was the most quietly assured man and she'd never met anyone like him. Yet still she knew nothing about him really. In the evenings, she had to stop herself pleading with him to stay and have some food with her and in the last few days she'd made an excuse to be out, so that he wouldn't think she was desperate. Now that he was leaving she realized how desperate she really was.

She spent the evening soaking in a bath, dreading her fortieth birthday, which was fast approaching. Her last birthday had been a week after David died and no-one had been in the mood to celebrate, least of all her. Even thinking about forty made her feel old and flabby.

'Stop thinking about it,' Annie had laughed when she mentioned it the other day. 'You've only just turned thirty-nine.'

Now she smothered her body in some wildly expensive French stuff, had a face pack, trimmed her eyebrows, painted her toenails, all things she'd normally have left to the slaves at the beauty salon. It was too difficult now to make idle conversation and anyway, she thought she'd probably have to cut back on such extravagant gestures in the future. Any thoughts of her finances made her run for cover so she poured herself another glass of wine and lay on the bed until a restless sleep finally claimed her.

Chapter Forty-Six

Next day she watched Andrew as he worked, wondering how they'd say goodbye. She had a horrible feeling it was more of a preoccupation for her than for him.

She kept finding excuses to go outside and when she finally came face to face with him she felt nervous and he looked relaxed.

'I picked you some of these, thought you might like them in the kitchen. The perfume is quite something.' He handed her an enormous basket of purple, scented cabbage roses. They were exquisite.

'I thought you didn't like to pick them?'

'I don't normally but there are so many in the rose garden they won't be missed, in fact it will encourage a new flush of late blooms.'

'I won't be here to see them.' She was sorry she'd never taken more interest in the garden now.

'Well, you can always plant some more in your new home. Any ideas yet on where that will be?'

'No. I'll wait until this place sells. I've already told them I want a long closing period or alternatively I'll rent until I find somewhere.'

'A new home is very exciting. A chance to start again.'

'I'll have to get you to sort out the garden for me.' She tried to be casual. It was the first mention of a future meeting and she hoped her longing didn't show.

'I'd pictured you not being interested in a garden, somehow.'

'Well, you've converted me.' He laughed and she wanted to say more, but it didn't seem appropriate.

They made small talk and she asked him what time he expected to finish.

'About six, I think. Not much left to do, really.'

'I have to pay you. I don't have enough cash.' It was an excuse to see him again and she felt he knew it.

'A cheque will be fine.' He smiled the lazy 'I've just had great sex' smile that she'd come to know so well. 'Or else I'll send you the bill. A famous client is always easy to track down.'

She could ignore the put-down, partly because it was so charmingly wrapped.

'Will you call in for a drink later? And maybe stay to supper?' she asked. Oh God, please don't let that sound as desperate to him as it does to me, she prayed and didn't look at him in case those brown eyes were pitying her. 'Although you may have other plans?' she felt compelled to add. She imagined he could see right through her.

'I'd like that. Or maybe you'd prefer to go out for a bite?'

'No, I feel like cooking, if you can bear it.'

'I can bear it.' He watched her the way he always did, then he smiled and resumed his work and she strolled off, happier.

When she returned home at around five he was still working so she jumped into the shower and changed into her comfiest jeans and a baby blue strappy T-shirt that she'd always loved. She wished she hadn't put on so much weight but there wasn't much she could do about that right now. 'I'll start tomorrow.' It was the same mantra every day.

At about six-thirty he still hadn't appeared so she went in search of him and found him putting his stuff away.

'Come on, a cold drink awaits you.'

'Thanks, I could do with one.'

They sauntered indoors in the balmy, fragrant air and again Libby wondered how she'd ever taken her idyllic life for granted.

'Glass of champagne? I think you deserve it.'

'A beer would be fine. I'm not really a champagne drinker.'

'Well, I insist. You've done an amazing job and I'd like to say thanks.' The truth was she already felt a bit light-headed, having him here again. They were almost like a couple and she felt young and heady and didn't want to think too much about it. The bubbles would intensify the giddiness she so wanted to savour.

'Sure, but could I have a quick shower first? Would that be OK? I brought a change of clothes just in case, because I thought of inviting you out for some dinner tonight anyway.' The idea of him thinking about her in that way was doing more than any bubbles ever could.

'Of course, you know where it is. Towels in the hot press on the left.'

When he returned he'd changed into another pair of jeans and a clean, soft blue shirt. His hair was wet and she could smell him and it was a raw, sun-dried smell.

She handed him a glass of Cristal and he smiled his thanks and asked, 'What are you cooking?'

'A chicken dish with glass noodles and lots of mint and coriander and lemon. Sort of Asian flavours, I think, although I never really know how it will end up. But you said you liked Thai so that's what I'm aiming for.'

'Can I help?' No-one had ever offered before. David had had no interest, preferring to sit and chat or watch sport on TV, and other visitors were mostly intimidated by her.

'Yes, great, you could chop some chillies and garlic. Do you like it spicy?'

'I love spicy food.' He grinned and she grinned back.

'How hot?'

'Very hot.'

'OK, you got it.'

As they talked and worked, Andrew was close by her and she felt much more relaxed.

'What's your next job?' Libby asked.

'I'm not sure if I'll take another one on. I need to make a few decisions. Knuckle down to some real work.' He changed the subject, something he was very good at doing. 'What about you?'

'I got asked today if I'd do the *Late Late* next week.' She thought for a second. 'Oh my God, I think Annie is on that night too.' She smiled. 'Now that would be fun.' She made a mental note to ring her later.

'God, you really are famous.'

'You mean you doubted it?'

He shook his head. 'Will you do it?'

'I think I have to. The series needs all the help it can get and a slot on that show virtually guarantees ratings.'

He didn't ask any more but the silence wasn't uncomfortable. They worked contentedly and sipped their drinks and the early evening radio kept them company and the late evening sun kept them warm. It was simple and uncomplicated and different from most other nights she'd known in this house. She was surprised to find that it suited her very well.

'Let's eat in the conservatory.' She grabbed cutlery and plates and all the bits and pieces. 'That OK by you?'

'Fine.'

Libby set up the table and opened the french doors and the heady scent of lemon and vanilla drifted in from the garden. She lit some candles and then felt silly and started to blow them out.

'Leave them. They make the place look magical.'

My God, he must think I'm a pathetic old widow, she thought, fleeing the room until her face had cooled.

They ate the delicious warm noodle salad with some good bread for mopping up the tangy dipping sauce and Libby poured some white wine.

'Enough – that champagne has already gone to my head.'

'Well, I presume you're not driving and some strong coffee will work wonders.'

'This tastes amazing. Thank you for cooking for me.'

'It's a pleasure.' She was proud as punch.

For pudding she had defrosted a lemon tart and now she served it warm with softly whipped cream and mascarpone. It was by far the easiest meal she'd had in a long time.

Afterwards, Andrew coaxed her back out to the garden.

'Don't you ever get fed up with it?'

'No, come on, I want you to smell some of the things that only give off scent at night.' He almost lifted her out of her chair and then made her take off her sandals as he guided her out through the doors with an arm not quite around her, but close enough for her to be able to feel him near.

As they walked and laughed she knew she was going to kiss him eventually and the thought terrified and tantalized.

She was down on all fours because he'd insisted

she sniff something very small and as she went to get up she was laughing so much she stumbled slightly. He reached out his hand to steady her. She took it and he pulled her up and she was very close to him and suddenly neither of them was smiling any more and, heart thumping, she leaned over and kissed him lightly on the lips. She knew he wasn't expecting it and he looked at her enquiringly but this time she brazened it out.

'Thank you.'

'For what?'

'For doing all this and being so nice and saving my sanity.'

'I think my fee has just gone up. That wasn't part of the original contract.'

They were very close, in the heady sweet smell of a summer twilight and Libby wanted to kiss him properly more than anything else right now, so she reached up and stroked his face with her hand and this time he made the first move. It was a long, slow, moist kiss and it made her insides melt.

When they broke apart he seemed to want to lighten the mood and she was sorry. 'Come on lazybones, there's more to see.' She entered into it a bit reluctantly this time, because now the only thing she wanted to do was to kiss him and touch him and have him close again.

Only when the sky had finally turned inky did they head back inside. 'I'll help you clear up,' Andrew said.

'I never clear up.'

'Well, I do. I don't want you grumbling about me in the morning.'

'Will I make some coffee?'

'I'd love some.'

They loaded the dishwasher and she was pleased when he hand-washed her copper pan. 'Are you sure you're not a chef yourself?' she asked.

'Uh-uh, but I know that good pots and pans are special so I didn't think you'd risk the dishwasher.'

'Most men would never have thought of that.'

'I'm not most men.' He was teasing but she knew it was true. They drank coffee and made chit-chat and finished their wine. At around eleven, Andrew stood up to leave.

'I'd better go. Lots to do tomorrow.'

'But you're not working?'

'Not officially, but I've a great deal of catch-up, bits and pieces to attend to.'

'Will I call you a cab? I don't even know where you live.'

'No, don't worry. I live in town and the walk will do me good.' He picked up his jacket and slung it over his shoulder, then lifted his rucksack. 'Thanks for dinner. I enjoyed it—' another slow, half-smile. 'And the company too.'

They strolled out the side door and Libby walked with him to the gate with a dry mouth and a heavy heart, now that the goodbye moment had come. She didn't want any more partings.

'Thanks for everything.' She looked at him and

hoped he could see something in her eyes, even if she wasn't sure what it was herself.

'I had a good time.' He gave her the grin that should never be allowed loose on vulnerable women. 'Once the first day was over, that is.' She thumped him and he reached out to protect himself and caught her hand, and she knew she made the first move again but all that mattered was that they were kissing. And this time he held on to her.

'I don't want you to go.' At least now she'd put words to it.

He looked at her for a long moment. 'I'm not sure that's a good idea.'

'Me neither.' She shrugged. But her eyes said please stay.

He took her hands in his and searched her face. 'Are you certain about this?'

'Yes.'

'It's not too soon?'

She knew it should be, didn't know why it wasn't, but the timing felt right and she didn't want to go to bed alone again with this longing.

She shook her head.

'In that case I'd like very much to stay.' The slow, deliberate way he said it made it sound like a lifelong commitment. After a moment they turned and walked in silence back to the house, not exactly holding hands but with arms touching and fingers wanting to.

Chapter Forty-Seven

'Come on and I'll show you the best view of the garden.' She was smiling at him as she flicked off the lights.

He halted her by turning her round to face him and putting his two hands on her shoulders.

'Sure you're sure?'

'Positive.' And she was.

It was odd to be climbing the stairs with him behind her. She walked over to the huge bay window, fingered a switch and the curtains drifted silently apart. Another flick and the garden resembled the Blackpool illuminations. Libby controlled the glow until the lights were like fallen stars. And as she looked out and wondered how on earth she'd got to where she was now, he turned her again to face him and ran one hand lightly from her shoulder to her earlobe. This time there was no doubting who kissed who. As it deepened and became more exploratory, she edged closer until it was impossible to tell where one body ended and the other began.

Instead of going straight to bed he led her to the big couch where she'd been lonely so many nights and pulled her down beside him, then he kissed her again and again and watched her in between. Although she had no recollection of wanting sex since David had died the urge now resurfaced as if it had been smouldering away for months and not dead, as she'd often feared. She couldn't wait to feel every bit of him naked and glued to her, yet still he made no move to do anything other than kiss her and touch her face and hair and arms and fully clothed back.

He looked at her and smiled. 'How are you feeling?'

She wanted to lie but it was out before she knew it: 'Horny.'

He threw back his head and laughed and when he looked at her again his eyes were dark and she realized she hadn't really touched him. Now she ran her fingers through his hair and kissed his eyes and his ears and his neck, breathing in the clean, healthy smell of him and giving full rein to feelings she'd had since she first saw him in her garden early that memorable morning. He looked so sexy sitting there, long lean body stretched out on her couch, eyes shining, hair that was too long and too tousled.

She stood up and pulled her T-shirt over her head and started to unbutton her jeans. He stopped her. 'No.'

She was flustered.

'I want to do that.' He was standing now too.

'Then please, please, touch me properly. I seem

to have been waiting for this for a long time.'

He ran his hands over her back then lightly up her arms, and kissed her neck and her shoulders and burnt a trail between her breasts, but it seemed like hours until he actually touched them and even before he did that he stood back to look at her and take in her shape as the now heavy breasts struggled to finally escape the bits of lace. He pushed the thin straps from her shoulders in slow motion and continued to look at her face as the garment fell away; his breath was audible as he cupped her in his hands and stroked her lightly with his thumb.

Still watching her intently, he knelt down and kissed each nipple with a feathery tongue then went further down and slipped off her jeans. And she stood there impatient to be rid of the final barrier but he made her wait, kissing her stomach before running his hands over her bottom, then down the back and up the inside of her legs. He continued his tortuous route, causing her to moan with pleasure when his hand came to a stop, and with frustration when it didn't try to go further. Only after another few minutes of torment did his fingers tug at her thong.

She stood in front of him feeling sexy as hell and then it was her turn to undress him and make him gasp as she slipped her hand inside his jeans. She played him at his own game now, bending down and staring at his swollen penis, not touching him until eventually her lips found the tip and she covered him with kisses. She could sense him trying to restrain himself and she pictured him coming in her mouth and it made her very wet. Without warning he pulled her to her feet and led her over to the bed where they faced each other.

'I don't think I can stand much more of that.' He rubbed her cheek lightly.

'I haven't even started.' She felt brazen and liked the power.

'You're beautiful.' He smiled at her but she shook her head.

'I used to be beautiful but the year has taken its toll and I sure as hell haven't helped. But tonight I feel gorgeous and sexy and I like it.'

He grinned at her. 'I'm glad. And you are beautiful, inside as well as out.' He kissed her again for the longest time.

'And in case I forget to tell you later, I had a great time tonight.'

He looked at her. 'The night hasn't started.'

'I know.'

His eyes narrowed. 'Oh Libby . . .' He stroked her hair and held her away from him and studied her carefully, taking it all in.

'You are one gorgeous-looking man.' She looked up at him as if seeing him properly for the first time. 'I hadn't realized quite how gorgeous.'

'Thank you.' He smiled but didn't look embarrassed, as most men would have.

'I want you so badly.' Her eyes seemed black and cloudy.

'Come here, I want to feel you close to me first.' He pulled her to him but they didn't kiss, and

finally she found the absolute skin on skin closeness she'd longed for.

It was different from any other sex she'd had.

When finally it was over, he pulled her down
beside him and wrapped her in the soft white cover
and they lay with their arms around each other and
exchanged silly grins and funny little secrets.

When Libby awoke the translucent, early morning
light greeted her and it took a second for her to
realize that she'd fallen asleep beside him, with her
back to him, spooned in close for added comfort.
It was the first time she hadn't felt the awful ache
of regret that had been her usual early morning
companion for so long.

His arm made escape impossible and when she
stretched tentatively he moved and turned her to
face him.

'Hi.'

'Hi.'

'Are you OK?' His favourite question.

She smiled and he kissed her and she looked
longingly and shyly at his body in daylight as they
explored each other, and made love again and she
didn't care about her tousled hair or early morning
breath or the faint traces of make-up she knew
must still be visible. It didn't seem to matter, in fact
the sleepy, dishevelled look of her seemed to
arouse him further.

When she awoke for the second time it was
much, much later and she was alone.

Chapter Forty-Eight

'I'm clever enough not to try and compete with a chef when it comes to cooking, but I thought I couldn't go wrong with coffee and toast.'

Andrew was standing over her, grinning. He was dressed and she wondered if it meant he was leaving. 'Thanks.' She hitched herself up against the pillows and pulled the sheet up around her, feeling very naked.

''Don't go all shy on me now, please.' He sat down on the bed beside her and poured the fragrant liquid into china cups that looked too delicate for his hands. 'How are you feeling after all that sleep?' His eyes were grinning at her.

'Fine. Thanks.' He seemed in control of the situation and Libby didn't like it. She took the offered cup and he sensed she needed space. 'OK if I have a quick shower?'

So he was leaving. 'Fine. In there. Towels on the left.' Libby pushed her hair back and added milk to her cup, anything to keep busy and avoid catching his eye.

She drank thirstily as insecurities she didn't even know she had came flooding in, swiftly followed by a cold feeling of apprehension. Her mind galloped along and all her thoughts were variations on a theme, helped along by the fact that he seemed too relaxed and confident; smug almost, she imagined.

Oh God, I was so easy. I practically begged him. I bet he can't wait to tell his friends.

It was gathering momentum and it was dangerous.

What if he talks about this? Worse, what if he goes to the papers?

She needed to chat to Annie about it, to try and make sense of it all. All the plans she'd carefully put into place to protect her privacy were suddenly threatened. She felt naïve and stupid. He was a gardener, for God's sake, a handyman. No formal training. This story could be worth a fortune.

It was building into a modern-day classic, rich older woman and her bit of rough. A small voice of reason tried hard to intrude but she was feeling panicky and pushed it away.

'Fancy going out for breakfast?' Or lunch, as it will be soon?'

He was back, looking even better with wet hair and gleaming skin and all she could think of was making her escape.

'Em . . . let me take a quick shower first.' She was out of bed in a flash.

She made her exit and jumped into the shower, then immediately imagined he might be seeing some of her personal stuff, letters she had lying on the table next to the bed, so she jumped out in record time and dried quickly, dressed and combed her hair and brushed her teeth. She was back in five minutes.

He was sitting on the bed watching Sky news.

'What do you think about an early lunch?' he asked.

Maybe he was hoping they'd be photographed together, had someone standing by, even. Don't be mad, he didn't know he'd be staying here last night, she told herself as the shrinking, sane bit of her brain finally broke through the paranoia.

'I'm not really hungry. How about another coffee?'

Anything to buy time.

'Fine. The newspapers have arrived downstairs, in case you fancy a browse, see if you're in them.' He was smiling, teasing. It was the worst thing he could have said at that moment.

What was he doing in the hall? Had he been in her study? Oh God, she'd told him some stuff about why she was selling the house last night. This would make a fantastic story.

'Libby, are you sure you're OK?' It was only the second time she could remember him using her name and he made it sound soft and sensuous, yet different from how it had sounded when he called out for her last night.

They were in the kitchen and she had her back to him. Now her heart was beating faster and her stomach was churning.

'I'm fine, Andrew, it's just that . . .' How could she explain it without sounding like a looper? 'I just think . . . we should take it slowly, that's all.'

'Fine by me.'

'That's if we're taking it anywhere at all.' She laughed to hide her nervousness.

'Is that what all this is about?'

If only it were that simple. She knew she must represent a great catch for him, even if only in the short term. She wasn't silly enough to believe he had any long-term intentions towards her.

She looked at him now, standing tall and healthy and uncomplicated in her 200,000-euro kitchen and wanted to believe that he was what he appeared to be. But somehow she doubted it.

'I suppose, it's just that . . . my life is very complicated and . . . I don't normally do what I did last night and I have to be careful, in my position . . .' She didn't elaborate, because it was all coming out the wrong way.

'What are you trying to say?' He had been flicking through the newspaper and now he came to stand beside her. He tilted her face up to look at him.

'Libby, I know this is hard for you but there's something going on in your head and you need to tell me so that we can sort it out.'

'I have to be careful about my privacy . . .'

'So, what, you think we shouldn't be seen in

public together?' He was grinning at her. 'We've already been out in public together. I'm suggesting brunch. I could be anyone, your brother even, and I promise not to kiss you or slap you on the bottom so no-one will get the wrong idea. How's that?' He winked at her.

'You don't understand, I . . .'

'Libby, we're friends, we have been almost from the start.' He was talking to her as if she were a child. 'And getting to know you was . . . different – at least it was for me. I liked the fact that it happened slowly, almost by accident. Anyway, you're not typical girlfriend material.'

'What exactly do you mean by that?'

'Well, I know you're . . . famous.' He was smiling again, indulging her. 'Your lifestyle is different from mine. And what happened last night changed things between us, I think we both know that. But what we need to do now is really get to know each other, spend some time together as a couple, when I'm not your gardener, your employee.' He paused briefly. 'There are lots of things about me I need to explain too. My job, for instance—'

'No. Please, I need to think about this, I . . .' Libby had a horrible feeling that maybe he was a journalist or something. What was it Annie had said about him? She cursed herself for not looking for references. This was turning into a nightmare.

'Let me explain.'

'No. Let's just take a bit of time, talk later in the week. Please.'

'OK, fine, I'll leave and we can meet in a couple of days, but only if you tell me what's really bothering you.'

She took a deep breath. She had to test out her theory, see his reaction. Then at least she'd know. 'The papers would pay big money for a story like this about me.'

Something flashed across his face, but his expression didn't change.

'You think I'd talk to the newspapers about us?' He looked puzzled, as if convinced he'd got it wrong, but then when she didn't deny it he looked hurt, then angry and she knew she shouldn't have said it.

'Have I given you any reason to think I'd behave in such a manner?'

'I don't know, it's just, I've been let down before . . .'

'And couldn't you have given me the benefit of the doubt, for a while at least, until you'd got to know me a bit better? Spent the weekend with me, asked me anything, checked me out, whatever it is you do with people before you decide whether they're good enough for you?' It was the first time she'd seen him really pissed off, but it was still a quiet, controlled emotion.

'Look, I know I'm being foolish and stupid,' Libby said. 'Why would you want to talk about us? It's mad, I know that now. After all, there isn't really an us, is there?' Her laugh was nervous and she was looking for reassurance.

None was forthcoming. He looked straight at

her for a long moment, then gave her what she later thought was a pitying look. He spoke slowly, but very deliberately, as if making his mind up as he went along. 'Up until a moment ago there was a definite possibility, but now . . . no. There isn't an us.'

The look of sadness, the lack of bitterness, the quiet, determined voice hit her right between the eyes and she knew she'd seriously misjudged him.

'Andrew, look, I'm sorry if I've offended you, it's just I've had so many bad experiences . . . and Annie said something . . . and I was afraid you might be a journalist because I don't think you've been a gardener all your life.'

'I'm a doctor.'

'*What?*'

'I studied medicine because it was what my father wanted. But horticulture is my passion, always has been. Then I got caught up with teaching and I went to North America to study for a couple of years and suddenly I was at the top of my profession and I'd never really stopped to think about whether it was what I really wanted. So, I took a year off, time out to see how it would work out if I indulged my hobby.' He was talking to her as if she was a stranger. 'That's all, nothing more sinister.'

'Why didn't you tell me?'

'It's a long story. And up until last night it wasn't important.' He sighed and seemed to come to a decision. 'I'd better go.'

'Please don't. Look, let's go out to brunch and talk. I'm really sorry, I know I was being ridiculous, I'll—' She was jabbering.

'No.'

'I've said I'm sorry. Now you're the one who's being stupid. I . . .' She struggled to make it OK, unused to not getting her own way.

'Stop.' He was staring at her intently. 'Either you trusted me or you didn't. It's a gut thing and it's really quite simple. I think you've made it clear where you stand.' He looked a bit lost, started to say something more, then shrugged and turned away. Picking up his bag that he'd abandoned so casually the night before, he walked out of her life and Libby let him because she was too proud to beg.

Chapter Forty-Nine

'He's a *what*?'

'Doctor.'

'I don't believe it.' Annie laughed. 'Or maybe I do. Now that I know him I think he'd make a perfect doctor.'

'I slept with him.'

'Ah here, this is too much for the telephone to take. It'll go up in smoke in a minute. Are you coming to me or I am going to you?'

'Put the kettle on, I'll be there in ten minutes.'

Annie was the only person in the world Libby knew wouldn't judge her. As usual she sat quietly and listened, then rallied round her friend.

'You poor thing, I can imagine what was going through your mind.' She gave Libby a hug.

'It was mad, I sort of freaked out while he was in the shower. I could feel it building up. I was convinced he was going to sell his story to the tabloids. Ruin whatever miserable chance I have of surviving this last few months and the lousy series that I can't wait to see the back of.'

Annie giggled. 'I don't think he was ever going to do anything to hurt you, Libby. He's too ... honest looking – sincere – self-confident. I dunno ...' she struggled to find the right word. 'Too nice, I suppose.'

'Much too nice. And I've ruined it.'

'Maybe not. I think we'll have to come up with a plan. First, coffee and some chocolate.'

'I forgot to tell you, by the way, I've been asked to do the *Late Late* as well this week.' Libby was glad to have some good news, even though she herself was dreading it. 'So let's get that out of the way first, before I screw anything else up.'

Annie danced around her tiny kitchen. 'I can't believe it. This makes it bearable, knowing you'll be there too.'

'Well, I'd have been there anyway. I was going with you, whether you liked it or not.'

The day of the show dawned and Annie was anxious, despite Libby's encouragement. On the surface at least, things had returned to normal. It was only a little over a week since the incident, but she had made a determined effort not to let it ruin her life. Max Donaldson was relieved and the show was providing her with a car to take her to and from the studio at all times. Mike Nichols had called around; he'd been calm and measured and had helped her considerably by assuring her that they would all do everything they could to help her recovery. Her new pal Orla sent a lovely card and telephoned regularly and the police were brilliant, especially John Reynolds, who had by now become a friend. She saw police cars almost every night in her estate and it was a comfort, but nothing could take away the fear that lurked at the back of her mind and turned silly, everyday things into a challenge, making her realize how much she'd taken freedom and peace of mind for granted.

Annie didn't walk alone any more, didn't browse or stroll or window-shop and never day-dreamed. She lived in a state of heightened alert and the tension never seemed to leave her stiff, taut back. Libby was minding her like a baby, turning up at all hours and bringing her shopping, and even going to the dentist with her. It was keeping her going.

Doing *The Late Late Show* was going to be a nightmare, however, and she cursed her stupidity over and over again. She should never have agreed to go on national TV and talk about herself. It was the most out of character thing she'd ever done. It was like showing off, name-dropping and bragging all rolled into one. It was like 'Look at me, aren't I terrific.'

Still, it should be short, that was the only con-solation. A quick chat about the part, another few minutes about the nomination and she'd be out of there like a shot. Max had kept his word: she now had a gorgeous, burnt-orange dress, sleeveless with a fitted top, long and well cut. It made her look tall and thin. It was easily the most elegant creation she'd ever seen and it was completely the opposite to what Bobby normally wore. She was ordered to get her hair done – 'have the works' – on the programme budget and Janey from make-up had promised to stay back and give her a soft, girl-next-door look without the hard lines and textures her character loved. Yet despite all the attention she was a bundle of nerves as she read through her notes that afternoon.

Libby was also feeling unusually nervous about doing the show, but then she'd had a faintly sick stomach since the frightful morning with Andrew. It was almost a week and she hadn't heard from him – not even a bill. When Mrs O'Connell returned Libby asked her casually how she'd found him.

'George met him at some night course and he'd just taken a year's sabbatical from the hospital, so George offered him some work. He's a doctor, you know,' she said and smiled smugly.

Now you tell me. Libby felt like slapping the grin off her face.

'Yes, so he said.' Eventually, she didn't add. 'Eh . . . do you have a number for him?'

The older woman was thinking. 'Well, George told me he'd be back in the hospital from next week, so I don't think he'll be available again, except maybe the odd day here and there. I'm sure I could get a number, I know they keep in contact. He seems to keep himself to himself, though,' she added approvingly. 'Nice man, very handsome. Good breeding, you can tell.'

Pity I couldn't. Libby was annoyed and ashamed all over again.

She left her housekeeper and went back to her study, cursing herself for not getting Andrew's home address and telephone number, at least. The more she thought about him, the more she realized how ridiculous she'd been: she knew now she'd been wrong not to trust her instincts. It was driving her mad.

The other nagging, uncomfortable thing about the whole episode was finding out how much she missed him. It was like a dull ache in her stomach. She'd got so used to having him in her life, to telling him things, stupid little nothings that she'd never have told anyone about, not even David. He'd become her friend and then her lover and the sex had been gentler and softer yet just as passionate as anything she'd experienced. Now, when it was maybe too late, she realized it was a powerful combination she wasn't prepared to live without easily.

'He suits me, somehow,' she told Annie one night. 'It's like he goes well with the person I now am, and that's very different to how I was when David was alive.'

'I think you suit each other.'

'I wish he thought so.'

'You're terrific and he must see that.' Annie was her usual loyal self. But Libby knew she'd been far too busy worrying about what 'everyone' would think if it came out that she was having an affair with the gardener. She felt like the worst snob now, especially as Annie already liked him and she knew her mother would never pass judgement without getting to know Andrew first.

She spent the day getting organized. A couple of her favourite boutiques had sent her several outfits on appro. They knew her taste exactly and she'd insisted it had to be black.

In the end she'd settled on a long tailored coat jacket that nipped in at her waist, or what was left of it, and flowed away at her hips. With it she wore a long black crumpled silk skirt with a chiffon wrap around the waist and a heavy lace corset-like bodice that made her boobs look huge.

Her hair had been expertly cut and her hair-dresser was to meet her at the station for a final fixing; so would her favourite make-up artist, who was flying in from London. She'd had a facial and manicure that morning. The only good thing about the week was that she'd eaten very little so her face had lost some of its puffiness. She whiled away the time getting her jewellery ready and organizing shoes, some glorious new French underwear and tights so sheer they were almost invisible.

She spent most of the day on the phone to Annie, who laughed at her preparations and refused the offer of a loan of her hair and make-up team.

'You're a big star, I'm only an actress with a tiny part.'

'Start as you mean to go on, darling.'

'I think I'll wait for a while before I start making demands.'

'You really are the most un-actressy actress I've ever met. You need to be more dramatic, throw a few tantrums. Make lots of demands. Get your agent to handle it. Mel organizes everything for me.'

'Listen I'm fine, Libby, honest. But I am so nervous.'

'Me too.'

They arranged to meet at the station before the show.

When the limousine arrived to collect her, Libby really wanted a glass of wine to steady her nerves but knew she couldn't indulge. At reception she was greeted by Leo Morgan and an array of producers.

'It's good to have you back.' He kissed her and as they made small talk, Libby realized he was another whose calls she'd never returned.

Her dressing room was the best they had and her agent had ensured that fresh flowers, fruit, magazines, a TV and a hundred other niceties vied for her attention along with a bottle of good champagne in an ice bucket. Libby knew she'd do justice to that afterwards.

'So, who else is on?' Annie asked the guy who came to meet her at reception. The cool, trendy researcher was happy to show her the running order. There were one or two major international names, a couple of bands she was really into and, of course, Libby.

'She's one of my heroes,' Annie said like a child. 'She is so gorgeous and, do you know something—'

'Well, between you and me she's been overindulging a bit lately, I'd say.' Annie never got to tell him they were friends; Dan Pierce was a talker, and not known for his discretion. 'Looks years older. Still, she's an audience-puller, that's for sure, although she won't talk about what everyone wants to know.'

'You mean her husband?' Annie couldn't believe what she was hearing. He gave a knowing nod.

'Well, why on earth should she? She doesn't need to do this and it's all very recent.' Annie was surprised at how fiercely protective she felt.

'Well, if you believe the rumours, her new series is a turkey, so I'd say she does need this.'

Annie decided she'd listened to enough: she was not taking any more shite from this horrible little man.

'It is not, I've seen it,' Annie lied. 'It's fantastic and so is she and what's more, she's a friend of mine so please don't say anything else, particularly as you seem to be talking through your arse.' Annie headed for her dressing room, feeling she'd just thrown the first tantrum of her career. The room was empty except for one fake leather chair and a lamp with a broken shade that had seen better days. She sat quietly and went through it all again in her head, just to be sure she wouldn't run out of things to say. Then she went in search of her friend.

Libby was putting pressure on the make-up artist. 'I think I need a stronger base and more well-defined eyes, Zoe darling.'

The younger woman, who'd known Libby Marlowe for years, had been shocked by her appearance and was trying to minimize the lines and soften the jowls.

'I don't want you to look too made-up.'

'Trust me – these days I need it.'

'No, you look great, but I was going for a soft, dewy look.'

'Not this time, Zoe. I need the works. Pile it on.'

It was an unusual situation, because in all the years she'd known Libby, Zoe had never known her to get it wrong. Normally, she knew exactly what worked and what didn't. But tonight she was already looking a bit too 'done'.

'Why don't I give you stronger lips and cheeks and see how it looks?' The artist was using all her powers of persuasion. She'd been working for an hour and a half now and still Libby wanted more emphasis on her gorgeous eyes, even though less was definitely the way to go.

Eventually, they compromised. Then her hair was fingered and waxed and Libby added some amazing jewellery and the overall effect was a sophisticated, confident, beautiful woman who, when you looked at her closely, seemed older and more tired than her legion of fans would remember.

Annie was totally taken aback when she saw the penthouse suite version of her bedsit dressing room. 'Hello, I don't think I'm on the same show as you, bitch.'

The styling team were startled at their easy familiarity.

'I did try to tell you but you ignored me as usual. Anyway, who are you again?' They hugged and Libby asked what she thought.

'You look fabulous, as always,' Annie insisted. 'I'm just sorry that I have to go on after you, you're a hard act to follow.'

'Make-up – too much, too little?'

'Well,' Annie wanted to be honest. 'I might take it down a bit round the eyes, but that's just me.'

Zoe wanted to hug her but instead seized the moment. 'I agree, so you're outnumbered.'

'OK, I know when I'm beaten.' Libby sighed and Annie settled down and watched, enjoying the build-up. Soon Libby was called and they promised to meet back in the room for a drink afterwards.

'Have mine poured, otherwise I might drink from the bottle and I'm sure you're not normally so gross,' Annie warned.

'Zoe, lock up the booze. This woman can't be trusted.' Libby laughed and blew her friend a kiss.

The interview was exactly as she expected. They plugged the new series and showed several clips. There were questions from the audience, which Libby had been shown in advance. She dealt with them easily. Towards the end came the bit she'd been expecting.

'We all know that this year has been perhaps the most difficult of your life, with the sudden death of your husband and I suppose I can't let you go without asking how you're coping.'

She couldn't imagine what the audience would think if she told the truth. That she hadn't been coping at all, except for the past few weeks. She wondered if Andrew was watching. 'I'm fine, getting there,' she said. 'It has been a very difficult time but I've been helped by the thousands of letters I've received and I'd like to say thank you to everyone who wrote and sent cards and flowers. Far too many to acknowledge.' She knew when to stop.

At last the charade was over. She got a huge round of applause and they immediately cut to a commercial break. She was indeed a hard act to follow.

Annie was waiting in the wings on the other side of the studio. Libby waved and held up two crossed fingers. 'Break a leg,' she mouthed.

'You were brill,' Annie mimed back.

'Do you two know each other?' The producer was surprised.

'Yes, we're best friends.' Libby felt like a child. 'She's great.'

'She sure is. Going places fast too, I'd say.'

Annie's nerves had vanished. Libby seemed to fill her with confidence. She chatted easily, as if she'd been on the champagne already, and was funny and natural and charming and the audience loved her. There were lots of questions about Bobby and she assured them she was nothing like her. Then they talked about the research she'd done for the part and she had them in fits telling them about turning up for the audition dressed like a hooker.

As it ended came the question she wasn't prepared for. 'So, how has all this changed your life?'

'I don't think it has, really.' She was still relaxed. 'I'm exactly the same as I was, I live in the same house, go about my life as normal.'

'And what advice would you give to a young girl starting off with all the same hopes and dreams as you've just told us about? Have there been any negatives, for instance, any bad experiences?' It was a totally innocent question, and if it took Annie by surprise then her answer nearly knocked her out.

It was the 'young girl' thing that did it. She felt a responsibility. Her mouth felt dry. She looked at him for what seemed like minutes, then said, 'I did have one bad experience, actually and I am only sharing it tonight in case it might help someone else, because I was pretty naïve, really.' She recounted the events of that night in a calm, flat voice, feeling the now familiar cold sensation slide down her spine and he had to tease out the details of the story very gently and was careful not to push when he saw she was close to tears.

'And has he been caught?' Annie shook her head and he sighed.

'Well, you are very brave to talk about it. I want to tell our viewers that I didn't know anything about this before now and I'd like to thank you for sharing it with us tonight. It must have been very painful for you.'

'It was.' She managed a weak smile. 'But I'm getting there and I'm determined not to let it take over my life.'

He paused to allow enough time to effect a change of tone. 'Can I finish by wishing you every success and good luck in the awards and we hope you'll come back and talk to us again soon. It's been a great pleasure to meet you. Annie Weller, ladies and gentlemen!'

One final, deafening round of applause which she couldn't hear properly because of the ringing in her ears, and then it was all over. She kept a smile pasted to her face until she heard the music that meant they were on a commercial break.

Chapter Fifty

Libby was waiting in the corridor as a pale-faced Annie almost fell into her arms.

'My God, you poor darling.' She was full of concern. 'What a brave thing to do. I can't imagine how you must have felt, talking about it again.' She shuddered and ushered the worn-out girl inside.

'I hadn't intended to, as you know.' Annie was still close to tears. Libby handed her a glass of champagne.

'Here, sit down. Don't talk for a minute or two. Just relax,' she ordered.

'I can't get over this dressing room. I don't even have toilet paper and you've got champagne in an ice bucket.' Annie looked around, still in shock.

It was a completely ridiculous conversation to be having after what had just happened. Libby looked almost as surprised to be told that all dressing rooms weren't the same. 'I thought you were exaggerating earlier.' They laughed together, as they seemed to often. It usually helped.

'You were extraordinarily brave. I couldn't have bared my soul like that.' Libby, suddenly wistful, was envious.

'Well, it wasn't in the plan. You were the only one I spoke to. Christ, my father was watching and he didn't even know,' Annie remembered, putting her face in her hands. 'Oh God.'

'Ring him now and get it over with. Then you can forget about it.' Libby thrust her mobile in Annie's direction. 'Would you like some privacy?'

Annie shook her head. This was going to be difficult.

The conversation was tearful. He was upset and bewildered. 'I'm sorry, I know I should have told you but I hadn't really come to terms with it myself yet,' she explained.

He struggled to understand. 'And you're sure he didn't . . . interfere with you in any way?' It was all he wanted to know.

'I'm sure, Dad.'

They talked for a while and she hung up, dejected and disheartened all over again.

'Look, why don't we get out of here? There's a car waiting outside. Will we go somewhere quiet, maybe grab a bite to eat?' Libby asked.

'I couldn't really touch food right now, to be honest. I feel sick. Christ, will this ever go away?'

'Right, that's settled, you're coming to my house and I'm minding you for the rest of the evening. Get your things.'

The stretch limo was another source of amazement to Annie, miles away from her smelly taxi where the only elastic was in the leopardskin covers.

Despite her earlier protests, Annie managed a small plate of the delicious tiger prawns with chilli and garlic that Libby produced effortlessly.

'Every time I eat with you here I wonder how I ever manage to go back to flat, brown burgers and flaccid chips.'

'That's another thing I keep meaning to say to you. I'm teaching you how to cook. No excuses. You need to stay healthy after your illness.' Annie wasn't about to protest. 'Anyway, I need something to keep my mind off doctors.'

'Maybe one of us will get food poisoning and he'll be the doctor on call at the hospital. I could cook a few of my specialities. That should put one of us in bed for a week, at least.'

They giggled and made mad plans until Annie yawned twice in as many minutes.

'My God, it's two-thirty. I'd better call a cab.' She couldn't believe they'd been talking for hours.

'Sure you won't stay?' Libby didn't want her to go.

'No, if it's OK with you I think I need to go home tonight. Sort of puts the incident into perspective.'

'I know.' Libby hugged her friend. 'The car's waiting outside to take you home.'

'What?'

'Why not? That's what he's there for.'

'You mean there's some poor eejit sitting in a car for all this time waiting on me? I feel terrible.'

Annie picked up her bag and scarpered. Libby followed.

'I'm telling you, he's fine.'

'I'll have to give him a tip.'

'You're mad. One doesn't tip a driver.'

'This one does. Goodnight darling.' Annie did her Libby impression, air-kissing her friend on both cheeks.

She hoped the neighbours could all see the limo. It meant she'd arrived. It said famous as clearly as if it was written in dust on the bonnet. She gave the driver a 10-euro note and legged it, still mortified at keeping the poor man from his bed. Her answering machine was winking at her as she opened the door and there were two messages to ring John Reynolds.

'John, hi, it's Annie Weller.'

'Annie, I was beginning to get worried about you. I called round earlier.'

'I was on the *Late Late*.' She was feeling very pleased with herself.

'So I hear. I believe you were brilliant. Where are you now?'

'At home. Where else would I be if I got your message? Not very good detective work, Garda Reynolds!'

'True enough. Well, young lady, you'll have to get yourself a mobile. I've been trying to get hold of you for hours.'

'I was with Libby.' Annie still loved telling people they were friends and now she sounded like

418

a child telling an adult she'd just been given a puppy.

'Wow, you really are becoming quite a celebrity. What d'you think of her now that you know her?'

'Listen, I've been in love with her for years. There's nowhere for this one to go except that we become lesbian lovers.'

He roared laughing. 'Have you been drinking?'

'Champagne. Dom P.'

'You're not cheap, I'll say that for you. Listen, could I call round in the morning?'

'Come now.'

'Sure?'

'I'm making tea and toasties.'

'I'm on my way so.' He was still smiling as he hung up. He hoped his news wouldn't upset her.

Twenty minutes later they sat by the glowing two-bar, munching and sipping. She told him all about the show and how she hadn't intended saying anything but it had all come out.

'Actually, that's what I wanted to talk to you about.' He watched her carefully. 'We've got someone in custody.'

The bubbles left her system in an instant. 'You caught him?'

'We think so.' He hesitated, not wanting to upset her. 'He was mouthing off in a bar in town when he saw you on the show. Seems he was out of it. The barman rang us and tipped us off.'

Annie was terrified all over again.

'He was . . . watching me?'

He nodded slowly.

'And bragging about . . . what he'd done to me?' It all came flooding back.

'You and a number of others, it seems.' He wasn't sure how much to tell her.

'There were others?' Her eyes filled up.

'Annie, don't let him get to you, please.' He wanted to hug her again. 'You were lucky. It seems not all of them got away.'

Annie cried when she heard it and he put his arm around her.

'I think it's the champagne. I'm sorry.'

'It's OK. Perhaps I should have left this until the morning but I thought you'd want to know that he's not a threat to you any more.'

'Or any other woman.'

'Or any other woman. There is one more thing . . .' He watched her closely again. She looked up sharply.

'What?'

'We need you to identify him.'

'No, please, don't ask me. I couldn't . . . look at him.'

'It's important, Annie. I wouldn't ask you otherwise.'

She sat and said nothing for a long time, staring into the plastic flames.

'OK.'

'Good girl. Don't worry, I'll be with you.'

'Will he be able to see me?'

He shook his head.

'When?'

'In the morning.'

'What time?'

'Say I call around about eleven?'

'OK.'

He stood up, knowing he'd spoiled her evening. Damn, he should have left it until morning. He cursed his lack of sensitivity.

'Thanks for telling me.'

'Are you sure you're OK?'

Annie nodded but didn't look it. He left her biting her lip. She wanted to ring Libby but didn't want to disturb her. She'd moaned enough at her for one night.

When she awoke she was surprised to discover she'd slept at all, but last time she'd looked it had been four-thirty and now it was after nine. She jumped up and into the shower, despite the headache that threatened to saw her head in half.

She shivered each time she thought about what she had to do today. Her phone rang non-stop, everyone calling to congratulate her and offer support. Very few on the show knew exactly what had happened and all her new friends were horrified. Marc Robinson was one of only half a dozen or so who didn't call.

John Reynolds arrived bang on time.

'Did you sleep?' he asked.

'Yes. I can understand why people get hooked on alcohol. It makes you forget.'

'Yes well, it's not a sedative I would recommend.'

'Yes sir.' She was smiling in spite of her nerves.

'How's the head?'

'Someone shoved a Black and Decker drill between my temples in the middle of the night.'

He handed her a packet. 'These might help.'

'You're an angel. I was just about to ask if we could stop off on the way.'

Minutes later they were in the car. 'God, the neighbours will be apoplectic. Last night a stretch limo left me home. This morning I'm taken away in a squad car.'

'I should have handcuffed you, just for effect.'

They drove the short journey in silence, with Annie getting more and more agitated.

'I'm really not sure I can do this.'

'It'll be all over in a few seconds.'

'You're positive he won't be able to see me?'

'Certain. All you need to do is call out his number. That should mean the end of him for a long time.'

'What do you know about him?'

'He's married with two small kids.' Annie sucked in her breath at the news. Somehow that made it worse.

'What about his wife?'

'It seems there's been a history of violence, although she has never made a formal complaint.'

'Where do they live?'

He mentioned a village on the outskirts of Dublin, a quiet area where everybody knew everybody else. Annie thought about how some poor woman with two babies must be feeling this morning. She wasn't quite sure if that strengthened or weakened her resolve.

She felt that everyone in the station was looking at her as she was led down a grimy, institutional corridor and into a small room. There were two other uniformed officers waiting, a man and a woman. The introductions were monosyllabic.

'Are you ready?'

Annie nodded. 'Just explain to me once more what will happen.' Anything to avoid coming face to face with him.

'I'll just pull up that blind–' John Reynolds pointed to a large square window – 'and all you have to do is tell us which one you think it is. They'll be holding cards numbered one to six.' He smiled reassuringly at her, then nodded to the woman, who slowly raised the grubby blind by pulling on a tatty cord.

Annie saw him immediately. His eyes were red rimmed, he had more stubble, but there was no doubt in her mind. The only thing that surprised her was that she didn't tell them straight away. Instead, she kept her eyes glued to his face, remembered again the shiny, scratchy cheap suit and the gloating eyes of someone relishing his power. But what got to her most of all was the smell of him that assailed her nostrils, even though she knew it was all in her head, because the room they were in was soundproofed, she'd been told earlier. But no amount of padding could keep out the stench, the sweat, the sickly sweet aftershave, the stale smoke that clung to him and had clawed its way beneath her skin and above all the sour, whiskey-laced, putrid breath.

'If he's not there, or if you're unsure, just say.' John Reynolds was watching her watching him.

'It's number two.'

'You're sure?'

'Certain. Can I go now?'

'Yes of course.' He nodded at his colleagues. 'I'll take you home.'

She wanted out of there as quickly as possible and didn't speak until the car had pulled away.

'Was he the one you arrested?'

'Yes.' She was relieved, even though there was no doubt in her mind.

'Will he go to prison?'

'Yes.'

'For how long?'

'For a very long time. For all his bragging, he wasn't so clever in the end. He gave a lot of detail to the guy in the pub. We've got loads on him. We're working on a couple of leads for other stuff as well. By the time we're finished with him he'll have confessed to a whole lot more, I'd say.'

She had a frightening thought. 'I won't have to go to court, will I?'

'Shouldn't think so. Forget about him, Annie. Start getting on with your life.' Easier said than done, he knew, but he smiled at her warmly and she was once more glad of his kindness.

'It was hard in there, I hadn't expected to feel so . . . raw. I could smell him, you know.'

'He won't harm you again. By the time we're through with him he won't be hurting any other woman either.'

'What about his wife and kids?'

'I haven't been across that end so I don't know much.'

In a way it suited Annie not to have to think about them. She was silent for most of the journey.

'Would you like to come in for some tea?' she asked quietly.

'I'd better be getting back to the station. There's a lot on. I'll check in with you later. Are you sure you're OK?'

'I'm fine, thanks.' But she wasn't really.

Chapter Fifty-One

'Hello.'

'Hi, it's me.'

'Annie, hi. Everything all right?' Libby didn't like the sound of the voice.

'Yeah. I was just wondering if you're free for lunch?'

'Come round. I'm making pizza.' Libby was trying to keep busy.

Annie hopped into a taxi immediately, wanting company.

Libby knew there was something wrong but sensed her friend wasn't quite ready to spill it out.

'Can I help?' Annie asked as they entered the kitchen.

Libby was about to refuse automatically, as other people's sloppy, inept ways of working irritated her. Something about her friend changed her mind. 'Yes, actually. Pizza and salad OK for lunch?'

'That'd be brilliant. But why didn't you just order in?'

Libby could feel her nose creasing. 'Ugh, I can't think of anything worse. All that thick, dry, doughy base and gloopy tomato sauce.'

'But that's what makes them so tasty.' Annie was amazed. 'When's the last time you had one?'

'I've never had one and please God I never will. Just the look of them is enough.'

Annie was giggling again.

'What's so funny?'

'That look on your face.'

'What look?'

'Like you've just stepped on a particularly runny dog pooh.'

Libby burst out laughing. Annie was the only one who ever slagged her and she liked it. It was all so easy with her. Somehow, the easiness bit reminded her of Andrew and she pushed the uncomfortable thought firmly away.

'Right, give me instructions.' Annie wiped her eyes and sipped the wine spritzer Libby handed her.

'Well, I've just softened the onions and garlic for the sauce. You could add a couple of tins of tomatoes, some dried oregano, then season it and oh, add a pinch of sugar. Then you could pick some fresh herbs from just outside the door and tear them up and we'll add them at the last minute.'

Annie was trying to remember it all. She was just about to throw in a heap of salt and pepper when Libby slapped her hand.

'Always taste before you season.'

'Yes, your majesty.' Annie was giggling again

and it was infectious. 'What herbs will I pick?'

'Any of the soft ones, parsley, basil, chives, maybe a bit of sage.' Libby was rolling out the bases she'd made earlier. She always made a pile and stuck them in her freezer.

'How will I know what's what? There are millions of them.'

'Smell them, taste them.' She watched her friend. 'Just make sure you don't eat the poisonous ones.' Now it was Libby's turn to take the piss and she fell about laughing as Annie spat out a mound of green slime.

They chatted as they each designed their own lunch, Libby having first spooned the aromatic tomato sauce onto the wafer-thin bases, and added pepperoni and chilli and a few black olives to hers, before smothering it in marshmallow-like, buffalo mozzarella.

'What are you having?'

'Everything.' Annie was like a child, heaping smoked ham and pineapple and peppers and even slivers of fish on the rapidly growing mound.

'Stop. You'll ruin it.' Libby could have kicked herself as Annie's face fell. 'Sorry, I'm always doing that. Pizzas are completely individual, so keep going.'

'Actually, I think I was getting carried away. Everything looks so good.' Annie was mortified.

'No please, have anything you like. I am far too precious.

'And I'm a muck savage,' Annie grinned and relaxed for the first time since that phone call last night.

After a bit more effort they tucked into the most delicious pizzas with a flavour unlike anything Annie had tasted before. 'My God, this is heaven,' she said and twisted the stainless steel pepper mill to within an inch of its life. Libby resisted the urge to grab it. Annie felt sophisticated.

'Do you not cook really or have you just been having me on all this time?'

'I never cook, you know that. I open tins and fry the occasional chop but it's mostly ready-prepared food, chicken Kiev, beans, chips, that sort of thing.'

Libby couldn't believe her ears, but she'd learned many lessons from Annie, so she adopted what she hoped was a casual tone.

'But don't you have to eat masses of fresh food – vegetables, salads, fish and the like – since your illness?'

'I tried in the early days. But I lived with my father at first and he's a very limited cook, and then later I could never afford all that stuff.'

'That's rubbish.' Libby couldn't help herself, she was on her hobby-horse. 'Processed foods are much more expensive. Some of those ready meals are a rip-off and you can never be sure what you're eating. Masses of sugar and salt, too.'

'But they taste great.' There was no arguing, but Libby tried.

'That's all those additives. Doesn't *this* taste good?'

'This tastes better than practically anything I've

ever eaten in my whole life.' Annie was grinning as she tucked in.

'That's it. I'm definitely taking you in hand. A few simple lessons and you'll be off.'

Later, as they sat in the garden sipping wine, Annie told Libby her news. Libby was shocked but relieved.

'Oh Annie, I am so glad he's behind bars. I knew there was something when I heard you earlier. How did you feel, seeing him again?' Libby put down her glass, turned to her friend and saw that the tears were streaming down her face. She knelt down on the grass beside her and held her hand and rubbed her hair and let her cry it all away.

Much later Annie asked about Andrew. She felt better now and she wasn't going to let Libby do nothing about him. 'Why don't you get in touch with him? Start again.'

'I'm not sure I want to.' Libby knew it was a lie and Annie would have bet her life on it.

'I think you do.' It was gently delivered.

'I was so stupid to panic and say all that stuff.'

'That's understandable. You're not an ordinary person. You're a star.'

'As soon as we'd had sex and he stayed the night, I started to imagine all sorts of scenarios . . . him selling his story. Pictures of us together.'

'Did you suck his toes or anything?' It was lost on Libby so she tried a different approach.

'Was it good?'

'What?'

'The sex.' They'd talked about it all before, but not the sex.

'It was fabulous.'

'The best ever?'

Libby had to think about that, she was defensive and it surprised her. 'It was different. David and I had a great sex life . . .'

'I'm sorry, I didn't mean to pry.'

'It's fine.' She stopped trying to justify it. 'David was . . . confident and assured. Andrew was tender – and passionate. It felt very intimate.' She smiled. 'And my God, he is one hell of a gorgeous-looking man, as you know.'

'What do you find attractive about him?' Annie was deliberately trying to encourage her.

'He's different from anyone else I've known. David was very suave and sophisticated. Handsome. You know that, you've met him.' She smiled at Annie and they both remembered.

'I always thought he was gorgeous. I think I even had a bit of a crush on him.'

Libby nodded. She was used to women fancying her husband. 'He was lovely. Andrew is different, he's more the rugged, outdoor type. He smells of soap rather than expensive aftershave.' Libby smiled. 'And I love the fact that his hair is longer and he doesn't look like anyone else and certainly not any doctor I've met. He's quietly confident. And I miss his voice, all soft and liquidy and gravelly. We seemed to fit so well together.' She sighed. 'There's something about him, something I can't quite put my finger on . . .'

'I'd say you've got it bad.' Annie grinned at her friend across the shadows.

'I miss him, that's the funny thing. Even though I hardly knew him, really. But we talked a lot. In a way I shared more little, stupid things with him, things David and I didn't have time for, I suppose. We were always out, socializing. Andrew's not really interested in all that. He really looks at you and listens when you talk and he considers his responses, doesn't come out with the glib remarks that most of my acquaintances find funny.'

'I think you need to go see him.'

Libby was silent for a long time. 'I think you're right.'

Chapter Fifty-Two

The week was not going well for Libby. The new series was on air and the ratings were poor. A leading and well-respected newspaper had savaged it, calling it pretentious and patronizing. One of the tabloids went further, describing it as 'up its own bum'. Everyone was running for cover. Carrie was the only one of her old friends who telephoned when she'd seen it. She hadn't heard a word from Moya.

As if that wasn't enough, the house had been sold, much more quickly than anyone thought it would. That meant Libby had to find a new home. She'd looked at several but after her mansion, they were all depressingly small and so dark. The gardens were tiny, some had no off street parking – and all this when Libby was still spending a small fortune compared to the average Joe Soap. The problem was that all her money was going on location, and nice neighbourhoods and panoramic views didn't come cheap. She had another appointment the next day and she'd sounded so depressed when Annie spoke to her that she had offered to go along with her to the next couple of houses, 'just to get a real perspective on things'.

'When are you going to talk to Andrew, by the way?'

'I don't even know what shifts he works.'

'I think you should just go there.'

'But how will I know where to find him?'

'Ask at the main reception.'

'What if he's not there?'

'Well then, they'll just tell you when he's on again. Hell, the porter on duty might be so taken with you that he'll give you his home number.'

'I feel sick just talking about it.'

'OK, give me the number.' Annie had had enough. 'I'll ring and find out what shift he's on this week.'

'You can't.'

'I can. Give me the number.'

'What if they put you through to him? What if he answers the phone himself?'

'I think I can cope.'

'He'll know it's me.'

'How can he? It's not you. I don't sound anything like you. I'll ask him to come and tidy my garden. That should take him all of ten minutes.'

Libby read out the number Mrs O'C. had given her only after Annie threatened to go and see him herself.

'I'll call you back in five minutes.'

'Please don't do anything stupid.'

'*Moi?* I'm an actress, darling. If I can't carry this off I'll eat my Lycra mini.'

'Call me immediately.'

'OK, bye.'

Libby felt sick as she waited. She leapt on the phone on the first ring. It was her mother. 'Can I call you right back?'

'That's what you always say, Elizabeth and then you don't.'

Libby closed her eyes in frustration and grovelled.

The second time it rang she was almost hysterical.

'Annie?'

'He's on tomorrow at ten or Friday after three.'

'What did they say?'

'Nothing much. The receptionist just checked. I said I wanted to make an appointment for my friend.'

'You don't even know if you *can* make an appointment. We don't even know what he does.'

'I asked. She said he specializes in broken hearts.'

'Very funny. How will I recognize him in good clothes? All those white coats. Or is it green?'

'He's a doctor, not a porter. You've been watching too much *ER*.'

'Well, I can't imagine him in a suit.'

'Don't be so patronizing. And ignore your imagination, it's what got you into this mess in the first place.' As she said it, Annie marvelled at how far they'd come in such a short time. A couple of months ago she'd have been afraid to say hello to the great Libby Marlowe: now she was telling her off.

'I can't do this.'

'It's your only chance.'

'I'll ring him.'

'Won't work. This is not a conversation for the telephone. It'll all go pear-shaped. Your only chance is to be eyeball to eyeball with him. You need to be very convincing and he needs to see you to know that. So go find a mirror and practise.'

Libby laughed in spite of her churning stomach.

'Personally, I'd give him ten minutes and I'd say he'll be putty in your pizza-making hands,' Annie insisted.

Libby wasn't so sure. 'You don't know him, Annie. He's very proud. He won't be easy.'

'I do know him, a bit. He's lovely. Anyway, I've been listening to nothing else for weeks now and my liver is shot because of him so I hope he's good at his job because he'll be wheeling me in for a transplant if you don't sort this out soon. Now, when are you going?'

'I'll go on Friday afternoon.' Libby knew Annie was right. She wanted him back. She'd been a fool. 'What if he can't talk?'

It was like dealing with a toddler. 'Then you simply tell him you'll go and have a coffee and wait for him. Or come back when he has a break. Bring a book with you. Now, they've just called me for a recording. I have to go and have sex with a barrister. So I suggest you toddle off and practise being sincere.'

Libby changed her clothes five times. This was excruciating.

She'd had her hair blow-dried and then tossed and her make-up done professionally. 'Be subtle with the war paint,' Annie had advised in her usual forthright manner.

Eventually, she settled on one of her old reliables, a black trouser suit that still fitted her. The jacket was long and unstructured, but it hung beautifully and she teamed it with a sexy little T-shirt, hoping she looked a bit funky and girly.

'No jewellery' – another warning from her new friend. 'The ice on your fingers is enough to intimidate Ms Dynamite.'

It was almost five by the time she pulled into the car park. She'd have given anything for a very large G & T but knew this was not the time to breathe alcohol fumes all over him – if he even spoke to her, that is.

Her heart was thumping a beat that was strong enough to set Ladysmith Black Mambazo dancing but she kept going simply because she couldn't face a build-up like this again. It was worse than anything that might happen later.

She nearly got caught in the swing doors, such was her attempt to appear nonchalant. The main reception was facing her but the walk was at least a mile and a half and she was convinced everyone was staring at her.

'Hello, I'm looking for Andrew Harrington.'

The receptionist was hassled, with phones in both hands. 'Second floor, take the lift over there and when you get out it's the third door on the right.'

'Thank you.' Libby scarpered.

As she pushed through the swing doors, and took the third on the right as instructed, Libby prayed with a fervour she rarely used that he wouldn't be here. The smell she would always associate with the night David had died invaded her nostrils and settled in her already queasy stomach.

It was a sort of waiting room, filled to capacity and noisy. Another reception desk loomed large on the horizon and she felt unsteady as she made her way there, with a hundred or so bored faces following her progress. She was sure she could spot him at the desk, wearing a white coat and stethoscope. His back was to her but she knew the back of that head from weeks of watching him gardening. She passed a man talking to a nurse and made a beeline for the counter before she threw up.

'Libby?' She was almost there when she heard her name and it took her a second to realize it was coming from the opposite direction to the desk. Oh God, please don't let me meet anyone I know. She kept her eyes firmly on the back of the neck she was looking at and when she heard her name again she turned aggressively to rid herself of the intruder.

438

Swinging round, she came face to face with him. Blankly she looked at the tall man she'd just passed, and was about to give him one of the special yeses she reserved for irritating fans when she realized it was Andrew. But not *her* Andrew. This one was still tall, still tanned, still had the same probing eyes but his hair wasn't tousled and he'd borrowed someone else's clothes. He looked sophisticated. Aloof. Different.

'What are you doing here?' He was surprised. The voice convinced her, yet still she looked around, afraid that someone was playing a trick on her. Where was the white coat?

'Hi.'

'Hi.'

The nurse was looking at her in an 'I've seen you somewhere before' way. Libby swallowed and licked her lips.

'How are you?'

'Fine. You?'

'Great. I, eh, came to see you, actually.' She laughed nervously. 'But I can see you're busy so I'll, em, ring you later.' Her eyebrows felt as if they were somewhere up around her hairline.

'No, it's fine. I'm just finished here.' He looked at the nurse. 'Could I talk to you about that again in the morning?'

'Sure.' She treated him to her brightest smile, then turned to Libby.

'You're Libby Marlowe.'

'Yes, I am.' Libby's smile begged her to go away.

'I love your shows. I've taped every one of them.'

'Thank you.' She just couldn't be polite any more so she turned away from the fawning young woman. 'Are you sure it's not a bad time?' she asked Andrew.

'No, it's fine. Thanks, Lorna. See you to-morrow.' He took Libby's arm and led her towards the door. 'Would you like a cup of coffee?'

'Yes, please.' Anything just to sit down quietly and talk to him and look at him properly. And not pretend.

He held open a door and as she walked through it the heat and the noise hit them both instantly.

'Feels like that restaurant all over again.' It was a feeble attempt to remind him that they'd once been close.

'On second thoughts, maybe a bit of fresh air would be better. There are lots of quiet places in the grounds. Would that be OK with you?'

She nodded and they walked towards the lift. It was full. Libby stood close to him and struggled to smell his normal, outdoorsy scent amidst the antiseptic.

He led her out a back door and over to a quiet corner where a bench nestled among the shrubbery. He waited for her to sit down, then sat beside her and slid his arm along the cold wrought iron. For a second Libby thought he was going to touch her and she had to stop herself sliding her arms around his neck. All her old longings returned, except now that she knew what he felt like to hold, the cravings were multiplied a thousand times.

'How have you been?' He was staring at her.

'Fine. You?'

'OK, I guess. How did you find me?'

'Mrs O'Connell knew all the details. I wasn't expecting to see you like . . . you look different.' It was the understatement of the year. He was wearing a dark grey suit that looked as if it was hand made. Armani, she suspected. A snow-white shirt deepened his tan and a gorgeous pale grey Hermès tie completed the look. Even his shoes must have cost a gardener's week's wages.

'I suppose I do. Still, I think I'd rather be in my jeans. Same person inside no matter what you dress them in, eh?'

'You're back working full time here?' He was staring again and it made her heart somersault, now that she'd recovered enough to really take him in.

'For the moment,' he said.

'I just . . . wasn't expecting you to be so . . .'

'So what?'

She wanted to say gorgeous or glamorous. 'Clean' was what came out, and he laughed.

'I scrub up well. Still, you've seen me clean before.' They were both remembering.

'What do you do?'

'I'm a surgeon.'

'Oh. In what area?'

'Cardiothoracic.'

'Sounds more like a plant. What does it mean?'

'Heart, lungs . . .'

'So what exactly was a heart surgeon doing

working as a handyman in my garden, earning a pittance?' She felt even more of a fool now for thinking he'd sell their story. He was probably worth much more than she'd ever been.

'As I think I told you, I took a year out. I've never been sure this was what I wanted to do. I'm not very happy cooped up indoors for hours on end, and being surrounded by people who are very ill can be difficult. Also, it's a hell of a lot of pressure sometimes.'

'So how did you end up here?'

'My father. Did I tell you that already?'

'Your father's a doctor?'

He nodded wryly. 'A cardiologist. He's a hard act to follow.'

'So why did you?'

'I resisted for a long time.'

'Why didn't you tell me all this when we met?'

He shrugged. 'I was going to, eventually. I hadn't really sorted out my job in my own head, I suppose. I'm getting a bit old to be still deciding on a career, aren't I?' He gave the half-smile she knew so well. 'Actually, I was all set to tell you the whole story on that famous morning after the night before. But things took a different turn.' His smile changed and he looked far away for a moment. 'When I met you I was just a gardener, and you know something? I liked it that way. What was amazing during the last year was how differently people treated me when I was nobody. Maybe it's crazy, but I expect people to take me as they find me. Too much bullshit otherwise.'

'You were never just a gardener.'

'Deep down that's exactly what I am. But after a year out I came back. I'm still not sure why. Maybe I don't have the courage. Maybe deep down I like the profile that goes with this job. Pretty sad, eh, if that's the case?' Libby didn't believe for a second that it was.

'All I know is that I've met more rich people in my life that I wouldn't spend a minute more than I have to with. Yet here I am, and my heart is elsewhere. I just don't know if I'll ever follow it.'

'You should.'

'Would you have treated me differently if you'd met me here, like today?'

'Probably not.' But they both knew she wasn't telling the truth.

'I don't think you'd have been as quick to judge me.' It wasn't nasty, it was nicely said and it made her more ashamed.

As they sat in silence Libby wanted to break down and tell him everything but couldn't find the courage. 'I shouldn't have said what I said that morning,' she began.

He shrugged. 'It doesn't matter any more.' He looked straight into her eyes. 'But it mattered a great deal at the time. You should have trusted me. You knew me well enough. But because you thought I didn't have any money you assumed I might be desperate enough to sell you off to the highest bidder.'

That was the moment, she knew later, when she

should have thrown herself at his feet and begged for forgiveness. But she didn't know how to, wasn't used to it, so she handled it in the only way she could. She backpedalled. 'No, you're wrong. It's just that I have to be careful. The media would have a field day . . . I know now, though . . .'

He shook his head. 'It doesn't matter.'

'Can't we try again?' She had to ask. And he'd probably never know how much it cost her to say those words. Now that it was probably too late she knew that maybe he was her one chance of salvation. He was honest and open and real and that was what had been missing in her past life. It was so easy once you recognized it. Even her beloved David had been a performer for a lot of his life.

She looked at him. He wasn't smiling.

'Please?'

'I'm sorry, but I think I'm going to have to pass on that one, Libby.' When he used her name it felt like a caress, but his next words felt more like a whip. He didn't take his eyes from her face and he was gentle. 'I suppose I'm not sure . . . at least I don't know if . . .' It was his turn to be lost for words and she could see him struggle. He sighed and it was long and painful. 'I suppose I think we missed our moment.'

Chapter Fifty-Three

'And what happened next?' Annie drew in her breath.

'Nothing, really. There wasn't anything else to say.' They were sitting in Libby's kitchen, their favourite haunt these days. 'I just wanted to get away. I stood up and he walked with me to my car. And he guided me out of the parking space, even though it was a mile wide.' She laughed. 'He was probably afraid I'd burst into tears and crash and he'd be stuck with me.'

'And he's really a doctor?'

'A cardiothoracic surgeon.' She looked lonely. 'God, you should have seen him. He made David Beckham seem like a wimp.'

'I think I feel a heart problem coming on.' Annie was trying to cheer her friend up. 'Shame I don't have private medical cover or I could book myself in there for a week.'

'Oh Annie, what am I going to do?' It was the million-dollar question and there was no answer that didn't involve a lot of heartache.

'I don't think there's much you can do, really, although I know that's not what you want to hear.' Annie was gentle. 'All you can do is hope that when he thinks about things he'll want to give it another chance too.'

'I just wish I'd really pleaded with him.' She looked at Annie. 'Does that sound demented?' The younger woman shook her head.

'I'm so afraid of looking stupid sometimes, that I skirt around saying outright that I was totally and utterly wrong. I think he saw through me today and that's what decided him.'

'Well, he's the loser. Just because you're vulnerable where the tabloids are concerned.'

'No, it's not that. I suppose I've always seen myself as a bit superior underneath it all. How tragic is that? He doesn't judge a person by what they are on the outside. I thought he was just a gardener and that he might need the money. I totally blew it. Does that all make sense?'

'Yes, in a way. But you're not like that, really – look at how you trusted me enough to invite me into your home so soon after we'd met.'

Libby looked at her friend and hoped she wouldn't lose her by what she said next. But she reckoned she had to start somewhere. 'The truth is, I think I did look down my nose at you a bit at the start. I was standoffish, don't you remember? And the funny thing is that now I can't imagine not having you in my life. You're the best friend I've ever had and I hope what I said doesn't send you packing.'

'I'm not going anywhere.'

'Thanks.'

Several big hugs later Annie came up with a plan. 'I think you need to get out of this house. Get settled. Start again. When do you have to be out of here?'

'I haven't confirmed it but they'd want me out tomorrow, if they could have their way. I guess I'll have to rent. You're right. I need to stop feeling sorry for myself and move on.' She looked like a child. 'I think I fell a little bit in love with him though, and that's what hurts the most. Especially as I never thought I'd feel that way about anyone after David.'

'It will happen again, so.' They were each lost in their own thoughts. 'So, what's the first thing on your new agenda?'

'See that little cottage I told you about tomorrow. I've an appointment at eleven.'

'OK, will you come to my house for breakfast? Tea and white rubber toast is all I'm promising, though. Then I'll come with you.'

'Thanks.'

Next morning, after a lazy breakfast they arrived at the cottage near Dalkey. They had approached it via a tiny road off the main street. It was one of just four identical cottages although the owners had treated them differently on the outside. They were detached and one was whitewashed, two had the

447

original brick exposed and the one they'd come to see was painted pale pink. It was just two windows and a door but they were the genuine Victorian article and the white facia boards under the eaves added to the charm. It had a small front garden, with a pretty little gate and room to park one car at the side of the house, accessed through a separate, wider entrance.

'This was done recently, obviously,' Annie said.

'Yes but they've done it well, the gate is a copy of the original front gate and they've used the same stone that's on the little path.'

It was neglected. The windows were dirty and the plastic windowboxes empty. A once healthy rambling rose hadn't been pruned in years and was now a leggy, sprawling mess without a single flower. Annie didn't like it, Libby could tell, but she saw its potential.

'It seems like a lot of money for what you're getting.' Annie was flicking through the brochure.

'I know. It's all about location.'

'Can you afford it?'

'Yes. Alex O'Meara has done the sums.'

The auctioneer greeted them at the door. Libby had used her married name so as not to attract unnecessary attention.

'Good morning. I'm Vince Jones. I hope you won't be put off but I'm afraid the vendor has decided to stay put.'

'That's fine, as long as we can look around freely.'

'Of course. Come in.'

The hall was quirky but still had the original wood panelling, unusual in a house this size. The wall facing them was ugly, as if it had been boarded up. There was a living room with original beams and a surprisingly big stone fireplace. The kitchen and dining room had been knocked into one room with a big, old, rectangular table at one end and gorgeous french doors leading to the garden. The kitchen part was a disaster: someone had tried to modernize it and had failed miserably. 'This makes my kitchen look like a show house,' Annie whispered, running her hands over the cracked brown sink.

'But look, it even has a pantry.' Libby was intrigued.

'That's not a pantry, it's a wardrobe,' Annie laughed, turning up her nose.

'No, look, it's stone with the original wooden shelves. It's lovely and cold – and imagine a granite work surface in here. Could be great.'

'I don't believe you, I've seen nicer dustbins.'

'Come on, let's look upstairs.' Libby dragged her friend by the arm.

There was one decent room, with a small fireplace and two good windows. 'My God, you can see the sea. Just what I've always wanted.'

'You'll be able to feel the sea too, I'd say. The gaps in these windows are bigger than the fillings in my teeth.'

The other two rooms were small. 'But that's all I need. One could be a study, this one, because it overlooks the garden. And this could be a spare bedroom.' Libby was beaming. 'For when you come to stay.'

'I like the bathroom, that's about all.'

The bathroom was indeed one of the better rooms. It still had its original claw-foot bath and more of the wood panelling, as well as a huge airing cupboard. 'There's also a small utility room out the back that you haven't seen,' the estate agent was quick to point out, 'and there's a small downstairs toilet.'

The old lady who owned the house was sitting on the veranda.

'Hello, my dears. I'm Eleanor.'

Libby and Annie shook hands with her and they chatted for a few minutes.

The garden wasn't huge, but it had a vegetable patch, a tiny greenhouse and some mature fruit trees and a south-facing raised patio.

'This garden gets the sun all day,' Eleanor told them. 'I'll be sorry to leave it.'

The estate agent had told them that she was going into a nursing home because she had no family and had never married. Both Annie and Libby took to her instantly.

'Are you that girl off the telly?' Eleanor was staring at Libby intently.

'Yes, I am and Annie here is also on TV.'

'Oh my, what programme do you do, my dear?'

'I'm in *Southside*, actually.' Annie was mortified.

'Oh.' She sounded disappointed. 'I'm afraid I never watch that rubbish.' Both women collapsed with laughter.

'So haven't you a big palace and plenty of money?' She was only interested in Libby. 'What would you want with my little house?'

Libby sat down beside her. 'My husband died earlier this year so I'm selling and looking for a smaller house just for myself.'

'Do you like this one?'

'Very much.'

'Would you look after my garden, keep the vegetables going and feed the roses?'

'Yes.' Libby had no idea how, but she knew she would.

The old lady nodded but said nothing.

They wandered around for a while and promised to ring the estate agent later.

'It's mingin',' Annie said as she got into the car. 'I can't get that awful musty smell out of my nostrils.'

'That's just stale air, no windows open.'

'Libby, it's damp. Did you feel that mattress in the spare room?'

'I think it's just right for me.'

'I can't believe you. How can you consider moving from one of the most beautiful houses in Dublin into that heap of shite?'

'It's like a doll's version of my house. It's perfect. A cosy sitting room, a big kitchen, a—'

'A big, manky kitchen.' Libby ignored her.

'A pantry that will house all my cooking stuff. A really good-sized bedroom, room for a study and a decent bathroom. All that plus a great garden that gets the sun, somewhere to park my car and a view of the sea when I wake up each day.'

'You are stark, raving mad. You could buy a six-bedroomed detached house closer to town for what they're asking here.'

'But I couldn't live in one of those. This has character.'

'Woodworm.'

'Interesting shapes . . .'

'Dry rot.'

'It's like a little cottage from a storybook. I could do lots with it. And the location is superb.'

'It would cost almost as much again.'

'No, you're wrong. Structurally it's good, from what I can see. The roof looks fine. It's been rewired and done properly. All it needs is central heating and a new kitchen and a big clean-out and redecorating. It's full of clutter. You can't see its true potential. Even empty would be a better way to sell that house. Anyway,' she grinned nervously, 'I kind of like that it has a history and that I met the old woman and that I'm sort of carrying on, like a relative or something.'

'You're losing it and I feel it my duty to stop you making a big mistake, just because of some stupid, romantic notion.'

But it was too late. Libby laughed and took out her phone and dialled John Simpson. She told him all about the house and he suggested they put in a considerably lower offer, given the state of the property.

'OK, but don't lose it on me. I want it. And I don't want to do the old lady out of a fair price,' she surprised herself by adding.

Chapter Fifty-Four

The day of Annie's awards ceremony was drawing closer and she was growing nervous. The newspapers were getting miles of headlines out of the event and she'd been interviewed four times. She'd spent more than a month's salary on a stunning dress and a matching bag and shoes that Libby had insisted she buy as well. Jewellery was courtesy of her new friend and when she'd tried it all on Annie didn't recognize herself.

Her only regret was that she didn't have a partner. She'd agonized over it for ages. Mike Nichols was a possibility and Annie knew he'd have jumped at the chance to go with her but she was afraid of giving him the wrong idea. Then she'd considered asking John Reynolds. Libby had approved of this, they'd had a long conversation about it. Annie felt safe with him but she didn't really fancy him. They'd had a drink together once or twice and initially she thought there was a spark. The trouble had started when he'd kissed her in his car the second time they were out. Annie wasn't prepared and found herself tensing up as soon as he came close. It felt like he was lunging at her, but she knew this wasn't so. She'd over-reacted, he'd been embarrassed and she'd said good night quickly and gone inside. The incident had troubled her ever since. She kept thinking of the night she'd been attacked and now she was worried that she was frigid. So far she hadn't told anyone this.

A couple of days before the event she asked Libby to go with her. They were eating, their favourite occupation since Libby had started on the lessons. Tonight it was Thai fishcakes with lime and coriander, fried until crisp and golden and served with parsley and watercress salad and a tangy sweet chilli dipping sauce. Annie was eating them as fast as Libby was taking them out of the pan.

If Libby was surprised by the invitation she didn't show it. 'I'd love to come, if you're sure? I won't know many people there so I might be more of a hindrance than a help to you.'

'No you won't. Please come.'

'OK, I will.' After they'd eaten they wandered around the house. Libby had asked Annie to take some furniture and there were so many beautiful things that she was paralysed, not wanting to appear greedy.

'Libby, all this stuff cost a fortune, I can't take it for nothing.'

'Nonsense, all the good stuff has gone to the

auction house, you really would be doing me a favour. And I have a load of kitchen stuff for you, most of it samples, all new. So, at last you've no excuse not to be making your own food every evening.'

Annie hugged her and said thanks. 'Will you be sorry to let all your stuff go?'

Libby was determined not to get maudlin. She'd shed enough tears to last a lifetime. 'I've taken everything I want for the cottage into storage. All that's left are some bits and pieces that won't fetch much so I want you to have anything you like first,' she said, and looked at her friend sadly. 'I have so much, let me share it, please.'

'OK then.' Annie had never known such generosity.

'Now, there are two small sofas that would be perfect in your front room, along with a lovely little table I bought in Italy. Then I kept back a rug that I thought would suit the room as well. And I think you should take that bookcase over there for all your files and scripts.'

Annie was speechless. 'I can't—'

'Yes you can. Now make a list of anything else you want. I have a van coming in a few days' time and they'll deliver to you and take away any stuff you want to get rid of.'

'That's everything in the house, basically. Most of it was bought in junk shops.'

'Well then, start again. You're going to be moving house shortly anyway, so think of a big apartment and take things you can bring with you.

And–' Libby grabbed her hand and dragged her into another room – 'I want you to have that picture. I kept it back specially.'

It was a small child on a beach and it reminded Annie of herself. 'It's probably worth a fortune. I can't possibly take it.'

'Yes you can. You've loved it since you first saw it. I've always hated it.'

The kindness was too much for Annie. She burst into uncontrollable sobs and Libby, who'd known for days that something was wrong, let her cry. Eventually, it all came out.

'I don't like anyone touching me. Men, I mean. They all remind me of . . . him. I'm afraid I'm frigid. I don't know what to do.'

'Oh darling, all this is normal. How could you not feel this way? You had a horrible, traumatic experience.' Libby felt like her mother as she held Annie and comforted her. 'I promise it will all be fine once you meet a guy you really like that way. And it will be someone you can talk to about it, and he'll understand and be gentle and it will all just fade away. Trust me.' She lifted Annie's face up and dried her eyes. 'I promise.'

'Thanks. I don't know what came over me just then. I suppose I've been bottling it up for days. I'm sorry, I haven't even asked you how you're feeling. This must be very hard for you to do.'

'Actually, it's not too bad. The toughest thing will be cleaning out the last of David's personal stuff. But in a funny way, I know it's time. And meeting Andrew made me realize what a sham my life had become. Now I want to simplify it.' She smiled. 'Also, I need a project. I've had no offers of work, very few invites out and I know I have to get my eating and drinking under control again.'

'I see a difference already.' Annie meant it. 'You're not comfort-eating like you used to. And you're definitely not a lush now.' She was teasing again.

'No, and I have lost a bit of weight too. And I have cut back on drink, although I haven't had a day yet without one. Speaking of which, let's not start being good tonight, you look like you could use one.'

'No, I'm fine now. In fact, I think that what I'd like is a big mug of drinking chocolate.'

Libby knew she was looking for an excuse to drink herself. 'I have some gorgeous stuff from Fortnum and Mason, 70 per cent cocoa solids. I'll show you how to froth it and float marshmallows on top. But only on condition that we drink it while you make that list. Then I'm sending you home to get organized. The van could even be with you tomorrow.'

Five minutes later they were giggling again. Each of them gave silent thanks for the presence of the other one in their lives and neither said anything.

Chapter Fifty-Five

Annie had never felt so good about herself and it was all down to a few pieces of furniture. The stuff from Libby had completely transformed the place and made her finally decide to move. Now that her little house reeked of good taste it gave Annie a longing for a place of her own, with freshly painted walls and a real bath and a shiny, new kitchen. Libby had thrown in masses of other things she thought would suit a new place and there were bits and pieces stacked everywhere. As soon as tonight was over, Annie decided, she was going to start looking seriously. She'd also booked a course of driving lessons, her first real extravagance.

The phone rang. It was her brother Tom from Australia, calling to wish her luck. Ever since her attack they'd all taken to phoning her occasionally, just to see how she was. It pleased her.

The programme had arranged for Annie to stay in a hotel beside the complex from where the awards show was being televised live. As she got ready she marvelled at how much her life had changed for the better. Even the events of that awful night were beginning to fade.

She hardly recognized the vibrant face and shining eyes that stared back at her from the mirror.

There was a knock at the door and Annie opened it eagerly.

'Wow, you look fabulous!' It was Libby, clutching several bags. 'I brought along my entire jewellery collection, but I see you need very little. You're stunning.'

Libby dived in, rummaging through exquisite beaded chokers, long earrings and magnificent pendants and crosses.

'Here's what I thought.' She handed Annie a pair of the most amazing diamond earrings and a long, heavily beaded cross that nestled between Annie's breasts. The result almost made her cry.

'No, please don't. You'll spoil your make-up. You look fabulous, darling.' Libby was being deliberately theatrical. 'Now let's go down, and to hell with our diets and my sobriety – we're having a glass of champagne.'

The evening passed in a blur. There were photographers everywhere and Annie was much sought after. Libby stayed well in the background and few people paid her any attention. She knew it was because the series had bombed and people were embarrassed and were pretending not to see her. She sipped her drink and watched, feeling distant from the world she'd inhabited for so long.

The ceremony itself was a dazzling affair and as the Best Newcomer category got closer Libby became more and more nervous for her friend. They were seated at one of the *Southside* tables in a prominent position. Annie was the star of the evening, their great white hope.

When the award for Best Newcomer was announced Libby reached under the table and squeezed Annie's arm. No-one saw but Annie shot her a grateful glance as she swallowed hard and tried to smile. As the list of nominees was read out, the cameras swung around to get all the close-ups. The others had told Libby that the likely winner was a young man from a top British police drama and she cursed herself for not watching any of them, to size up the competition. The programme then cut to excerpts by each of the nominees. Annie's was the famous scene with Marc Robinson and Libby had tears in her eyes. When her clip ended Annie got the most defeaning cheer from the hall. When the camera cut to her for a reaction she was biting her lip and trying not to cry. It was an endearing shot and Libby wanted to hug her, but she also wanted to stay out of the way.

The award was being presented by the Best Actress winner from last year. Libby knew none of the other nominees but she applauded with gusto. Opening the envelope seemed to take five minutes. 'For her sensitive . . .' – a woman, anyway '. . . portrayal of a difficult character . . .' – could that be a prostitute? '. . . and for bringing warmth and passion to even the most harrowing scenes . . .' Libby's eyes were darting around the table, waiting for a reaction. Annie's head was firmly down. '. . . For the first time this year the judges' decision was unanimous . . .' A three-minute pause, at least: 'This award goes to Annie Weller!'

All hell broke loose. Everyone jumped up and tried to grab her but Annie headed for Libby and the two hugged till they bruised each other. It was the shot that made the front pages of the three leading newspapers the following morning.

Annie's speech was the shortest of the night.

'This means more to me than anyone will ever know. Thank you to my family, especially my dad, and my best friend Libby.' She fled the stage as flashes went wild, ''Cause I could feel the tears starting,' she later told a jubilant Libby.

Marc Robinson's congratulatory kiss startled Annie. It was full on the lips and quite possessive, Libby thought, watching carefully. She'd decided she didn't like him the instant they were introduced. There was something very false about him. He came and sat beside Annie while Libby was in the loo and when she returned he made no effort to move, assuming Libby would use the next available chair. She was having none of it, and stood between the two of them just to thwart him. It took a while but he got the message in the end. 'I'll see you later,' he said. He had eyes only for Annie.

'If you go back to him I'll throttle you.'

'He is very cute, isn't he?'

'He is the biggest fake I've seen tonight, and there are quite a few here.'

'You really think so?' Annie was intrigued.

'I really think so.' Libby laughed. 'You can do much better for yourself I think. I like Mike Nichols, though, and he really likes you,' she whispered later.

'I know, but it's not happening for me. Pity, he's a dote and a great friend and I owe him a lot.'

'Don't even think about it. Life's too short. I know.'

When the ceremony was over they all adjourned to the upmarket hotel next door for the party. It took nearly twenty minutes to make the one-minute journey, as Annie was stopped by almost everyone they met. Libby beamed like a mother hen.

As they made their way in through the swing doors Libby stiffened, causing Annie to glance sharply in her direction. Four people were waiting to come out. It took a minute for Annie to recognize him.

'Hi, Libby.'

'Andrew, how are you?'

He smiled at her. 'Fine, thanks. You?'

'I'm good. Annie's just won the Best Newcomer award next door. It's huge, and now so is she. Annie, you remember Andrew Harrington.'

'Of course. Hi Andrew. Nice to see you again.'

'Congratulations, Annie. I'm so pleased. I remember you telling me how difficult it was to get recognition as a new actress.' Annie was surprised he'd remembered. His eyes were twinkling at them. 'My God, there's a pair of you in it. I'd say you're dynamite together.' All three of them laughed.

Andrew introduced his parents. She could see where he got his smile.

'Libby, hello, I'm a great fan of yours,' his mother told her as she shook hands with both girls.

'And this is a friend of mine, Andrea Stephens.'

'Hello.' She smiled at Libby but Annie was her focus of attention. 'Congratulations. I love you in *Southside*. Bobby is a great character. She's one of my favourites.' Annie smiled, mortified and didn't say anything, determined not to spoil Libby's moment.

'So are you celebrating?' His smile was warm and he looked interested.

'We certainly are! No man is safe tonight.' Annie wanted to let him know that he wasn't the only fish in the sea, but looking at him tonight, she could see why Libby had fallen so hard. He was wearing expensive black jeans, a lightweight, beautifully cut jacket and his pale shirt was open at the neck. He was tanned and his hair was still tousled and still too long and he looked way too trendy for a cardiowhatever.

'How's the garden?' He hadn't taken his eyes off Libby.

'It looks great.' She smiled up at him. 'But I'm leaving it tomorrow.'

'The house sold?'

'It did. But I've found a great new place with a slightly more manageable garden.' She was not going to ask for his help. 'Now, we'd better head on in before the photographers run riot looking for this lady.' She smiled at Annie and then at his parents and saved her cheesiest smile for the pretty young woman. 'It was nice to meet you.'

'Take care of yourself.' That look again, the one that always caught her by surprise.

'You too.' She legged it, as Annie would say.

'Into the ladies', quick.'

They disappeared round the corner. Annie was worried. 'Are you OK?' she asked.

'I am now. God I nearly fainted when I saw him. What did you think when you saw him again?'

'I have to say you sure know how to pick 'em, Ms Marlowe.'

'He's lovely, isn't he?'

'He is. That voice. Those eyes. I'd almost forgotten how powerful he is. And seeing him dressed up, he does look different, you're right.' Libby was pleased. 'It's quite a combination. I could almost smell the heather. He definitely doesn't belong in a place full of sick people.' Annie made a face.

Libby laughed in spite of her misery. She was glad her friend had had a real chance to see how gorgeous Andrew was and how stupid she'd been.

'What about your woman? Any ideas?'

'No.' Libby was deflated. 'I guess he's well and truly over me.'

'Huh, he couldn't take his eyes off you.'

'He's always like that with people. When he's with you, you get his full attention. Can you believe I had that opportunity and I threw it away?'

'It's his loss as well.'

'Listen, he's younger than me and even as a gardener he was a great catch. How attractive do you think he is as a surgeon, with all that money, not to mention power? And then there's the charisma.'

Annie hugged her.

'And how old was she – the girl? Eighteen?'

'At least twenty-two, I'd say,' Annie said.

'Very attractive, though.'

'Come on. Let's have a drink.' Annie knew there was nothing else to talk about on that score.

'I'm really glad we saw him again. I wanted you to see him at his best,' Libby whispered as they were drawn into the mêlée.

At one-thirty Libby slipped off home. 'I've booked a cab,' she told a protesting Annie. 'You'll be partying all night anyway. I have the removal men coming at eight.'

Annie insisted on seeing her into the taxi. 'Sure you're all right?' It was the younger woman's turn to play mother. Libby nodded brightly.

Back home she wandered around, burying her head in some of David's things, trying to recall every detail of his face. Then she strolled barefoot in the garden and sat where she'd sat many times with Andrew and saw him as clearly as if he was standing directly in front of her. It was a night for remembering.

Chapter Fifty-Six

Annie arrived unannounced shortly after eight o'clock, ahead of the removal van, carrying her overnight bag on her shoulders and clutching her award and some orange juice and croissants in her arms.

Libby was taken aback. 'What are you doing here? Are you mad? What time did you get to bed?'

'Five,' Annie said, her eyes still shining. 'You?'

'Four.'

'Tough?'

'Lonely.'

'Make me some coffee and tell me all about it. Then I'm here to work. Oh, I almost forgot!' she screamed delightedly. 'Have you seen the papers?'

Libby hadn't. There they were on the front of all of them, laughing, screaming, hugging, looking as if they hadn't a care in the world.

Over coffee and croissants Annie told her all the gossip. Most of the names meant nothing to Libby, but she listened as if they were her closest friends. All that was required was an occasional 'really' or a 'wow' here and there, enough to keep Annie going for minutes at a time.

'The only thing is I'm not sure if I'm a luvvie or a darling. I've never been air-kissed so many times in my life. Luvvies are all plunging necklines and too much jewellery – and that's only the men. Darlings are less ostentatious and more dramatic.' They giggled and gossiped some more.

'And I met someone.' Now she had all of Libby's attention.

'Please don't say his name was Marc Robinson or I really will throw up.'

'Not on your nellie, Sheila.' Annie's Australian accent was perfect.

'Tell me quick.'

'His name is Gary Bryson. He's a movie producer. Tall. Ish. Fair hair. Blue eyes. Very cute.'

'I want to know everything.'

'Nothing happened, actually.' Annie looked a bit deflated herself. 'But we talked. He asked for my number, wanted to meet me for a drink.' She cheered up just thinking about him. 'But best of all, I sort of imagined him kissing me and I felt all tingly.'

Libby hugged her. 'That is the best news. I hope that awful Aussie was watching everything.'

'He was. He sort of followed me around most of the evening.' Annie's grin was as wide as a canal.

The arrival of the troops at nine-fifteen sent

them scurrying around. Libby gave the orders just as she'd been doing all her life.

'What can I do?'

'Help me pack the last of David's things.' It was a plea.

'If you're sure?'

Libby nodded. She had decided to give them all to charity. Now she and Annie worked in silence, packing them into boxes and labelling them. All went well until Libby found his wallet, with its carefree picture of the two of them taken on their last holiday together. She stared at it for ages.

Annie let her be, and was just about to go quietly outside for a minute or two when Libby looked up. 'He was my best friend and now some days I have difficulty remembering what he looked like.'

'He'll always be right there in your heart.' Annie wished she could say more.

'I know.' Libby wiped her eyes. 'And then when I met Andrew, I felt that same pull.'

Annie understood.

It was easier after that. There were a few other moments when she stumbled across the unexpected, but none to rival finding the photo in his wallet. In a couple of hours it was all over and Annie left her to say goodbye to the house while she waited in the car.

Libby was staying at her mother's for two weeks and she was dreading it. She dropped Annie home then dumped her stuff and headed into town to meet John Simpson, to close the sale on the house. She was also finalizing the purchase of the cottage. It had all gone remarkably smoothly. When the other solicitor handed her the keys to her new home she felt a small surge of hope and it gave her some comfort. She and Annie were going to christen it later that evening.

Avoiding heavy conversations with her mother became a daily chore. Quickly Libby developed a routine. She got up early every morning and headed out to White Linen Cottage, as she discovered it had once been called because of its proximity to a laundry more than a hundred years ago. The builders had moved in. Her contacts had proved invaluable, and John Clancy and his team set about checking everything and making the few changes they'd discussed.

On the second day he had good news for her.

'Guess what I found?'

'What?'

'In the hall, behind that funny-looking plywood.'

'Tell me, please.'

He led her proudly in.

'Oh my God!'

They'd stripped back the wall that had been badly boarded up to reveal a dinky little fireplace.

'Once that's cleaned up it will look gorgeous. It even has the original brass hood. I'll take it off and have it properly polished. And I think you need a new slate hearth. You should also have a look-out for a good set of fire irons.'

'I can do better than that. I have an original high fender, you know, with a leather seat. It's adjustable and I think it will fit perfectly.' She hugged the older man. 'Thanks, John, that's cheered me up no end.'

Libby was cleaning down all the wood panelling herself and her days were spent knee deep in dust and grime. The workmen were amazed to see a 'celebrity' up to her neck in dirt and enjoying it. It was hard, the toughest physical work she'd ever done, but it kept her mind off food and drink. She was too tired in the evenings to do anything but have a hot bath and fall into bed – and straight into dreams of Andrew.

Chapter Fixty-Seven

Things simply couldn't get much better for Annie. Since winning the award, her agent had been bombarded with scripts for her to read. One or two were long-term projects still in development. Some would require her to move to the UK, but she wasn't prepared to think that far ahead yet.

Gary Bryson had phoned as promised and they'd met for a drink. He was funny and laid-back and really cool and Annie was mad about him. Based between Dublin and London, he worked hard and took life as it came. Annie felt totally relaxed with him and found herself telling him everything. He was in awe of the way she'd handled so many setbacks and when she told him about the attack he reached over and pulled her close and stroked her hair. It was so gentle, so comforting, so non-sexual in a way, that she didn't feel any tension or fear. He stroked the top of her head as if kissing a child's wound. After a while she looked up at him. 'So you see, I'm not really in the market for a heavy relationship just at the moment. I think it's only fair to tell you now, not waste your time.'

'Listen Annie, chill, will you? Let's just have some fun. I like being with you. You're smart and funny and cute. We can go places and party or just stay home and eat popcorn and watch movies. I'm not looking for a heavy scene either, OK?'

'OK.'

'So we have a deal?'

'Deal.' She laughed as he shook her hand. He was quirky and a little bit mad and just what she needed at the moment.

Marc Robinson was also calling her, leaving messages, trying to get her to meet him for a drink. She hadn't bothered replying to any of them. That gave her a great deal of satisfaction.

On the home front, she'd rung two agents. Both of them recognized her name and were now anxiously hunting around for an apartment for her. She had to do none of the legwork, which was just as well as she was working six-day weeks at the moment as *Southside* tried to up her profile fast in the current episodes, in order to capitalize on her win. Sundays, her only free days, were spent reading new scripts, learning lines and visiting her father occasionally. She hadn't seen Libby for a few weeks and she really missed her, although they spent hours on the phone late at night. She teased her about getting her hands dirty and Libby gave back as good as she got. 'Just you wait until you see it, Annie Weller, you'll eat your words.'

It was true enough. The place was shaping up nicely. The outside had been brushed down and given a fresh coat of the pale pink paint, with all the woodwork done in matt white. The windows sparkled thanks to vinegar and newspaper, a tip she'd been given by one of her neighbours, an elderly man named Walter, who'd stopped to welcome her to the neighbourhood. Libby didn't know it but she was the subject of many a chat among the locals, either over tea and scones or a creamy pint, depending on the time of day and whether they were male or female. The men all fancied her and the women wanted to be her.

She'd cleaned up the front garden, reading books on pruning in bed in the evenings and even planting up some new windowboxes with autumn colour and trailing ivy. By the front door stood two clipped box pyramids in large Victorian planters, and two standard bay trees framed the front gate. Even at this late stage in the year the garden was scented with pink roses and late-flowering clematis.

The new kitchen had been fitted. Libby had gone for free-standing units, all different sizes, some in a clotted cream colour and others in raspberry with thick maple work surfaces. Although it looked and felt as if it had been there for years, the lines were smooth and sleek and behind the doors lay every modern convenience, including a state of the art cooker and a walk-in fridge-freezer. She'd found a big old polished french table in an antique shop; now it glistened in the slanted autumn sunshine and was home to a huge porcelain jug filled to overflowing with raspberry-coloured flowers from the local flower shop where the staff seemed to delight in finding exactly what she was looking for. What pleased Libby most about the kitchen was that she'd done it all on a budget and had even managed to kit out the pantry and the utility room, buying the best appliances and decorating in a fresh, simple, country style.

Her bedroom was furnished sparsely with an oversized french bed, one they'd had in a spare room in the old house. She'd dressed it in white with a fat eiderdown and an antique throw and plumped it up with bolsters and huge square pillows in various shades of copper and gold. All over the house were her gorgeous lamps and rugs and the floorboards had been sanded and polished by a professional. In the bathroom the old bath had been resurfaced and the taps restored. The wood panelling was painted in the palest blue limewash that reminded Libby of the sea. Everywhere stood jugs and buckets filled with flowers, most from the garden.

The sitting room was the last to be finished, mainly because the beams had to be sanded to remove the awful black tarry substance that had made them seem dark and low. The stone fireplace also needed work. Libby was ecstatic when at last she could bring in her two big squashy couches and settle her Edwardian table under the window.

* * *

Annie telephoned one night when she was admiring her handiwork.

'Hi, stranger.'

'Hi yourself. How's it all going in fantasy land?' It was strange that their roles were now reversed. Annie was the star and Libby knew little or nothing about what was happening in the world of telly.

'Great. Busy. But listen, I've got a day off on Friday and I'm finished at about four on Thursday. Fancy meeting up?'

'Why don't you come here and I'll cook you dinner?' Libby was suddenly excited. 'You could even stay over.'

'On that damp smelly mattress? No chance!'

'Well, bring an overnight bag and if you don't want to stay I'll drop you home myself. How's that for an offer you can't refuse?'

'Best one I've had for weeks. I can't wait to see what you've done. When are you moving in?'

'Thursday. You've just made the decision for me.'

'Oh my God, that is so cool. Your first night and I'll be there. I can't wait. I've lots of gossip to tell you.'

'OK, come about eight.'

The push was exactly what Libby needed. She urged John Clancy to get all her pictures up and add the final touches to her study.

No-one had seen it finished, not even her

mother, who'd been horrified when Libby had taken her to see it originally. Christina Marlowe had begged her daughter to move home permanently until she found 'a more suitable place': it only made Libby more determined than ever to make a new life for herself.

She did a big grocery shop on-line and arranged delivery for Thursday morning. She arrived at the cottage with bags of the fresh ingredients that she preferred to choose herself from small specialist shops. Clearing out her larder in the old house, she'd been amazed at the amount of obscure ingredients she'd collected over the years. Now it was all stripped back to basics, just like her life, and as she stocked the cupboards sparingly she felt much less cluttered inside and out.

The morning was spent cooking and she was amused at how well she could improvise, using an old milk bottle when she couldn't find a rolling pin and substituting lime juice and zest for the hard to find kaffir lime leaves normally used in the delicate chicken starter she'd invented years ago. It was still the one she was most often asked for at parties.

For dinner itself she was roasting a good, old-fashioned loin of pork with succulent white fat. She crushed some garlic and crumbled a few bay leaves, added some good olive oil and seasoned it well, then worked the whole thing into a gloopy mush. She massaged the meat with the aromatic oil and left it to do its work for a couple of hours.

The crackling she scored with one of the

builder's knives and scattered some salt flakes to help it crisp up.

The only accompaniment was to be some roast potatoes, cooked with the meat to suck up all the juices. A simple salad and some gravy made with the roasting pan scrapings, a glass of Vermouth and a good crack of pepper completed the feast.

For pudding she was preparing a simple fruit crumble to make the most of the wonderful blackberries and plums in season. It had a sublime, almost toffee-apple crust and needed nothing except a jug of pouring cream to set it off.

Just before eight Libby went outside and looked at her new home, seeing it as Annie would when she arrived. It was a chilly autumn evening so she'd lit the lamps and candles but left the curtains open to reveal a soft orange light that contrasted with the curls of powder-grey smoke spiralling from her chimney. The air was heavy with scent after the earlier showers and she felt calm and peaceful as she went indoors to touch up her make-up and wait for her friend. She switched on the outside Victorian lanterns to complete the welcome.

'Oh my God, oh my God!' Annie was squealing with delight and doing an obscure African tribal dance outside while the taxi man looked on in amusement. Libby dashed out. They hadn't seen each other in over three weeks.

'You've cheated. I know you. You've demolished that grotty old place and had a chocolate box cottage imported from, I dunno,

Cornwall or Switzerland or somewhere.'

'I wish.' Libby beamed. 'No, actually I don't. I've enjoyed every minute of this one.'

Annie grinned at her. 'Well, not many things confound me but you've left me speechless this time.' She took a long look at Libby. 'You look different. You've lost weight and the ... tiredness has gone from your eyes.'

'You mean puffiness. Go on, say it.' They laughed and linked arms and went inside.

The hall was Libby's favourite room. Annie's mouth was that of a goldfish. The wood panelling gleamed following many hours of TLC. The banisters that had been enclosed in the cheapest MDF were now liberated and had rewarded Libby with elegant, hand-turned spirals and a little squiggly bit at the top and bottom. The walls, paintwork, ceiling – everything had been painted in an old Regency rich cream, in order to maximize the space and height and show off the gleaming wood-work. But the star feature was the newly exposed fireplace, carefully restored and home tonight to a mound of logs that sputtered and glowed in the soft lamplight. Above it was a bevelled mirror and a row of fat candles on the mantel. The furniture was simple, an old chair that had belonged to Libby's grandmother, a Victorian gateleg table with a pitcher of flowers on top and an antique rug in shades of warm rust, biscuit and chocolate.

Annie just kept looking around, taking it all in.

'My God, girl, whatever style is, you've got it in buckets.'

'Do you like it?'

'Like it? It's incredible. If you can do this in a couple of weeks then there's hope for everyone else on the planet. And I want you to promise to help me with mine when the time comes. I'm getting in early, 'cause I'd say you'll be in big demand.'

'Of course, don't be stupid. Now, come on up and see your smelly old room.'

Annie wandered around the rest of the house in a dream and when she saw the kitchen her expression made Libby laugh out loud.

'Have a drink,' she offered.

'I tell you I need one, or else I'll need smelling salts to revive me. This is fab. It's all so amazing. I have never seen anything like it in my life.'

They settled in and had a great chat and every scrap of food was eaten and only a little wine drunk.

'How come you're looking so well?' Annie wanted to know as they sat in front of the fire later.

'Well, I've been so busy here and I only got the cooker a couple of days ago, so I've been living on soup and fruit and vegetables and in the evenings I've been so tired that I've fallen into bed in Mum's house, not even stopping to pour myself a drink in case we got stuck into another heart-to-heart.'

'How are things on that front?'

'Just about OK. David's father has been phoning her a lot and they're both asking questions about the business. He's coming home in a few weeks and I know I'm going to have to sit down and explain at least some of it then. I suppose I'm afraid they'll rush in and try to help, although at that stage it will be too late. I signed most of the papers yesterday and the company's no longer operational.'

'Are you OK about all of this?'

'Yes, I'm relieved in a way. It's another chapter closed. And that's why it's been so important to get my base here set up. It'll keep me grounded. It's what I need right now.'

Chapter Fifty-Eight

Next morning they went for a long walk after a breakfast of juice and pancakes and coffee.

'You haven't said much about you. What's happening?' Libby asked as she pulled on her jacket against the breeze.

'Do you know something, everything's so good I'm starting to get scared. The upcoming scripts are really great, my personal profile has increased dramatically and my agent rings me every other day with some sort of offer.'

'Yeah, I keep reading about you every time I open a newspaper or magazine and it's all good.' Libby put her arm around Annie. 'It's great having a famous friend.'

'What about some of the rubbish I've been reading about you this week?' They'd already talked about it a lot but it wasn't dying down.

'Now that's what's really worrying Mum, I think. Since the series has done so badly the papers have really turned, as you well know. Funny, isn't it? I suppose I thought it would never happen to me. And maybe with David around it wouldn't have. He was sort of untouchable. People didn't mess with him easily. He was too powerful, I guess. Now it's open season, with all sorts of innuendo and speculation about the business, even about our relationship. Most of it I don't read. But it kind of gets me down now and then, which is a pity because otherwise I feel calm and peaceful and more in control since I stopped using alcohol as a crutch.' She shuddered. 'It makes me really scared to realize how near I came to having a real problem. I was becoming very dependent.'

'No news from Andrew?'

Libby shook her head. 'And now that I've moved he doesn't know where I am.'

'He'd find you.' Annie was gentle in her usual forthright way.

'I know that.' Libby squeezed her arm. 'I still get lonely for him sometimes but I can cope with it. Anyway, I'm old enough not to believe in fairytales.'

'We all need our dreams. Let's never stop making each other believe in movie endings. OK?'

'Deal.'

'And for me, having you as my best friend is just like in the movies. Remember that one with Bette Midler about the two best friends and a cat called Pouncer?'

'Please – didn't one of them die?' Libby was horrified.

'That wasn't important. It was all about their

relationship. They were lucky to have each other. And that's what I feel about you.'

'Me too.' They stood and looked out to sea with their arms around each other, causing a few kettles to boil dry in the neighbourhood as speculation about their celebrity neighbour intensified.

Annie left later for a date with Gary.

'How's it all going?' Libby wanted to know everything.

'Great. We kiss and hug and snog, sort of like teenagers. For now at least he seems content with that. And I know I am.'

'Good girl. You have it all sussed.'

Annie's mobile rang. After a short conversation she turned to Libby with shining eyes. 'That was the estate agent. He's found me a place that he thinks is ideal.'

They jumped up and down like kids. 'Perfect timing. I'm ready for a new project.' They went on the Internet to look at the property and it seemed ideal, a stylish, modern two-bedroomed apartment in a beautifully proportioned building with fabulous facilities. It had two terraces and a decent bathroom and the kitchen was 'ideal for advanced lessons', according to Libby. 'And the rooms are a good size, so we'll be able to go to town on the décor and some of the stuff you took from me will look great there too. I can't wait.'

They made an arrangement to go and see it together, then Annie left, asking Libby about work on her way out the door.

'I've nothing lined up, but I need to get something soon. I've been putting a few ideas on paper. Leo Morgan promised me another series but Melanie's been trying to get a commitment out of him for ages, with no success. I'm more difficult to sell now that I have a dud on my hands.'

'Don't give up.'

'I won't.'

When Annie had gone, Libby tidied up. Her pottering was interrupted by a whining noise at the front door. Outside in the rain sat the saddest little dog she'd ever seen. It was a mongrel, clearly, roughly the shape and size of a cocker spaniel. Its paws were thick and padded and its wheaten coat was a cross between a poodle and the Dulux dog, which made it long and shaggy and extremely matted.

'Go away. Shoo.' Libby, who didn't like dogs, was freaked. It refused to budge. Sitting there, it stared up at her with a face that would make even a boxer pup look cheerful.

She closed the door but kept her eye on him or her and about an hour later a middle-aged man came and tried to coax the animal away.

'Hello.' Libby felt she'd better make an effort.

'I'm very sorry. I'm afraid he wants to come back here. Every time we open the door he bounds out and hides when we try and get him to come back home. He always sits at this door.'

'But who is he?' Libby didn't like this story one bit.

'He was owned by Eleanor, the lady who's now

in the nursing home. She wouldn't give him up so we offered to take him. We have two other dogs so it didn't really matter. But he won't settle and we keep finding him here, usually hiding from us. We've been down every day but I didn't realize you'd moved in until just now. I'm Alan O'Rourke, by the way. Welcome.'

'Libby Marlowe.' She shook hands. 'Is there anything I can do?'

He shook his head. 'Not unless you fancy a pet?'

'Afraid not. I'm allergic.' She smiled as he dragged a very stubborn animal down the path.

'What's his name, by the way?' she called.

'Cookie Monster.' He looked mortified.

She was still laughing as she settled down to do some work at the computer. It was tough, trying to put together ideas to get Leo Morgan to commit. The clock had just struck five, almost knocking-off time, when she decided to call him and bully him into a meeting. He agreed, very reluctantly she thought, and she printed off pages of notes to bring with her the following day.

'Look, Leo, I know what we should be doing.' The idea had come to her at six o'clock that morning and she'd been working on it ever since. 'We need a series that gives people at home all the tips that professional chefs use. Most punters don't have the kitchens, or equipment, or "essential" ingredients that we use. I want to show the audience how to build up a basic cooking repertoire – how to make a simple gravy, a good loaf, a couple of easy sauces for pasta and some of the best salad dressings I've ever come across.'

'I don't know, Libby. Maybe we should wait a year or so till all this stuff dies down.' He smiled at her. 'Right now you're up there with Saddam Hussein and Osama bin Laden in the popularity stakes.' He saw her flinch and could have kicked himself. 'Only joking,' he said, trying to lighten the atmosphere.

'I can't afford to wait twelve months. I need to work, both financially and for my own sanity.' Libby played her best card. 'You owe me, Leo. I was unsure about this series from the beginning, you know that. I only agreed to get the station out of a hole. It was the worst possible time for me personally and now I need to work for reasons you know nothing about.'

He looked uncomfortable. 'Give me a day or two. I'll see what I can do.'

When she told Annie, her friend was thrilled. 'Good for you. That son-of-a-bitch. He owes you bigtime. So, tell me about the new series.'

Libby started to fill her in and Annie interrupted her. 'That's it, Libby. Teach them what you're teaching me. OK, not all your fans are as bad as I am but we all want the tips, the shortcuts, the stripped-down versions of the classics.'

'Do you really think so?'

'Yes I do.'

'The problem is, who do I get to produce it?'

'Do it yourself.'

'What?'

'Produce it yourself. That way you avoid the pitfalls. Take a cut in salary, put together a team and do it.'

Libby's mind was going into overdrive. 'You know something? You just might be right. All I'd need is a good director, a researcher, a PA and a food stylist. I have my own company.'

'I'll help, for free. In fact, maybe we could do an episode together. You could bring me on as the classic example of someone who couldn't boil an egg before they met you.'

Libby was immensely touched by her offer, knowing that Annie's appearance would make the series infinitely more appealing to the station.

'I might hold you to that. Sometimes it's great having a name on the first running order.'

'Well, I'm all yours. Just give me dates as soon as you have them. I could probably rope in one or two others from the show if that would help? Oops, gotta go. They've just called my next scene.'

'How's it going?'

'I'm getting too old for six-inch stilettos and minis no wider than an elastic band.'

'You should try being forty. I've just got a bunion. My dentist tells me my gums are shrinking with age. I need glasses but I'm too proud and all I have the energy to do these nights is flop into bed at nine-thirty. Buy me a flannelette nightie, please.'

'When's your birthday? Not for ages yet?'

'A couple of months. And stop laughing, it'll

come to you, too. Just wait for that cellulite to appear overnight.'

'Ouch. You bitch. Talk later.' She blew a kiss and was gone.

Leo Morgan rang the next day. 'I think I can sell them the idea, Libby. But they're worried about all this negative publicity. There've been rumours about your business affairs now for months and they're not going away.'

'What can I do? And it's David's affairs they're hinting at, not mine. You think I need this?'

'What about doing one major interview? On one of the big chat shows?'

'I was on the *Late Late* a while ago. They won't want me back.'

'Leave that to me. Will you do it?'

'I don't know, Leo.'

'Libby, I always try and advise you in the best way I can. I think it's the only way to start afresh.'

'Oh Libby, I really don't know.' Annie didn't like the idea.

'That's what I thought at first. But, thinking about it, maybe he's right.'

'What would you talk about?'

'David's death. How it changed my life.'

'What about the business?'

'I'd say enough to let them know that it wasn't all plain sailing. But they've nothing on me, nothing on him either and I'd put an end to it once and for all, that's for sure.'

'And the series?'

'I think I'd have to be honest about it.'

'Sounds like you've already made up your mind.'

'Yeah.'

'I'll come in with you on the night.'

'Thanks.'

The only thing left to do was to talk to her mother and David's father beforehand. First, she rang John Simpson.

'I've been thinking about it for a while, Libby. The rumours aren't going to go away and they're beginning to damage you. I think your instinct is right.'

'I would need to have a session with you first, though, just so I know what I should and shouldn't say.'

'Of course.'

'And I'm determined not to say anything that would tarnish his reputation.' Another thought occurred to her. 'How are things your end?'

'Fine. Alex is just preparing a final set of accounts. That's it. The office has been closed as you wanted and everyone's been well looked after.'

'And all the clients are all right?'

'Yes, we've had a meeting with every one of them.'

'That's great, John. Thanks.'

'It was all your doing, Libby.' He admired the way she'd taken control of a very difficult situation.

'I'm just glad it's over. Now I can really move on.'

'Let me know when you finally make up your mind about the show.'

'I think I already have.'

Libby decided to send an e-mail to Charles English. It was one of the hardest things she'd ever had to write. She didn't tell him everything, just enough to let him know that she'd done what she had to do.

Talking to her mother was less easy.

'I can't believe what you're telling me, Elizabeth.'

'I know. It's a lot to take in.'

'But he was one of the top financial brains in the country. How could he leave you so badly provided for?'

'He didn't think he was going to die. He thought he had years and years to sort it out. So did I. So did John Simpson, who was advising him.'

'So that's why you sold the house and all the paintings that you loved so much.'

'Actually Mum, I didn't need them. And do you want to know something I couldn't have said six months ago?' She gave a sad little smile. 'I'm glad it's turned out like this. Not his . . . dying or anything. It's just that I think I was becoming a very large pain in the arse.' She grinned. Bits of Annie were beginning to rub off on her.

'You know that all this is yours when I die. And there's money invested for you as well. I'll do anything I can – sell the house now, if necessary.'

Libby wanted to cry and run to her mummy, as she had done many times as a little girl. 'I appreciate it, Mum, but I'm fine. I won't starve.'

'What about your future?'

'I have a good pension, thanks to him. My own business account couldn't be touched. I have my cottage, my friends . . .' She smiled, just thinking about Annie. 'And most of all I have my health.'

'Any new men friends?' It was a question she wouldn't have dared ask the old Libby.

An image of Andrew came into her head. It was the only cloud on her horizon. She shook her head and looked away. 'I'm luckier than most, Mum. So don't worry about me. I'm content with my lot.'

Chapter Fifty-Nine

The Late Late Show was delighted to have her as a
guest and showtime came around again much too
soon for the frightened has-been that Libby felt
she had become. She was relieved to at least be
looking better than on her last outing.

This time she was determined to keep it simple.
Her hair was hand-dried and waxed and left untidy
and natural. She'd decided on the absolute minimum make-up possible and her old friend Janey
offered to stay back and ensure she didn't go overboard. What to wear was easy: a long dark blue
linen pinafore that she'd seen in a local boutique. It
was sleeveless, fitted at the top with a super cut and
an unusual detail at the hips. Young and trendy, it
flattered her curvy figure and made her eyes look
even darker. Libby decided to team it with high
leather boots and to wear no jewellery.

It was early morning on D-Day and she was
mooching around the house, her stomach in a bit
of a knot, when the phone rang.

'Libby–' the voice sounded odd. 'I think I might be in trouble.'

Libby's stomach did a somersault. Her tone remained dead calm. 'Annie, what's wrong? Have you been in an accident?' She knew her friend was taking driving lessons, she'd teased her often enough.

'No. Nothing like that.'

'What is it then?' No reply. 'Annie, please tell me.'

'I think I may have found a lump.'

Libby swallowed. Hard. She bit her lip. 'When?'

'This morning. In the shower. Oh Libby, I'm so scared.'

'Don't be. You've got to ring your doctor.'

'I just have. They're trying to get me a bed. It may take days, weeks even.'

'Did they say that?'

'No. But I've been through this before. The public health service is already bursting at the seams.'

'Leave it to me. Stay where you are. Pack a bag. I'll call you back as soon as I know anything.'

Libby used every contact she had. Her number one was away on holiday. Number two was playing golf for the weekend. She cursed them both.

On and on it went until she thought she'd go mad. She left messages on two mobile phones. No response. And she was dealing with the top brass.

Half an hour later, she slammed down the phone. All of a sudden, heart hammering, she picked it up again, flicking through the phone book for the number she wanted.

'I'd like to speak to Andrew Harrington, please.'

'Just a moment.'

Same request three more times.

'Good afternoon, Mr Harrington's secretary.'

'Hello, I need to speak with Andrew. It's urgent.'

'I'm afraid he's in a meeting.'

'Can you interrupt him? Tell him it's Libby Marlowe.'

'Well, I—'

'Please. I think he'd want to talk to me.'

'Hold a moment, please.' She did as she was told, for what felt like an hour.

'Libby?'

'Andrew?'

'Libby, what's wrong?'

'Andrew, I know I've a cheek but I need a favour and I need it today.' She explained about Annie in a panicky voice.

'Give me a few minutes. I'll call you back. Let me have your number. Has she private medical insurance, by the way?'

'No, but that won't be a problem.' Brief silence.

'I'll call you right back.'

He did, several endless minutes later.

'Can you get her in here, to the clinic, in the next hour?'

'Yes.'

'Right, here are the details. They're standing by to do some tests. I'm in surgery shortly but I'll come and see you as soon as I can.' He knew everything he needed to know from her voice. 'Libby, try not to worry. It may be nothing.'

'Andrew, I have no job, I've just lost my home, I'm about to go on national TV and spill my guts.' She paused for breath. 'And I don't care a toss. But if anything happens to her, I don't know what I'll do.'

'I understand.'

'Thank you.'

'Get her here as soon as you can.'

'I will.'

'Drive carefully.'

But she'd already gone.

'How did you manage this?' Annie was pale and looked lost.

Libby, trying to appear normal, grinned at her as they got into her car. 'All my super-duper contacts failed. So, guess who came up trumps?'

'Who?'

'Andrew.'

'Andrew who?'

'My Andrew.'

'Oh my God. We're going to his clinic?'

'Well, he doesn't exactly own it, as far as I know.' She was trying to be nonchalant. 'But yes, you wanted to see him up close and personal. Now's your chance.'

'Libby, I can't afford this. On second thoughts, I probably can. No point in worrying about an apartment I might never get to live in.'

'Don't think like that now.'

'I have to.'

'Look, Annie, we need to get a handle on this. If it's serious, we can reassess the situation.'

'That's the worst thing about it. The waiting.'

Libby stared straight ahead. It was her coping mechanism. 'I realize that. At least this way we'll find out quickly.'

'I'll never be able to thank you enough.'

'Thank me by being my friend for a long time.'

The waiting had only just begun. As soon as she checked in they took Annie for tests. Libby tried to read, paced, switched on the TV, paced some more, bought grapes and minerals, paced again. On and on it went and still no-one came. Eventually, she couldn't stand it any longer. 'Can you tell me anything about Annie Weller?' she asked a passing nurse.

'She's still having some tests. Why don't you go home and we can call you later? It might take a few hours.'

'No, it's OK.' She smiled at the tired-looking woman. 'I'll wait.'

Two hours later they wheeled Annie back, looking pale and sounding a bit groggy.

'Hi.'

'Hi, Libby. How come you're still here?'

'Nowhere else to go.'

'Don't you have a *Late Late Show* home to go to?'

'Later.'

Annie smiled and nodded off. Libby settled down. Nurses popped in, checked her, offered tea and coffee. No sign of a doctor and soon Libby would have to leave. Annie was still sleeping.

'Will she be all right?' she asked.

'Of course.' The nurse smiled brightly. 'Will you call back in the morning?'

'No. I'll come back later tonight, if that's all right?'

'That's fine, but we probably won't have all the tests back until the morning.'

'It doesn't matter.'

'Well, try not to worry. She's in good hands.'

Chapter Sixty

'. . . Ladies and gentlemen, please welcome Libby Marlowe!'

She could vaguely hear the applause. It sounded subdued. She walked out into the light and prepared to face the firing squad. Suddenly, it didn't seem important.

The interview started routinely enough – some general questions about her style of programming.

'Well, moving on to your current series, just finished its run on Channel 1, I think it's fair to say that the critics have been less than kind?'

'That's true.' Libby ploughed straight in. 'I think what we tried to do was very ambitious and looking back I feel we underestimated the audience. I've spoken to some women and what they really want is to go behind the scenes in a restaurant. They lead busy lives. They don't always have time to source specialist ingredients. But they know what they like. That's why we've decided to try a completely different approach this time.' She took a deep breath and, on the spur of the moment, put Leo Morgan on the spot.

'We're about to go into production on a new series where we give people inside information, teach them the best-kept secrets and show them what every good home cook needs to have as a basis for everyday living.'

'But that's not a new idea, surely?'

'No, but our approach will be entirely different from anything that's been done before, I can assure you.'

They chatted about it for a while. The audience asked questions and appeared keen.

Eventually, it came down to her personal life, which was why she was here.

'On a more serious note, you lost your husband earlier this year. That must have had a devastating effect on your life?'

'It was the worst thing that ever happened to me.' Talking about it made it seem like two weeks ago. 'I loved him very much. When he died, a part of me died too. I found it hard to cope.'

'So that must make the rumours that have been circulating in some of the tabloids hard to bear?'

'I suppose I've grown used to speculation about my personal life over the years. But it has been hard on my family: my mother, for instance, and David's mum and dad.'

'What about the stories about his business acumen?'

Libby was ready for this and she handled it with ease, confronting the innuendo head on.

'So there's no truth in the speculation that his business was in trouble?'

'David's business went through a difficult time after his death. I think that was to be expected. He was a financial genius. Without him it was always going to be tough.' She looked the audience straight in the eye. 'But the business was healthy and solvent when I made the decision to close it recently. It was a tough decision but I'm not David and I don't have his brains for finance. I am the only other partner and I want to pursue other interests. I have my own company to run.'

He left it there and came to the other point that had been the subject of speculation.

'So selling the family home was not a decision that was forced on you?' Fair play, Libby thought, this is great television. I just wish I was at home watching.

'The decision to sell was entirely mine. I think it's fair to say that those around me, both personally and professionally, advised against it. But it was too big for me and, more importantly, I needed to make a fresh start. There were too many memories already.'

'So you've bought a new house, I believe.'

'Yes, much smaller. The whole of my little cottage would fit into the hall of my old home.' She smiled at the memory of Annie's face as she stepped inside for the first time. 'But it has lots of character and I love it. It's perfect for me. Apart from one thing . . .' It was her first genuine smile of the evening.

'Oh. What's that?'

'No-one told me it came complete with a dog. He wasn't in the deeds.' She told the story. 'Last night, he hid under a tree in the front garden, directly in front of the window. It was pelting rain and he was soaked. Now, I make no apologies. I'm not a dog lover. I got up and callously closed the curtains.' The audience groaned. 'When I went to make a cup of cocoa he was outside the french doors.' The audience clapped. 'I pretended I didn't see him and drew the blind.' Another groan. 'When I went to bed he had managed to manoeuvre himself directly into my line of vision again, except by this time he looked as if he'd been put through a wringer.'

'So what did you do?'

'I turned up the electric blanket.' The men mostly clapped and laughed. A few pet lovers took her seriously and gasped in indignation.

'You know he's going to win, don't you?' It was asked in a fashion that suggested he had 'dog lover' tattooed across his chest, underneath his immaculate shirt.

'He already has. When I left home today he was stretched out on my Persian rug, chewing my slipper.' The audience roared their approval.

'Sounds like a clever dog. What's his name, by the way?'

'I believe he's known as Cookie Monster.' It was at least ten seconds before the laughter and applause died. But they were laughing with her. It was a side of Libby Marlowe they'd never seen before.

*　*　*

As the interview drew to a close and just as Libby was beginning to breathe normally, a question caught her unawares. 'So, what are your plans for the future?'

She thought for a second.

'I've no great ambitions any more, really. I don't pray often, but when I do it's for good health. I want to live peacefully. I hope to continue working. Most of all I intend to spend time with the people who are important in my life, my mother' – she wouldn't have thought of that as a priority before – 'and my best friend, Annie.'

'And has there been anyone special in your life, since . . . since your husband died?' It was a natural conclusion to what, from his point of view, had been one of the most successful interviews of the season.

Libby started to laugh it off and then decided, what the hell. She owed it to Andrew to tell him on national TV what she couldn't admit to his face. 'There was someone, actually. I met him a couple of months ago.' It all came flooding back. 'He was warm and funny and kind –' she smiled – 'and gorgeous.'

The audience all went 'woo'.

'And are you still seeing him?' This was more than the presenter could ever have hoped for.

'Ah,' Libby gave a small smile. 'That's where it all unravels, I'm afraid. You see, I mucked it up. I was stupid and very short-sighted and I made one of my biggest mistakes yet. I underestimated him.'

She tried to look philosophical. 'And he left. And when I tried – very badly – to explain, he said thanks, but no. Very nicely, it must be said.'

'And you had great hopes for this relationship?'

'No, I don't think either of us had got that far. But now, looking back, I think it had great potential.' You could hear a pin drop as people strained forward in their seats. This was dynamite.

'And what does he do? Is he in the media business?'

'No actually, he's a gardener.'

Chapter Sixty-One

Libby pulled up in the private car park with the applause still ringing in her ears. It had that eerie, late-night hospital feel, where time always seems suspended, as if there are much more important things.

Inside, all was quiet, the Friday night peace contrasting sharply with the world she'd left behind, the stillness belying the turmoil she knew existed in many rooms in the building.

When she entered Annie's room, the electric atmosphere hit her like a brick, and that was before she noticed Andrew sitting beside her friend.

'You were brill.'

'Was I? Thanks.' She looked at the quiet, gorgeous man she'd lost and was able to smile, because she knew that compared with what her friend was facing, it didn't really matter. It calmed her.

'Hi.'

'Hi.'

'How are you?' She included him. 'Both?'

'I'm fine.' Annie sat up in bed. 'It's not back.'

It took a second to sink in. 'What do you mean?'

'It's not the cancer back.'

'But I thought . . . they said it would be morning before . . .'

'Andrew pulled some strings.'

She wasn't prepared to buy it so easily. 'So what is it, then?'

'I've no idea. I didn't hear anything after the words "not" and "cancerous". They're just waiting on the results of one more test in the morning. But I'm in the clear.' She looked at Libby with shining eyes. 'It was probably just a piece of gristle from all those fancy steaks you've been making me eat lately in an effort to keep me healthy.'

The three of them burst out laughing. It was warm and easy. 'Anyone for coffee?' Andrew stood up, as if aware that they needed to be alone.

'I'd murder a cup.' Libby looked tired.

'Black for me, thanks, no sugar. I'm on a diet. Got to look super for the rest of my life.' Annie looked like a brazen child. Andrew touched her hair, hinting at a closeness that made Libby feel like the odd one out. She didn't mind.

'You were fantastic. I'm in awe of you,' Annie told her as soon as he'd left.

'Did I do OK?'

'You were amazing. I was so proud of you.'

'Today I learned another lesson.'

'Me too.'

'Do you know if he saw any of it?'

'He saw it all. He was right here beside me.'

It didn't surprise, or upset her. 'What did he say?'

'Nothing.'

'Nothing?'

'No.'

'What do you mean "no"? That's it?'

'Yeah, 'fraid so. But I think he was pleased.'

'How do you know?'

'I'm a cancer victim, I know these things.'

'I meant every word.'

'I know you did. You handled it all fantastically well. It was a very difficult interview.' She looked happy. 'Thanks for the mention, by the way. Made me feel all warm and runny inside. Just like that fantastic fruit crumble you made the other night.'

'You're welcome.' Libby was trying not to laugh. 'Just don't go scaring me like that again.'

'I'll try not to,' Annie grinned. 'He's yummy, you know. You'd better get him quick, otherwise I might be in there,' she warned.

'Over my dead body.'

'Well, definitely not over mine.' Annie made a face and Libby slapped her.

'By the way, I forgot to tell you, I had sex with Gary the other night.' She laughed at the look on her friend's face.

'That's brilliant, I told you it would happen. Was it good? How could you keep this from me?'

'I didn't want to tell you over the phone and then today, other things sort of took over. And yes, it was good.'

'Great or just good?'

'I'll tell you after I've done it a couple more times.'

They were still teasing when Andrew returned with plastic coffee and cellophane biscuits. They pounced on him as if he was carrying Cristal and caviar.

The three of them talked for hours. All around them the clinks of hospital life reassured them that they weren't entirely in a vacuum.

It was after three when Andrew returned for the second time, having taken advantage of being in the clinic to check on some of his patients. Another injection of caffeine followed.

'Don't you have anything stronger?' Annie complained.

'Aren't you supposed to be ill?' Libby demanded.

'Haven't you two mucked up my Friday night enough already?' Andrew enquired.

The sun was almost rising on a near-perfect, warm still autumn Saturday when Libby and Andrew left the hospital.

'Are you OK?' It was still his favourite question where she was concerned.

'Yeah. I'm fine.' She stopped and turned to face him. 'Thanks for what you did today.'

'My pleasure.'

'I didn't know who to turn to.' He strolled over to that same park bench. Libby followed and sat down. She let out a deep breath. 'I guess I panicked a bit. She's become very important to me.'

'I can see why. She's lovely.'

'She is, isn't she?' Please God let him not fancy her.

All around them birds chirped, at least the ones that hadn't yet flown south. For Libby it was a totally different experience from when she'd sat with him before. Maybe it helped that this time she had no agenda, and anyway his hair was ruffled, his immaculate tie had long since been wrenched loose and his designer suit looked as if it had been on him for far too long. He was much more like the old Andrew and not the newer, sophisticated version that she was still in awe of.

'Busy day?'

'Yeah.'

'What time did you start?'

'This time yesterday.'

'Oh my God, you must be tired.'

'Knackered. You?'

'Yep. It's been a long day.'

'The show went well?'

'I think so.'

'You were happy with what you said?'

'Yeah, I was.'

Later, when she was trying to remember every detail of their conversation, it seemed to her that he'd just been double-checking. Slowly, he reached out and gripped her shoulders and turned her towards him.

'You hurt me a lot.'

'Yes.'

'Don't do it again.' It was the shortest, sternest reprimand.

'No.'

He nodded and seemed to accept her word.

'Come on, I'll walk you to your car.' He held out his hand and she knew it was going to be OK.

The sun came up as they strolled out of the tiny garden, across the mass of concrete and clay to the grey, almost deserted car park. Suddenly Libby ached for her cottage, and her dog, and his arms around her. It was the strongest feeling and maybe, because of the witching hour, she found the courage she needed. Or maybe it was just that she felt so close to him, holding his hand for the very first time, as if they were a real couple.

'Would you come home with me? Just for what's left of the night?'

He shook his head.

She didn't feel rejected. He stopped.

'This time you're not calling the shots,' he said and looked at her for the longest time.

'All right.'

'I'll phone you.'

'Fine.' They continued in silence.

She'd reached her car and was just about to open the door when he grabbed her hand and pulled her to him. He gave her the most fleeting, yet permanent kiss and she had to stop herself from dragging him into the car. Then he leaned back and looked at her, smiled and said nothing.

There was one other question. 'That girl I saw

510

you with the night Annie won the award. Is she important?'

'No.'

'Thank you.'

'You're welcome.' He was teasing her. She reached up and touched his face lightly and couldn't resist kissing him once more and it felt like coming home. This time he held her very close and she wrapped her arms around his neck and ran her fingers through his hair and indulged all of her senses. It was the most powerful feeling, smelling him and being able to touch him, and it lingered long after he'd pulled back.

'Get some rest. I'll talk to you later.'

'I'd like that.'

He stood back to wait until she'd manoeuvred out of the parking space. It was wider than a plane hangar.

'After you.' She opened her window, determined not to let him have it all his own way. He grinned at her and moved away. She pressed a button and the roof of her car opened to reveal a brand new day and she watched him finally discard his tie and sling the million-dollar jacket over his shoulder. And she hoped that the Cookie Monster would be awake, and wouldn't have pooed on her Persian rug. She needed someone to stroke and tell stories to.

She waited while he drove out ahead of her, and she followed, hair streaming in the light breeze of a morning that suddenly oozed possibilities.

He drove behind her down the dual carriageway

and she liked looking at him in her mirror. She turned on some music and grinned at nothing and saw that he was smiling too. And she watched intently as he slowed and indicated to turn right. She waved frantically at him and he grinned and waved back until eventually he disappeared out of her sight but not, she hoped, out of her life.

THE END